*Sooner or Later
Everything
Falls
into
the
Sea*

Sooner or Later Everything Falls into the Sea

— stories —

Sarah Pinsker

Small Beer Press
Easthampton, MA

Small Beer Press
150 Pleasant Street #306
Easthampton, MA 01027
smallbeerpress.com
weightlessbooks.com
info@smallbeerpress.com

Distributed to the trade by Consortium.

Library of Congress Cataloging-in-Publication Data

Names: Pinsker, Sarah, author.
Title: Sooner or later everything falls into the sea : stories / Sarah
  Pinsker.
Description: Easthampton, MA : Small Beer Press, 2019.
Identifiers: LCCN 2018050543 (print) | LCCN 2018051754 (ebook) | ISBN
  9781618731562 | ISBN 9781618731555 (alk. paper)
Classification: LCC PS3616.I579 (ebook) | LCC PS3616.I579 A6 2019 (print) |
  DDC 813/.6--dc23
LC record available at https://lccn.loc.gov/2018050543

Set in Centaur 12 pt.

Printed on 30% PCR recycled paper by Versa Press in East Peoria, IL.
Cover illustration "Kurosawa" copyright © 2018 by Matt Muirhead (mattmuirhead.co).
All rights reserved.

— Contents —

To my parents, for feeding me stories.

— A Stretch of Highway Two Lanes Wide —

Andy tattooed his left forearm with Lori's name on a drunken night in his seventeenth year. "Lori & Andy Forever and Ever" was the full text, all in capital letters, done by his best friend, Susan, with her home-made tattoo rig. Susan was proud as anything of that machine. She'd made it out of nine-volt batteries and some parts pulled from an old DVD player and a ballpoint pen. The tattoo was ugly and hurt like hell, and it turned out Lori didn't appreciate it at all. She dumped him two weeks later, just before she headed off to university.

Four years later, Andy's other arm was the one that got mangled in the combine. The entire arm, up to and including his shoulder and right collarbone and everything attached. His parents made the decision while he was still unconscious. He woke in a hospital room in Saskatoon with a robot arm and an implant in his head.

"Brain-Computer Interface," his mother said, as if that explained everything. She used the same voice she had used when he was five to tell him where the cattle went when they were loaded onto trucks. She stood at the side of his hospital bed, her arms crossed and her fingers tapping her strong biceps as if she were impatient to get back to the farm. The lines in her forehead and the set of her jaw told Andy she was concerned, even if her words hid it.

"They put electrodes and a chip in your motor cortex," she continued. "You're bionic."

"What does that mean?" he asked. He tried to move his right hand to touch his head, but the hand didn't respond. He used his left and encountered bandages.

His father spoke from a chair by the window, flat-brimmed John Deere cap obscuring his eyes. "It means you've got a prototype arm and a whole lot of people interested in how it turns out. Could help a lot of folks."

Andy looked down at where his arm had been. Bandages obscured the points where flesh met prosthetic; beyond the bandages, the shine of new metal and matte-black wire. The new arm looked like their big irrigation rig, all spines and ridges and hoses. It ended in a pincer, fused fingers and a thumb. He tried to remember the details of his right hand: the freckles on the back, the rope-burn scar around his knuckles, the calluses on the palm. What had they done with it? Was it in a garbage can somewhere, marked as medical waste? It must have been pretty chewed up or they would have tried to reattach it.

He looked at the other arm. An IV was stuck in the "Forever" of his tattoo. He thought something far away was hurting, but he didn't feel much. Maybe the IV explained that. He tried again to lift his right arm. It still didn't budge, but this time it did hurt, deep in his chest.

"Can't prosthetics look like arms these days?" he asked.

His practical mother spoke again. "Those ones aren't half as useful. You can replace this hand with a more realistic one later if you want, but to get full use of the arm they said to go with the brain interface. No nerves left to send the impulses to a hand otherwise, no matter how fancy."

He understood. "How do I use it?"

"You don't, not for a while. But they were able to attach it right away. Used to be they'd wait for the stump to heal before fitting you, but this they said they had to go ahead and put in."

"You don't have a stump, anyway." His father chopped at his own shoulder as an indicator. "You're lucky you still have a head."

He wondered what the other options had been, if there had been any. It made sense that his parents would choose this. Theirs had always been the first farm in Saskatchewan for every new technology. His parents believed in automation. They liked working the land with machines, gridding it with spreadsheets and databases, tilling the fields from the comfort of the office.

He was the throwback. He liked the sun on his face. He kept a team of Shires for plowing and used their manure for fertilizer. He had his father's old diesel combine for harvest time, his biggest concession to speed and efficiency. And now it had taken his arm. He didn't know if that was an argument for his horses and tractors or his parents' self-guided machines. The machines would take out your fence if you programmed the coordinates wrong, but unless your math was really off they probably wouldn't make it into your office. On the other hand—now a pincer—it had been his own stupid fault he had reached into the stuck header.

Andy's world shrank to the size of the hospital room. He stood by the window and read the weather and fought the urge to call his parents, who were taking care of his small farm next to theirs in his absence. Had they finished harvesting before the frost? Had they moved the chicken run closer to the house? He had to trust them.

The doctor weaned him off the pain medications quickly. "You're a healthy guy," she said. "Better to cope than get hooked on opiates." Andy nodded, figuring he could handle it. He knew the aches of physical labor, of days when you worked until you were barely standing, and then a Shire shifted his weight and broke your foot, and you still had to get up and work again the next day.

Now his body communicated a whole new dialect of pain: aches wrapped in aches, throbbing in parts that didn't exist anymore. He learned to articulate the difference between stinging and stabbing pains, between soreness and tenderness. When the worst of it had broken over him, an endless prairie storm, the doctor gave the go-ahead for him to start using his arm.

"You're a fast learner, buddy," his occupational therapist told him when he had mastered closing the hand around a toothbrush. Brad was a big Assiniboine guy, only a couple of years older than Andy and relentlessly enthusiastic. "Tomorrow you can try dressing yourself."

"Fast is relative." Andy put the toothbrush down, then tried to pick it up again. He knocked it off the table.

Brad smiled but didn't make a move for the fallen toothbrush. "It's a process, eh? Your muscles have new roles to learn. Besides, once you get through these things, the real fun begins with that rig."

The real fun would be interesting, if he ever got there. The special features. He would have to learn to interpret the signal from the camera on the wrist, feeding straight to his head. There were flashlights and body telemetry readings to turn off and on. He looked forward to the real tests for those features: seeing into the dark corners of an engine, turning a breach calf. Those were lessons worth sticking around for. Andy bent down and concentrated on closing his hand on the toothbrush handle.

Just before he was due to go home, an infection sank its teeth in under his armpit. The doctor gave him antibiotics and drained the fluid. That night, awash in fever, he dreamed his arm was a highway. The feeling stuck with him when he woke.

Andy had never wanted much. He had wanted Lori to love him, forever and ever, but she didn't and that was that. As a child, he'd asked for the calf with the blue eyes, Maisie, and he kept her until she was big enough to be sold, and that was that. He'd never considered doing anything except working his own land next to his parents' and taking over theirs when they retired. There was no point in wanting much else.

Now he wanted to be a road, or his right arm did. It wanted with a fierceness that left him baffled, a wordless yearning that came from inside him and outside him at once. No, more than that. It didn't just want to be a road. It knew it was one. Specifically, a stretch of asphalt two lanes wide, ninety-seven kilometers long, in eastern Colorado. A stretch that could see all the way to the mountains, but was content not to reach them. Cattleguards on either side, barbed wire, grassland.

Andy had never been to Colorado. He'd never been out of Saskatchewan, not even to Calgary or Winnipeg. He'd never seen a mountain. The fact that he was able to describe the contours of the mountains in the distance, and the tag numbers in the ears of the bald-faced cows, told him he wasn't imagining things. He was himself, and he was also a road.

"Ready to get back to work, buddy? How's it feeling?" Brad asked him.

Andy shrugged. He knew he should tell Brad about the road, but he didn't want to stay in the hospital any longer. Bad enough that his parents had been forced to finish his harvest, grumbling the whole time about his archaic machinery. There was no way he would risk a delay.

"Infection's gone, but it's talking a lot. Still takes some getting used to," he said, which was true. It fed him the temperature, the levels of different pollutants in the air. It warned him when he was pushing himself too hard on the treadmill. And then there was the road thing.

Brad tapped his own forehead. "You remember how to dial back the input if it gets too much?"

"Yeah. I'm good."

Brad smiled and reached for a cooler he had brought with him. "Great, man. In that case, today you're going to work on eggs."

"Eggs?"

"You're a farmer, right? You have to pick up eggs without cracking them. And then you have to make lunch. Believe me, this is expert level. Harder than any of that fancy stuff. You master eggs with that hand, you graduate."

Brad and the doctors finally gave him permission to leave a week later.

"You want to drive?" asked his father, holding out the keys to Andy's truck.

Andy shook his head and walked around to the passenger side. "I'm not sure I could shove into second gear. Might need to trade this in for an automatic."

His father gave him a once-over. "Maybe so. Or just practice a bit around the farm?"

"I'm not scared. Just careful."

"Fair enough, fair enough." His father started the truck.

He wasn't scared, but it was more than being careful. At first, the joy of being in his own house eclipsed the weird feeling. The road feeling. He kept up the exercises he had learned in physical therapy. They had retaught him how to shave and cook and bathe, and he retaught himself how to groom and tack the horses. He met up with his buddies from his old hockey team at the bar in town, to try to prove that everything was normal.

Gradually, the aches grew wider. How could you be a road, in a particular place, and yet not be in that place? Nothing felt right. He had always loved to eat, but now food was tasteless. He forced himself to cook, to chew, to swallow. He set goals for the number of bites he had to take before stopping.

He had lost muscle in the hospital, but now he grew thinner. His new body was wiry instead of solid. Never much of a mirror person, he started making himself look. Motivation, maybe. A way to try to communicate with his own brain. He counted his ribs. The synthetic sleeving that smoothed the transition from pectorals to artificial arm gapped a little because of his lost mass. If anything was worth notifying the doctors about, it was that. Gaps led to chafing, they had said, then down the slippery slope to irritation and abrasion and infection. You don't work a horse with a harness sore.

In the mirror, he saw his gaunt face, his narrowed shoulder, the sleeve. His left arm, with its jagged love letter. On the right side, he saw road. A trick of the mind. A glitch in the software. Shoulder, road. He knew it was all there: the pincer hand, the metal bones, the wire sinew. He opened and closed the hand. It was still there, but it was gone at the same time.

He scooped grain for the horses with his road hand, ran his left over their shaggy winter coats. He oiled machinery with his road hand. Tossed hay bales and bags of grain with both arms working together. Worked on his truck in the garage. Other trucks made their slow way down a snowy highway in Colorado that was attached to him by wire, by electrode, by artificial pathways that had somehow found their way from his brain to his heart. He lay down on his frozen driveway, arms at his sides, and felt the trucks rumble through.

The thaw came late to both of Andy's places, the farm and the highway. He had hoped the bustle of spring might bring relief, but instead he felt even more divided.

He tried to explain the feeling to Susan over a beer on her tiny screen porch. She had moved back to town while he was in the hospital, rented a tiny apartment on top of the tattoo parlor. A big-bellied stove took up most of the porch, letting her wear tank tops even this early in the season. Her arms were timelines, a progression of someone else's skill; her own progression must be on other arms, back in Vancouver. She had gone right after high school, to apprentice herself to some tattoo bigshot. Andy couldn't figure out why she had returned, but here she was, back again.

The sleeves of his jacket hid his own arms. Not that he was hiding anything. He held the beer in his left hand now only because his right hand dreamed of asphalt and tumbleweeds. He didn't want to bother it.

"Maybe it's recycled," Susan said. "Maybe it used to belong to some Colorado rancher."

Andy shook his head. "It isn't in the past, and it isn't a person on the road."

"The software, then? Maybe that's the recycled part, and the chip was meant for one of those new smart roads near Toronto, the ones that drive your car for you."

"Maybe." He drained the beer, then dropped the can to the porch and crushed it with the heel of his workboot. He traced his scars with his fingertips: first the scalp, then across and down his chest, where metal joined to flesh.

"Are you going to tell anybody else?" Susan asked.

He listened to the crickets, the undertones of frog. He knew Susan was hearing those, too. He didn't think she heard the road thrumming in his arm. "Nah. Not for now."

Andy's arm was more in Colorado every day. He struggled to communicate with it. It worked fine; it was just elsewhere. Being a road wasn't so bad, once he got used to it. People say a road goes to and from places, but it doesn't. A road is where it is every moment of the day.

He thought about driving south, riding around until he could prove whether or not the place actually existed, but he couldn't justify leaving after all that time in the hospital. Fields needed to be tilled and turned and seeded. Animals needed to be fed and watered. He had no time for road trips, no matter how important the trip or the road.

Susan dragged him to a bonfire out at the Oakley farm. He didn't want to go, hadn't been to a party since he had bought his own land, but she was persuasive. "I need to reconnect with my client base and I don't feel like getting hit on the whole time," she said. He hung his robot arm out the window to catch the wind as she drove. Wind twenty-one kilometers per hour, it told him. Twelve degrees Celsius. In the other place, five centimeters of rain had fallen in the last two hours, and three vehicles had driven through.

The bonfire was already going in a clearing by the barn, a crowd around it, shivering. Doug Oakley was a year older than Andy, Hugh still in high school. They both lived with their parents, which meant this was a parents-out-of-town party. Most of the parties Andy had ever been to were like this, except he had been on the younger side of the group then instead of the older side. There's a point at which you're the cool older guy, and then after that you're the weird older guy who shouldn't be hanging with high school kids anymore. He was pretty sure he had crossed that line.

Susan had bought a case of Molson to make friends and influence people. She hoisted it out of the backseat now and emptied the beers into a cooler in the grass. She took one for herself and tossed one to him, but it bounced off his new hand. He glanced around to see if anybody had noticed. He shoved that can deep into the ice and freed another one from the cooler. He held it in the pincer and popped the top with his left, then drained half of it in one chug. The beer was cold and the air was cold and he wished he had brought a heavier jacket. At least he could hold the drink in his metal hand. His own insulator.

The high school girls all congregated by the porch. Most of them had plastic cups instead of cans, for mixing Clamato with their beer. Susan looked at them and snorted. "If I live to be two hundred, I will never understand that combination."

They walked toward the fire. It blazed high, but its heat didn't reach far beyond the first circle of people knotted around it. Andy shifted from foot to foot, trying to get warm, breathing in woodsmoke. He looked at the faces, recognizing most of them. The Oakley boys, of course, and their girlfriends. They always had girlfriends. Doug had been engaged at one point and now he wasn't. Andy tried to remember details. His mother would know.

He realized that the girl on Doug's arm now was Lori. Nothing wrong with that—Doug was a nice guy—but Lori had always talked about university. Andy had soothed his broken heart by saying she deserved more than a farmer's life. It hurt him a little to see her standing in the glow of the flame, her hands in her armpits. He didn't mind that he was still here, but he didn't think she ought to be. Or maybe she was just leaning against Doug for warmth? It wasn't his business anymore, he supposed.

Lori slipped from under Doug's arm and into the crowd. She appeared next to Susan a moment later.

"Hey," she said, raising a hand in greeting, then slipping it back under her armpit, either out of awkwardness or cold. She looked embarrassed.

"Hey," he replied, nodding his beer toward her with the robot hand. He tried to make it a casual movement. Only a little beer sloshed out of the can.

"I heard about your arm, Andy. I felt terrible. Sorry I didn't call, but the semester got busy . . ." She trailed off.

It was a lousy excuse, but his smile was genuine. "It's cool. I understand. You're still in university?"

"Yeah. Winnipeg. I've got one more semester."

"What are you majoring in?" Susan asked.

"Physics, but I'll be going to grad school for meteorology. Climate science."

"Awesome. You know what would make a cool tattoo for a climate scientist?"

Andy excused himself to get another beer. When he came back, Susan was drawing a barometer on the back of Lori's hand. She and Lori had never been close, but they had gotten on okay. Susan had liked that Lori had ambition, and Lori had liked dating a guy whose best friend was a girl, which she said was pretty unusual. If they had moved to the same city, CTV could have made some cheesy buddy comedy about them, the small town valedictorian and the small town lesbian punk in the big city. He would make a one-time appearance as the guy who had stayed behind.

After his fifth beer he couldn't feel anything but the road in his sleeve. The air in Colorado smelled like ozone, like maybe a storm was about to hit. That night, after Susan had drawn marker tattoos onto several of their former classmates and invited them to stop at her shop, after promises of email were exchanged with Lori, after the hazy drive home, he dreamed the highway had taken him over entirely. In the nightmare, the road crept up past his arm, past his shoulder. It paved his heart, flattened his limbs, tarred his mouth and eyes, so that he woke gasping before dawn.

He set up an appointment with a therapist. Dr. Bird's broad face was young, but her hair was completely silver-white. She nodded sympathetically as she listened.

"I'm not really here to give my opinion, but I think maybe you were rushed into this BCI thing. You didn't have a part in the decision. You didn't have any time to get used to the idea of having no arm."

"Did I need to get used to that?"

"Some people do. Some people don't have a choice, because their bodies need to heal before regular prosthetics can be fitted."

What she said made sense, but it didn't explain anything. It would have explained phantom pains, or dreams that his arm was choking him. He had read about those things. But a road? None of her theories jibed. He drove home on flat prairie highway, then flat prairie two-lane, between fallow fields and grazing land. The road to his parents' farm, and his own parcel of land in back of theirs, was dirt. His new truck had lousy shock absorbers, and every rut jolted him on the bench.

He had lived here his whole life, but his arm was convinced it belonged someplace else. On the way home it spoke to him without words. It pulled him. Turn around, it said. South, south, west. I am here and I am not here, he thought, or maybe it thought. I love my home, he tried to tell it. Even as he said it, he longed for the completion of being where he was, both Saskatchewan and Colorado. This was not a safe way to be. Nobody could live in two places at once. It was a dilemma. He couldn't leave his farm, not unless he sold it, and the only part of him that agreed with that plan was not really part of him at all.

That night he dreamed he was driving the combine through his canola field when it jammed. He climbed down to fix it, and this time it took his prosthetic. It chewed the metal and the wire, and he found himself hoping it would just rip the whole thing from his body, clear up to his brain, so he could start afresh. But then it did keep going. It didn't stop with the arm. It tore and ripped, and he felt a tug in his head that turned into throbbing, then a sharp and sharp and sharper pain.

The pain didn't go away when he woke. He thought it was a hangover, but no hangover had ever felt like that. He made it to the bathroom to throw up, then crawled back to his cell phone by the bed to call his mother. The last thing he thought of before he passed out was that Brad had never taught him how to crawl on the prosthetic. It worked pretty well.

He woke in the hospital again. He checked his hands first. Left still there, right still robot. With the left, he felt along the familiar edges of the prosthetic and the sleeve. Everything was still there. His hand went up to his head, where it encountered bandages. He tried to lift the prosthetic, but it didn't move.

A nurse entered the room. "You're awake!" she said with a West Indian lilt. "Your parents went home, but they'll be back after feeding time, they said."

"What happened?" he asked.

"Pretty bad infection around the chip in your head, so they took it out. The good news is that the electrodes all scanned fine. They'll give you a new chip when the swelling goes down, and you'll be using that fine bit of machinery again in no time."

She opened the window shade. From the bed, all Andy saw was sky, blue and serene. The best sky to work under. He looked down at the metal arm again, and realized that for the first time in months, he saw the arm, and not Colorado. He could still bring the road—his road—to mind, but he was no longer there. He felt a pang of loss. That was that, then.

When the swelling went down, a new chip was installed in his head. He waited for this one to assert itself, to tell him his arm was a speedboat or a satellite or an elephant's trunk, but he was alone in his head again. His hand followed his directions, hand-like. Open, close. No cows, no dust, no road.

He asked Susan to get him from the hospital. Partly so his parents wouldn't have to disrupt their schedules again, and partly because he had something to ask her.

In her car, driving home, he rolled up his left sleeve. "Remember this?" he asked.

She glanced at it and flushed. "How could I forget? I'm sorry, Andy. Nobody should go through life with a tattoo that awful."

"It's okay. I was just wondering, well, if you'd maybe fix it. Change it."

"God, I'd love to! You're the worst advertisement my business could have. Do you have anything in mind?"

He did. He looked at the jagged letters. The *I* of *LORI* could easily be turned into an *A*, the whole name disappeared into COLORADO. It was up to him to remember. Somewhere, in some medical waste bin back in Saskatoon, there was a computer chip that knew it was a road. A chip that was an arm that was Andy who was a stretch of asphalt two lanes wide, ninety-seven kilometers long, in eastern Colorado. A stretch that could see all the way to the mountains, but was content not to reach them. Forever and ever.

— *And We Were Left Darkling* —

I don't remember her birth. My dream baby, the baby I have in my dreams, the one who crashed into my head one night and took roost. She is a day old, a week old, a year old, eight years old, three weeks old, a day old. She has fine blond hair, except when she has tight black curls. Once she had cornrows that lengthened every time I looked away.

"Her hair grows faster than I can cut it," I said to my dream family.

My family in my dream is my family in real life, but less helpful. In my dream, they are standoffish. They offer advice or jokes or criticism. They never take the baby from my arms. Even my wife, my dream version of my real wife, sits on a couch on the far side of the room. She smiles and gives me the occasional thumbs-up. I am supported and loved. I am panicked and out of sorts.

The dreams are so powerful my real breasts fill with milk. They ache. In the dream, nobody gives me any instruction on how to nurse, but we find our way. She never cries.

During the day, I try to explain to Taya. She doesn't understand. Doesn't understand the dream baby, the real milk, the disorientation I carry into my morning.

"What do you mean 'she's real'?" Taya asks. "Does this have anything to do with giving up on getting pregnant?"

We tried and failed for five years. We're too old, too broke for the treatments that might get us there. Can't afford to adopt. In the last year we've just stopped talking about it entirely.

"It's different," I tell her. "It doesn't feel like a wanting. It feels like she exists already. She's real."

I start taking naps. I go to sleep as soon as I get home from the store, setting an alarm so that I wake a few minutes before Taya gets home from the veterinary clinic. I hide what I can. I don't know how to say that this is my baby, not ours.

It's a variation on the same dream every time. Every night and every nap. I am holding my baby, cradling her [blond dark fine napped curly] head. My sisters are there, my parents, my wife. I remark that if I had known the baby was coming, I would have cleaned the floors, run a bath, made some food.

"When was the last time I bathed her?" I ask, though her head smells sweet and clean. Nobody answers.

She reaches for me and I fumble with my shirt. I'm unprepared, awkward. I look to my sister for advice, but she shakes her head and smiles. While the baby nurses, I look out the window at a composite of Georgia O'Keeffe's 1920s skyscrapers. They gleam silver against the velvet night. Giant windup toy monsters stalk the spaces between [the paintings the towers]. They are genial monsters despite their occasional exhalations of sparks. No buildings are stomped.

My dream baby grows older except when she grows younger. She is sometimes a toddler, except when she's not. She has left home twice, but each time returned to be a baby the next night. I greet her with relief. I am always surprised to see her. For the first moment, I always wonder that she is mine, even as I know it is true. I try to remember giving birth, but that's not part of [the plan the dream]. She is always here. She was always here. She is [fourteen eighteen one day] old.

I look online, using the search terms "dream symbolism" and "infants." The results scroll past. Dreams of great earth changes, the divine child, responsibility, innocence. I dismiss most of it, but one link catches my eye: a bulletin board comment asking for other people who have had extended, repeating, real-feeling dreams of a baby. I click, scroll through the responses. There are hundreds. I don't read them. I don't want to find out if I share her. I don't want to share her.

The third time she leaves home, she leaves for good. For the first time in a year I sleep without dreams. Waking is easier, bedtime is sadder. I miss her. I find the website with the dream babies again. There's a follow-up post by the same woman, and I read it this time. She is no longer having the dream, either. Two hundred and seventy-two others report the same thing. I should add my voice to theirs, but I don't want to share the loss any more than I wanted to share my child.

When the babies come back, they all return at once. I recognize mine when I see her on the news. They come out of the ocean, our dream children, naked and beautiful, all different ages. They appear on the rocks off southern California with the sea lions. I would know mine anywhere, even through the television. Her hair is chest-nut, like mine. She looks to be eight years old. I remember all the times she was eight in my dreams. The year she broke her arm, the year we made chocolate-chip cookies and let the windup monsters bake them with their breath. She has freckles and skin that browns quickly in the California sun.

I want to book a flight, but Taya refuses. "It's too weird. And we can't afford it."

"The other parents are gathering, though. They're flying in from all over the world. What if she needs me?" I ask. "What if she needs me and I'm not there?"

Taya shakes her head and scratches at a stain on her green scrub pants. "I'm trying to understand, Jo." I know she's trying. I see the worry in her eyes. I book the flight anyway, maxing out our credit card for a same-day ticket. It's irresponsible. I shouldn't do it. I don't even say goodbye.

I'm not the only one. There are other dreamers at the airport. We're all easy to spot. The security lines loop back on themselves as the agents pull us aside for intrusive searches. We look too vacant, too gone. None of us have luggage. We accept the pat downs without complaint. We watch out the airplane windows, no books or tablets or crosswords in our hands. We're the ones with our faces in the clouds, clouds in our faces.

We take cabs from the airport in Los Angeles, grouping in twos and threes and fours, telling the confused cab drivers to drop us by the ocean, by the niños del mar. Emphasizing niños, niños. They drop us at the beaches and piers, at the rocky cliff tops. Surfers stare at us with idle curiosity. We only see the figures off the shore.

My boss calls to ask whether I'm sick. I mean to lie, say yes, but what comes out is, "I had to leave town."

She tells me not to bother coming back. I should mind, but I don't.

We wait. It's June, and the evening is crisp but not cool. The air smells like salt. We search our bags and pockets for airline peanuts, for apples and protein bars and whatever we stashed on our way out the door. Concerned locals bring us pizzas and bottled water. We eat with our eyes on the sea, even in the fading light.

The sunset reminds me for a moment that I have never before seen the Pacific, never seen this particular sinking sun. I feel a pang of guilt that I'm watching this without Taya. The children on the rocks are lit from behind, then fall into shadow. The sunset takes them from us afresh.

We tell each other stories about our dream children. They are different and the same. None of us have children of our own outside of dreaming. Those with families always report that our families appear in the dreams. I'm the only one with Georgia O'Keeffe skylines, the only one with windup monsters. Others have Chagalls and Rothkos and that overdramatic painter of light; they have Donkey Kong and Space Invaders and Looney Tunes characters.

"Like Mad Libs," someone says. "We each fill in the blanks differently."

It's easy to poke at the other aspects of the dreams. Nobody pokes at the parts about the children. I don't know how many others are doing the math that I am doing in my head. There are far more parents on this beach than there are children on the rocks. Does that mean some of us share? Are we all even seeing the same thing? We don't ask those questions.

A group of reporters camps near us, their vans circled like covered wagons, their giant antennae piercing the sky. Occasionally one approaches us, but we don't speak to them. It takes just a few minutes to discover the one who tries to infiltrate our group. Her details are wrong. She refers to "the baby," not "my baby." Her eyes aren't haunted. When we ask her to leave, she smirks. I guess that she recorded us, and I wonder what she captured.

A woman arrives on foot. It's unclear where she walked from, but her face blisters with sunburn. Heat radiates from her skin, even this long after nightfall. We lay her on the cool sand and pour a slow trickle of water into her cracked lips.

"Do you need a doctor? Medico?" Someone asks.

She shakes her head and points toward the dark sea. "Mijo."

She is one of us.

I sleep dreamless on the damp sand. I'm wakened by a familiar hand, a familiar voice. I curl into Taya for a moment before I realize where I am.

"What are you doing here?" My throat is scratchy and sore from sleeping outdoors.

"I could ask you the same fucking thing."

I hear the betrayal in her voice. Ordinarily, I would hate to be the cause of that hurt.

"How did you get here?" I ask.

"I sold the car to pay for a ticket. We'll have to figure that out when we get back. Come on, babe. Let's go get breakfast or something." She holds out her hand to help me stand.

I shake my head. "I can't go anywhere. Not without her."

She rocks back on her heels.

"I would leave if I could, Tay. But I need to be here when they—"

"When they what? You're acting crazy. What are we doing here?"

I wrap my arms around my knees and look out at the ocean. The children sit on the rocks, watching us. She's right, but it doesn't matter. I ought to leave. I can't leave. I still can't explain.

She sits down next to me. "Okay, if you're staying, I'm staying, too. We're both going to get fired, but we've got no way to get home and no way to get to work, so we're screwed either way. But you're still with me, yeah?"

"Yeah," I say. I don't tell her I've already been fired. I know I should put an arm around her, but I don't. I'm glad she's here, but I wish she wasn't.

The others stir and turn to face the water, to check that they are still out there.

"They're talking about you on the news, you know." Taya doesn't look at me when she speaks. Her eyes are on the children, as ours are.

"Me? What are they saying?"

"Not you specifically. All of you. They're calling it 'mass hallucination.'"

"Hallucination? But they can see them too, right? Our babies were on TV."

She winces when I say "our babies," and doesn't speak for a moment. When she does, her words are carefully chosen. "We see them. But nobody but you claims to recognize them. They've been taking photos of them since they showed up, comparing the photos to databases, missing persons, driver's licenses. None of them are anybody."

"Of course they're not," says the man sitting on Taya's other side. I had spoken with him the previous evening; he had flown down from Vancouver. Mark somebody. "Why would they match your databases? They aren't lost. We've been waiting for them to find us again."

Taya sneaks me a look of "this guy is nuts." How many times has it been me and her against the rest of the world? I know it hurts her when I take his side. If he's crazy, I am, too. I don't feel crazy. "What else are they saying, Tay?"

"There are only about two hundred and fifty children out there. There are more than three hundred of you on the shore, and more still arriving. There are people at airports all over the world screaming that they need to get over here, but a lot of them don't have visas, or any way to pay for tickets. Some of us are throwing off the count, though. Me, I mean. For example."

Mark doesn't mince words. "Why don't you leave, then? We don't need you here."

"I'm glad she's here. I'm glad you're here." I direct the second one at her.

"So she can call us all crazy? There aren't enough people doing that." I guess he caught her "crazy" look at me a moment before.

"Maybe so she can explain that we're not."

He stands up in pretext of a stretch, then moves away.

"Asshole," I say. Taya smiles.

A few more of us arrive, from much farther away. One woman came from Namibia via Johannesburg, Dakar, Amsterdam, New York. She braces in the sand as if she's still on an airplane. Others from Belize, Iceland, Sri Lanka. Some of the wealthier among us have arranged for food and water to be brought to us. I'm grateful. The sight of food reminds me to eat, but I'm not hungry. The children on the rocks haven't eaten. They look happy.

Taya leaves after three days. "I love you," she says. "I love you and I'm worried about you. I would stay, but we can't afford for me to lose my job, too. And I think this is something you need to finish for yourself."

I kiss her. I want her to stay, but not as much as I want her to leave.

"I love you, too. I'll see you soon," I tell her. She turns away with tears in her eyes. Things we don't mention: I have no return ticket; I have no money for a return ticket; I am waiting for my dream baby; I don't know what happens next.

After she leaves, I find a note from her in my pocket. It reads:

> 1. The California ground squirrel disguises its own scent by chewing the discarded skins of the rattlesnakes that would kill it, then licking itself and its pups.
> 2. The cuckoo is a brood parasite. It lays its eggs in the nests of other birds, leaving them to do the hard work of raising the chicks.
> 3. I do not consider myself an unreasonable person. I make rational decisions in my everyday life. You do, too. We make reasonable, rational decisions together. Come back soon. Please. I miss you.

I fold the note up and put it back where I found it.

We are there for a full week before the children finally leave the rocks. Our numbers have dwindled by then, but only somewhat. A couple of people have been dragged away forcibly. Others have been persuaded by their loved ones to return home. They don't go willingly, but they go. I wonder what the rest of their lives will be like: if they will always wonder if they had stayed. I guess that depends on what happens next.

What happens next is the children dive into the water. We track their progress with whispered pleas, under breath. I am taken in.

"Come on," we call to them. "We miss you."

I realize my child doesn't have a name. It's the first thing that gives me pause in any of this. How am I here, in California, calling to somebody I am so sure is my own child, but I can't say her name? I think she had one. She may have had many. It bothers me how I can't remember.

Memories of my baby's childhood flood through me. Her third birthday party, with the cake shaped like a rabbit; she refused to let me cut it. Her school play, where she played a queen and wouldn't take off the crown for a week afterward. Looking for shapes in the perfect O'Keeffe clouds. I wonder how these memories will reconcile with the girl swimming toward me now. Will she be eight for me again? Did those things happen, or are they yet to happen? I don't even know if she'll recognize me.

I put my hand in my pocket and feel the folded note. I'm not sure what Taya meant, not sure if I'm the squirrel, the snake, the cuckoo, the other bird. I want to go back to the minute before I had that thought. I try to picture how she'll fold into our life back home. How will Taya treat her? What will they be to each other? We don't even have a second bedroom. None of this was thought through. None of it was meant for thinking.

They're getting closer. They're so beautiful.

I realize I never taught her to swim. They swim like Olympians, like fish, like creatures of the ocean, like they have always been swimming and have never stopped swimming. I'm scared now. She's so beautiful, and she's reached the shore, and she's inescapably mine.

— Remembery Day —

I woke at dawn on the holiday, so my grandmother put me to work polishing Mama's army boots.

"Try not to let her see them," Nana warned me. I already knew.

I took the boots to the bathroom with an old sock and the polish kit. I had seen Nana clean them before, but this marked the first time I was allowed to do it myself. Saddle soap first, then moisturizer, then polish. I pictured Nana at the ironing board in our bedroom, pressing the proper creases into Mama's old uniform.

The door swung open, and I realized too late that I had forgotten to lock it. Mama didn't often wake up this early on days she didn't have to work.

"Whose are those?" my mother asked, yawning.

"Uh—" I didn't know what to say, which lie I was supposed to tell.

Nana rescued me from the situation, coming up behind Mama. "Those were your father's, Kima. I asked Clara to clean them for me."

Mama's gaze lingered on the boots. Did she think they were the wrong size for Grandpa? Did she recognize them?

"I need the bathroom," she said after a moment. "Do you mind doing that somewhere else, Clara?"

I pinched the boots together and lifted them away from my body so I wouldn't stain my clothes, gathering up the polish kit with my other hand. Mama waited until I slipped past before she wheeled in.

Her indoor chair was narrow, but not narrow enough for both of us to fit in the small bathroom.

"I'm sorry," I whispered to Nana once the door closed.

"No harm done," Nana whispered back.

I finished on the kitchen floor, now that there was no reason to hide. It was almost time, anyway. The parade would start at ten by us. In some places, people had to get up in the middle of the night.

Mama came in to breakfast, and I put the boots in a corner to dry. Nana had made coffee and scrambled eggs with green chiles, but all I could smell was the saddle soap on my hands. We all ate in silence: Mama because she wasn't a morning person, and Nana and I because we were waiting. Listening. At eight the sirens went off, just the expected short burst to warn us the Veil would be lifting.

Mama whipped her head around. "What was that? Oh."

The lifting of the Veil always hit her the same. My teacher said each vet reacted in a different way, but my friends never discussed what it was like for their parents. Mama always went "Oh" first, lifting her hand to her mouth. Her eyes flew open as if they were opening for the first time, and for one moment she would look at me as if I were a stranger. It upset me when I was little. I think I understand now, or anyway I'm used to it.

"Oh," she said again.

She studied her hands in her lap for a moment, and I saw they were shaking. She didn't say anything, just wheeled herself into the bathroom. I heard the water start up, then the creak as she transferred herself to the seat in the shower. Nana came around the table to hug me. When she got up to lay Mama's uniform on her bed, I followed with the boots I had shined. We waited in the kitchen.

Showering and dressing took her a while, as it did on any day, but when she appeared in the kitchen doorway again, she had her uniform on. It fit perfectly. Mama didn't need to know that Nana had let it out a little. I had never seen a picture of her as a young soldier, but it wasn't hard to imagine. I only had to strip away the chair and the burn on her face. This was the one day I looked at her that way; on all other days, those were just part of her.

"Did you shine these for me?" She pointed to her boots.

I nodded.

"They're perfect. Everyone will be so impressed." She pulled me onto her lap. I was getting too old for laps, but today she was allowed. I stayed for a minute then stood again. When she laughed it was a different laugh from the rest of the year, a little lower and softer. I've never been sure which is her real laugh.

At nine, we all got in the van, and Mama drove us downtown.

"Mama, can I ask you a question?"

"Yes?"

"What did you do in the War?"

I saw her purse her lips in the mirror. "There's a long answer to that question, mija, and I don't think I can answer it right this moment while I'm driving. Can we talk more in a while?"

I knew how this worked. "In a while" didn't always come. Still, this was her day. "I guess."

A few minutes later Mama took an unexpected right turn and pulled the van over. "How about if we skip it this year? Go get some ice cream or sit on the pier or something?"

"Mama, no! This is for you!" I didn't understand why she would suggest such a thing. My horror welled up before I thought to see what Nana said first.

She turned to Nana next, but my grandmother just shrugged.

"You're right, Clara. I don't know what I was thinking." Mama sighed and put the van back into gear.

Veterans got all the good parking in the city on the holiday. Mama's uniform got us close. The wheelchair sticker got us even closer. I didn't understand how they all knew where to go, how to find their regiments, but they did. Nana and I stood near the staging area and watched as the veterans hugged each other and cried. Mama pointed to me and waved. I smiled and waved back.

We found seats in the grandstand, surrounded by other families like ours. I recognized a couple of the kids. We had played together beneath the stands when we were little, when we called it Remembery Day because we didn't know better. Now that I was old enough to understand a little more, I wanted to sit with Nana. The metal bench burned my legs even through my pants. A breeze blew through the canyon created by the buildings. It rustled the flags on the opposite side of the street, and I tried to identify the different states and countries.

A marching band started to play, and we all sang "The Ones Who Made it Home" and then "Flowers Bloom Where You Fell." At school I learned that parades used to include national anthems, but since the War our allies everywhere choose to sing these two songs. I can sing them both in four different languages. The band stopped in front of each stand to play the two songs again. It was always a long parade.

Behind them came six horses the color of Mama's boots and every bit as shiny. Froth flew from their mouths as they tossed their heads and danced sideways against their harnesses. Their bits and bridles gleamed with polish, but they pulled a plain cart. It rolled on wooden wheels and carried a wooden casket. The young man driving wore the new uniform designed after the War, light gray with black bands around the arms. Nobody who hadn't fought was allowed to wear the old one anymore.

Then came the veterans. Fewer every year. Nana has promised me Mama was never exposed to the worst stuff; I worry anyway. I imagine there will be a time when there aren't enough of them to form ranks, but for now there were still a good number. Some, like my mother, rode in motorized wheelchairs. Some had faces more scarred than hers. Others waved prosthetic hands. Those too weak were pushed by others or rode on floats down the boulevard. I saw my teacher march past. I had never noticed him in the ranks before, but I guess he wasn't my teacher until this year, so I wouldn't have known to look for him. The way he talked in class I would never have guessed he was a veteran. Of course, that was the case with all of them since the Veil was invented. I don't know why I was surprised.

When Mama passed I mustered a little extra volume, so everyone would know she was mine. She spotted me in the crowd and pointed and waved. We cheered until our throats were raw. It was the least we could do, the only thing we could do.

The same thing was happening at the same time in all the cities and countries left. I pictured children and grandparents cheering under dark skies and noonday sun. It was summer here, but winter in the northern hemisphere, so I pictured the other kids bundled up, their bleachers chilling their legs while the bench I sat on made me sweat behind my knees.

The last soldiers passed us, and we made sure we had enough voice left to show our appreciation to them as well. Behind them, another horse, saddled but riderless, with fireweed braided into his mane. He was there to remind us of the clean-up crews, those who had been exposed after the treaty. None of them were left to march.

We waited in the stands after the parade ended. Nana spoke with some people sitting nearby. Some families left, but others lingered like us. We knew it would be a while. The veterans had gone off to gather at their arranged meeting places as they were supposed to do, in bars or parks or coffee shops at the other end of the route. A couple of people in uniform walked back in our direction and slipped away with family, ignoring the looks we gave them. We all knew they were supposed to be at the vote.

"What do you think they'll decide this year?" asked a boy around my age. I had met him before, but I didn't remember his name, only that both his parents were in the parade. He sat alone.

I shrugged and gave my teacher's answer. "That's up to them. It's not for us to approve or disapprove."

He moved away from me. Nana was still talking. The bench had cleared and I lay back on it despite the heat. We were lucky to have had such beautiful weather. The sky was a shade of blue that got deeper the more I looked at it, like I could see through the atmosphere and into space. I thought about the other girls like me in a hundred other cities, waiting for their mothers and lying on benches and looking up at the sky.

We waited a long time. Nana pulled out her book. Her finger didn't move across the page the way it usually did, so I guessed she wasn't really reading. I closed my eyes and listened to the sweepers come to clear the streets, and the other stragglers chatting with each other. Now and again the bleachers clanged and shook as small children chased each other up and down.

Eventually, I heard the whine of a wheelchair operating at its highest speed. I shaded my face and looked down. Mama. Her eyes were puffy like she had been crying. Some years she smelled like beer, but this year she didn't.

I sat in the backseat and counted all the flags hanging from houses and shops.

"And?" Nana asked after we had ridden in silence for several minutes.

"No."

"Was the vote close?"

Mama sighed, her voice so soft I strained to hear it. "It never is."

Nana put her hand on Mama's arm. "Maybe someday."

"Maybe."

Back at the house, we took in the flag. Mama changed her clothes. She sat in her recliner with her hands folded in her lap, while Nana took the uniform from her to hide until next year. I went to get my father's photo from my drawer. I didn't see Nana on her bed across from mine until I stood up. She was holding her face in her hands.

"That damned Veil," she said. "I'll never understand why they vote for the Veil, year after year."

"Because the memories are too strong." I repeated what my teacher told me. "The war was too brutal."

"But she wants to remember."

"It wouldn't do anyone any good if she ran into one of her friends in the grocery store who didn't remember her. It has to be everybody or nobody, Nana."

"But they push down so many good memories along with the bad ones."

"I think the good memories hurt too." I had seen the tears in my mother's eyes.

"Tell me something about him that I don't know." I climbed onto the arm of the recliner.

My mother smiled and took the photo from me, tracing his jaw-line and then the buttons on his dress uniform.

"I met him in the gym on base. He was the only guy who would spot me while I lifted without making comments."

"I know, Mama. What else?" I didn't mean for the impatience to show in my voice. "I'm sorry. I don't mean to rush you."

"He liked to play games with the village children outside the compound where we were stationed. The officers hated it, told him he would get kidnapped, but he sneaked out whenever he could."

I smiled. "I didn't know that. What games did they play?"

"The first week we were there, he brought chalk with him. He said there was one little boy, and he went to give him a piece of chalk, and suddenly he had two dozen children climbing all over him with their hands out. He was lucky it was chalk, so he was able to break it into smaller pieces. Some of the little ones tried to eat it. 'At least they got their calcium,' he told me later. After that, he didn't bring them anything, since he didn't have anything else to split so many ways. He made me teach him hopscotch, so he could teach it to them. Can you imagine that? This big soldier playing hopscotch? Then four square, football, anything they could play with a stick or a line in the dirt or the ball they already had. He would sneak back in with his eyes glowing like he had forgotten where we were and why we were there. Then the first attack—" She twisted her hands in her lap.

"Why were you there, Mama?"

A church bell began to chime, and another one, and another.

"Tell me more, Mama, quick!"

There was so much I wanted to know. A tear rolled down her cheek, and she pulled me close. She didn't answer, and I knew it was too late. I thought of my father, the man in the uniform, and tried to picture him teaching hopscotch to me instead of village children. It was hard to imagine somebody I had never known, never could know. I should have started with her instead of my father.

Minutes passed, and the bells stopped. Mama's face closed down like a shutter. She fumbled in the pocket on the side of her chair. The photo of my father slid off her lap and to the floor.

"I don't know why, but I'm in the mood to watch something funny before we make dinner," she said. "Do you want to watch with me?"

"Sure. I'll be right back." I picked up the fallen photograph.

"Who's that?" she asked, glancing up.

"Somebody who fought in the war."

"A school project?"

"Yeah," I said.

"I'm proud of you." She smiled. "Those soldiers deserve to be remembered."

Nana was asleep on her bed. I hid the photo back in my drawer where Mama couldn't reach it or find it accidentally. Why had I asked about him first? I could never know him. He was gone and she was here and I still didn't know any more about the parts of her that went away.

Mama's voice carried down the hall. "Clara, are you watching with me?"

"Coming."

I pulled a chair up beside Mama's and leaned up against her. She leaned back. This was the Mama I knew best. The one who couldn't quite remember why she was in a wheelchair, who thought war was something that had happened to other people. The one who laughed at pet videos with me.

Some year, maybe the old soldiers would vote to lift the Veil. Maybe I'd get to know the other Mama, too: the one who remembered my father, who had died before I was born. The one who could someday tell me whether it had been worth everything she had lost. Next year, I would try to remember to ask that question first.

— *Sooner or Later Everything Falls into the Sea* —

The rock star washed ashore at high tide. Earlier in the day, Bay had seen something bobbing far out in the water. Remnant of a rowboat, perhaps, or something better. She waited until the tide ebbed, checked her traps and tidal pools among the rocks before walking toward the inlet where debris usually beached.

All kinds of things washed up if Bay waited long enough: not just glass and plastic, but personal trainers and croupiers, entertainment directors and dance teachers. This was the first time Bay recognized the face of the new arrival. She always checked the face first if there was one, just in case, hoping it wasn't Deb.

The rock star had an entire lifeboat to herself, complete with motor, though she'd used up the gas. She'd made it in better shape than many; certainly in better shape than those with flotation vests but no boats. They arrived in tatters of uniform. Armless, legless, sometimes headless; ragged shark refuse.

"What was that one?" Deb would have asked, if she were there. She'd never paid attention to physical details, wouldn't have recognized a dancer's legs, a chef's scarred hands and arms.

"Nothing anymore," Bay would say of a bad one, putting it on her sled.

The rock star still had all her limbs. She had stayed in the boat. She'd found the stashed water and nutrition bars, easy to tell by the wrappers and bottles strewn around her. From her bloated belly and cracked lips, Bay guessed she had run out a day or two before, maybe tried drinking ocean water. Sunburn glowed through her dark skin. She was still alive.

Deb wasn't there; she couldn't ask questions. If she had been, Bay would have shown her the calloused fingers of the woman's left hand and the thumb of her right.

"How do you know she came off the ships?" Deb would have asked. She'd been skeptical that the ships even existed, couldn't believe that so many people would just pack up and leave their lives. The only proof Bay could have given was these derelict bodies.

Inside the Music: Tell us what happened.

Gabby Robbins: A scavenger woman dragged me from the ocean, pumped water from my lungs, spoke air into me. The old films they show on the ships would call that moment romantic, but it wasn't. I gagged. Only barely managed to roll over to retch in the sand.

She didn't know what a rock star was. It was only when I washed in half-dead, choking seawater, that she learned there were such things in the world. Our first attempts at conversation didn't go well. We had no language in common. But I warmed my hands by her fire, and when I saw an instrument hanging on its peg, I tuned it and began to play. That was the first language we spoke between us.

A truth: I don't remember anything between falling off the ship and washing up in this place.

There's a lie embedded in that truth.

Maybe a couple of them.

Another lie I've already told: We did have language in common, the scavenger woman and me.

She did put me on her sled, did take me back to her stone-walled cottage on the cliff above the beach. I warmed myself by her wood-stove. She didn't offer me a blanket or anything to replace the thin stage clothes I still wore, so I wrapped my own arms around me and drew my knees in tight and sat close enough to the stove's open belly that sparks hit me when the logs collapsed inward.

She heated a small pot of soup on the stovetop and poured it into a single bowl without laying a second one out for me. My stomach growled. I didn't remember the last time I'd eaten. I eyed her, eyed the bowl, eyed the pot.

"If you're thinking about whether you could knock me out with the pot and take my food, it's a bad idea. You're taller than me, but you're weaker than you think, and I'm stronger than I look."

"I wouldn't! I was just wondering if maybe you'd let me scrape whatever's left from the pot. Please."

She nodded after a moment. I stood over the stove and ate the few mouthfuls she had left me from the wooden stirring spoon. I tasted potatoes and seaweed, salt and land and ocean. It burned my throat going down; heated from the inside, I felt almost warm.

I looked around the room for the first time. An oar with "Home Sweet Home" burnt into it adorned the wall behind the stove. Some chipped dishes on an upturned plastic milk crate, a wall stacked high with home-canned food, clothing on pegs. A slightly warped-looking classical guitar hung on another peg by a leather strap; if I'd had any strength I'd have gone to investigate it. A double bed piled with blankets. Beside the bed, a nightstand with a framed photo of two women on a hiking trail, and a tall stack of paperback books. I had an urge to walk over and read the titles; my father used to say you could judge a person by the books on their shelves. A stronger urge to dive under the covers on the bed, but I resisted and settled back onto the ground near the stove. My energy went into shivering.

I kept my eyes on the stove, as if I could direct more heat to me with enough concentration. The woman puttered around her cabin. She might have been any age between forty and sixty; her movement was easy, but her skin was weathered and lined, her black hair streaked with gray. After a while, she climbed into bed and turned her back to me. Another moment passed before I realized she intended to leave me there for the night.

"Please, before you go to sleep. Don't let it go out," I said. "The fire."

She didn't turn. "Can't keep it going forever. Fuel has to last all winter."

"It's winter?" I'd lost track of seasons on the ship. The scavenger woman wore two layers, a ragged jeans jacket over a hooded sweatshirt.

"Will be soon enough."

"I'll freeze to death without a fire. Can I pay you to keep it going?"

"What do you have to pay me with?"

"I have an account on the Hollywood Line. A big one." As I said that, I realized I shouldn't have. On multiple levels. Didn't matter if it sounded like a brag or desperation. I was at her mercy, and it wasn't in my interest to come across as if I thought I was any better than her.

She rolled over. "Your money doesn't count for anything off your ships and islands. Nor credit. If you've got paper money, I'm happy to throw it in to keep the fire going a little longer."

I didn't. "I can work it off."

"There's nothing you can work off. Fuel is in finite supply. I use it now, I don't get more, I freeze two months down the line."

"Why did you save me if you're going to let me die?"

"Pulling you from the water made sense. It's your business now whether you live or not."

"Can I borrow something warmer to wear at least? Or a blanket?" I sounded whiny even to my own ears.

She sighed, climbed out of bed, rummaged in a corner, and pulled out a down vest. It had a tear in the back where some stuffing had spilled out, and smelled like brine. I put it on, trying not to scream when the fabric touched my sunburned arms.

"Thank you. I'm truly grateful."

She grunted a response and retreated to her bed again. I tucked my elbows into the vest, my hands into my armpits. It helped a little, though I still shivered. I waited a few minutes, then spoke again. She didn't seem to want to talk, but it kept me warm. Reassured me that I was still here. Awake, alive.

"If I didn't say so already, thank you for pulling me out of the water. My name is Gabby."

"Fitting."

"Are you going to ask me how I ended up in the water?"

"None of my business."

Just as well. Anything I told her would've been made up.

"Do you have a name?" I asked.

"I do, but I don't see much point in sharing it with you."

"Why not?"

"Because I'm going to kill you if you don't shut up and let me sleep."

I shut up.

Inside the Music: Tell us what happened.

Gabby Robbins: I remember getting drunk during a set on the Elizabeth Taylor. *Making out with a bartender in the lifeboat, since neither of us had private bunks. I must have passed out there. I don't know how it ended up adrift.*

I survived the night on the floor but woke with a cough building deep in my chest. At least I didn't have to sing. I followed the scavenger as she went about her morning, like a dog hoping for scraps. Outside, a large picked-over garden spread around two sides of the cottage. The few green plants grew low and ragged. Root vegetables, maybe.

"If you have to piss, there's an outhouse over there," she said, motioning toward a stand of twisted trees.

We made our way down the footpath from her cottage to the beach, a series of switchbacks trod into the cliffside. I was amazed she had managed to tow me up such an incline. Then again, if I'd rolled off the sled and fallen to my death, she probably would've scraped me out of my clothes and left my body to be picked clean by gulls.

"Where are we?" I had managed not to say anything since waking up, not a word since her threat the night before, so I hoped the statute of limitations had expired.

"Forty kilometers from the nearest city, last I checked."

Better than nothing. "When was that?"

"When I walked here."

"And that was?"

"A while ago."

It must have been, given the lived-in look of her cabin and garden. "What city?"

"Portage."

"Portage what?"

"Portage. Population I don't know. Just because you haven't heard of it doesn't make it any less a city." She glanced back at me like I was stupid.

"I mean, what state? Or what country? I don't even know what country this is."

She snorted. "How long were you on that ship?"

"A long time. I didn't really pay attention."

"Too rich to care."

"No! It's not what you think." I didn't know why it mattered what she thought of me, but it did. "I wasn't on the ship because I'm rich. I'm an entertainer. I share a staff bunk with five other people."

"You told me last night you were rich."

I paused to hack and spit over the cliff's edge. "I have money, it's true. But not enough to matter. I'll never be rich enough to be a passenger instead of entertainment. I'll never even afford a private stateroom. So I spend a little and let the rest build up in my account."

Talking made me cough more. I was thirsty, too, but waited to be offered something to drink.

"What's your name?" I knew I should shut up, but the more uncomfortable I am, the more I talk.

She didn't answer for a minute, so by the time she did, I wasn't even sure if it was the answer to my question at all.

"Bay."

"That's your name? It's lovely. Unusual."

"How would you know? You don't even know what country this is. Who are you to say what's unusual here?"

"Good point. Sorry."

"You're lucky we even speak the same language."

"Very."

She pointed at a trickle of water that cut a small path down the cliff wall. "Cup your hands there. It's potable."

"A spring?"

She gave me a look.

"Sorry. Thank you." I did as she said. The water was cold and clear. If there was some bacterium in it that was going to kill me, at least I wouldn't die thirsty.

I showed my gratitude through silence and concentrated on the descent. The path was narrow, just wide enough for the sled she pulled, and the edge crumbled away to nothing. I put my feet where she put hers, squared my shoulders as she did. She drew her sweatshirt hood over her head, another discouragement to conversation.

We made it all the way down to the beach without another question busting through my chapped lips. She left the sled at the foot of the cliff and picked up a blue plastic cooler from behind a rock, the kind with cup holders built into the top. She looked in and frowned, then dumped the whole thing on the rocks. A cascade of water, two small dead fish. I realized those had probably been meant to be her dinner the day before; she had chosen to haul me up the cliff instead.

This section of beach was all broken rock, dotted everywhere with barnacles and snails and seashells. The rocks were wet and slick, the footing treacherous. I fell to my hands several times, slicing them on the tiny snails. Could you catch anything from a snail cut? At least the ship could still get us antibiotics.

"What are we doing?" I asked. "Surely the most interesting things wash out closer to the actual water."

She kept walking, watching where she stepped. She didn't fall. The rusted hull of an old ship jutted from the rocks down into the ocean; I imagined anything inside had long since been picked over. We clambered around it. I fell farther behind her, trying to be more careful with my bleeding palms. All that rust, no more tetanus shots.

She slowed, squatted. Peered and poked at something by her feet. As I neared her, I understood. Tidal pools. She dipped the cooler into one, smiled to herself. I was selfishly glad to see the smile. Perhaps she'd be friendlier now.

Instead of following, I took a different path from hers. Peered into other pools. Some tiny fish in the first two, not worth catching, nothing in the third. In the fourth, I found a large crab.

"Bay," I called.

She turned around, annoyance plain on her face. I waved the crab and her expression softened. "Good for you. You get to eat tonight too, with a nice find like that."

She waited for me to catch up with her and put the crab in her cooler with the one decent-sized fish she had found.

"What is it?" I asked.

"A fish. What does it matter what kind?"

"I used to cook. I'm pretty good with fish, but I don't recognize that one. Different fish taste better with different preparations."

"You're welcome to do the cooking if you'd like, but if you need lemon butter and capers, you may want to check the pools closer to the end of the rainbow." She pointed down the beach, then laughed at her own joke.

"I'm only trying to be helpful. You don't need to mock me."

"No, I suppose I don't. You found a crab, so you're not entirely useless."

That was the closest thing to a compliment I supposed I'd get. At least she was speaking to me like a person, not debris that had shown an unfortunate tendency toward speech.

That evening, I pan-fried our catch on the stovetop with a little bit of sea salt. The fish was oily and tasteless, but the crab was good. My hands smelled like fish and ocean, and I wished for running water to wash them off. Tried to replace that smell with wood smoke.

After dinner, I looked over at her wall.

"May I?" I asked, pointing at the guitar.

She shrugged. "Dinner and entertainment—I fished the right person out of the sea. Be my guest."

It was an old classical guitar, parlor sized, nylon stringed. That was the first blessing, since steel strings would surely have corroded in this air. I had no pure pitch to tune to, so had to settle on tuning the strings relative to each other, all relative to the third string because its tuning peg was cracked and useless. Sent up a silent prayer that none of the strings broke, since I was fairly sure Bay would blame me for anything that went wrong in my presence. The result sounded sour, but passable.

"What music do you like?" I asked her.

"Now or then?"

"What's the difference?"

"Then: anything political. Hip-hop, mostly."

I looked down at the little guitar, wondered how to coax hip-hop out of it. "What about now?"

"Now? Anything you play will be the first music I've heard other than my own awful singing in half a dozen years. Play away."

I nodded and looked at the guitar, waiting for it to tell me what it wanted. Fought back my strange sudden shyness. Funny how playing for thousands of people didn't bother me, but I could find myself self-conscious in front of one. "Guitar isn't my instrument, by the way."

"Close enough. You're a bassist."

I looked up, surprised. "How do you know?"

"I'm not stupid. I know who you are."

"Why did you ask my name, then?"

"I didn't. You told it to me."

"Oh, yeah." I was glad I hadn't lied about that particular detail.

"Let's have the concert, then."

I played her a few songs, stuff I never played on the ship.

"Where'd the guitar come from?" I asked when I was done.

An unreadable expression crossed her face. "Where else? It washed up."

I let my fingers keep exploring the neck of the guitar, but turned to her. "So is this what you do full time? Pull stuff from the beach?"

"Pretty much."

"Can you survive on that?"

"The bonuses for finding some stuff can be pretty substantial."

"What stuff?"

"Foil. Plastic. People."

"People?"

"People who've lost their ships."

"You're talking about me?"

"You, others. The ships don't like to lose people, and the people don't like to be separated from their ships. It's a nice change to be able to return someone living for once. I'm sure you'll be happy to get back to where you belong."

"Yes, thank you. How do you alert them?"

"I've got call buttons for the three big shiplines. They send 'copters."

I knew those copters. Sleek, repurposed military machines.

I played for a while longer, so stopping wouldn't seem abrupt, then hung the guitar back on its peg. It kept falling out of tune anyway.

I waited until Bay was asleep before I left, though it took all my willpower not to take off running the second she mentioned the helicopters. I had nothing to pack, so I curled up by the cooling stove and waited for her breathing to slow. I would never have taken her food or clothing—other than the vest—but I grabbed the guitar from its peg on my way out the door. She wouldn't miss it. The door squealed on its hinges, and I held my breath as I slipped through and closed it behind me.

The clifftop was bright with stars. I scanned the sky for helicopters. Nothing but stars and stars and stars. The ship's lights made it so we barely saw stars at all, a reassurance for all of us from the cities.

I walked with my back to the cliff. The moon gave enough light to reassure me I wasn't about to step off into nothingness if the coastline cut in, but I figured the farther I got from the ocean, the more likely I was to run into trees. Or maybe an abandoned house, if I got lucky. Someplace they wouldn't spot me if they swept overland.

Any hope I had for stealth, I abandoned as I trudged onward. I found an old tar road and decided it had to lead toward something. I walked. The cough that had been building in my chest through the day racked me now.

The farther I went, the more I began to doubt Bay's story. Would the ships bother to send anyone? I was popular enough, but was I worth the fuel it took to come get me? If they thought I had fallen, maybe. If they knew I had lowered the lifeboat deliberately, that I might do it again? Doubtful. Unless they wanted to punish me, or charge me for the boat, though if they docked my account now, I'd never know. And how would Bay have contacted them? She'd said they were in contact, but unless she had a solar charger—well, that seemed possible, actually.

Still, she obviously wanted me gone or she wouldn't have said it. Or was she testing my reaction? Waiting to see if I cheered the news of my rescue?

I wondered what else she had lied about. I hoped I was walking toward the city she had mentioned. I was a fool to think I'd make it to safety anywhere. I had no water, no food, no money. Those words formed a marching song for my feet, syncopated by my cough. No water. No food. No money. No luck.

Bay set out at first light, the moment she realized the guitar had left with the stupid rock star. It wasn't hard to figure out which way she had gone. She was feverish, stupid with the stupidity of someone still used to having things appear when she wanted them. If she really expected to survive, she should have taken more from Bay. Food. A canteen. A hat. Something to trade when she got to the city. It said something good about her character, Bay supposed, down below the blind privilege of her position. If she hadn't taken Debra's guitar, Bay's opinion might have been even more favorable.

Inside the Music: Tell us what happened.

Gabby Robbins: My last night on the ship was just like three thousand nights before, up until it wasn't. We played two sets, mostly my stuff, with requests mixed in. Some cokehead in a Hawaiian shirt offered us a thousand credits each to play "My Heart Will Go On" for his lady.

"I'll give you ten thousand credits myself if you don't make us do this," Sheila said when we all leaned in over her kit to consult on whether we could fake our way through it. "That's the one song I promised myself I would never play here."

"What about all the Jimmy Buffet we've had to play?" our guitarist, Kel, asked her. "We've prostituted ourselves already. What difference does it make at this point?"

Sheila ignored Kel. "Dignity, Gab. Please."

I was tired and more than a little drunk. "What does it matter? Let's just play the song. You can mess with the tempo if you want. Swing it, maybe? Ironic cheesy lounge style? In C, since I can't hit those diva notes?"

Sheila looked like she was going to weep as she counted off.

I ran into Hawaiian Shirt and his lady again after the set, when I stepped out on the Oprah deck for air. They were over near the gun turrets, doing the "King of the World" thing, a move that should have been outlawed before anyone got on the ship.

"You know who that is, right?" I looked over to see JP, this bartender I liked: sexy retro-Afro, sexy swimmer's build. It had been a while since we'd hooked up. JP held out a joint.

I took it and said he looked familiar.

"He used to have one of those talk radio shows. He was the first one to suggest the ships, only his idea was religious folks, not just general rich folks. Leave the sinners behind, he said. Founded the Ark line, where all those fundamentalists spend their savings waiting for the sinners to be washed away so they can take the land back. He spent the first two years with them, then announced he was going to go on a pilgrimage to find out what was happening everywhere else. Only, instead of traveling the land like a proper pilgrim, he came on board this ship. He's been here ever since. First time I've seen him at one of your shows, though. I guess he's throwing himself into his new lifestyle."

"Ugh. I remember him now. He boycotted my second album. At least they look happy?"

"Yeah, except that isn't his wife. His wife and kids are still on the Ark waiting for him. Some pilgrim."

The King of the World and his not-wife sauntered off. When the joint was finished, JP melted away as well, leaving me alone with my thoughts until some drunk kids wandered over with a magnum of champagne. I climbed over the railing into the lifeboat to get a moment alone. I could almost pretend the voices were gulls. Listened to the engine's thrum through the hull, the waves lapping far below.

Everyone who wasn't a paying guest—entertainers and staff—had been trained on how to release the lifeboats, and I found myself playing with the controls. How hard would it be to drop it into the water? We couldn't be that far from some shore somewhere. The lifeboats were all equipped with stores of food and water, enough for a handful of people for a few days.

Whatever had been in my last drink must have been some form of liquid stupid. The boat was lowered now, whacking against the side of the enormous ship, and I had to smash the last tie just to keep from being wrecked against it. And then the ship *was pulling away, ridiculous and huge, a foolish attempt to save something that had never been worth saving.*

I wished I had kissed JP one more time, seeing as how I was probably going to die.

Gabby hadn't gotten far at all. By luck, she had found the road in the dark, and by luck had walked in the right direction, but she was lying in the dirt like roadkill now. Bay checked that Deb's guitar hadn't been hurt, then watched for a moment to see if the woman was breathing, which she was, ragged but steady, her forehead hot enough to melt butter, some combination of sunburn and fever.

The woman stirred. "Are you real?" she asked.

"More real than you are," Bay told her.

"I should have kissed JP."

"Seems likely." Bay offered a glass jar of water. "Drink this."

Gabby drank half. "Thank you."

Bay waved it away when the other woman tried to hand it back. "I'm not putting my lips to that again while you're coughing your lungs out. It's yours."

"Thank you again." Gabby held out the guitar. "You probably came for this?"

"You carried it this far, you can keep carrying it. Me, I would have brought the case."

"It had a case?"

"Under the bed. I keep clothes in it."

"I guess at least now you know I didn't go through your things?"

Bay snorted. "Obviously. You're a pretty terrible thief."

"In my defense, I'm not a thief."

"My guitar says otherwise."

Gabby put the guitar on the ground. She struggled to her feet and stood for a wobbly moment before leaning down to pick it up. She looked one way, then the other, as if she couldn't remember where she had come from or where she was going. Bay refrained from gesturing in the right direction. She picked the right way. Bay followed.

"Are you going to ask me why I left?" Even this sick, with all her effort going into putting one foot in front of the other, the rock star couldn't stop talking.

"Wasn't planning on it."

"Why not?"

"Because I've met you before."

"For real? Before the ships?" Gabby looked surprised.

Bay shook her head. "No. Your type. You think you're the first one to wash ashore? To step away from that approximation of life? You're just the first one who made it alive."

"If you don't like the ships, why did you call them to come get me?" Gabby paused. "Or you didn't. You just wanted me to leave. Why?"

"I can barely feed myself. And you aren't the type to be satisfied with that life anyhow. Might as well leave now as later."

"Except I'm probably going to die of this fever because I walked all night in the cold, you psychopath."

Bay shrugged. "That was your choice."

They walked in silence for a while. The rock star was either contemplating her choices or too sick to talk.

"Why?" Bay asked, taking pity.

Gabby whipped her head around. "Why what?"

"Why did you sign up for the ship?"

"It seemed like a good idea at the time."

"Sounds like an epitaph fitting for half the people in this world."

Gabby gave a half smile, then continued. "New York was a mess, and the Gulf states had just tried to secede. The bookers for the Hollywood Line made a persuasive argument for a glamorous life at sea. Everything was so well planned, too. They bought entire island nations to provide food and fuel."

"I'm sure the island nations appreciated that," said Bay.

The other woman gave a wry smile. "I know, right? Fucked up. But they offered good money, and it was obvious no bands would be touring the country for a while.

"At first it was just like any other tour. We played our own stuff. There were women to sleep with, drugs if we wanted them, restaurants and clubs and gyms. All the good parts of touring without the actual travel part. Sleeping in the same bed every night, even if it was still a bunk with my band, like on the bus. But then it didn't stop, and then they started making us take requests, and it started closing in, you know? If there was somebody you wanted to avoid, you couldn't. It was hard to find anyplace to be alone to write or think.

"Then the internet went off completely. We didn't get news from land at all, even when we docked on the islands. They stopped letting us off when we docked. Management said things had gotten real bad here, that there was for real nothing to come back to anymore. The passengers all walked around like they didn't care, like a closed system, and the world was so fucking far away. How was I supposed to write anything when the world was so far away? The entire world might've drowned, and we'd just float around oblivious until we ran out of something that wasn't even important to begin with. Somebody would freak out because there was no more mascara or ecstasy or rosemary, and then all those beautiful people would turn on each other."

"So that's why you jumped?"

Gabby rubbed her head. "Sort of. I guess that also seemed like a good idea at the time."

"What about now?"

"I could've done with a massage when I woke up today, but I'm still alive."

Bay snorted. "You wouldn't have lasted two seconds in a massage with that sunburn."

Gabby looked down at her forearms and winced.

They walked. Gabby was sweating, her eyes bright. Bay slowed her own pace, in an effort to slow the other woman down.

"Where are you hurrying to, now that I've told you there's nobody coming after you?"

"You said there was a city out here somewhere. I want to get there before I have to sleep another night on this road. And before I starve."

Bay reached into a jacket pocket. She pulled out a protein bar and offered it to Gabby.

"Where'd you get that? It looks like the ones I ate in the lifeboat."

"It is."

Gabby groaned. "I didn't have to starve those last two days? I could've sworn I looked every place."

"You missed a stash inside the radio console."

"Huh."

They kept walking, footsteps punctuated by Gabby's ragged breath.

"We used to drive out here to picnic on the cliff when my wife and I first got married," Bay said. "There were always turtles trying to cross. We would stop and help them, because there were teenagers around who thought driving over them was a sport. Now if I saw a turtle I'd probably have to think about eating it."

"I've never eaten a turtle."

"Me neither. Haven't seen one in years."

Gabby stopped. "You know, I have no clue when I last saw a turtle. At a zoo? No clue at all. I wonder if they're gone. Funny how you don't realize the last time you see something is going to be the last time."

Bay didn't say anything.

The rock star held Deb's guitar up to her chest, started picking out a repetitive tune as she walked. Same lick over and over, like it was keeping her going, driving her feet. "So when you said you traded things like aluminum foil and people, you were lying to me, right? You don't trade anything."

Bay shook her head. "Nobody to trade with."

"So you've been here all alone? You said something about your wife."

Bay kicked a stone down the road in front of her, kicked it again when she caught up with it.

The rock star handed her the guitar and dropped to the ground. She took off her left shoe, then peeled the sock off. A huge blister was rising on her big toe. "Fuck."

Bay sighed. "You can use some of the stuffing from your vest to build some space around it."

Gabby bent to pick a seam.

"No need. There's a tear in the back. Anyhow, maybe it's time to stop for the night."

"Sorry. I saw the tear when you first gave me the vest, but I forgot about it. How far have we traveled?"

"Hard to say. We're still on the park road."

"Park road?"

"This is a protected wilderness area. Or it was. Once we hit asphalt, we're halfway there. Then a little farther to a junction. Left at the T used to be vacation homes, but a hurricane took them twenty years ago. Right takes you to the city."

Gabby groaned. She squinted at the setting sun. "Not even halfway."

"But you're still alive, and you're complaining about a blister, not the cough or the sunburn."

"I didn't complain."

"I don't see you walking any farther, either." Bay dropped her knapsack and untied a sleeping bag from the bottom.

"I don't suppose you have two?"

Bay gave Gabby her most withering look. What kind of fool set out on this walk sick and unprepared? Then again, she had been the one who had driven the woman out, too afraid to interact with an actual person instead of the ghosts in her head.

"We'll both fit," she said. "Body heat'll keep us warm, too."

It was warmer than if they hadn't shared, lying back to back squeezed into the sleeping bag. Not as warm as home, if she hadn't set out to follow. The cold still seeped into her. Bay felt every inch of her left side, as if the bones themselves were in contact with the ground. Aware, too, of her back against the other woman, of the fact that she couldn't remember the last time she had come in physical contact with a living person. The heat of Gabby's fever burned through the layers of clothing, but she still shivered.

"Why are you living out there all alone?" Gabby asked.

Bay considered pretending she was asleep, but then she wanted to answer. "I said already we used to picnic out here, my wife and I. We always said this was where we'd spend our old age. I'd get a job as a ranger, we'd live out our days in the ranger's cabin. I pictured having electricity, mind."

She paused. She felt the tension in the other woman's back as she suppressed a cough. "Debra was in California on a business trip when everything started going bad at a faster rate than it'd been going bad before. We never even found out what it was that messed up the electronics. Things just stopped working. We'd been living in a high-rise. I couldn't stay in our building with no heat or water, but we couldn't contact each other, and I wanted to be someplace Debra would find me. So when I didn't hear from her for three months, I packed what I thought I might need into some kid's wagon I found in the lobby and started walking. I knew she'd know to find me out here if she could."

"How bad was it? The cities? We were already on the ship."

"I can only speak for the one I was living in, but it wasn't like those scare movies where everyone turns on one another. People helped each other. We got some electricity up and running again in a couple weeks' time, on a much smaller scale. If anything, I'd say we had more community than we'd ever had. But it didn't feel right for me. I didn't want other people; I wanted Deb."

"They told us people were rioting and looting. Breaking into mansions, moving dozens of people in."

"Would you blame them? Your passengers redirected all the gas to their ships and abandoned perfectly good houses. But again, I can only speak to what I saw, which was folks figuring out the new order and making it work as best they could."

Gabby stayed silent for a while, and Bay started to drift. Then one more question. "Did Debra ever find you? I mean I'm guessing no, but . . ."

"No. Now let me sleep."

Inside the Music: Tell us what happened.

Gabby Robbins: You know what happened. There is no you anymore. No reality television, no celebrity gossip, no music industry. Only an echo playing itself out on the ships and in the heads of those of us who can't quite let it go.

Bay was already out of the sleeping bag when I woke. She sat on a rock playing a simple fingerpicking pattern on her guitar.

"I thought you didn't play," I called to her.

"Never said that. Said I'm a lousy singer, but didn't say anything about playing the guitar. We should get moving. I'd rather get to the city earlier than late."

I stood up and stretched, letting the sleeping bag pool around my feet. The sun had only just risen, low and red. I could hear water lapping on both sides now, beyond a thick growth of brush. I coughed so deep it bent me in two.

"Why are you in a hurry?" I asked when I could speak.

She gave me a look that probably could have killed me at closer range. "Because I didn't bring enough food to feed both of us for much longer, and you didn't bring any. Because I haven't been there in years, and I don't know if they shoot strangers who ride in at night."

"Oh." There wasn't much to say to that, but I tried anyway. "So basically you're putting yourself in danger because I put myself in danger because you made me think I was in danger."

"You put yourself in danger in the first place by jumping off your damn boat."

True. I sat back down on the sleeping bag and inspected my foot. The blister looked awful. I nearly wept as I packed vest-stuffing around it.

I stood again to indicate my readiness, and she walked back over. She handed me the guitar, then shook out the sleeping bag, rolled it, and tied it to her pack. She produced two vaguely edible-looking sticks from somewhere on her person. I took the one offered to me.

I sniffed it. "Fish jerky?"

She nodded.

"I really would've starved out here on my own."

"You're welcome."

"Thank you. I mean it. I'd never have guessed I'd have to walk so long without finding anything to eat."

"There's plenty to eat, but you don't know where to look. You could fish if you had gear. You might find another crab. And there are bugs. Berries and plants, too, in better seasons, if you knew what to look for."

As we walked she meandered off the road to show me what was edible. Cattail roots, watercress. Neither tasted fantastic raw, but chewing took time and gave an excuse to walk slower.

"I'm guessing you were a city kid?" she asked.

"Yeah. Grew up in Detroit. Ran away when I was sixteen to Pittsburgh because everyone else ran away to New York. Put together a decent band, got noticed. When you're a good bass player, people take you out. I'd release an album with my band, tour that, then tour with Gaga or Trillium or some flavor of the month."

I realized that was more than she had asked for, but she hadn't told me to shut up yet, so I kept going. "The funny thing about being on a ship with all those celebrities and debutantes is how much attention they need. They throw parties or they stage big collapses and recoveries. They produce documentaries about themselves, upload to the ship entertainment systems. They act as audience for each other, taking turns with their dramas.

"I thought they'd treat me as a peer, but then I realized I was just a hired gun and they all thought they were bigger deals than me. There were a few other entertainers who realized the same thing and dropped down to the working decks to teach rich kids to dance or sing or whatever. I hung on to the idea longer than most that my music still meant something. I still kinda hope so."

A coughing spell turned me inside out.

"That's why you took my guitar?" Bay asked when I stopped gagging.

"Yeah. They must still need music out here, right?"

"I'd like to think so."

I had something else to say, but a change in the landscape up ahead distracted me. Two white towers jutted into the sky, one vertical, the other at a deep curve. "That's a weird-looking bridge."

Bay picked up her pace. I limped after her. As we got closer, I saw the bridge wasn't purposefully skewed. The tower on the near end still stood, but the road between the two had crumbled into the water. Heavy cables trailed from the far tower like hair. We walked to the edge, looked down at the concrete bergs below us, then out at the long gap to the other side. Bay sat down, her feet dangling over the edge.

I tried to keep things light. "I didn't realize we were on an island."

"Your grasp of geography hasn't proven to be outstanding."

"How long do you think it's been out?"

"How the hell should I know?" she snapped.

I left her to herself and went exploring. When I returned, the tears that smudged her face looked dry.

"It must've been one of the hurricanes. I haven't been out here in years." Her tone was dry and impersonal again. "Just goes to show, sooner or later everything falls into the sea."

"She didn't give up on you," I said.

"You don't know that."

"No."

I was quiet a minute. Tried to see it all from her eyes. "Anyway, I walked around. You can climb down the embankment. It doesn't look like there's much current. Maybe a mile's swim?"

She looked up at me. "A mile's swim, in clothes, in winter, with a guitar. Then we still have to walk the rest of the way, dripping wet. You're joking."

"I'm not joking. I'm only trying to help."

"There's no way. Not now. Maybe when the water and the air are both warmer."

She was probably right. She'd been right about everything else. I sat down next to her and looked at the twisted tower. I tried to imagine what Detroit or Pittsburgh was like now, if they were all twisted towers and broken bridges, or if newer, better communities had grown, like the one Bay had left.

"I've got a boat," I said. "There's no fuel, but you have an oar on your wall. We can line it full of snacks when the weather is better, and come around the coast instead of over land."

"If I don't kill you before then. You talk an awful lot."

"But I can play decent guitar," I said. "And I found a crab once, so I'm not entirely useless."

"Not entirely," she said.

Inside the Music: Tell us what happened.

Gabby Robbins: I was nearly lost, out on the ocean, but somebody rescued me. It's a different life, a smaller life. I'm writing again. People seem to like my new stuff.

Bay took a while getting to her feet. She slung her bag over her shoulder, and waited while Gabby picked up Deb's guitar. She played as they walked back toward Bay's cottage, some little riff Bay didn't recognize. Bay made up her own words to it in her head, about how sooner or later everything falls into the sea, but some things crawl back out again and turn into something new.

— *The Low Hum of Her* —

Father built me a new grandmother when the real one died. "She's not a replacement," he said, as if anything could be. This one was made of clay and metal all run through with wires to conduct electricity, which Father said made her a lot like us. At her center, where we have hearts and guts, she had a brass birdcage. I don't know how he made her face look right. He put my real Bubbe's clothing on her, and wrapped one of my real Bubbe's headscarves around her iron-gray hair, and put Bubbe's identification papers into her skirt pocket, and told me to call her Bubbe.

"Does it cook?" I asked him. "Does it bake, or sing?"

"She can," said Father. "Those are exactly the things she can do. You just have to teach her. She can look after you and keep you company when I'm working."

"I won't call it Bubbe."

"Call her what you like. Maybe you can say 'the new Bubbe' and 'she' when you're around me, though. I worked hard to make her for you."

He had spent months at his workbench. Long evenings after days spent teaching, and then long days after he was no longer allowed to work at the university. I had heard him cry sometimes, when he thought I was asleep. "She," I repeated, eyeing the machine.

That night, it offered help as I prepared beets for soup.

"Just stand in the corner and watch," I said. "You don't know how."

57

It followed my instructions. I stained the kitchen red with my messy chopping while it stood in the corner. How strange to see something that looked so much like Bubbe lurking in the dark corner where Bubbe never would have been found. "Too much to do," she would have said. "I'll rest when I'm dead." Now she was dead, and her absence was an ache in my chest.

The fake Bubbe was quiet for a while, then spoke again. "Teach me the songs you're singing, Tatiana. We can sing together while you cook."

I hushed it and sang the old songs softly to myself, imitating my grandmother's quavering soprano. There was no "we," I told myself. There was Father and there was me and there was the hole that Bubbe had left. No machine could replace her, even one that looked and sounded like her. It didn't even know to call me my nickname, Tania. Or perhaps Father told it that would be too familiar.

I had started a notebook of recipes and songs back before my real Bubbe took ill. She hated that notebook. She said I should remember with my hands and heart and not leave a book to do the remembering for me. Each night after she was gone, I flipped through the pages and chose something to make, trying to re-create her recipes precisely. I made new notes to myself when the recipes went wrong, trying to recapture the little details that hadn't made it to the page. On the page for challah, my original transcription said "knead." "Use your back to knead," I remembered Bubbe saying when she first showed me how. "Your hands will get tired without the help of your back." She threw her whole body into the effort. Her whole front was coated in flour by the end. "Bosoms," she sighed in false despair, dusting herself off.

I wrote "use back" next to "knead." Still, the dough never worked out as well for me as it had for her. The other recipes were the same way. My father ate each meal without complaint, but I longed to make us something that tasted as good as my grandmother's cooking. I tried and tried, with the new Bubbe looking on from her corner.

And then Father came rushing home early one afternoon. "Tania, we must leave the house now as if we are going for an afternoon stroll. We can take only what we can fit into Bubbe." I started to correct him, to say "new Bubbe," but something in his tone silenced me.

The new Bubbe unbuttoned its blouse and opened the birdcage for us. For the first time, I understood what it was for. Father filled it with what little gold we had: my real Bubbe's rings and necklaces and the shabbos candlesticks, all wrapped in headscarves so they wouldn't rattle. Father's prayer book. I put in the picture of my parents at their wedding, and a portrait of Bubbe with the grandfather I never knew, and my book of songs and recipes.

I saw my father glance back, just once, and I looked back too. The house looked sad. The eaves drooped and the window boxes sagged empty. Father had been too busy to fix the eaves, and I had not known when to plant seeds for spring flowers. Bubbe had always done that. What if my memories of my mother and grandmother were so tied to that house that they stayed behind? I whispered one of Bubbe's songs under my breath, to show the memories they could come with us.

We walked away. The trees still had more flowers than leaves, but rain the night before had driven some of the petals to the ground. The petals were soft underfoot and muted our footsteps on the cobblestones. The streets smelled like lilacs and rain and I listened for screams and jackboots that I never heard and the three of us strolled down to the river and along its bank as if there were no hurry in the world. We walked away from home, just like that, just kept walking with nothing but the valuables that traveled inside the cage of the new Bubbe's chest.

One of Father's friends met us outside the city as evening fell. He gave us black bread and cheese and drove us through the night. We stopped once to show papers. A soldier shined a light into the car and looked at our documents while another held a rifle at the ready. They opened all of the doors and the boot of the automobile.

"Where are you going, Grandmother?" the one soldier asked the new Bubbe. I held my breath.

"My son, he has all the answers," she said. It was something Bubbe had always said. I didn't even know this one knew how to say it. I didn't hear Father's explanation for our travel over the pounding of my heart. The light lingered in our faces another moment, then went out.

"No bags," said the one soldier to the other. They raised the gate to let us through.

We drove on. I wished Father had sat in the backseat with me, to stroke my hair and reassure me. Instead, the new Bubbe reached for my hand in the darkness of the car; for the first time, I let it. I fell asleep on its lap listening to the low hum of it and pretending it was a lullaby.

Father's friend left us in a strange city in the morning. There, Father purchased a small trunk and a suitcase and clothing for us, then tickets aboard a steamship for the following day. He only bought two tickets. I watched from our hotel room's single sagging bed as he dismantled the new Bubbe.

"I'm sorry I have to do this," he said to it. It shrugged and sighed a very Bubbe-like sigh, weighted with suffering and understanding. I shivered when the light went out of its eyes.

"Why didn't you just buy it—her—a ticket?" I asked.

"There will be closer quarters on the next part of our journey, Tania, and inspections. She can fool anyone who is not expecting a person to be something other than a person, but she would not pass a medical examination."

He separated it into several parts, tying and braiding wires back in on themselves in neat bundles. I averted my gaze when he took its face. He left the torso intact, like a dressmaker's form, with its bird-cage core and all of our valuables hidden within. Disassembled, she fit into the small trunk he had purchased that afternoon.

At the docks, we were assigned numbers and a group. We descended a steep staircase to the steerage compartment, pushed and prodded the whole way like cattle. Father needed both hands for the trunk that contained the new Bubbe, so I gripped his coat with one hand and the suitcase with the other, trying not to get separated from him in the crush of people. Two more levels down we found the family quarters, where we were permitted to claim two iron bunks and the narrow gap between them.

That night, Father placed the trunk at the foot of his straw mattress. He slept curled up like a baby in the space that remained. I tried not to think about the collection of parts in the trunk, which had once seemed so close to alive. Life was a fragile thing. I had seen my grandmother's body after her passing, but I was not there to witness the light leaving her eyes.

Our quarters smelled like sweat and wet wool and sick. And so many noises! Other families murmured. Babies cried, and somewhere an old woman moaned. The steam engine churned and clanked. I struggled to sleep at first, but I soon learned to tune out the families and let the sounds of the ship lull me. The engine sounds from the deepest parts of the ship's belly reminded me of the new Bubbe, and that in turn reminded me of my own Bubbe's voice. I let the sounds blur together: real and imaginary, alive and almost alive.

I did not count the days, but gave over to the indignities of the situation. We had no dining area, but ate on the floor or on our bunks. We gnawed hard biscuits and picked insects out of our soup. My cooking was fit for royalty compared to the ship's fare, and at least I had never lost a hairpin into my stew. After each meal I waited in line to dunk our tin plates in a basin of seawater, and in another line to wash my face and hands. I considered the new Bubbe, in pieces in the trunk, whenever I felt too cramped.

We arrived in the place Father said would be our new home. As he had warned, there were physical inspections. They checked our hair, face, neck, and hands, which the new Bubbe might have passed, then our eyes, which she might not have. The doctors had chalk in their hands, and marked the clothing of some. I tried to regulate my breathing, tried to turn myself into a machine incapable of weakness, and hoped Father was doing the same. We passed the doctors, and the interrogators, and then we were in the new place with nothing but our trunk and our suitcase.

Father had the address of a colleague from his old university, and we walked for an hour to reach his house. Mr. Levitan embraced my father despite what must have been the overwhelming stink of us. He helped us secure an apartment that very day. Perhaps the odor sped his actions. Still, he took the time to ask me questions about our journey, and he gave me a candy that tasted both sweet and citrus-sour at once.

The new apartment was much smaller than our old house. That didn't matter, since we had fewer things. The building smelled like lemons and pickles and cigarettes, and the sunlight that filtered through the windows was more intense than the light where we had come from. Bells rang often throughout the day.

Father reassembled the new Bubbe. I did not admit it to him, but when he reconnected her circuits I was relieved to see that she had survived her travel without any damage. I listened as he explained our new situation. She shrugged and nodded.

Father said not to leave the apartment, which was easy since we had no place to go. The new Bubbe was my only company now that Father was away working even longer hours than he had at home. She had not asked her questions since we moved to the new place. Father brought home only bread and herring, so she had no reason to help with the cooking. He bought me a radio. I listened to that in place of singing, though I recognized few of the songs and didn't know the language the announcers spoke.

The electricity in our building was inconsistent, surging and dropping at various points throughout most days. For the most part the power would resume mere moments after the interruption, but one morning it went out and didn't come back on. My radio cut out in mid-song. I paced the floor, at first in boredom and then in fear. Hours passed, and the room grew dark.

"What if something happened and Father can't come home?" I asked the new Bubbe. "What if we're alone?"

"Ssha," she said. For the first time since the car ride, I let her take me in her arms. The whir of her inner workings reassured me; she was something the outage couldn't touch.

It took a minute to realize she was singing. Quietly at first, then louder when I didn't make her stop. She sang one of Bubbe's songs, the ones I had sung under my breath when I didn't want her to hear. Her voice cracked like porcelain on the high notes.

I wanted her to sing another, and she seemed pleased when I asked her to do so. I joined her on the chorus. We sang another, and another, the old songs and the ones from the radio, and passed the day in that way. I didn't even notice when the electricity came back on.

Late that night, Father arrived with a chicken and an onion and a sack of kasha.

"Get your recipe book, Tania," he said. "We'll have a feast."

I shook my head.

The real Bubbe said to remember with my hands, so I showed the new Bubbe how the secret to kasha was to mix in the chicken fat. She got grease on her blouse, like the real Bubbe. I taught her to say "bosoms," and sigh, as the real Bubbe always had.

My thought that day was if I taught her hands the recipes, if her lips knew Bubbe's songs, then there would always be two of us to remember, even when Father was away. My real grandmother had been my teacher, but this one needed me to teach her.

"You can call me Tania," I said to her. It might have been my imagination, but I thought she looked pleased.

"What will you call me?" she asked. I considered. Bubbe did not fit any longer, nor "the new Bubbe," as I had addressed her with such derision.

"What would you like to be called?"

She shrugged. "You choose. Call me something with meaning to you."

I gave her the name Chaya, *alive*. She was no longer just a reminder of the grandmother I had lost, but her own thing.

She will be with me always, I hope. Someday she and I will show my children and grandchildren how to make kreplach and kasha varnishkes. Someday they will wonder at the birdcage in her chest, which still holds my old book of recipes and the photo of my grandparents. Someday I will have hair as gray as hers, and then grayer. I will lean over the table and cover my own blouse with flour, and sigh and say "bosoms" with the right note of false despair, so the children around me will giggle. When the others go to sleep, she and I will remember together, and I will listen to the low hum of her, and we will sing each other lullabies.

— Talking with Dead People —

Yes, I was the one who came up with the name "House of Whacks," as in "Lizzie Borden took an ax . . ." Like I was someone who could joke about that kind of thing. And yes, it's true that Elizabeth Mint offered me a partnership in the business and I turned her down. We were college roommates, and I feel comfortable saying I had no business sense whatsoever. If I had seen the same potential in the idea that she did, if I had taken her up on the offer, if I hadn't called it quits on working with her, I would be a millionaire now.

She called herself Eliza then. Made sure you knew it was EE-LIES-AH and nothing else. She had a weird love-hate relationship with the whole Lizzie Borden thing. Her family lived in South Jersey when she was a kid, and she was a Lizzie then without anyone making a fuss about it. They moved an hour upstate to Teaneck right before she started high school, right when that big Lizzie Borden movie came out. The next thing she knew, she was Lizzie-from-Bordentown and everybody was going around asking her how her parents were. After four years of teasing, she was happy to get a fresh start in college.

Despite all that, or maybe because of it, the story held a fascination for her. I didn't understand, but I was used to sharing space with people who couldn't let something go. She dragged me on more than one road trip from Rochester to Fall River, Massachusetts. Dragged me to some other creepy places, too: abandoned sanatoriums, murder sites, serial-killer homes. I had no idea how many people made pilgrimages to those places. At least Eliza's interest was pragmatic; not that I knew it at first.

I went along because she paid for gas and I had never been more than a hundred miles from home. Having somebody who wanted to go places with me was a novelty, too, though in retrospect that may have been her own self-interest reflecting off me.

On the way back from one of those places in my old Ford Fiesta—she was the only moneyed person I ever met who didn't drive—she always sat silent while I searched my phone for the cheeriest songs I could think of. Then the questions inevitably came.

"Hey, Gwennie, why do you think there was no water in the swimming pool?"

"It's October?"

"Not now. Then. He was found in an empty swimming pool in July."

I'd mull it over. "Do they know whether it was emptied before or after he wound up in there?"

"He didn't drown or fall in. He was dead already. Weren't you paying attention?"

The answer to that was always, "No." I'd had enough of murders and missing people by then. I wandered through the sites with the goal of learning as little as possible about the mystery at hand. The whole thing felt voyeuristic to me, lurid; to my mind, what went on behind a family's closed doors wasn't meant to be seen, much less solved. Instead of paying attention to the clues, I concentrated on the architecture, interior design, gardening, art. I studied the books on the bookshelves, the furniture, the cutlery. Imagined how I'd replicate them in miniature if I were adding that house to the train towns I'd built in my parents' basement.

She'd answer her own question after a while.

"I'll bet the pool was empty because somebody had convinced old Mr. Haygood that there was some expensive repair that needed to be done while the rest of the family was on vacation. Maybe somebody convinced him that a whole bunch of things needed fixing, the pool needed to be drained, and that he had to pay in advance. Then the family got home and discovered he'd been taken advantage of, and—"

"That's what brought down the most popular American politician of the twenty-first century? A scam? They had money. How does that explain his son in the pool, or Senator Haygood disappearing for three weeks?" I didn't need to pay attention on a tour to know any of that.

"If you don't see it, I'm not going to spell it out, Gwen."

Then I'd skip to a song I could sing along with, and before too long she'd apologize and change the subject to make me stop singing. She covered all this in the memoir, the road trips and the questions she asked herself afterward, though she left me out of that part. More introspection, less interrogation.

I pretty much got one scene in the book. In her telling, we were on the Mass Pike, an hour into the six-hour drive back to school from Fall River, when she turned to me and said, "What if we could ask them questions?"

In real life, I said, "Who?" and she said, "Them. You know." And I said, "I have no idea what you're talking about," and then we played a round of total exasperation. She tightened up the conversation in *Talking with Dead People* for clarity's sake.

In her version, she said, "What if we could ask them questions?"

The fictionalized me, with perfect grasp of her concept, answered, "That would be awesome."

What she meant, of course, was, "What if we gave them a voice?" That was her idea. Asking questions of murderers and monsters and the unjustly accused.

"Like a séance?" I suggested when I got her implication, also after a much briefer period in her book than in real life.

"A séance, but better. You go to Fall River and ask Lizzie Borden actual questions and get actual answers in reply."

I humored her. "You could call it 'House of Whacks.' Get it?"

"That's the best idea you've ever had." I could hear the grin behind her words. For the rest of the drive we tried to come up with better names, but that one stuck from the beginning.

The name helped focus the project, too. I think her original idea had been animatronic busts of the killers, which to her mind was cool and to mine was a cross between the Hall of Presidents and the Oz witch with the interchangeable heads. Creepy as hell, uncanny.

She might have stuck with that, but for the fact we didn't know anybody who made the type of sculptures needed to bring those busts to life. Eliza was always good at adapting to what was on hand, and what was on hand was me.

Model making was always my thing. First, broccoli-tree dioramas and ranch dressing dyed river-blue. Then whole train towns in the basement with my parents, before my brother, Tristan, disappeared, then every shop and engineering class my high school offered. Making murder houses wasn't that different; the architectural models I construct now aren't that different, either, for that matter. People ask, "Why houses? Why not the people themselves?" The answer is: we had a choice between fake-looking models of people or real-looking models of houses.

I built the first one in the campus theater's set shop, where I had my work-study gig that year. It was a good job; I liked making things, and I liked that the schedule was a sporadic one, even if that meant I never had much money. Nothing new there.

The prototype was the Borden house, of course. Not Maplecroft, her later home: 92 Second Street. On all our visits, Eliza made reservations for us at the bed and breakfast that operates there now; she'd book early enough to request the room where Lizzie's stepmother was found murdered. I'd always wandered the halls with an eye toward the house itself rather than the murders, but once she'd explained my role in her plan, I paid even more attention. The stairs' width, the orientation of the windows to the day's changing sunlight. It was easy enough to find floor plans and photos online, but my own experience of the rooms and hallways suffused the project.

"Jesus, Gwen," said Eliza when I showed her the model she'd commissioned.

The west wall swung open on hinges. Every room was in there, in perfect proportion. Tiny replicas of the murder couch, the mirrors, the railings. Functional windows and doors. It stood a foot tall, not including the base, which added about four inches. The Borden house didn't have electricity so I installed fake miniature gas lamps on the tables and the walls.

"It's what you asked for, right?"

"Well, yes. But how long did it take you?"

I added up the days and hours in my head, then shrugged. She'd been working on the programming and the electronics for exactly as long as I'd been building the model. She'd bought all my supplies as I worked on it, too, so she ought to know.

She turned it around, peered in through the windows. "She made all the furniture," she whispered to herself, like I couldn't hear her. "Amazing."

I had left the base hollow, as she'd requested, and she skipped classes the next day to add her electronics. When I got back to the room after dinner, she was lying on her bed reading.

"Turn it on," she said, rolling over to face me.

Her desk was always a mess, in stark contrast to mine; the model sat in the center, with tools scattered around it. One shutter was missing, which gave me a pang of anxiety. I felt around on the base until I found a switch. Nothing happened.

"Now what?" I asked.

"Ask her a question."

Nothing came to my mind, and after a moment Eliza groaned and asked in my place. "Abby, which way were you facing when you were attacked?"

I peered into the house, half-expecting to see figures inside. "Wait. Why Abby? I thought you were questioning Lizzie?"

"When we switched to houses instead of busts, I realized we could put everyone in there."

She repeated her question. A woman's voice came through the speakers. I recognized Eliza's friend Angie. "I was facing my attacker."

"Abby, where was the first place you were hit?"

"I was hit in the guest room."

I giggled, and Eliza gave me a hatchet-shaped look. This was a glitch.

"Abby," she tried again. "Where was the first place on your body you were hit?"

"I was hit on the side of my head."

Eliza smiled in triumph and continued. "Andrew, where did you go when you left the house the morning of your death?"

A male voice now, one I didn't recognize. A professor, maybe? The voice sounded older than our friends. "I went for my morning walk."

"Who attacked you?" I asked. No answer.

"You have to use a name first," Eliza said.

I felt suddenly shy, formal. "Um, Mr. Borden, who attacked you?"

"I was asleep."

I cocked my head at Eliza. "What happens if I ask Mrs. Borden that question? Or if I ask Lizzie directly?"

"Try it."

"Lizzie Borden, did you kill the people you were accused of killing?"

Lizzie Borden answered in Eliza's awful attempt at a Massachusetts accent. "I was acquitted of those crimes."

The same voice, lying on the other bed, said, "Cool, huh?"

Something tapped against the window behind my bed: a bee caught between the screen and the glass. I crossed the room to free it.

It glanced off the window a couple more times before bumbling its way down the side of the building. I flopped onto my bed.

"I still don't get it," I said. "It doesn't know any more than anybody else does. It can only say what you've programmed it to say. If you don't know who did it, it won't know, either."

Eliza sighed. "This is a prototype. It can only answer questions I programmed in. But I'm pretty sure that if I give the AI enough information, if I feed it every single known detail about every victim and every suspect, I can get it to a point where it'll be able to answer questions I don't know the answer to. Make connections I haven't made, based on what's been input. Maybe. And even if it doesn't, people will buy it anyway."

"But what's the point?"

"People love unsolved murders," she said, a line she repeated and expanded upon in her memoir. "And they love murder houses. I—we—are going to make these and sell them to murder-house museums. This one is museum quality. And then we're going to make smaller, cheaper ones, without furniture or tiny working shutters that fall off when I'm soldering."

That stung more than I let on. Nothing fell off my models if they were handled right. My little brother, Tristan, wrecked more than his share, before he wasn't around to do that anymore, but the fault was never in my workmanship. "*We*, huh?"

"We."

I stood and poked around the desk until I found the missing shutter amid Eliza's clutter. Fished among my model supplies for the tiny pin that would secure it back in place. "The other voices are good, but your Lizzie sounds fake."

Two weeks later, she updated the base. The house gave a wider variety of answers. She replaced her own voice with someone who sounded more like the accents we heard in Fall River. On spring break, while

I was home, she took a bus to Massachusetts with the house on her lap. She sold it to a general store in town for a thousand dollars.

She tossed the money on my bed my first day back at school. They'd paid her online, but she'd taken it out of the bank in twenties.

"Gwennie, I need to know if we're partners in this."

"I thought we already were?"

"We can be. I need you to build the models, but I see a couple of ways this can go. Either we're partners and we both put up money to get this business going, and we both make decisions, and we split everything fifty-fifty, or you let me pay you for the models, but it's my business."

"How much would you pay me? For the models?"

"That first one was a work of art. We'll need a few more like that—I've got a list of houses—and then some mini-versions with no frills. No furniture. No working shutters. For the big ones, you'd get six hundred dollars each, plus materials. For the little ones, um, fifty dollars each. I'd pay you for each one, regardless of whether I was able to sell it or not.

"There's nine hundred dollars in that stack, for your hard work on the first one. None of this could happen if I hadn't been able to sell that first one. You can have nine hundred for it if you want to just work for hire. Otherwise I'll take that money back and invest it in the next step and we're fifty-fifty partners. Succeed or fail, equal share."

I looked at the bills stacked on my bed. I'd never seen that much money in my life, and she knew it. My parents weren't particularly well-off, and after the police stopped looking for Tristan, they spent every penny on private investigations. Nine hundred would let me buy new tires and a muffler for my car. With more payments like that, I could cover my own fees for the next semester and not need to ask my parents for money they didn't have. Or I could partner with her. But if nobody actually wanted to buy tiny murder houses with tiny murder voices, I'd be left with said murder houses. Money for work, no accountability, or money for a share, with a stake I wasn't sure I could afford not to pocket.

"I'll work for you," I said.

She reached into her bag and pulled out a contract. "Let's make it official, then."

I never found out whether there was a second contract for if I'd answered the other way.

"People love solving mysteries," she wrote in her book. "It makes them feel smart."

She had a lot of ideas about what people liked and didn't like, maybe because she saw everybody else as extensions of herself. That part isn't in her book, of course. That's my own theory.

We turned our dorm room into a production factory. When the orders started coming in, she rented space in a warehouse and we moved everything there. It was a sauna in summer and freezing in winter, but nobody complained. She hired other friends to handle different aspects of the business, including a cast of voice actors and a couple of electronics people. Mo Bara painted my models. Samia Gilman built us a website and established a social-media presence.

Whatever the reason, Eliza was right. People wanted the murder houses. Just a few at first, but then someone solved the Haygood murder of 2021 using our model. Got the case reopened, found a way to prove their hypothesis using the actual evidence, exonerated the family. Senator Haygood even wrote to thank us.

After that, the orders came in faster than we could fill them. The waiting list only made them more desirable. We offered a range of houses we could assemble in bulk quantities, then another higher-priced tier for custom jobs. We did a Lindbergh, a Ramsey. I saved up enough money to pay my own tuition the next semester, since I was making more than anyone other than Eliza.

Once in a while I wondered if I'd made a mistake in not taking the partnership. I still wonder. I think I would have enjoyed the houses she built for forensic schools and the FBI, the case-study puzzles they commissioned, like the Nutshell Studies down in Maryland, but with voices and an AI that could follow lines of questioning. I would have been on board with the murder-house owners who paid Eliza for AIs that wired into intercoms or smartphones, so they could charge admission to people walking through the actual rooms.

Even if we hadn't fallen out when we did, we'd probably have fought over some of the other commissioned work she took, which I would have refused. Sensationalist TV shows that licensed our houses to provoke and harass people who had long since been acquitted. Dictators, current cases, things that felt too raw to be examined. At the time, my reason for wanting to stay with work-for-hire was simpler. I saw how much time Eliza spent on all the aspects that weren't craft; I was happy enough making my models and ignoring the business side.

We probably could have continued that way indefinitely if she hadn't gone and done the thing that ended our friendship. She didn't include that anecdote in *Talking with Dead People*, either . . . In the book she skips from our frigid warehouse space to her dropping out before senior year.

What she omitted was her present to me on my twentieth birthday. Our birthdays were fairly close to each other, so all three of the Decembers we roomed together we threw a joint party just before winter exams started, crowded and intimate, filled with our friends and business partners, more or less the same people. She drank Genny Light and I drank cider. I even remember that detail, mostly because later that night I got sick to my stomach, and I haven't been able to touch cider since.

Anyway, a few drinks in, she stood up on my desk and called for attention. Somebody—Mo Bara, I think, though that part is hazy—somebody handed her a canvas shopping bag. She plugged in a cable dangling from it before she passed it to me. I remember that, too, so I already knew what sort of present it was even if I didn't know the specifics.

I pulled it from the shopping bag. With its plywood base two feet by one foot and sewing-machine-sized building, it was much larger than even my high-end models. The details were crude, and it took me a minute to recognize my own childhood home, but when I did, I had a pretty clear idea what she had done.

In a shaky voice, not yet slurring, I asked the model, "What's your name?"

A voice from inside—not mine, since I hadn't recorded this particular surprise—answered, "Gwen." I couldn't tell who it was. One of the acting-school kids we sometimes paid to do the job, probably.

I looked over at Eliza then. I don't know why she expected me to be excited that she had programmed my life's details as she knew them into an AI box. I guess maybe she wouldn't have minded one of herself, to interrogate and get her own answers back, so she didn't understand how I wouldn't feel the same. But I looked at her, and in that moment I think she realized that maybe it had been a mistake. I glared until the smile died on her face.

Too late, though. People were already pushing past to ask the fake me questions. Did I sleep with Caz Mendelson last year? What about Samia? Did I really flunk Ethics in Engineering? The answers were eerily correct. No. Yes. No—I got an extension to finish it over the summer because I'd been too busy making murder houses, and the professor said I could turn in an essay on the ethics of making murder houses, which I did. These were all things Eliza knew about me from two and a half years in close proximity. The voice, though not my own, carried my speech patterns, my inflections.

The questions took other turns. I waited for the voice to make a mistake, to prove it wasn't me, but it knew my home address, my parents' names, the name of my favorite teacher in high school. I pictured Eliza secretly reaching out to my family, my online friends, asking them if they wanted to be in on a birthday surprise. I'll bet if anyone said they didn't think I enjoyed surprises, she probably just fed that information into the AI, too.

"How many siblings do you have?" somebody asked, and I think I stopped breathing. They were just asking random questions, I told myself.

"None," the AI said, then paused. "None anymore."

I grabbed my backpack from under my bed, made sure I had keys and wallet and computer, and walked out the door. I could have stayed and kicked everyone else out, but I left them interrogating me. All I knew was that I had to go before I heard any follow-up questions, or worse yet, answers.

I tried knocking on some doors to find a place to crash, but everybody was either at our party or gone from campus already. Freezing rain fell as I headed for my car, but it wasn't unbearably cold. My father made me keep an emergency blanket in the trunk, and I pulled my arms and legs up into my clothes. I woke up once in the middle of the night to vomit by my back tire, slipping on the ice that had accumulated and nearly wiping out in my own sick.

I stayed in other people's rooms for the rest of the exam period and applied to move over the winter break. The school assigned me to another junior whose roommate was studying in Rome for the spring.

I knew I was leaving the company in the lurch in terms of models, but at that point I didn't care. I was done with murder houses. Done with AI voices that knew too much. In my ethics essay, I had justified what we were doing. "In some cases, we're giving voice to the voiceless," I wrote. "The AI can represent all the players in the case. There's no speculation. If it doesn't know an answer, it says 'I don't know' or 'I don't remember.' And sometimes it makes intuitive leaps that somebody involved in the case should have made but didn't. It remains to be seen whether any of those inferences can be proven, but the possibility of serving justice is exciting and may outweigh any moral or ethical qualms."

I drove two hours up to Rochester on Christmas, in order to pack up my stuff at a time I knew she wouldn't be there. We had cleared all the Christmas orders before the party—yes, people buy each other murder houses for Christmas—and everyone had been rewarded with two whole weeks off. I was pretty sure she was in Barbados with her family.

The room looked exactly as it had when I'd left, minus the people. Red plastic cups and beer bottles everywhere, along with a yeasty smell that said they'd been left where they fell and not rinsed out.

My so-called present was on the desk where I'd abandoned it. Still plugged in. I shouldn't have asked, but I was the only one in the building and I had to know.

"What happened to your brother, Gwen?"

"I don't know," the House of Whacks said.

"But you were watching him that day?"

"Yes."

"And what happened?"

"He was playing in the yard, and I was playing a game on my phone. And then I went upstairs, and he was gone." My words in the police report, verbatim.

"You didn't hear anything?"

"I told the police 'no.'"

"Repeat that answer, please," I said.

"I told the police. No."

I didn't know if I'd imagined the different inflection the first time. Terrifying how that nuance changed my words' meaning. *Its* words. What line of code made the difference between the two? I had one more question.

"What video game were you playing?"

The machine paused. That information had never been in any articles.

"I don't remember," it said at last.

That "I don't remember" kept me from smashing the thing, though I probably should have. I had been playing *Karmic Warrior*. My highest level yet. My highest level to date, I should say, since I never played it again. The machine wasn't me. Eliza hadn't re-created me. It was just an approximation.

It didn't know Tristan had begged me to teach him how to play *Karmic Warrior*. It knew he was wearing his Tyrannosaurus T-shirt and jeans with a torn right knee and sneakers that were starting to pinch his toes—he'd complained about them just that morning—because I told the police exactly what he was wearing. It knew he had a tiny white patch of hair at the crown of his head where he'd earned eight stitches on the corner of the coffee table the year before, because that had fallen under "distinguishing marks."

It didn't know he snorted when he laughed. It didn't know he ran like a tiny drunk, weaving and listing. Nobody had told it about his strange fascination with bees, which he captured gently but sometimes accidentally set loose in the house, and that he had gotten all of us stung more times than we could count. It didn't know I had been chasing my high score in *Karmic Warrior* and told him to get lost. Those exact words, "Get lost," and I never saw him again.

Before I made my final trip across campus with my final box, I unplugged the Gwen AI. I was halfway down the hall when I changed my mind and went back. There was a screwdriver in the top desk drawer; I flipped the model over and unscrewed the base. Removed the chip, shoved it in my pocket. Stopped in the kitchen on the first floor to microwave it. Didn't stick around to see the fireworks.

That party was the last time I ever spoke to Eliza. She tried calling several times, but I didn't answer and eventually she gave up. Going by what I heard from Samia and a couple of the others who were still on the HoW payroll, she couldn't understand what had offended me, which told me I had made the right choice. To Eliza there was no difference between Lizzie Borden and the Haygood scandal and Tristan's disappearance. We were all just mysteries waiting for her to solve us.

— *The Sewell Home for the Temporally Displaced* —

Judy says, "It's snowing."

I look out the window. The sky is the same dirty gray as the snow left from last week's storm. I stand up to look closer, to find a backdrop against which I might see what she sees. The radiator is warm against my knees.

"You don't mean now." It's not really a question, but she shakes her head. She looks through me, through another window, at other weather. She smiles. Whenever she is, it must be beautiful.

"Describe it for me," I say.

"Big, fluffy snow. The kind that doesn't melt when it lands on your gloves. Big enough to see the shapes of individual flakes."

"Do you know when you are?"

She strains to catch a different view. "1890s, maybe? The building across the street hasn't been built yet. I wish I could see down to the street, Marguerite."

Judy isn't supposed to leave her bed, but I help her into her yellow slippers, help her to her feet. I try to make myself strong enough for her to lean on. We shuffle to the window. She looks down.

"There's a brougham waiting at the front door. The horse is black, and he must have been driven hard, because the snow that's collecting elsewhere is just melting when it hits him. There's steam coming off him."

I don't say anything. I can't see it, but I can picture it.

"Somebody came out of the building. He's helping a woman out of the carriage," she says. "Her clothes don't match the era or the season. She's wearing jeans and a T-shirt."

"A Distillers T-shirt," I say.

"Yes! Can you see her too?"

"No," I say. "That was me, the first time I came here. I didn't stay long, that first time."

I hear the creak of the door. It's Zia, my least favorite of the nurses. She treats us like children. "Judy, what are we doing up? We could get hurt if we have an episode."

She turns to me. "And you, Marguerite. We should know better than to encourage her."

"Your pronouns are very confusing," I tell her.

She ignores me. "Well, let's get down to lunch, since we're both up and about."

Zia puts Judy in a wheelchair. I follow them down to the dining room, slow and steady. She pushes Judy up to the first available space, at a table with only one vacancy. I'm forced to sit across the room. I don't like being so far away from her. I would make a fuss, but I try to tell myself we can stand to be apart for one meal. I keep an eye on her anyway.

Judy isn't fully back yet. She doesn't touch her food. Mr. Kahn and Michael Lim and Grace de Villiers are all talking across her. Mr. Kahn is floating his spoon, demonstrating the finer points of the physics of his first time machine, as he always does.

"Meatloaf again," mutters Emily Arnold, to my left. "I can't wait until vat protein is invented."

"It tastes good enough, Emily. The food here is really pretty decent for an industrial kitchen in this time period." We've all had worse.

We eat our meatloaf. Somebody at the far end of the room has a major episode, and we're all asked to leave before we get our jello. I can't quite see who it is, but she's brandishing her butter knife like a cutlass, her legs braced against a pitching deck. The best kind of episode, where you're fully then again. We all look forward to those. It's funny that the staff act like it might be contagious.

I wait in Judy's room for her to return. Zia wheels her in and lifts her into the bed. She's light as a bird, my Judy. Zia frowns when she sees me. I think she'd shoo me out more often if either of us had family that could lodge a complaint. Michael and Grace are allowed to eat together but not to visit each other's rooms. Grace's children think she shouldn't have a relationship now that she lives in so many times at once. Too confusing, they say, though Grace doesn't know whether they mean for them or for her.

"How was your dinner?" I ask Judy.

"I can't remember," she says. "But I saw you come in for the first time. You said, 'How is this place real?' and young Mr. Kahn said, 'Because someday all of us will build it.'"

"And then I asked, 'When can I get started?' and he said, 'You already did.'"

I can see it now. The dining room was formal, then. Everyone stared when I came in, but most of the smiles were knowing ones. They understood the hazards of timesling. They had been there, or they were there, or they were going to be.

Judy takes my hand. I lean over to kiss her.

"It's snowing," I say. "I can't wait to meet you."

— In Joy, Knowing the Abyss Behind —

"Don't leave."

The first time he said it, it sounded like a command. The tone was so unlike George, Millie nearly dropped her hairbrush. They were in their bedroom, in their home of sixty-six years. Outside the French doors, fresh snow settled on top of old snow. The lights in George's sprawling tree house made it stand out against the otherwise unbroken white. George sat in the chair at the telephone desk. He was in the middle of changing his socks, one leg crossed over the other, when he dropped the new sock to the floor and coughed once. Millie glanced in the mirror on her vanity, caught him staring at her.

"Don't leave," he said again.

She turned around to face him.

The third time it arrived as a question, a note of confusion lurking in the space between his words. "Don't leave, please?"

He seemed to struggle with the next sentence, his last. "I'm sorry."

"What are you talking about, old man?" she asked, but he was already someplace else. He opened his mouth as if to say more, but no words came out.

She had always been calm in the family's minor medical crises, but this time the words *this is it* blazed across her brain and crowded everything else out. She took deep breaths and tried to remember what she should do. She crossed to his chair, put her hand on his chest, felt the rise and fall. That was good. She didn't think she could get him to the floor, much less perform chest compressions. She stooped to put the clean sock on his bare foot, then reached across him to pick up the phone and dial for an ambulance. Should those actions have been the other way around? Possibly. *This is it.*

"I'll be right back," she told him before leaving the room to unlock the front door. He was still in the same place when she returned, collapsed slightly to the right in the chair. His left eye looked panicked, his right eye oddly calm. She dragged the chair from her vanity over and sat down facing him. Behind him the snow continued to fall.

"I wonder if this will be the storm that proves too heavy for that poor old sycamore," she said, taking her husband's hand in hers and looking out at the tree house. "I think this is going to be a big one."

It had snowed the day they met. Chicago, Marshall Field's, December 1944. He had held the door for her as they both exited onto State Street.

"Ladies first," said the young man in the army overcoat, gesturing with the fat notebook in his free hand. He was shorter than her by a few inches, and she was not terribly tall; if he hadn't been wearing the uniform she would have mistaken him for a boy.

"Thank you," she said, giving him a smile over her shoulder. She didn't see the patch of ice beyond the vestibule. Her left foot slipped out from under her, then her right. He caught her before she landed, losing his own footing in the process. The pages of his notebook fluttered to the ground around them as he broke her fall with his body. They both scrambled to their feet, red-faced and breathless.

"Thank you again," she said.

He brushed snow off his backside and bent to grab several loose pieces of paper from the pavement. She picked at one that had plastered itself to her leg.

He pointed at it. "It likes you. You should probably keep it."

She peeled the page from her nylon and examined it. Even as the ink blurred and ran she could tell it had been a skillful sketch of the grand staircase and the Tiffany dome at the library. The soaked paper tore in two in her hands.

"It's ruined!"

"It's okay, I have more." He held out the others. She saw the Field Museum, the Buckingham Fountain, the building they had just left, all bleeding away.

She put her hand to her mouth. "Your drawings are ruined, and you've torn your coat, too."

He shrugged, touching the ragged edges at his elbow. "Don't worry about it. These were just for fun. Practice. I'm an architect. George Gordon. You don't have to memorize it. Everybody'll know it someday."

"Millicent Berg. Nice to meet you. And I'm sorry about your drawings, even if they were only for fun. Can I make it up to you?"

He scratched his head in a pantomime of contemplation. "I'd ask you to have lunch with me, but I've already eaten. You might let me draw another for you over coffee, I suppose."

Millie glanced up at the clock jutting out from the building. She shook her head. "I'm afraid I'm already late to meet a friend."

"Another time?" he persisted, rubbing his elbow in an obvious fashion. In another man she might have found it rude, but there was something about him that she liked. Too bad.

"Sorry. I'm only visiting Chicago until Tuesday. I go to college in Baltimore," she said.

His grin chased everything ordinary from his face. "You may not get out of this so easily, then. I'm stationed in Maryland. Fort Meade."

Out of such coincidences, lives were built.

∽∾

The emergency workers tore two buttons off of George's pajama top. Millie, who had dressed while she waited for them to arrive, slipped the buttons into the pocket of her cardigan. The EMTs checked George's pulse and vital signs. They talked to each other but not to her. She hovered behind them as they worked.

"Will he be okay?" she asked. Nobody answered her, and after a moment she wondered if she had asked out loud. She glanced at herself in the mirror. The old woman who had stolen her reflection several years ago stared back at her. They nodded to each other in greeting.

When one of the paramedics finally spoke to Millie, it was to tell her they didn't want her to ride in the ambulance with George.

"There isn't room," said the young one, the girl.

What she meant, thought Millie, was that they didn't want to have to worry about her, too. She was spared the trouble of arguing when Raymond and his boyfriend, Mark, arrived.

"Don't worry, Grandma," Ray said. "We can ride behind them."

Mark helped her into the passenger seat of their Toyota. They were good boys. They took her to the salon, took her and George to dinner and to plays and concerts. Of all the children and grandchildren, she was glad that Ray was the one who lived nearby. He was the one she trusted most to actually listen to her if she said something.

Mark dropped Millie and Ray at the emergency bay. After filling out insurance paperwork, they sat in a waiting room until a tired-eyed woman in scrubs appeared. An ischemic stroke, the doctor said, on the left side of George's brain. They had stabilized him. She could see him if she liked. Millie wondered about the phrasing. Did anyone ever say no, thank you very much, I've waited all day, but on second thought, I wouldn't like to see him? After so many hours in one position she struggled to get to her feet. Raymond offered his arm, and she leaned on him all the way down the hallway to Intensive Care.

The right side of George's face sagged, the eye tugging downward at the outside corner. His right hand lay limp on his hip. His left hand busied itself, roaming the white sheets in sweeping motions.

"He's awake, but not really responding to anyone," the doctor told her. What was the doctor's name? DeSoto, like the mouse dentist in the book she had read to the grandchildren. She could remember that. "The stroke was on the left side, so we're looking at right-side hemiparesis, possibly hemiplegia. He probably will need therapy to regain speech, and that may be a long way off. For now, we'd like to see if he acknowledges you in any way."

Millie approached with delicate steps. The man in the bed looked like George with all of the Georgeness scooped out.

"Hello, old man," she whispered, just for him. A little louder she said, "Hi, George. It's me, Millie." That felt oddly formal, like an introduction. She didn't want to touch the dead hand, and reached instead for the roving one, his left.

He brushed her away with a force she hadn't expected and then resumed his interrupted motions. Millie fought back tears. He hadn't meant it, couldn't mean it, but the insult still bruised her.

"Believe it or not, that's a positive sign, Mrs. Gordon. That's the first time he's responded to stimulus."

Ray rested a hand on her shoulder. "He probably didn't know it was you, Grandma. He wasn't pushing you away."

Millie looked at the doctor. "Doctor Gordon," she said.

"No, I'm Dr. DeSoto." The young woman glanced at Ray.

"And I'm Dr. Gordon," Millie said. "Just so you know."

She lowered herself into the chair by the bedside, then looked up at the doctor and her grandson. They both knew everything, and knew nothing.

"He's drawing," said Millie. "All that motion. He's trying to draw. He's left-handed."

In their first months of courtship, she had once asked him to show her his designs.

"They're just buildings," he said. "Nothing special."

She couldn't believe that anything he did might be less than special. As far as she was concerned, everything about him was clever and funny and attentive and romantic. He had called her father to ask permission to see her, and replaced the ruined picture of the Tiffany dome with one of her college's stately main hall. He brought her handmade bouquets of paper roses, since it was still winter. Her friends buzzed about the fact that she had found an older man, a qualified architect, twenty-four to her twenty. They all dated Hopkins boys, rich and bland.

"Bring me some of your blueprints," she begged him one night in her dormitory's well-policed lounge. "I know it can't be the ones you work on for the army, but maybe something from when you were in school? I want to see what you do."

"Really, they'll bore you," he said, but he looked pleased. The next time he visited, he had a leather portfolio tucked under one arm. He spread the diagrams on the table in the visiting room.

"Is this a skyscraper?" Millie traced the outlines.

He grinned his charming grin, with a touch of sheepishness built in. "Yes—but that one isn't being built or anything. Not yet, anyway."

"I can tell it's going to be beautiful. The doorways, the decorative touches. It's lovelier than the Chrysler Building!"

He leaned over to kiss her, though a sharp cough from the dormitory matron interrupted his course. "The Chrysler Building was what inspired me to do this, you know," he said, pushing his drawings slightly to the side to sit on the corner of the table, facing her. The enthusiasm in his eyes lit his whole face. "That and the Empire State Building. We lived in New York back then, and I would slip out of school to watch them going up. Nine, ten years old, and I knew right then that I was going to make things that people would want to see."

He pointed to other drawings in the portfolio: towers, mansions, a stadium. Millie was amazed at his vision.

"When do you get to start making these?"

"As soon as the army's done with me."

"I'll bet they don't have you designing anything as beautiful as this. Just barracks and bases."

"There are some interesting projects. Hypothetical stuff, with the engineers."

"Hypothetical?"

"Made up. Like out of the pulps. Barracks for soldiers who are ten feet tall, prisons built into the side of mountains, guard houses underwater. I know it's all ridiculous stuff, kid stuff, but it's fun to imagine. The engineers tell me what is and isn't possible. I draw, and then they take my sketches away or tell me things to change. Mill, I thought my skyscrapers would be the future, but they're showing me all kinds of futures I hardly know how to think about."

When he proposed to her a month later, she said yes. She loved the sweet touches, but also the dreamer architect. She wanted to be part of the future he envisioned.

A nurse brought a piece of butcher's paper into George's hospital room, and Dr. DeSoto put a fat marker in his hand. Millie sat in the chair by his bedside. Their son Charlie, Charles now, brought in a second chair to sit next to her. Jane was due on a flight that evening. The room was getting crowded, but Millie didn't know whom she could ask to leave. She contemplated stepping out, excusing herself to go to the bathroom or the vending machine and not coming back. No, she would never get away with it. Charlie had become a hoverer, attending to needs she didn't have, fetching her tea and a pillow for her chair and antibacterial sanitizers that turned her skin to paper.

The odor of the marker cut through the hospital smells. Why was it only the acrid scents that came on so forcefully? Charlie had brought two huge bouquets, but Millie couldn't smell the flowers at all. Then again, it was winter, and these bouquets must have come from a supermarket or the hospital gift shop; they were probably scentless. She thought for a moment of the paper flowers that George used to make for her during the months that nothing bloomed.

George's good eye opened. He didn't seem to focus on anything in particular, but he began to draw again. Quick, sure strokes.

"The marker's going to bleed through the paper!" Charlie half rose from his chair.

"Let it," said Millie. "White sheets are boring anyway."

"Wait until the hospital bills you for them," her son said under his breath. He had perfected that stage mutter at the age of five. She ignored it, as she always had.

Millie had seen enough of George's blueprints over the years to know that this was an unusual one. He started from the center, instead of the perimeter. The sweeping motions he had made without the pen in his hand now transformed into curved walls. Thick walls, judging from the way he returned to them over and over. Shapes she had never seen him draw in any of his professional work.

He labored for an hour. Dr. DeSoto excused herself, saying she would be back.

"Should we stop him?" Charlie asked at one point. "He's exhausting himself."

"He's almost finished, I think," said Millie. His hand was slowing down, making finer adjustments now. The thickness of the marker obscured the delicacy of his sketching. What was going on in his head?

Someone echoed that thought, and she looked up to see that the doctor had returned. Dr. DeSoto gently took the marker from George's hand, which trembled now. She held up the drawing.

"What did he draw?" Millie strained, but was unable to see well enough at that distance. The doctor brought it closer.

Charlie was the one to say it out loud. "I think it's some kind of prison."

Examining the sketch up close, she knew he was right. Thick concentric walls, ramps that suggested someplace far underground.

No windows, no doors, except to and from the central guard tower. This was a place nobody was meant to leave.

In the early years, when he and the other junior architects were first throwing their hats into the partnership ring, George often stayed out for a drink after work or a late night in the office. They attended dinner parties and groundbreakings. Millie loved the meetings with new clients and their wives. She liked to watch George sell them on his vision for their buildings as if his ideas were their own.

"When I make partner, I'll build us our dream house," he said. In the meantime, they moved out to the county. He did his best to balance work and new fatherhood, though it was clear that fatherhood was tipping the balance. He started the tree house when Charlie was still an infant, making preliminary drawings with the baby asleep in the crook of his right arm. Millie would wake up to find the two of them in George's office. "We couldn't sleep, so we thought we'd get some work done," he would say. The early years were all sketches and crumpled paper, false starts and fresh ones.

"They're too young to ask for a tree house," Millie said once, after Jane was born. "How do you know they want one?"

"Look at that tree," George said, pointing to the enormous sycamore in their yard. Its leaves blazed gold and orange in the soft October sun. "How could they not?"

He started the actual construction when Jane was a year old and Charlie was three, working through the weekends and summer evenings. Millie didn't help with the tree house. Instead, she lingered in the garden, seeding and weeding and nurturing her flowers. She had only recently discovered the joys of gardening, but already it was becoming a passion for her. More than that, it was a chance for them all to be together, even if they were involved in different projects. She dug to a soundtrack of hammer and saw. A slight note of sawdust drifted in the air beneath the heady aroma of her roses and peonies.

She liked listening to George explain to Charlie what he was doing, and loved the ways in which he involved Charlie, starting a nail and then inviting the boy to finish it. "You're some builder, kid. Look at that workmanship." If Millie could have bottled a moment, it might have been one of these.

As the children grew older, George allowed them to assert their own personalities on the design.

"I want a giraffe," said four-year-old Charlie, and so George tore out the conventional ladder and constructed a wooden giraffe with stairs built into the neck. When Jane wanted a Rapunzel tower, George built a platform accessible only by a thick flaxen braid. Long after the structure was completed, if one of them asked for a new element he found a way to incorporate it.

"Someday they'll stump you," said Millie.

"They haven't yet," her husband replied. He was right; they never did. The project that she had envisioned as a simple *Our Gang* style fort began to assert itself in contrast to her manicured flowerbeds. Over the years he created a pirate-ship deck, a *Pippi Longstocking* wing, a *Swiss Family Robinson* addition, byzantine passages and secret compartments, and a crow's nest high in the branches. He wired it with thousands of lights, which switched on by timer every evening and danced like fireflies in all seasons.

He didn't let the sycamore limit his vision. He strayed yards from the tree in some directions, like an invasive vine. The tree was merely a guide; Millie suspected that if the tree were hit by lightning, George's structural supports would hold it in place. Some additions were more aesthetically pleasing than others, and some looked better in one season or another, but George didn't care about the aesthetics of the project; he seemed happiest when the whole thing was overrun with children, theirs and others, which was most of the time. The only thing he ever refused them was a rocket. "Spaceships aren't made of wood," he said, with more seriousness than Millie thought the topic was due. "It wouldn't make any sense."

≋ ≋

Jane arrived from Seattle, buzzing into the room with the manic exhaustion of air travel. Hugs all around. Millie marveled, as always, at the fact that two such quiet people had created two such loud ones. Five of the six grandchildren were loud too, everyone but Raymond. Maybe silence was a recessive trait.

Charlie and Jane spent ten minutes arguing over who would stay the night and who would take Millie home. Millie wasn't sure if she was the prize or the punishment. In the end, Jane said she wanted to spend some time alone with her father, since she had only just gotten there, and Charlie said that he and Millie could both use some proper sleep in proper beds, and it was all decided. Millie considered arguing that she wanted to stay at the hospital as well, to make the point that she had a say in the matter. Truth be told, she did want to leave. Too much time in a hospital wasn't good for anyone, even a visitor.

She took George's sketch with her, folding it across her lap for the ride home. Charlie was a good driver, but everything felt too fast. The car was some strange rental, full of glowing buttons and gauges, like the cockpit of an airplane.

"We're going to have to make some plans," said George—no, Charlie. How strange that her son was now older than her husband when she pictured him in her mind. She knew he was Charlie. George never took his eyes off the road, but Charlie stared at her now, waiting for her response to his statement. What kind of response did he expect? She fought the urge to say "duuuuh," as the great-grandchildren did.

"Look where you're going, Charles." Millie pointed at the windshield. Charlie shifted his eyes to the road, but continued throwing glances her way.

"You've done a great job of staying independent, but if he needs rehab you won't be able to take care of him."

"I know," said Millie.

"And I'm not sure it's wise for you to stay in that big house all by yourself."

"Raymond checks on me."

"He's a good boy. I'm glad he lives so close to you. Still, he can't be expected to take on all the responsibility."

"I'll be fine," said Millie.

"You have to consider—"

"I'll consider."

"You're eighty-eight years old. The fact that the two of you have been able to live on your own for this long is a minor miracle."

"I'll consider," she said with finality.

They drove the rest of the way in silence. The snow that had fallen the day before had compacted. Charlie left her in the car with the engine running while he shoveled and de-iced the walk. Even from a distance she saw his exertion. How strange to watch her son grow old. Did he consider himself old? If he was old, what did that make her? Red-faced and sweaty, he helped her up the salted steps.

Later, alone in her bedroom, Millie reached into the pocket of her cardigan and pulled out the two buttons from George's pajama top. She wondered what had happened to his pajamas now that he was in a hospital gown. These would be easy enough to sew back on for him, if they would only give her back the shirt. George was forever losing buttons, busting them off outgrown pants or catching his shirt on the edge of his drafting table. This time it wasn't his fault, of course.

She went through the motions: brushed her teeth, changed into her nightgown, walked her brush through her hair. No need to look in the mirror; she knew she was a mess. Instead, she looked out at the illuminated tree house. What would happen if George wasn't around to change the lights? She couldn't bear the thought of it going dark for a single night.

Maybe Charlie was right, and they should consider moving someplace easier to maintain. If George passed, maybe it would be better to be elsewhere than to live with the memories that suffused each corner of this house. She couldn't think of a time when she had spent a night in the bed alone. No, that wasn't true. How had she forgotten? There had been a whole month in 1951, the year everything changed.

George had only ever taken one trip without Millie, in the fall of 1951. A letter had arrived from the army asking him to fly to New Mexico.

"You don't have to go," she said. "You're not a soldier anymore. They don't even tell you in the letter what they want you to go for. Just 'project maintenance.'"

"I suppose I'll find out. Maybe one of those theoretical designs actually got built. Maybe I'll fly into George Gordon Airport." He swooped Jane into his arms and then up into the air. "Maybe they want to give your daddy a medal! Valor in the face of bureaucracy!" Jane giggled.

He was gone two weeks, then three weeks, then four. They picked him up at Friendship on the afternoon of Jane's third birthday. Up until the moment she loaded the children into the Packard, Millie kept expecting the telephone to ring and George's tired voice to say he had been delayed yet again and would she get by for another week. She attacked the ingredients for Jane's birthday cake, the batter fleeing up the sides of the bowl. Don't ring, she willed the telephone.

But no, he was already there when she drove up, his suit rumpled and his shoulders sagging. He looked every bit as exhausted as he had sounded. She had been prepared to let him know the stress his absence had caused her, but instead she kissed his stubbled cheek. The kids leaned in to hug or possibly strangle him from the backseat.

"Sit down, both of you," he said, slapping their hands from his neck.

"Do you have presents for us?" Charlie reached over the seatback for the blueprint tube George was holding between his knees.

"Don't touch that! Sorry, kid. No presents."

Millie saw Jane building up a wail, and tried to head it off. "I have a lovely dinner planned for tonight. All of Jane's favorites, and steak for you."

"Jane's favorites?"

"Yes, she got to pick for her birthday dinner, of course. Like a big girl."

He scratched at two days' growth of beard.

"Janie's birthday dinner. Of course," he repeated. "Janie, how would you like to pick your own present out tomorrow? Big girls do that."

The tantrum dissipated. In the backseat, Charlie began to run down a list of toys he thought Jane might like, all of which were actually toys he would like better. Millie glanced over at George, who was pinching the bridge of his nose between his fingers. She hoped to get a chance to ask him what was wrong, but when they got home he disappeared into his office. She busied herself making dinner. He snapped at the children twice for fidgeting over the meal; after losing patience a third time, he excused himself before they could sing to Jane.

That night, Millie rolled over in the bed to find George wasn't there. She checked his office, the kitchen, the children's rooms, the den, before finally noticing the unlatched patio door. The air and grass were already laced with frost. She wore a flannel robe, but wished she had put on shoes. George's sobs traveled down from the tree house and across the lawn.

She climbed the giraffe's-neck ladder, crossed the bridge of the pirate ship. The first fallen leaves made some of the steps slippery. George cried like a child in the crow's nest above her. She wasn't sure which frightened her more, his strange mood earlier in the day or his tears now. Maybe he'd rather she climbed down, slipped back into bed, and pretended she had heard nothing.

Her foot crunched a leaf as she took her first step backward.

"Don't leave," he said.

She stopped. "George, what's the matter?"

"Don't leave, please," he said. "I had no idea. I had no choice."

She wanted him to continue. It wouldn't take much to keep him from speaking. One wrong word, one wrong step. She stood still, trying to figure out how close he was from the ragged sound of his breath.

"They said the scenarios were hypothetical."

She waited.

"They were real, Mill. Defenseless, harmless things. Their ship was destroyed. They've been in there four years, and the army wants me to design a newer, better place, to make sure they're stuck 'for the indefinite future.' I should have said no and gotten right back on the plane. 'For the security of the country,' the lieutenant said. He said to think of you, and Charlie, and Jane. I had to, you see?"

She didn't see. She waited for him to say more. She asked questions in her mind: who were "they" and why were they stuck and why couldn't they go back and where couldn't they go back to? Why did he call them things? Was it better to know or not to know? She decided he would tell if he wanted to tell. Minutes passed. Shivering, she climbed four wooden rungs bolted to the trunk. An ungraceful shimmy brought her into the crow's nest. George, in his striped pajamas, sat in the corner, his knees to his chest like a child.

She wanted to go to him, to hold him as he had always held her, to tell him to put it behind him. Instead, she kissed him on the top of his head and leaned out over the edge. She had never been all the way to the top of the tree house before. From this solid perch she could see the delicate curves of her dormant gardens. Then past that, over the rooftops, past the lamplit neighborhood, out to the dark farmland beyond. She didn't know what time it was, but the faintest glimmer of dawn colored the place where the earth met the sky. Even at this height she trusted his workmanship. The platform was steady, the railing secure.

She sat down beside him. "You're a good man, and a good husband, and a good father," she said. "Whatever you did, I'm sure you had to do it."

After a moment, he put his arm around her. She knew that whatever he had allowed to surface he now had buried. Who would have imagined that such an intimate moment would become the line between before and after? Maybe she should have asked more, pushed more, given more comfort. How had it taken sixty years to come back around to the things he had spoken of that night? That night, she had no idea what he was talking about. She had let it go, let him carry it alone.

Millie dialed Raymond first thing when she woke up. Mark answered the phone, half asleep, and she realized she had no idea what day of the week it was. If it was a weekend she was calling far too early. Mark put Ray on.

"I think I lost a day at the hospital," she said by way of apology.

"It's okay, Grandma. What's up?"

She took a deep breath. "I was wondering if you would do me a favor if you're planning on coming . . . no, actually, that part doesn't matter. Regardless of whether you're coming to the hospital today, I was wondering if you would stop by the house and help me look for something."

"No problem. What and where?"

"I'm not sure exactly what, and I'm guessing at the where. There may be nothing. I'm just curious, and I can't go up there myself."

"Up there?" he asked.

"The top of the tree house."

When Charlie woke, Millie insisted that he leave for the hospital without her. "Raymond is on his way," she said. "He'll take me."

"Why are you dragging him over here?" Charlie poured coffee into a mug for her, then rummaged in the cupboard until he found a travel cup for himself. He took the milk from the fridge, sniffed it, and then splashed some into her coffee and some into his own.

"He's going to help find some paperwork I misplaced." Before Charlie offered his own assistance, she added, "I had asked him to put it in a safe place for me, so it makes sense for him to be the one to figure out where he put it."

He clapped the lid onto his cup and gave her a smile of sympathy. "Like his uncle, huh? Do you remember all the stuff I never saw again that I had put away for safekeeping? I still expect you to call someday to say you found my Brooks Robinson rookie card."

She kissed him goodbye and managed to push him out the door. Poor Raymond didn't deserve to be lumped in with Charlie on this one. Nobody lost things like Charlie.

When Ray arrived, she explained what she wanted him to search for, or rather the fact that she had no idea what he was searching for, but he would know it if he found it. She made him put on one of George's hats and a pair of gloves before sending him out to the tree house.

Once he had stepped outside, Millie set about her own search. She made her way down the hallway and pushed open the door to the office. The air in the room was cold and stale; though Millie would be sitting at the drafting table in a few weeks to plan her spring gardens, neither she nor George had much use for the room in the winter. As in their bedroom next door, the windows faced the backyard. She watched Raymond's progress through the snow before turning to the task at hand. She didn't know if George had kept anything here that might explain his actions, but it was worth looking.

She started with the file cabinets: not hers with the house bills and contracts and warranties and receipts, but the wood-faced one he had built for himself. The drawer slid open easily. The plans inside were neatly labeled, arranged alphabetically. What might she find here? "S" for "secret." "P" for "prison." Unlikely.

The phone rang. Once, twice. Why had they never put a telephone in the office? Three times, four. The bedroom was closer than the kitchen, but she wasn't yet ready to sit at the desk where George had been. Five rings, six, seven. The ringing paused, then began again. She wasn't sure she wanted to speak to anybody who wanted to reach her that badly.

She lifted the phone from its cradle.

"He had another stroke, Ma. They don't know if he's going to wake up." Jane was crying. Millie tried to comfort her, feeling absurd in doing so. How could she explain that she had already begun mourning George as she had picked the buttons of his pajama top off the floor?

"Hang on, Janie," Millie said. "We'll be there as soon as we can. I have to wait for Raymond to come back inside."

She hung up and leaned against the doorframe. From the kitchen doorway, she saw into the den. George's childhood desk stood in a dark corner beside the stairs; he had brought it back to the house after his mother's death in 1969. Funny, the things that become background, beneath notice. She hadn't given that desk a second thought in years.

The writing surface swung upward on protesting hinges, revealing layers of children's hidden treasures: a princess doll from some Disney movie or another, a metal car, a comic book, some foreign coins, the joke wrappers from several pieces of Bazooka gum. Beneath three generations of lost toys, she discovered something else: a piece of plywood. It took her some effort to pry loose the false bottom.

Inside, she found a small leather-bound notebook of the type George had carried when they first met. George had signed and dated the inside of the front cover, 1931. Each page was filled with diagrams. Castles, skyscrapers, scaled city maps, all done in a more fanciful version of George's trained hand. Everything he had put away of himself, bound into one sketchbook.

∞∞

In retrospect, Millie was able to look back on that single trip and the confession in the upper branches of the sycamore as a turning point. They climbed down as the sun rose, dressed the children, drove downtown to run some errands, went to Hutzler's for an early lunch and a belated birthday present for Jane. Life seemed back to normal. Millie put George's upset out of her mind over shrimp salad on cheese toast. Later there were other conversations, bigger battles. It was easy enough to say in hindsight that George had become different overnight, but by the time she noticed, the changes had already taken root. By the time she noticed, the architect was gone.

The man who replaced him was similar in most ways, but without any hint of boyishness. The only remnant of the child who had sketched skyscrapers was in his work on the tree house; he still mustered enthusiasm when planning something with Charlie and Jane. He ceased to bring designs home from the office at all.

"Work can stay at work," he said.

She was baffled that someone who still poured so much of himself into a project for his children had stopped putting anything into his occupation. She watched as he was passed over for promotion after promotion, never progressing beyond junior partner at any of the firms he worked for.

They wanted me to work overtime," he'd say after leaving another job. Or, "They wanted me to travel."

"So travel! The kids are old enough that I can manage for a few days on my own."

He just shook his head. It was as if he knew every trick for self-promotion and then set about sabotaging himself. Millie didn't complain. When money was tight, when Jane needed braces or when a storm blew the roof off the garage, Millie found work. She tried not to resent the change. Whatever it was the other architects had that drove them to create no longer seemed to be a part of George. He designed bland suburban houses, and later strip malls and office parks. The high-rises and mansions and museums went to other, more ambitious draftsmen.

"Show me your designs," she begged him. "The projects you want to work on."

"They're only buildings," he said, shrugging. This time it was true.

"A new subdivision?" She tried to ask in a way that sounded excited.

"Yes. A whole neighborhood, but just three different house designs."

"Are you designing all of them?"

"No, I'm in charge of the four bedroom, but I have to work with another fellow so that they look like they came from the same brain."

"You're very talented, you know." She said this as often as possible without sounding trite. "I wish you would get a chance to make all those things you used to talk about."

He laughed and turned away from the drafting table. "You're sweet to say so, but it's not art. It's just my job. I make what they want me to make."

When the wives of the firm's partners mentioned their husbands' latest endeavors, she smiled and volunteered nothing. If he didn't want to be an artist, he didn't have to be, but she couldn't understand how he took pride in his draftsmanship and dismissed it at the same time. Try as she might, she was unable to put her finger on what exactly he had lost. How could she complain about a man who helped with the dishes every night, who read to the children, who taught them to measure twice and cut once? She tried to encourage him, but he turned everything around.

"Why don't you get another degree?" he asked one day, after the children had both started high school. "You've always wanted to learn more about your plants."

She did it, half hoping to motivate him again as well. She had a master's degree and a doctorate in botany by the time she realized she would never goad him into competing with her. He let her take over his office and his drafting table when she needed them for her garden designs. He corrected others when they assumed he was the doctor in the family, and spoke of her accomplishments, but never said a word about his own. When she tried to brag to others about his work, he responded with self-deprecation. She hated herself for wishing him to be anything other than what he had become, and worked on loving him for the person that he was. He was a match that refused to ignite; she felt selfish for wanting him to burn brightly.

Over time, it ceased to matter as much. Her career bloomed, and she learned not to press him about his. The children grew up and left and came back and left and had children of their own. In retirement she found him to be much easier company. She enjoyed watching his comfortable way with the grandchildren and great-grandchildren, and loved it when he began to design new tree-house additions for the new generations.

She wasn't sure if it was fair to judge anyone by the man he had been in his twenties. The person you marry is not the same person you grow old with. She was sure he could say the same thing about her. She was sorry it had taken her so long to learn that, to stop pushing him, but that was probably the way of it.

Raymond drove her to the hospital, then returned to the house. "I'm on to something," he said, kissing her on the forehead and dashing out again. Millie watched reruns from the straight-backed chair beside George's bed. Jane and Charlie took turns beside her, occasionally slipping out to talk in the hallway. She thought she heard Charlie say "retirement community" at least twice.

She let the TV distract her. Every man on television seemed to be an architect. Every sitcom and every movie, from the *Brady Bunch* on, seemed to feature some young man with blueprints and skyscraper dreams. Why was that? It was artsy but manly, she supposed. Sensitive without being soft. A perfect occupation for a man with a creative side who also wanted to support his family, at least until the day he decided he didn't want to do it anymore. That didn't seem to happen on television.

Raymond arrived back late in the evening, the glow of success evident in his face. It only took him a moment to convince his mother and uncle to go grab some dinner before the cafeteria closed.

"I think I found what you were looking for, Grandma." It was amazing how much he looked like a young George when he smiled. Taller, thankfully for him, and with a strange lop-sided haircut, but with the same rakish confidence that she had so admired. She returned the smile. She hadn't really thought there would be anything to find, but it had been worth a shot.

"There are a bunch of compartments all over the tree house, but most of them are still filled with toys and baseball cards and stuff. Anyway, I remembered that one time my cousin Joseph was chasing me 'cause he wanted my Steve Austin action figure. I didn't know where to put it that he wouldn't find it. I was almost to the top when I realized that the metal struts that support the crow's nest are hollow, if you have something to pry them open with. I had my pocket knife with me. The first one I opened had something wedged in it, so I stashed Steve Austin in the second one until Joseph went home. Never thought to look at what was in that first one until now."

With a flourish, he produced a blueprint tube from behind his back. "I opened it to make sure there was something in it—there is—but I didn't look at what's inside."

She tried to keep her voice from quavering. She hoped the others would stay away from the room a little longer. "Shall we?"

Ray slid the rolled paper out, laying the drawing across George's legs.

"George, we're looking at the blueprints you hid." She thought it was only fair to explain what was going on.

This was the same prison he had drawn on the butcher paper. Done on proper drafting paper, and more detailed, but still with an unfinished quality. He wouldn't have been allowed to bring the actual plans home; he must have sketched it again later. Her eye roved the paper, trying to understand the nuances of the horrible place. She had seen enough of George's plans that they rose from the paper as fully formed buildings in her mind.

"It's the same," she said, but as she said it, she caught the flaw that she had missed in the cruder drawing. She looked closer, but there was no mistaking it. In this all-seeing prison, a small blind spot. To her knowledge, George had never made an error on a blueprint. Had he done the same thing on the original? Had anyone else noticed, in the engineering or the construction? She had no way of knowing if this sketch was true to the thing that had been built, or if he had changed the design in retrospect. She could still only guess at what to say to ease his mind.

Millie leaned over to kiss George's stubbled cheek. She whispered in his ear. "Maybe you did it, old man. Maybe you gave them a chance."

Jane spent the drive home updating her mother on her own work and the escapades of various children and grandchildren. Millie lost track, but appreciated the diversion. When they got to the house, her daughter headed straight for the kitchen.

"Tea?" Jane was already picking up the kettle.

"Tea would be wonderful," Millie agreed, before excusing herself to the bedroom.

She crossed the room in the dark and opened the French doors, letting the winter air inside. She had never tired of this view, not in any season. Tonight, the light of the full moon reflected off the snow and disappeared in Raymond's footprints. The naked branches of the sycamore were long white fingers outlined in light; they performed benedictions over the empty platforms of the tree house.

Millie stepped through the doorway and onto the patio. The drifts were nearly up to her knees. She took two more steps, toward the tree. The cold made her eyes water.

She wished she could go back to that night in 1951, ask George what he had done and how she might share his burden. She was too late for so much. She allowed herself to grieve it all for a moment: her husband, their life together, the things they had shared and the things they had held back. It surrounded her like the cold, filling up the space expelled by her breath, until she fixed her eyes again on the tree house. Everything missing from the body in the hospital was still here. The Georgeness.

"Oh," she whispered, as the day hit her.

"I won't leave," she said to the tree. Raymond would help her, maybe, or she would hire someone who would. The lights continued to dance after she had made her way back inside. They danced behind her eyelids when she closed her eyes.

Millie remembered the dream house that George used to promise her, back when this was a passing-through place, not their home. She was suddenly glad he had never gotten the chance to build it, that he had instead devoted himself to countless iterations of one mad project. Even the best plans get revised.

In the morning, there were pamphlets for a retirement village on the kitchen table.

Jane looked apologetic. "Charlie says we should talk about your options."

"I know my options," Millie said, setting a mug down on one of the smiling silver-haired faces.

She refused to let Jane help with the briefcase she carried with her to the hospital. When they got to George's room, she sent Charlie and Jane to get breakfast.

"I'd like some time with my husband," she said.

Then they were alone again, alone except for the noisy machines by the bedside and the ticking clock and the television and the nurses' station outside the door. None of that was hard to tune out.

"We're going to draw again, old man."

She opened the briefcase and pulled out a drawing board, a piece of paper, and a handful of pencils. She managed to angle a chair so that she was leaning half on the bed. George's hand closed around the pencil when she placed it against his palm. All the phantom energy of two days previous was gone. Her movement now led his, both of her hands clasped around his left.

He was the draftsman, but she knew plants. They started with the roots. She guided him through the shape of the tree, through the shape of his penance. Through every branch they both knew by heart, through every platform she had seen from her vantage point in the garden. The firehouse pole, the puppet theater, the Rapunzel tower. The crow's nest, which had kept his secret. Finally, around the treehouse, they started on her plans for the spring's gardens. All that mattered was his hand pressed in hers: long enough to feel like always, long enough to feel like everything trapped had been set free.

— No Lonely Seafarer —

On the nights Mrs. Wainwright let me work in the barn instead of the tavern, I used to sing to the horses. They would greet me with their own murmurs, and swivel their ears to follow my voice as I readied their suppers. That was where Captain Smythe found me: in the barn, singing a song of my own making. I shut up as soon as I heard the door squeal on its hinges.

"You're Freddy Turlington's boy, aren't you?" His voice was rummy but not drunk. There were men around I felt the need to hide from, but he didn't seem like one of them.

"Turlington was my father."

I watched him from one of the stalls. He sat down heavily on a bale of bedding straw, grunting as if the effort pressed all the air from his lungs. He wore a well-fitted blue coat and his boots still shone with care, which set him apart from most of our patrons these days.

"You must be, what, ten now?"

I didn't answer, but resumed my feeding rounds. Thirteen. Close enough. The horses rumbled their *pleases* and *thank yous.*

"What's your name, child?"

"Alex," I answered.

"Alex, do you know who I am?"

"Captain Smythe. My father sailed with you."

"Freddy was a good sailor and a good cook. I was sorry he got himself killed."

That one didn't really have an answer, so I left it. I climbed up into the loft, dangling my legs over. He looked up at me. His face was red, but less from drink than from exposure, as far as I could tell from the uniformity of the color. His skin had the look of leather left out in the sun.

"Can you sail, child?"

"Yes, sir."

I wished he would get to his point, whatever it was, but he was in no hurry. He closed his eyes. I thought for a moment he had fallen asleep, but then he addressed me again.

"I'd like you to sail out with me next week."

I assessed him again. I hadn't thought him drunk, but he had to know we couldn't sail anywhere. I chose to take the practical tack first. "I can't. My father bonded me to Mrs. Wainwright when he left me here."

"I spoke with Mrs. Wainwright about buying your bond. Or leasing it, I should say. I'll only have need of you for a short trip. I need somebody your age on board. Do you know why?"

I considered for a moment. "You think I can get you past the sirens?"

He smiled. "Well done. Yes. We must get past the sirens, and beeswax doesn't bloody well do it, contrary to anything Homer said. Bright child."

It didn't take intelligence. There wasn't a person in Dog's Bay who hadn't heard about the sirens now nesting on the headland, singing at anyone who tried to pass, keeping ships from getting in or out. The streets and the taverns and the boardinghouses were all clogged with sailors, who were in turn clogged with their desire to be back on the sea. It was part of why I felt so much safer in the barn. The Salt Dog tavern became rowdier with each passing night. Fights and fires would come next, according to Mrs. Wainwright. She said she was old enough to have seen it all before.

"What about sirens?" I had asked her.

She shook her head. "Not personally, but search the sea long enough and you'll see most stories have some truth to them."

Everyone in port had an opinion on how to get past the sirens. In recent evenings past, clearing tables, I had heard debate after debate on the matter. Lucius Nickleby had been the first to try to leave. He and his men had stuffed their ears with beeswax, the way the Greeks had done. John Harrow watched through his spyglass on shore as they threw themselves from the deck. Ahmed Fairouz, with his fluyt *Mahalia*, had attempted to outrun the bewitching songs. The *Mahalia* was dashed to splinters on the rocks below the promontory. A month later, pieces were still washing to shore with each tide.

"You understand what I'm proposing, boy?" Smythe asked.

"You're hoping that their voices don't work on a child."

"I'm betting my life on it."

I dropped down from the loft and walked over to where he was sitting. He was not a large man, though I was much smaller. Up close, his blue coat was stained and split-seamed. It made me bolder than I might have been otherwise. "You're betting my life on it as well. Do you expect to rouse an entire crew of children, then? Or am I to tie all your men to the masts until we pass?"

He was silent as he appraised me afresh. Maybe my voice was older than he expected, or maybe he caught a glimmer of what Mrs. Wainwright called "the off thing" about me. When he spoke again, the false cheer was gone from his voice. "I'm thinking it would be the two of us, in a small fishing boat I purchased for the purpose. And yes, I would have you tie me up, but no use risking my men or my ship if I'm wrong. If I'm right, we can pass unharmed, then return to port. If I'm mistaken, well, at least I die at sea, as I was meant to do."

"As you were meant to do," I echoed, emphasizing the "you." His chosen destiny, not mine. Not that I had any reason to expect a choice. If Mrs. Wainwright wanted to sell or rent my bond, she had every right. Then again, I liked that Smythe had come to me as if it were a question. I liked the idea of seeing something beyond Dog's Bay, even if only briefly. I had never considered myself an heir to my father's wanderlust, but maybe some small sliver of it in me begged to be entertained. I wanted to see how the ocean differed from the cove, and why it called to all of the men of our town as persuasively as any siren.

"If you've already spoken with Mrs. Wainwright and she's said I'm to go, I've no business saying otherwise." His rough hand dwarfed mine when we shook on it.

I waited until the next day to seek out Mrs. Wainwright. I found her overseeing the morning meal, making sure the twins ladled each customer exactly the right amount of porridge. She rarely cheated a patron, just made sure they got what they had paid for and nothing more. It had taken a long time to get the twins to understand that nuance; now, at seven, they needed only minimal supervision.

I waved a greeting. Eliza waved back, but Simon was clearly using all his attention to make sure the spoon got to the bowl and back without making a mess.

I came around the bar and Mrs. Wainwright swatted me with a towel. The gesture was friendly, her tone only mock stern.

"Don't be distracting them now. I might allow them to serve stew if this comes off right. Are the horses fed and watered?"

"Yes, ma'am. That little chestnut that came in with the knife salesman is still not drinking, though."

"Hopefully he'll leave again before he notices. Bit of a fool in any case. Try giving it some beer in its water when you go out next. Maybe the water here tastes different from the other side of the island. I'll tell you, I'll be happy when all of these opportunists hitch up and drive away and things get back to normal."

She squinted at me, tucking a stray lock of hair behind her ear. "Something bothering you, Alex?"

"That captain you sent out to the barn last night?"

She nodded. "Smythe. Good man. Used to come around a fair bit back in the day. Bad luck for him that the first time he swings out our way in a dog's year is when those screechy biddies settle down to roost. Here, make yourself useful."

I took the rag she held out, and began to wipe the closest unoccupied table. A couple of groggy sailors sat on the fringes of the room and one at the far end of the bar. I lowered my voice so the discussion could continue without them or the twins overhearing. "But—why'd you send him to me?"

"His idea is better than anything the rest of these fools came up with. Silas Hill—that fellow in the far corner—he's trying to work up the dash-fire to make himself deaf, if he can figure out how. Only he'll have to deafen his whole crew as well, won't he?" She made sure Silas Hill heard her. He stared into his ale.

"But Smythe's idea is to have a young boy take him, and you know I'm not as young as that, and," I walked to her side to whisper, "you know I'm not exactly the boy we say I am."

"All the better for it," she whispered back. "I think you have more chance than anyone, and this has to happen soon, before things get out of control."

"Why not one of those lady captains that come in here sometimes?"

She shook her head. "One of them tried as well, not two days ago. That's her mast sticking out of the rocks like a flagpole. But you're no lady captain."

"So you're trying to kill me. You want me out of here. Sold to the highest bidder." I swiped at a sticky spot on the bar with my rag until she stopped my hand.

"I have a right to do that if I want, but you've always worked hard, and I'm not of a mind to lose your help. I think you'll survive because you're not like any of the others who have tried."

"I see," I said in mock comprehension, not bothering to hide my anger. "Then it's because I'm neither-nor?"

She took the rag from my hand. "No. Because you know what you are, in a way that most people don't ever have to think about. Now take those fool children and clean them off before I'm tempted to beat them."

I looked over to see that the twins had managed to knock over the vat of porridge in their own direction. They were working together to right the pot, but wearing most of the dregs.

I wasn't going to win any argument here. "Come on, you two. Looks like you're getting a scrubbing, but it's better than a beating."

They followed me outside. Simon's left foot squished as he walked. Step, squish. Step, squish. Even in my dark mood, I found it hard not to laugh.

"Fetch two buckets each," I said, sliding the barn door open wide enough for them to wriggle through. They returned a moment later, and we went to the pump. I took pity on them and carried two back myself, leaving each of them with one full bucket. Sometimes two is better than one, though. Balance. Eliza lost half of hers on the walk back, most onto her own shoes and trousers. Simon trailed us, careful not to spill a drop.

The day was mild enough, so I poured the four buckets into the barnyard trough.

"Empty your shoe into one of those buckets," I told Simon. "And both of you, any porridge you can scrape off yourselves."

They did as they were told.

"Now into the trough with you ducklings." They both hesitated, then Simon shrugged and climbed over the edge, and his sister followed with a whimper. I slipped into the barn to give the shoe-porridge to the little chestnut mare that wouldn't drink.

When I returned to the barnyard, I heard the twins bickering. Eliza sounded more put upon, so I suspected the accident had been her fault. They were both still in their clothing, but I figured that needed washing, too.

I had been in charge of their baths and their nappies from the time they had arrived, when I was seven. The smooth cleft between

Eliza's legs and the nub between Simon's taught me everything that I was supposed to be and wasn't. I suspected later that was part of the reason Mrs. Wainwright had put me to the task.

"Why?" I asked the first time she showed me how to clean each of them properly.

"Why are they different from each other, or why are you different from both of them?"

I considered. "Yes."

"Most everyone is born into this world a boy, like Simon, or a girl, like Eliza. I guess there are some people in the world born like you, with boy parts and girl parts that don't really add up to either. That isn't really a why, but I'm not sure there is one. You've seen that tabby cat running around with the extra toes? That doesn't bother her none, so I guess you have to make up your mind that this won't bother you neither."

The cat in question unlatched box stalls and unscrewed jars. She did pretty well for herself.

"It won't bother me neither," I echoed.

"Do you feel more like one than the other?"

I looked at the two babies. Up until that point I hadn't really thought about it either way. It didn't seem to make much difference.

"I don't know," I answered honestly.

"It'll be safer for you to live as a boy. You can piss standing up, and you won't get pawed by as many of the drunks so long as your chest stays flat, and they won't get any surprise sticking a hand down your skirt someday. Though that would serve them right. I wouldn't mind teaching that lesson myself."

"I can be a boy." More than anything, I wanted to please her. I was rewarded with a smile.

"You're a good child, Alex. Whatever else you are doesn't matter to me."

I had one more question. "Is that why my father left me here?"

She gave Simon a final powdering of wood dust and put him into my arms. "Yes and no. Your father left you because a seafaring man can't be expected to care for a baby, and he knew I'd raise you and give you work. How he wound up with you? I would guess that the woman that bore you, whoever she was, got a little put out by that collection of parts you're carrying and decided to wash her hands of you. No matter, though. It's just an odd thing, and one better not to discuss with anyone else. You understand?"

I nodded, bouncing Simon on my knee. He giggled. I made a face, and he copied it. That would be how I would learn, too.

I draped the wet clothing over a rail to dry, and bade the two naked children to sit on an old blanket while I cleaned stalls.

"Why do you sing to the horses?" Eliza asked, tucking in her toes to stay clear of my wheelbarrow.

"To let them know where I am, and to keep them calm while I work around them. And because I like it. There, that's three reasons."

"Are we allowed to sing?"

"Always, little duck. Pick a song."

I dumped the barrow outside, then joined my voice with theirs as I hoisted my pitchfork again.

By the time I finished all fourteen occupied straight stalls and the two boxes, the sun was well past noon. I much preferred the horse waste to human waste, but most of the guests would be out by now, and chamber pots needed emptying. The twins levered themselves into clothes half dry and stiffened in the sunlight.

My intention was to head straight back, but a commotion in the square distracted me. "Run home and start on the chamber pots," I told Eliza and Simon. "Take care not to mess."

I crept closer to the source of the sounds, staying up against the buildings in case it was a fight. Silas Hill, who looked to be even more in his cups than he had that morning, stood on the edge of the old well.

"How much longer are we going to stare at our ships as they rot in this bay? How much longer will we spend away from our homes?"

Hill swayed as he talked; he was probably lucky the well had been bricked over when the pumps were installed. The crowd murmured and swayed with him. They sounded like they agreed on the sentiment, even if they couldn't put an actual number on it.

I noticed my friend Ginny, the baker's daughter, and went to stand by her. "What's he on about?"

She flashed me a smile. "Alex! He's trying to get a party together—a troop, I think he said—to sneak up on the sirens over land."

"Can he do that? The sneaking up part, not the over land part."

She blushed, and I looked down. We both knew it was possible to climb up to the headland, and to sit in the rocky meadow and watch the ships come and go, and to share a single kiss before scrambling back down with our hearts hammering out of our chests. We hadn't spoken of it since.

"He thinks he can. The question is how many he'll rally, I suppose. And what weapons they'll bring."

"Weapons?"

"That's why they're sneaking up. To shoot the sirens before they can sing."

The idea of killing them wasn't one I had heard before. I knew the seamen needed to get back out to sea and that we needed supplies to come in. Still, I had figured the sirens would find some other place to nest at some point, and leave us alone. Or Captain Smythe's idea would work, and ships could get by again. I wasn't sure it was fair that they should have to die for doing what was their nature.

Ginny and I watched as Hill rounded up eleven men, all as drunk or drunker than he was. "Cowards!" he shouted at the rest. None of them seemed to mind. Somebody put a rifle in his hand and he swung it like a sword. Another man raised a bow and a handful of arrows. The group stumbled down the cobblestones in the right general direction. A couple of snickers came from the larger crowd.

"Bunch of suicides," said a woman standing at the back.

"If you're going to get yourself killed by sirens, it's only proper to go by ship," agreed a man standing next to her. "I'm working up to it myself."

I saw Captain Smythe at that moment, facing me from the other side of the well. He had heard the other man too, but he caught my eye and shook his head. He believed in his solution. The others had too, of course.

"Hey! Boy!" A hand clamped down on my shoulder, though the derision in the voice had already rooted me to the spot. Ginny's mother, Mrs. Arietti. "Aren't you supposed to be working? You aren't needed here."

I threw an apologetic glance at Ginny as her mother marched me away. Had she noticed the way her mother said "boy"? My cheeks burned.

"What have I said about speaking to my daughter?" she whispered when we were out of Ginny's earshot.

"D-don't do it."

"So what makes you think I didn't mean it?" Each of her fingers was like a separate nail biting into my collarbone. "You're not the type I want sweet on my daughter."

I wondered what the type was. In this town, her choice was pretty much one of the seafaring men or me, or one of the island's few inland farmers. Maybe she was waiting for some rich merchant to roll in and whisk Ginny away to a better life. It wouldn't happen so long as the sirens had us locked in and the world locked out.

She rounded on me one last time outside the tavern. She crooked a finger at my face, the knuckles swollen from kneading dough. "If you so much as walk on the same side of the street as Ginny, I'll make sure you regret it."

Somebody stumbled out of the Salt Dog at that moment, and I took the opportunity to squirm from Mrs. Arietti's grasp and duck inside. For the next minute my breath came in gasps as I waited for her to follow.

The tavern was full that night and the next, and for once I was grateful to have no time to think about anything but chores. Even the twins were called to duty. They kept busy fetching empties and unwatched half-empties, and giving us a running tally of what was going on in the corners we couldn't see.

The patrons fell into two categories, surly and morose. Nobody sang, nobody played card games. I broke up one fight, earning myself a black eye in the process, and Mrs. Wainwright broke up two more. She sent Simon and Eliza back to her rooms upstairs.

Not long after, a sober and ragged-looking man slunk through the door. I recognized him as the one who had brandished the bow and arrows the day before. Someone at the closest table stood up to let him have a chair, and someone else handed him a mug of ale, which he drained in one draught.

"What happened?"

"Are the sirens dead?"

"Quiet, all of you," said Mrs. Wainwright, banging on the bar. "Let him have another drink. Can't you see his tail's down? Give him a moment and he'll speak when he's ready."

They grew silent. Another mug appeared in front of the man. He drank that one slowly, sighing when he reached the bottom. I expected a long story, but he didn't have much to say.

"They're all dead, the men I left with. We went to sneak up, only they must have heard us coming, 'cause they started singing. We heard 'em, the sirens, like, and every man among us dropped his weapons and started running toward 'em."

"How did you get away?" asked the sailor who had hit me a few minutes before.

"I tripped and hit me head on a rock." The man tipped his cap to show a gash and bruise on his temple. "Knocked meself out cold."

A laugh went round the room. "That sounds about right for old Charley," someone shouted.

"What did you do when you woke up?"

"I left, of course, before those bitches got to thinking I was trying to pass them and started singing at me. Only I was a little confused, see, and when I got to the bottom I got turned around and went the wrong way. Took me half a day to realize I was walking away from the port."

Almost everyone laughed.

"What did they sing?" Smythe asked, his voice cutting through the chuckles. I hadn't even realized he was in the room.

Old Charley looked confused.

Smythe repeated himself, then rephrased the question. "The sirens. What did they sound like? You're the first person we know who has heard them and lived. I've heard different stories, but most of them say if anyone hears their song and resists the temptation, the sirens fall away or die."

Charley touched a hand to his bruise. "I'm sorry. I didn't resist. And I don't have much of a head for a tune on the best of days."

"That's no lie," someone shouted from the back of the room. More laughter.

"Not the tune, then. The words? Anything?" Smythe's voice held no humor.

"It was about singing, I think." Charley frowned. "They were singing about singing. I remember that much. Not too many songs are about singing. Most of them are about women or ships."

Someone launched into "Married to a Mermaid," and for the first time all night the customers sang. Mrs. Wainwright joined in, and I would have liked to, but I made sure not to sing where strangers might hear. I noticed Captain Smythe wasn't singing either. He pushed his way through the crowd to talk to me.

"I've had enough of this, Alex. We'll go tomorrow morning. Out and back, to show it can be done."

"Yes, sir."

The mood in the tavern brightened. Mugs were raised to Old Charley and to Silas Hill and the other dead men.

"We're leaving in the morning," I told Mrs. Wainwright.

"Feed the horses before you go, then, and you'll be back to feed them again come evening." She turned away from me quickly, but not before I noticed tears in her eyes.

I slipped upstairs to her rooms, where Simon and Eliza were playing jacks on the floor. I sat down beside them.

"I have to go away tomorrow."

Eliza cocked her head at me. "Go away?"

"With one of the captains."

"But I thought nobody could leave. Not by ship."

"We're going to show there's a way to leave by ship and come back."

Simon's hug surprised me, coming out of nowhere. "I hope you come back."

I hugged him. "I hope so too."

"Do we have to do your chores if you don't?" Eliza asked.

"I imagine you do. But I'll be back." I tried to keep my tone light.

I spent the night in their bed with them, and extricated myself from their little bodies at the first light of dawn, having not slept a minute myself. I went through my rounds in the barn, feeding and watering the horses, singing them "Married to a Mermaid," and giving each an extra pat and scratch behind the ears. The chestnut mare had finally drunk. If we reopened the port, the knife salesman would be on his way, and she could go home to where she liked the water better. If we reopened the port, I'd be back here to see her off. I tried not to think about the other option.

Captain Smythe met me at the docks. I had expected a crowd, but I was happy to see only his own men had gathered to see him off. I wasn't much for attention. I only wished Mrs. Wainwright had come. Maybe the previous night was as much goodbye as she could stand to say. I knew she cared about me, even if she didn't say it outright.

Smythe's rented fishing boat was as small as he had said, though it had a small cabin and sails. He was chatting with his men, so I jumped on board and began looking over the rigging, to show him I knew a little bit. Not that I knew much. I had only sailed around the bay now and again with some friend or another of Mrs. Wainwright. One had actually taken the time to teach me.

"It's not right to live in a port town and not know how to sail," she said. So I checked the lines and the cleats, and felt pleased with myself.

Smythe joined me a few minutes later, with one last wave to his men. I imagined he had charged them to watch and report back if we didn't return, or to serve as our witnesses if we made it back and nobody believed us.

He cast off with practiced hands. I left him alone while he worked. When he finally addressed me, he did so without looking in my direction, pointing to a heavy iron lock on the outside of the cabin and a key on a hook beside it.

"I'm going to go below as soon as I can, and you're to lock me in. No sense in risking getting any closer when we don't know how far their voices carry."

I nodded.

"You're not to let me out, no matter how much I beg. Not until we're out of the bay."

I nodded again, and watched as he lashed the tiller to hold direction. He didn't say another word, but gave an ambiguous gesture in my direction as he went below. Goodbye, perhaps, or good luck, or don't wreck us, or just get on with it. I closed the lock and hung the key back on the peg.

I had never been alone on the deck of a boat before. It felt strange to sit at the tiller as if I were a captain. Powerful. How much more so would it feel to succeed in our task? Maybe if I returned a hero, Ginny's mother would let us speak again.

A mast stuck out between the rocks. Here and there, pieces of other ships that had preceded us. Ahead lay the mouth of the bay, wide and glittering gold-blue where the morning sun hit the water. The two rocky promontories that sheltered us loomed taller than I had ever seen them before.

The one to the starboard side was the one I watched now. I didn't know what to expect. Would the sirens appear? Would they sing first? What did it feel like to be lured by a song, lulled by a song? What went through the heads of the captains as they dashed their own ships on the rocks? I wanted to know. I didn't want to know.

There was a decent breeze by the shore, but it lessened as we sailed toward the open sea. I hummed to myself to pass the time. The air now hung like a woolen blanket on a washline. I took my hand off the tiller; I was only pretending to be a captain. Really, I had no clue what to do if we were becalmed.

"Let me out!"

I spoke to the locked door. "Captain, I'm not supposed to let you out. But do you hear them? I don't."

He moaned in response. I scanned the rocks for any sign of the sirens.

And then I heard them.

Their voices were hideously beautiful. I made out some of the words. As Old Charley had said, it was a song about the song itself, daring the listener to listen, as if anyone had a choice. The words drifted in the air.

"Listen to our two voices," they said, and I did.

"Sweet coupled airs we sing," and something about a green mirror, and the whole time they were singing, I kept expecting some key to turn in my own lock, something to make my hand move on the tiller. And the whole time they were singing, I kept thinking: I know this song. I knew it in my bones, knew it though I had never heard it. Not the words, but the challenge behind them.

The sail moved of its own accord, fighting any direction. A new wind swirled, pushed about by the force of enormous wings. Wings that blocked the sun and sent the boat rocking. The sirens landed on the deck, feather light, and I saw them for the first time.

They were like me. Or I thought they were, for a moment of wishful thinking. They weren't, but I found it hard to look at them straight on. They were naked, and they had wings, or they didn't, and they threw their shoulders back and their chests forward like strutting birds. I understood the two voices, understood the mirror, understood.

Smythe still moaned in the cabin, but with luck the tide would bring the boat safely to shore even if I didn't return. His men could pry the door.

I took off my shirt and unwrapped the binding round my small breasts. I removed one boot, then the other, then my trousers. I dared them to look at me, and they did it as if it wasn't a dare at all. Like nothing I had ever wanted in my life, I suddenly knew I wanted to grow wings and scales. I wanted to roost with them on rocks in their green meadow.

No. What about Mrs. Wainwright and Captain Smythe? Roost with the sirens in some other green meadow, overlooking some other sea. Teach them new songs that didn't sing sailors to their graves.

"Draw near, bring your ship to rest," they sang. They never stopped singing. "No man passes without hearing the sweet sound from our lips."

I am not a man, some small part of me said. I am but I am not. But the female captain had run aground as well, and I knew I wasn't exactly a woman either. While I puzzled, each of them took one of my arms. They lifted me into the sky. I squeezed my eyes shut.

It took me a moment to work up the nerve to look. Everything appeared much smaller viewed from above. I saw the shape of the whole island, the rocky cliffs that made any other landing impossible. The bay really was shaped like a dog's head, pinched by the collar of the two headlands. Our town, the dog's snout. I saw the town square, and the tavern, and the barn, where I had sung only to horses. I pictured Mrs. Wainwright starting the porridge, and the twins stirring in their bed, and Ginny's lips on mine, and I missed them all as if I already gone.

"Wait," I said. What belonging could the sirens offer me? I wasn't one of them. Whatever they were offering wasn't love, or furtive kisses, or even the satisfaction of a job done well. If I went with them, what would Mrs. Wainwright think of me? The choice overwhelmed me. I wasn't sure if it even was a choice. Maybe I was already another sailor lost to the sirens.

I didn't know what else to do, so I sang. The sirens closed their mouths and listened as I sang their own song back at them, and then shifted the tune to one of my own, keeping some of their words. Their two voices? I lived that story every day. They sang that no life could be hid from their dreaming, so I offered mine as proof. I thought maybe they had never heard a creature such as I was: alone in my knowing, alone of my kind. I sang another song, turning their mirror back on them.

"But we can tell you everything that will ever happen in the world. All the secrets." Their voices had lost some luster.

"I already know what happens. Everybody lives until they die, and most have hard lives, and some have easy ones, and some give up their children and some take them in, and some get a home even with an odd thing about them."

"Come with us. No lonely seafarer rows past our green mirror."

"I'm not lonely. They're the lonely ones, all these sailors that long for the sea when they're home and their homes when they're at sea. They're stuck in between. I'm in between, but I'm not stuck. I just am."

Their wings beat slower now, and we descended a bit. The hesitation gave me confidence. "I think I won. I heard your song, but mine was better. I'm not going with you. I'm staying here, and you're leaving, because I won."

The sirens dropped me over open water. I might have taken that for a kindness, but it didn't feel intentional. By the time I hauled myself onto the boat, they were specks on the horizon. Someone else's problem. I lay naked for a moment on the deck, basking in the bright sunlight. Then I clothed myself and unlocked the cabin. The horses would be waiting for me, swiveling their ears to catch my song over top of the breeze that would bring our small boat back to shore.

— *Wind Will Rove* —

There's a story about my grandmother Windy, one I never asked her to confirm or deny, in which she took her fiddle on a spacewalk. There are a lot of stories about her. Fewer of my parents' generation, fewer still of my own, though we're in our fifties now; old enough that if there were stories to tell they would probably have been told.

My grandmother was an engineer, part of our original crew. According to the tale, she stepped outside to do a visual inspection of an external panel that was giving anomalous readings. Along with her tools, she clipped her fiddle and bow to her suit's belt. When she completed her task, she paused for a moment, tethered to our ship the size of a city, put her fiddle to the place where her helmet met her suit, and played "Wind Will Rove" into the void. Not to be heard, of course; just to feel the song in her fingers.

There are a number of things wrong with this story, starting with the fact that we don't do spacewalks, for reasons that involve laws of physics I learned in school and don't remember anymore. Our shields are too thick, our velocity is too great, something like that. The Blackout didn't touch ship records; crew transcripts and recordings still exist, and I've listened to all the ones that might pertain to this legend. She laughs her deep laugh, she teases a tired colleague about his date the night before, she even hums "Wind Will Rove" to herself as she works—but there are no gaps, no silences unexplained.

Even if it were possible, her gloves would have been too thick to find a fingering. I doubt my grandmother would've risked losing her instrument, out here where any replacement would be synthetic. I doubt, too, that she'd have exposed it to the cold of space. Fiddles are comfortable at the same temperatures people are comfortable; they crack and warp when they aren't happy. Her fiddle, my fiddle now.

My final evidence: "Wind Will Rove" is traditionally played in DDAD tuning, with the first and fourth strings dropped down. As much as she loved that song, she didn't play it often, since re-tuning can make strings wear out faster. If she had risked her fiddle, if she had managed to press her fingers to its fingerboard, to lift her bow, to play, she wouldn't have played a DDAD tune. This is as incontrovertible as the temperature of the void.

And yet the story is passed on among the ship's fiddlers (and I pass it on again as I write this narrative for you, Teyla, or whoever else discovers it). And yet her nickname, Windy, which appears in transcripts starting in the fifth year on board. Before that, people called her Beth, or Green.

She loved the song, I know that much. She sang it to me as a lullaby. At twelve, I taught it to myself in traditional GDAE tuning. I took pride in the adaptation, pride in the hours I spent getting it right. I played it for her on her birthday.

She pulled me to her, kissed my head. She always smelled like the lilacs in the greenhouse. She said, "Rosie, I'm so tickled that you'd do that for me, and you played it note perfectly, which is a gift to me in itself. But 'Wind Will Rove' is a DDAD tune and it ought to be played that way. You play it in another tuning, it's a different wind that blows."

I'd never contemplated how there might be a difference between winds. I'd never felt one myself, unless you counted air pushed through vents, or the fan on a treadmill. After the birthday party, I looked up "wind" and read about breezes and gales and siroccos, about haboobs and zephyrs. Great words, words to turn over in my mouth, words that spoke to nothing in my experience.

The next time I heard the song in its proper tuning, I closed my eyes and listened for the wind.

"*Windy Grove*"

Traditional. Believed to have travelled from Scotland to Cape Breton in the nineteenth century. Lost.

"*Wind Will Rove*"

Instrumental in D (alternate tuning DDAD)

Harriet Barrie, Music Historian:

"*The fiddler Olivia Vandiver and her father, Charley Vandiver, came up with this tune in the wee hours of a session in 1974. Charley was trying to remember a traditional tune he had heard as a boy in Nova Scotia, believed to be 'Windy Grove.' No recordings of the original 'Windy Grove' were ever catalogued, on ship or on Earth.*

"*'Wind Will Rove' is treated as traditional in most circles, even though it's relatively recent, because it is the lost tune's closest known relative.*"

The Four Deck Rec has the best acoustics of any room on the ship. There's a nearly identical space on every deck, but the others don't sound as good. The Recs were designed for gatherings, but no acoustic engineer was ever consulted, and there's nobody on board with that specialty now. The fact that one room might sound good and one less so wasn't important in the grander scheme. It should have been.

In the practical, the day to day, it matters. It matters to us. Choirs perform there, and bands. It serves on various days and nights as home to a Unitarian church, a Capoeira hoda, a Reconstructionist synagogue, a mosque, a Quaker meetinghouse, a half-dozen different

African dance groups, and a Shakespearean theater, everyone clinging on to whatever they hope to save. The room is scheduled for weeks and months and years to come, though weeks and months and years are all arbitrary designations this far from Earth.

On Thursday nights, Four Deck Rec hosts the OldTime, thanks to my grandmother's early pressure on the Recreation Committee. There are only a few of us on board who know what OldTime refers to, since everything is old time, strictly speaking. Everyone else has accepted a new meaning, since they have never known any other. An OldTime is a Thursday night is a hall with good acoustics is a gathering of fiddlers and guitarists and mandolinists and banjo players. It has a verb form now. "Are you OldTiming this week?" If you are a person who would ask that question, or a person expected to respond, the answer is yes. You wouldn't miss it.

On this particular Thursday night, while I wouldn't miss it, my tenth graders had me running late. We'd been discussing the twentieth and twenty-first century space races and the conversation had veered into dangerous territory. I'd spent half an hour trying to explain to them why Earth history still mattered. This had happened at least once a cycle with every class I'd ever taught, but these particular students were as fired up as any I remembered.

"I'm never going to go there, right, Ms. Clay?" Nelson Odell had asked. This class had only been with me for two weeks, but I'd known Nelson his entire life. His great-grandmother, my friend Harriet, had dragged him to the OldTime until he was old enough to refuse. He'd played mandolin, his stubby fingers well fit to the tiny neck, face set in a permanently resentful expression.

"No," I said. "This is a one-way trip. You know that."

"And really I'm just going to grow up and die on this ship, right? And all of us? You too? Die, not grow up. You're already old."

I had heard this from enough students. I didn't even wince anymore. "Yes to all of the above, though it's a reductive line of thinking and that last bit was rude."

"Then what does it matter that back on Earth a bunch of people wanted what another group had? Wouldn't it be better not to teach us how people did those things and get bad ideas in our heads?"

Emily Redhorse, beside Nelson, said, "They make us learn it all so we can understand why we got on the ship." She was the only current OldTime player in this class, a promising fiddler. OldTime players usually understood the value of history from a young age.

Nelson waved her off. "'We' didn't get on the ship. Our grandparents and great-grandparents did. And here we are learning things that were old to them."

"Because, stupid." That was Trina Nguyen.

I interrupted. "Debate is fine, Trina. Name-calling is not."

"Because, Nelson." She tried again. "There aren't new things in history. That's why it's called history."

Nelson folded his arms and stared straight at me. "Then don't teach it at all. If it mattered so much, why did they leave it behind? Give us another hour to learn more genetics or ship maintenance or farming. Things we can actually use."

"First of all, history isn't static. People discovered artifacts and primary documents all the time that changed their views on who we were. It's true that the moment we left Earth we gave up the chance to learn anything new about it from newly discovered primary sources, but we can still find fresh perspectives on the old information." I tried to regain control, hoping that none of them countered with the Blackout. Students of this generation rarely did; to them it was just an incident in Shipboard History, not the living specter it had been when I was their age.

I continued. "Secondly, Emily is right. It's important to know why and how we got here. The conventional wisdom remains that those who don't know history are doomed to repeat it."

"How are we supposed to repeat it?" Nelson waved at the pictures on the walls. "We don't have countries or oil or water. Or guns or swords or bombs. If teachers hadn't told us about them we wouldn't even know they existed. We'd be better off not knowing that my ancestors tried to kill Emily's ancestors, wouldn't we? Somebody even tried to erase all of that entirely, and you made sure it was still included in the new version of history."

"Not me, Nelson. That was before my time." I knew I shouldn't let them get a rise out of me, but I was tired and hungry, not the ideal way to start a seven-hour music marathon. "Enough. I get what you're saying, but not learning this is not an option. Send me a thousand words by Tuesday on an example of history repeating itself."

Before anyone protested, I added, "You were going to have an essay to write either way. All I've done is changed the topic. It doesn't sound like you wanted to write about space races."

They all grumbled as they plugged themselves back into their games and music and shuffled out the door. I watched them go, wishing I'd handled the moment differently, but not yet sure how. It fascinated me that Nelson was the one fomenting this small rebellion, when his great-grandmother ran the OldTime Memory Project. My grandmother was the reason I obsessed over history, why I'd chosen teaching; Harriet didn't seem to have had the same effect on Nelson.

As Nelson passed my desk, he muttered, "Maybe somebody needs to erase it all again."

"Stop," I told him.

He turned back to face me. I still had several inches on him, but he held himself as if he were taller. The rest of the students flowed out around him. Trina rammed her wheelchair into Nelson's leg as she passed, in a move that looked one hundred percent deliberate. She didn't even pretend to apologize.

"I don't mind argument in my classroom, but don't ever let anyone hear you advocating another Blackout."

He didn't look impressed. "I'm not advocating. I just think teaching us Earth history—especially broken history—is a waste of everybody's time."

"Maybe someday you'll get on the Education Committee and you can argue for that change. But I heard you say 'erase it all again.' That isn't the same thing. Would you say that in front of Harriet?"

"Maybe I was just exaggerating. It's not even possible to erase everything anymore. And there's plenty of stuff I like that I wouldn't want to see erased." He shrugged. "I didn't mean it. Can I go now?"

He left without waiting for me to dismiss him.

I looked at the walls I'd carefully curated for this class. Tenth grade had always been the year we taught our journey's political and scientific antecedents. It was one of the easier courses for the Education Committee to re-create accurately after the Blackout, since some of it had still been in living memory at the time, and one of the easier classrooms to decorate for the same reason. I'd enlarged images of our ship's construction from my grandmother's personal collection, alongside reproductions of news headlines. Around the top of the room, a static quote from United Nations Secretary-General Confidence Swaray: "We have two missions now: to better the Earth and to better ourselves."

Normally I'd wipe my classroom walls to neutral for the continuing education group that met there in the evening, but this time I left the wall displays on when I turned off the lights to leave. Maybe we'd all failed these children already if they thought the past was irrelevant.

The digital art on the street outside my classroom had changed during the day. I traced my fingertips along the wall to get the info: a reimagining of a memory of a photo of an Abdoulaye Konaté mural, sponsored by the Malian Memory Project. According to the description, the original had been a European transit station mosaic, though they no longer knew which city or country had commissioned it. Fish swam across a faux-tiled sea. Three odd blue figures stood tall at the far end, bird-like humanoids. The colors were soothing to me, but the figures less so. How like the original was it? No way to tell. Another reinvention to keep some version of our past present in our lives.

I headed back to my quarters for my instrument and a quick dinner. There was always food at the OldTime, but I knew from experience that if I picked up my fiddle I wouldn't stop playing until my fingers begged. My fingers and my stomach often had different agendas. I needed a few minutes to cool down after that class, too. Nelson had riled me with his talk of broken history. To me that had always made preserving it even more important, but I understood the point he was trying to make.

By the time I got to the Four Deck Rec, someone had already taken my usual seat. I tuned in the corner where everyone had stashed their cases, then looked around to get the lay of the room. The best fiddlers had nabbed the middle seats, with spokes of mandolin and banjo and guitar and less confident fiddlers radiating out. The only proficient OldTime bass player, Doug Kelly, stood near the center, with the ship's only upright bass. A couple of his students sat behind him, ready to swap out for a tune or two if he wanted a break.

The remaining empty seats were all next to banjos. I spotted a chair beside Dana Torres from the ship's Advisory Council. She was a good administrator and an adequate banjo player—she kept time, anyway. I didn't think she'd show up if she were less than adequate; nobody wants to see leadership failing at anything.

She had taken a place two rings removed from my usual seat in the second fiddle tier. Not the innermost circle, where my grand-mother had sat, with the players who call the tunes and call the stops; at fifty-five years old, I still hadn't earned a spot there yet. Still, I sat just outside them and kept up with them, and it'd been a long time since I'd caught a frown from the leaders.

A tune started as I made my way to the empty chair. "Honey-suckle." A thought crossed my mind that Harriet had started "Hon-eysuckle" without me, one of my Memory Project tunes, to punish me for being late. A second thought crossed my mind, mostly because of the conversation with my students, that probably only three other people in the room knew or cared what honeysuckle was: Tom

Mvovo, who maintained the seed bank; Liat Shuster, who worked in the greenhouse—in all our nights together, I never thought to ask her about the honeysuckle plant; Harriet Odell, music historian, last OldTime player of the generation that had left Earth. To everyone else, it was simply the song's name. A name that meant this song, nothing more.

When I started thinking that way, all the songs took on a strange flat quality in my head. So many talked about meadows and flowers and roads and birds. The love songs maintained relevance, but the rest might as well have been written in other languages as far as most people were concerned. Or about nothing at all. Mostly, we let the fiddles do the singing.

No matter how many times we play a song, it's never the same song twice. The melody stays the same, the key, the rhythm. The notes' pattern, their cadence. Still, there are differences. The exact number of fiddles changes. Various players' positions within the group, each with their own fiddle's timbral variances. The locations of the bass, the mandolins, the guitars, the banjos, all in relation to each individual player's ears. To a listener by the snack table, or to someone seeking out a recording after the fact, the nuances change. In the minutes the song exists, it is fully its own. That's how it feels to me, anyway.

Harriet stomped her foot to indicate we'd reached the last go-round for "Honeysuckle," and we all came to an end together except one of the outer guitarists, who hadn't seen the signal and kept chugging on the last chord. He shrugged off the glares.

"Oklahoma Rooster," she shouted, to murmurs of approval. She started the tune, and the other fiddles picked up the melody. I put my bow to the strings and closed my eyes. I pictured a real farm, the way they looked in pictures, and let the song tell me how it felt to be in the place called Oklahoma. A sky as big as space, the color of chlorinated water. The sun a distant disk, bright and cold. A wood-paneled square building, with a round building beside it. A perfect carpet of green grass. Horses, large and sturdy, bleating at each other across the fields. All sung in the voice of a rooster, a bird that served as a wake-up alarm for the entire farm. Birds were the things with feathers, as the old saying went.

It was easy to let my mind wander into meadows and fields during songs I had played once a week nearly my whole life. Nelson must have gotten under my skin more than I thought: I found myself adding the weeks and months and years up. Fifty times a year, fifty years, more or less. Then the same songs again alone for practice, or in smaller groups on other nights.

The OldTime broke up at 0300, as it usually did. I rolled my head from side to side, cracking my neck. The music always carried me through the night, but the second it stopped, I started noticing the cramp of my fingers, the unevenness of my shoulders.

"What does 'Oklahoma Rooster' mean to you?" I asked Dana Torres as she shook out her knees.

"Sorry?"

"What do you think of when you play 'Oklahoma Rooster?'"

Torres laughed. "I think C-C-G-C-C-C-G-C. Anything else and I fall behind the beat. Why, what do you think of?"

A bird, a farm, a meadow. "I don't know. Sorry. Weird question."

We packed our instruments and stepped into the street, dimmed to simulate night.

Back at my quarters, I knew I should sleep, but instead I sat at the table and called up the history database. "Wind Will Rove."

Options appeared: "Play," cross-referenced to the song database, with choices from several OldTime recordings we'd made over the years. "Sheet music," painstakingly generated by my grandmother and her friends, tabbed for all of the appropriate instruments. "History." I tapped the last icon and left it to play as I heated up water for soporific tea. I'd watched it hundreds of times.

A video would play on the table. A stern-looking white woman in her thirties, black hair pulled back in a tight ponytail, bangs flat-cut across her forehead. She'd been so young then, the stress of the situation making her look older than her years.

"Harriet Barrie, Music Historian," the first subtitle would say, then Harriet would appear and begin, "*The fiddler Olivia Vandiver and her father, Charley Vandiver, came up with this tune in the wee hours of a session in 1974 . . .*" Except when I returned, the table had gone blank. I went back to the main menu, but this time no options came up when I selected "Wind Will Rove." I tried again, and this time the song didn't exist.

I stared at the place where it should have been, between "Winder's Slide" and "Wolf Creek." Panic stirred deep in my gut, a panic handed down to me. Maybe I was tired and imagining things. It had been there a moment ago. It had always been there, my whole life. The new databases had backups of backups of backups, even if the recordings we called originals merely re-created what had been lost long ago. Glitches happened. It would be fixed in the morning.

Just in case, I dashed off a quick message to Tech. I drank my tea and went to bed, but I didn't sleep well.

"Wind Will Rove"

Historical re-enactment. Windy Green as Olivia Vandiver, Fiddler:

"We were in our ninth hour playing. It had been a really energetic session, and we were all starting to fade. Chatting more between songs so we could rest our fingers. I can't remember how the subject came up, but my father brought up a tune called 'Windy Grove.' Nobody else had ever heard of it, and he called us all ignorant Americans.

"He launched into an A part that sounded something like 'Spirits of the Morning,' but with a clever little lift where 'Spirits' descends. My father did things with a fiddle the rest of us could never match, but we all followed as best we were able. The B part wasn't anything like 'Spirits,' and we all caught that pretty fast, but the next time the A part came round it was different again, so we all shut up and let him play. The third time through sounded pretty much like the second, so we figured he

had remembered the tune, and we jumped in again. It went the same the fourth and fifth times through.

"It wasn't until we got up the next day that he admitted he had never quite remembered the tune he was trying to remember, which meant the thing we had played the night before was of his own creation. We cleaned it up, called it 'Wind Will Rove,' and recorded it for the third Vandiver Family LP."

My grandmother was an astronaut. We are not astronauts. It's a term that's not useful in our vocabulary. Do the people back on Earth still use that word? Do they mention us at all? Are they still there?

When our families left they were called Journeyers. Ten thousand Journeyers off on the Incredible Journey, with the help of a genetic bank, a seed bank, an advisory council. A ship thirty years in the making, held together by a crew of trained professionals: astronauts and engineers and biologists and doctors and the like. Depending on which news outlet you followed, the Journeyers were a cult or a social experiment or pioneers. Those aren't terms we use for ourselves, since we have no need to call ourselves anything in reference to any other group. When we do differentiate, it's to refer to the Before. I don't know if that makes us the During or the After.

My mother's parents met in Texas, in the Before, while she was still in training. My grandfather liked being married to an astronaut when the trips were finite, but he refused to sign up for the Journey. He stayed behind on Earth with two other children, my aunt and uncle, both older than my mother. I imagine those family members sometimes. All those people I have no stories for. Generations of them.

It's theoretically possible that scientists on Earth have built faster ships by now. It's theoretically possible they've developed faster travel while we've been busy travelling. It's theoretically possible they've built a better ship, that they've peopled it and sent it sailing past us, that they've figured out how to freeze and revive people, that those who stepped into the ship will be the ones who step out. That we will be greeted when we reach our destination by our own ancestors. I won't be there, but my great-great-great-great-great-great-grand-children might be. I wonder what stories they'll tell each other.

This story is verifiable history. It begins, "There once was a man named Morne Brooks." It's used to scare children into doing their homework and paying attention in class. Nobody wants to be a cautionary tale.

There once was a man named Morne Brooks. In the fourth year on board, while performing a computer upgrade, he accidentally created a backdoor to the ship databases. Six years after that, an angry young programmer named Trevor Dube released a virus that ate several databases in their entirety. Destroyed the backups too. He didn't touch the "important" systems—navigation, life support, medical, seed and gene banks—but he caused catastrophic damage to the libraries. Music gone. Literature, film, games, art, history: gone, gone, gone, gone. Virtual reality simulation banks, gone, along with the games and the trainings and the immersive re-creations of places on Earth. He killed external communications too. We were alone, years earlier than we expected to be. Severed.

For some reason, it's Brooks' name attached to the disaster. Dube was locked up, but Brooks still walked around out in the community for people to point at and shame. Our slang term "brooked" came from his name. He spent years afterward listening to people say they had brooked exams and brooked relationships. I suppose it didn't help that he had such a good name to lend. Old English, Dutch, German. A hard word for a lively stream of water. We have no use for it as a noun now; no brooks here. His shipmates still remembered brooks, though they'd never see one again. There was a verb form already, unrelated, but it had fallen from use. His contemporaries verbed him afresh.

It didn't matter that for sixteen years afterward he worked on the team that shored up protection against future damage, or that he eventually committed suicide. Nobody wanted to talk about Dube or his motivations; all people ever mentioned was the moment the screens went dark, and Brooks' part in the whole disaster when they traced it backward.

In fairness, I can't imagine their panic. They were still the original Journeyers, the original crew, the original Advisory Council, save one or two changes. They were the ones who had made sure we had comprehensive databases, so we wouldn't lose our history, and so they wouldn't be without their favorite entertainments. The movies and serials and songs reminded them of homes they had left behind.

The media databases meant more to that first generation than I could possibly imagine. They came from all over the Earth, from disparate cultures; for some from smaller sub-groups, the databases were all that connected them with their people. It's no wonder they reacted the way they did.

I do sometimes wonder what would be different now if things hadn't gone wrong so early in the journey. Would we have naturally moved beyond the art we carried, instead of clinging to it as we do now? All we can do is live it out, but I do wonder.

I don't teach on Fridays. I can't bounce back from seven hours of fiddling, or from the near-all-nighter, the way I did at twenty or thirty or forty. Usually I sleep through Friday mornings. This time, I woke at ten, suddenly and completely, with the feeling something was missing. I glanced at the corner by the door to make sure I hadn't left my fiddle at the Rec.

I showered, then logged on to the school server to see if any students had turned in early assignments—they hadn't—then checked the notice system for anything that might affect my plans for the day. It highlighted a couple of streets I could easily avoid, and warned that the New Shakespeare and Chinese Cultural DBs were down for maintenance. Those alerts reminded me about the database crash the night before. My stomach lurched again as I called up "Wind Will Rove," but it was there when I looked for it, right where it belonged.

The door chimed. Fridays, I had lunch with Harriet. We called it lunch, even though we'd both be eating our first meal of the day. She didn't get up early after the OldTime either. Usually I cut it pretty close, rolling out of bed and putting on clothes, knowing she'd done the same. I glanced around the room to make sure it was presentable. I'd piled some dirty clothes on the bed, but they were pretty well hidden behind the privacy screen. Good enough.

"You broke the deal, Rosie," she said, eyeing my hair as I opened my door. "You showered."

"I couldn't sleep."

She shrugged and slid into the chair I'd just been sitting in. She had a skullcap pulled over her own hair, dyed jet black. Harriet had thirty years on me, though she still looked wiry and spry. It had taken me decades to stop considering her my grandmother's friend and realize she'd become mine as well. Now we occupied a place somewhere between mentorship and friendship. History teacher and music historian. Fiddle player and master fiddler.

I handed her a mug of mint tea and a bowl of congee, and a spoon. My dishware had been my grandmother's, from Earth. Harriet always smiled when I handed her the chipped "Cape Breton Fiddlers Association" mug.

She held the cup up to her face for a moment, breathing in the minty steam. "Now tell me why you walked in late last night. I missed you in the second row. Kem Porter took your usual seat, and I had to listen to his sloppy bow technique all night."

"Kem's not so bad. He knows the tunes."

"He knows the tunes, but he's not ready for the second row. He was brooking rhythms all over the place. You should have called him out on it."

"I wouldn't!"

She cradled the mug in her hands and breathed in again. Liat and I hadn't been a couple for years, but she still brought me real mint from the greenhouse, and I knew Harriet appreciated it. "I know. You're too nice. There's no shame in letting someone know his place. Next time I'll do it."

She would, too. She had taken over the OldTime enforcer job from my grandmother, and lived up to her example. They'd both sent me back to the outer circles more than once before I graduated inward.

"I'll tell you when you're ready, Rosie," my grandmother said. "You'll get there."

"You know Windy would have done it," Harriet said, echoing my thoughts.

The nickname jogged my memory again. "'Wind Will Rove!'" I said. "Something was wrong with the database last night. The song was missing."

She pushed the cups to the side and tapped the table awake.

"Down for maintenance," she read out loud, frowning. She looked up. "I don't like that. I'll go down to Tech myself and ask."

She stood and left without saying goodbye.

Harriet had a way of saying things so definitively you couldn't help agreeing. If she said you didn't belong in the second row, you weren't ready yet. If she said not to worry over the song issue, I would have been willing to believe her, even though it made me uneasy. Hopefully it was nothing, but her reaction was appropriate for anyone who'd lived through the Blackout. I hadn't even gotten around to answering her first question, but I wasn't really sure what I would have told her about Nelson in any case.

I went to pick up my grandchildren from daycare, as I always did on Friday afternoons, Natalie's long day at the hospital. If anything could keep me out of my head, it was the mind-wiping exhaustion of chasing toddlers.

"Goats?" asked Teyla. She had just turned two, her brother, Jonah, four.

"Goats okay with you, too, buddy?" I asked Jonah.

He shrugged stoically. He didn't really care for animals. Preferred games, but we'd played games the week before.

"Goats it is."

The farm spread across the bottom deck, near the waste processing plant. We took two tubes to get there, Jonah turning on all the screens we passed, Teyla playing with my hair.

I always enjoyed stepping from the tube and into the farm's relatively open spaces, as big as eight rec rooms combined. The air out here, pungent and rich, worked off a different circulator than on the living decks. It moved with slightly more force than on the rest of the ship, though still not a wind. Not even a breeze. The artificial sun wasn't any different than on the other decks, but it felt more intense. The textures felt different too, softer, plants and fur, fewer touch screens. If I squinted I could imagine a real farm, ahead or behind us, on a real planet. Everything on every other deck had been designed to keep us healthy and sane; I always found it interesting to spend time in a place dedicated to keeping another animal alive.

The goats had been a contentious issue for the planners in my grandmother's generation. Their detractors called them a waste of food and space and resources. Windy was among those who argued for them. They could supplement the synthetic milk and meat supplies. They'd provide veterinary training and animal husbandry skills that would be needed planetside someday, not to mention a living failsafe in case something happened to the gene banks. It would be good to have them aboard for psychological reasons as well, when people were leaving behind house pets like cats and dogs.

She won the debate, as she so often did, and they added a small population of female African Pygmy goats to the calculations. Even then there were dissenters. The arguments continued until the

Blackout, then died abruptly along with the idea the journey might go as planned.

She told me all of that three weeks after my mother left, when I was still taking it personally.

"Have you ever tried to catch a goat?" she asked.

I hadn't. I'd seen them, of course, but visitors were only supposed to pet them. She got permission, and I spent twenty minutes trying to catch an animal that had zero interest in being caught. It was the first thing that made me laugh again. I always thought of that day when I brought my grandchildren to pet the goats, though I hoped I never had any reason to use the same technique on them.

I had wrapped up some scraps for Jonah and Teyla to feed the nippy little things. Once they'd finished the food, the goats started on Teyla's jersey, to her mixed delight and horror. I kept an eye on goat teeth and toddler fingers to make sure everybody left with the proper number.

"Ms. Clay," somebody said, and I glanced up to see who had called me, then back at the babies and the fingers and the goats. They looked vaguely familiar, but everyone did after a while. If I had taught them, I still might not recognize a face with twenty more years on it, if they didn't spend time on the same decks I did.

"Ms. Clay, I'm Nelson's parent. Other parent. Lee. I think you know Ash." Ash was Harriet's grandkid. They'd refused to play music at all, to Harriet's endless frustration.

Lee didn't look anything like Nelson, but then I recalled Harriet saying they had gone full gene-bank. The incentives to include gene variance in family planning were too good for many people to pass up.

"Nice to meet you," I said.

"I'm sorry if he's been giving you any trouble," Lee said. "He's going through some kind of phase."

"Phase?" Sometimes feigning ignorance got more interesting answers than agreeing.

"He's decided school is teaching the wrong things. Says there's no point in learning anything that doesn't directly apply to what will be needed planetside. That it puts old ideas into people's heads, when they should be learning new things. I have no idea where he came up with it."

I nodded. "Do you work down here?"

Lee gestured down at manure-stained coveralls. "He likes it here, though. Farming fits in his worldview."

"But history doesn't?"

"History, classic literature, anything you can't directly apply. I know he's probably causing trouble, but he's a good kid. He'll settle down once he figures out a place for himself in all this."

Teyla was offering a mystery fistful of something to a tiny black goat. Jonah looked like he was trying to figure out if he could ride one; I put a hand on his shoulder to hold him back.

"Tell me about the Blackout," I say at the start of the video I made while still in school. Eighteen-year-old me, already a historian. My voice is much younger. I'm not on screen, but I can picture myself at eighteen. Tall, gawky, darker than my mother, lighter than my father.

"I don't think there was anybody who didn't panic," my grandmother begins. Her purple hair is pulled back in a messy bun, and she is sitting in her own quarters—mine now—with her Cape Breton photos on the walls.

"Once we understood that the glitch hadn't affected navigation or the systems we rely on to breathe and eat, once it became clear the culprit was a known virus and the damage was irreparable, well, we just had to deal with it."

"The 'culprit' was a person, not a virus, right?"

"A virus who released a virus." Her face twisted at the thought.

I moved back to safer ground. "Did everyone just 'deal with it'? That isn't what I've heard."

"There are a lot of people to include in 'everyone.' The younger children handled it fine. They bounced and skated and ran around the rec rooms. The older ones—the ones who relied on external entertainments—had more trouble, and got in more trouble, I guess." She gave a sly smile. "But ask your father how he lost his pinkie finger if you've never asked."

"That was when he did it?"

"You bet. Eighteen years old and some daredevil notion to hitch a ride on the top of a lift. Lucky he survived."

"He told me a goat bit it off!"

She snorted. "I'm guessing he told you that back when you said you wanted to be a goat farmer when you grew up?"

No answer from younger-me.

She shrugged. "Or maybe he didn't want to give you any foolish ideas about lift-cowboys."

"He's not a daredevil, though."

"Not anymore. Not after that. Not after you came along the next year. Anyway, you asked who 'just dealt with it,' and you're right. The kids coped because they had nothing to compare it to, but obviously the main thing you want to know about is the adults. The Memory Projects."

"Yes. That's the assignment."

"Right. So. Here you had all these people: born on Earth, raised on Earth. They applied to be Journeyers because they had some romantic notion of setting out for a better place. And those first years, you can't even imagine what it was like, the combination of excitement and terror. Any time anything went wrong: a replicator brooked, a fan lost power, anything at all, someone started shouting we had set our families up for Certain Death." She says "certain death" dramatically, wiggling her fingers at me. "Then Crew or Logistics or Tech showed them their problem had an easy fix, and they'd calm down. It didn't matter how many times we told them we had things under control. Time was the only reassurance.

"By ten years in, we had finally gotten the general populace to relax. Everyone had their part to do, and everyone was finally doing it quietly. We weren't going to die if a hot-water line went cold one day. There were things to worry over, of course, but they were all too big to be worth contemplating. Same as now, you understand? And we had this database, this marvelous database of everything good humans had ever created, music and literature and art from all around the world, in a hundred languages.

"And then Trevor Dube had to go and ruin everything. I know you know that part, so I won't bother repeating it. Morne Brooks did what he did, and that Dube fellow did what he did, and all of a sudden all of these Journeyers, with their dream of their children's children's children's et cetera someday setting foot on a new planet, they all have to deal with their actual children. They have to contemplate the idea the generations after them will never get to see or hear the things they thought were important. That all they have left is the bare walls. They wait—we wait—and wait for the DB to be restored. And they realize: hey, I can't rely on this database to be here to teach those great-great-great-grandchildren."

She leans forward. "So everyone doubles down on the things that matter most to them. That's when some folks who didn't have it got religion again. The few physical books on board became sacred primary texts, including the ones that had been sacred texts to begin with. Every small bit of personal media got cloned for the greater good, from photos to porn—don't giggle—but it wasn't much, not compared to what we'd lost.

"Cultural organizations that had been atrophying suddenly found themselves with more members than they'd had since the journey started. Actors staged any show they knew well enough, made new recordings. People tried to rewrite their favorite books and plays from memory, paint their favorite paintings. Everyone had a different piece, some closer to accurate than others. That's when we started getting together to play weekly instead of monthly."

"I thought it was always weekly, Gra."

"Nope. We didn't have other entertainments to distract us, and we were worried about the stories behind the songs getting lost. The organized Memory Projects started with us. It seemed like the best way to make sure what we wanted handed down would be handed down. The others saw that we'd found a good way to approach the problem and to keep people busy, so other Memory Projects sprung up too. We went through our whole repertoire and picked out the forty songs we most wanted saved. Each of us committed to memorizing as many as we could, but with responsibility for a few in particular. We knew the songs themselves already, but now people pooled what they knew about them, and we memorized their histories, too. Where they came from, what they meant. And later, we were responsible for re-recording those histories, and teaching them to somebody younger, so each song got passed down to another generation. That's you, incidentally."

"I know."

"Just checking. You're asking me some pretty obvious stuff."

"It's for a project. I need to ask."

"Fine, then. Anyhow, we re-recorded all our songs and histories as quick as possible, then memorized them in case somebody tried to kill the DBs again. And other people memorized the things important to them. History of their people—the stuff that didn't make it into history books—folk dances, formulae. Actors built plays back from scratch, though some parts weren't exactly as they'd been. And those poor jazz musicians."

"Those poor jazz musicians? I thought jazz was about improv."

"It's full of improv, but certain performances stood out as benchmarks for their whole mode. I'm glad we play a music that doesn't set much stock in solo virtuosity. We recorded our fiddle tunes all over again, and the songs are still the songs, but nobody on board could play "So What" like Miles Davis or anything like John Coltrane. Their compositions live on, but not their performances, if that makes sense. Would have devastated your grandfather, if he'd been on board. Anyway, what was I saying? The human-backup idea had legs, even if it worked better for some things than others. It was a worst-case scenario."

"Which two songs did you memorize history for?"

"Unofficially, all of them. Officially, same as you. 'Honeysuckle' and 'Wind Will Rove.' You know that."

"I know, Gra. For the assignment."

"Windy Grove"

Historical Re-enactment: Marius Smit as Howie McCabe, Cape Breton Fiddlemaker:

"Vandiver wasn't wrong. There was a tune called 'Windy Grove.' My great-grandfather played it, but it was too complicated for most fiddlers. I can only remember a little of the tune now. It had lyrics, too, in Gaelic and English. I don't think Vandiver ever mentioned those. There was probably a Gaelic name too, but that's lost along with the song.

"My great-grandfather grew up going to real milling frolics, before machines did the wool-shrinking and frolics just became social events. The few songs I know in Gaelic I know because they have that milling frolic rhythm; it drives them into your brain. 'Windy Grove' wasn't one of those. As far as I know, it was always a fiddle tune, but not a common one because of its difficulty.

"All I know is the A part in English, and I'm pretty I wouldn't get the melody right now, so I'm going to sing it to the melody of 'Wind Will Rove':

> *"We went down to the windy grove*
> *Never did know where the wind did go*
> *Never too sure when the wind comes back*
> *If it's the same wind that we knew last."*

Nelson's essay arrived promptly on Monday. It began "Many examples of history repeating itself can be seen in our coursework. There are rulers who didn't learn from other ruler's mistakes."

I corrected the apostrophe and kept reading. "You know who they are because you taught us about them. Why do you need me to say them back to you? Instead I'm going to write about history repeating itself in a different way. Look around you, Ms. Clay.

"I'm on this ship because my great-grandparents decided they wanted to spend the rest of their lives on a ship. They thought they were being unselfish. They thought they were making a sacrifice so someday their children's children's children to the bazillionth or whatever would get to be pioneers on a planet that people hadn't started killing yet, and they were pretty sure wouldn't kill them, and where they're hoping there's no intelligent life. They made a decision which locked us into doing exactly what they did.

"So here we are. My parents were born on this ship. I was born here. My chromosomes come from the gene bank, from two people who died decades before I was born.

"What can we do except repeat history? What can I do that nobody here has ever done before? In two years I'll choose a specialty. I can work with goats, like my parents. I could be an engineer or a doctor or a dentist or a horticulturist, which are all focused on keeping us alive in one way or another. I can be a history teacher like you, but obviously I won't. I can be a Theoretical Farmer or a Theoretical something else, where I learn things that will never be useful here, in order to pass them on to my kids and my kid's kids, so they can pass them on and someday somebody can use them, if there's really a place we're going and we're really going to get there someday.

"But I'm never going to stand on a real mountain, and I can't be a king or a prime minister or a genocidal tyrant like you teach us about. I can't be Lord Nelson, an old white man with a giant hat, and you might think I was named after him but I was named after a goat who was named after a horse some old farmer had on Earth who was named after somebody in a book or a band or an entertainment who might have been Lord Nelson or Nelson Mandela or some other Nelson entirely who you can't teach me about because we don't remember them anymore.

"The old history can't repeat, and I'm in the next generation of people who make no impact on anything whatsoever. We aren't making history. We're in the middle of the ocean and the shore is really far away. When we climb out the journey should have changed us, but you want us to take all the baggage with us, so we're exactly the same as when we left. But we can't be, and we shouldn't be."

I turned off the screen and closed my eyes. I could fail him for not writing the assignment as I had intended it, but he clearly understood.

"Wendigo"
Traditional. Lost.
Harriet Barrie:
"Another tune we have the name of but not much else. I'm personally of the belief 'Wendigo' and 'Windy Grove' are the same song. Some Cape Bretonians took it with when they moved to the Algonquins. Taught it to some local musicians who misheard the title and conflated it with local monster lore. There's a tune called 'When I Go' that started making the rounds in Ontario not long after, though nobody ever showed an interest in it outside of Ontario and Finland."

If we were only to play songs about things we knew, we would lose a lot of our playlist. No wind. No trees. No battles, no seas, no creeks, no mountaintops. We'd sing of travellers, but not journeys. We'd sing of middles, but not beginnings or ends. We would play songs of waiting and longing. We'd play love songs.

Why not songs about stars, you might ask? Why not songs about darkness and space? The traditionalists wouldn't play them. I'm not sure who'd write them, either. People on Earth wrote about blue skies because they'd stood under gray ones. They wrote about night because there was such thing as day. Songs about prison are poignant because the character knew something else beforehand, and dreamed of other things ahead. Past and future are both abstractions now.

When my daughter Natalie was in her teens, she played fiddle in a band which would be classified in the new DB as "other/unde-fined" if they had uploaded anything. Part of their concept was that they wouldn't record their music, and they requested that nobody else record it either. A person would have to be there to experience it. I guess it made sense for her to fall into something like that after listening to me and Gra and Harriet.

I borrowed back the student fiddle she and I had both played as children. She told me she didn't want me going to hear them play.

"You'll just tell me it sounds like noise or my positions are sloppy," she said. "Or worse yet, you'll say we sound exactly like this band from 2030 and our lyrics are in the tradition of blah blah blah and I'll end up thinking we stole everything from a musician I'd never even heard before. We want to do something new."

"I'd never," I said, even though a knot had formed in my stom-ach. Avoided commenting when I heard her practicing. Bit my tongue when Harriet complained musicians shouldn't be wasting their time on new music when they ought to be working on preserving what we already had.

I did go to check them out once, when they played the Seven Deck Rec. I stood in the back, in the dark. To me it sounded like shouting down an elevator shaft, all ghosts and echoes. The songs had names like "Because I Said So" and "Terrorform"; they shouted the titles in between pieces, but the PA was distorting, and even those I might have misheard.

I counted fifteen young musicians in the band, from different factions all over the ship: children of jazz, of rock, of classical music, of zouk, of Chinese opera, of the West African drumming group. It didn't sound anything like anything I'd ever heard before. I still couldn't figure out whether they were synthesizing the traditions they'd grown up in or rejecting them entirely.

My ears didn't know what to pay attention to, so I focused on Nat. She still had decent technique from her childhood lessons, but she used it in ways I didn't know how to listen to. She played rhythm rather than lead, a pad beneath the melody, a staccato polyrhythm formed with fiddle and drum.

I almost missed when she lit into "Wind Will Rove." I'd never even have recognized it if I had been listening to the whole instead of focusing on Nat's part. Hers was a countermelody to something else entirely, the rhythm swung but the key unchanged. Harriet would have hated it, but I thought it had a quiet power hidden as it was beneath the bigger piece.

I never told Nat I'd gone to hear her that night, because I didn't want to admit I'd listened.

I've researched punk and folk and hip-hop's births, and the protest movements that went hand in hand with protest music. Music born of people trying to change the status quo. What could my daughter and her friends change? What did people want changed? The ship sails on. They played together for a year before calling it quits. She gave her fiddle away again and threw herself into studying medicine. As they'd pledged, nobody ever uploaded their music, so there's no evidence it ever existed outside this narrative.

My grandmother smuggled the upright bass on board. It's Doug Kelly's now, but it came onto the ship under my grandmother's "miscellaneous supplies" professional allowance. That's how it's listed in the original manifest: "Miscellaneous Supplies—1 Extra-Large Crate—200 cm x 70 cm x 70 cm." When I was studying the manifest for a project, trying to figure out who had brought what, I asked her why the listed weight was so much more than the instrument's weight.

"Strings," she said. "It was padded with clothes, and then the box was filled with string packets. For the bass, for the fiddles. Every cranny of every box I brought on board was filled with strings and hair and rosin. I didn't trust replicators."

The bass belonged at the time to Jonna Rich. In my grandmother's photo of the original OldTime players on the ship, Jonna's dwarfed by her instrument. It's only a 3/4 size, but it still looms over her. I never met her. My grandmother said, "You've never seen such a tiny woman with such big, quick hands."

When her arthritis got too bad to play, Jonna passed it to Marius Smit, "twice her size, but half the player she was." Then Jim Riggins, then Alison Smit, then Doug Kelly, with assorted second and third stand-ins along the way. Those were the OldTime players. The bass did double duty in some jazz ensembles, as well as the orchestra.

Personal weight and space allowances didn't present any problems for those who played most instruments. The teams handling logistics and psychological welfare sparred and negotiated and compromised and re-compromised. They made space for four communal drum kits (two each: jazz trap and rock five-piece) twenty-two assorted amplifiers for rock and jazz, bass and guitar and keyboard. We have two each of three different Chinese zithers, and one hundred and three African drums of thirty-two different types, from djembe to carimbo. There's a PA in every Rec, but only a single tuba. The music psychologist consulted by the committee didn't understand why an electric bass wasn't a reasonable compromise for the sake of space. Hence my grandmother's smuggling job.

How did a committee on Earth ever think they could guess what we'd need fifty or eighty or one hundred and eighty years into the voyage? They set us up with state of the art replicators, with our beautiful, doomed databases, with programs and simulators to teach skills we would need down the line. Still, there's no model that accurately predicts the future. They had no way of prognosticating the brooked database or the resultant changes. They'd have known, if they'd included an actual musician on the committee, that we needed an upright bass. I love how I'm still surrounded by the physical manifestations of my grandmother's influence on the ship: the upright bass, the pygmy goats. Her fiddle, my fiddle now.

I arrived in my classroom on Thursday to discover somebody had hacked my walls. Scrawled over my photoscreens: "Collective memory ≠ truth," "History is fiction," "The past is a lie." A local overlay, not an overwrite. Nothing invasive of my personal files or permanent. Easy to erase, easy to figure out who had done it. I left it up.

As my students walked in, I watched their faces. Some were completely oblivious, wrapped up in whatever they were listening to, slouching into their seats without even looking up. A few snickered or exchanged wide-eyed glances.

Nelson arrived with a smirk on his face, a challenge directed at me. He didn't even look at the walls. It took him a moment to notice I hadn't cleaned up after him; when he did notice, the smirk was replaced with confusion.

"You're wondering why I didn't wipe this off my walls before you arrived?"

The students who hadn't been paying attention looked around for the first time. "Whoa," somebody said.

"The first answer is that it's easier to report if I leave it up. Vandalism and hacking are both illegal, and I don't think it would be hard to figure out who did this, but since there's no permanent damage, I thought we might use this as a learning experience." Everyone looked at Nelson, whose ears had turned red.

I continued. "I think what somebody is trying to ask is, let's see, 'Ms. Clay, how do we know that the history we're learning is true? Why does it matter?' And I think they expect me to answer, 'Because I said so,' or something like that. But the real truth is, our history is a total mess. It's built on memories of facts, and memories are unreliable. Before, they could cross-reference memories and artifacts to a point where you could say with some reliability that certain things happened and certain things didn't. We've lost almost all of the proof."

"So what's left?" I pointed to the graffitied pictures. "I'm here to help figure out which things are worth remembering, which things are still worth calling fact or truth or whatever you want to call it. Maybe it isn't the most practical field of study, but it's still important. It'll matter to you someday when your children come to you to ask why we're on this journey. It'll matter when something goes wrong and we can look to the past and say 'How did we solve this when we had this problem before' instead of starting from scratch. It matters because of all the people who asked 'why' and 'how' and 'what if' instead of allowing themselves to be absorbed in their own problems—they thought of us, so why shouldn't we think of them?

"Today we're going to talk about the climate changes that the Earth was experiencing by the time they started building this ship, and how that played into the politics. And just so you're not waiting with bated breath through the entire class, your homework for the week is to interview somebody who still remembers Earth. Ask them why they or their parents got on board. Ask them what they remember about that time, and any follow-up questions you think make sense. For bonus points upload to the oral history DB, once you've sent your video to me."

I looked around to see if anyone had any questions, but they were all silent. I started the lesson I was actually supposed to be teaching.

I'd been given that same assignment at around their age. It was easier to find original Journeyers to interview back then, but I always turned to my grandmother. The video is buried in the Oral History DB, but I'd memorized the path to it long ago.

She's still in good health in this one, fit and strong, with her trademark purple hair. For all our closeness, I have no idea what her hair's original color was.

"Why did you leave?" I ask.

"I didn't really consider it leaving. Going someplace, not leaving something else behind."

"Isn't leaving something behind part of going someplace?"

"You think of it your way, I'll think of it mine."

"Is that what all the Journeyers said?"

My grandmother snorts. "Ask any two and we'll give you two different answers. You're asking me, so I'm telling you how I see it. We had the technology, and the most beautiful ship. We had—have—a destination that reports perfect conditions to sustain us."

"How did you feel having a child who would never get to the destination?"

"I thought 'My daughter will have a life nobody has ever had before, and she'll be part of a generation that makes new rules for what it means to be a person existing with other people.'" She shrugs. "I found that exciting. I thought she'd live in the place she lived, and she'd do things she loved and things she hated, and she'd live out her life like anybody does."

She pauses, then resumes without prompting. "There were worse lives to live, back then. This seemed like the best choice for our family. No more running away; running toward something wonderful."

"Was there anything you missed about Earth?"

"A thing, like not a person? If a person counts, your grandfather and my other kids, always and forever. There was nothing else I loved that I couldn't take with me," she says, with a far-away look in her eyes.

"Nothing?" I press.

She smiles. "Nothing anybody can keep. The sea. The wind coming off the coast. I can still feel it when I'm inside a good song."

She reaches to pick up her fiddle.

There was a question I pointedly didn't ask in that video, the natural follow-up that fit in my grandmother's pause. I didn't ask because it wasn't my teacher's business how my mother fit into that generation 'making new rules for what it means to be a person existing with other people,' as my grandmother put it. If I haven't mentioned my mother much, it's because she and I never really understood each other.

She was eight when she came aboard. Old enough to have formative memories of soil and sky and wind. Old enough to come on board with her own small-scale fiddle. Fourteen when she told my grandmother she didn't want to play music anymore.

Eighteen when the Blackout happened. Nineteen when she had me, one of a slew of Blackout Babies granted by joint action of the Advisory Council and Logistics. They would have accepted anything that kept people happy and quiet at that point, as long as the numbers bore out its sustainability.

My grandmother begged her to come back to music, to help with the OldTime portion of the Memory Project. She refused. She'd performed in a Shakespeare comedy called *Much Ado About Nothing* just before the Blackout, while she was still in school. She still knew Hero's lines by heart, and the general Dramatists and Shakespeareans had both reached out to her to join their Memory Projects; they all had their hands full rebuilding plays from scratch.

The film faction recruited her as well, with their ridiculously daunting task. My favorite video from that period shows my twenty-year-old mother playing the lead in a historical drama called *Titanic*. It's a re-creation of an old movie, and an even older footnote in history involving an enormous sea ship.

My mother: young, gorgeous, glowing. She wore gowns that shimmered when she moved. The first time she showed it to me, when I was five, all I noticed was how beautiful she looked.

When I was seven, I asked her if the ocean could kill me.

"There's no ocean here. We made it up, Rosie."

That made no sense. I saw it there on the screen, big enough to surround the ship, like liquid, tangible space, a space that could chase you down the street and surround you. She took me down to the soundstage on Eight Deck, where they were filming a movie called *Serena*. I know now they were still triaging, filming every important movie to the best of their recollection, eight years out from the Blackout, based on scripts rewritten from memory in those first desperate years. Those are the only versions I've ever known.

She showed me how a sea was not a sea, a sky was not a sky. I got to sit on a boat that was not a boat, and in doing so learn what a boat was.

"Why are you crying, Mama?" I asked her later that evening, wandering from my bunk to my parents' bed.

My father picked me up and squeezed me tight. "She's crying about something she lost."

"I'm not tired. Can we watch the movie again?"

We sat and watched my young mother as she met and fell in love with someone else, someone pretend. As they raced a rush of water that I had already been assured would never threaten me or my family. As the ship sank—it's not real, there's no sea, nothing sinks anymore—and the lifeboats disappeared and the two lovers were forced to huddle together on a floating door until their dawn rescue.

When I was sixteen, my mother joined a cult. Or maybe she started it; NewTime is as direct a rebuttal to my grandmother's mission as could exist. They advocated erasing the entertainment databases again, forever, in the service of the species.

"We're spending too much creative energy re-creating the things we carried with us," she said. I listened from my bunk as she calmly packed her clothes.

"You're a Shakespearean! You're supposed to re-create." My father never raised his voice either. That's what I remembered most about their conversation afterward: how neither ever broke calm.

"I was a Shakespearean, but more than that, I'm an actress. I want new things to act in. Productions that speak to who we are now, not who we were on Earth. Art that tells our story."

"You have a family."

"And I love you all, but I need this."

The next morning, she kissed us both goodbye as if she were going to work, then left with the NewTime for Fourteen Deck. I didn't know what Advisory Council machinations were involved in relocating the Fourteen Deck families to make room for an unplanned community, or what accommodations had to be made for people who opted out of jobs to live a pure artistic existence. There were times in human history where that was possible, but this wasn't one of them. Those are questions I asked later. At that moment, I was furious with her.

I don't know if I ever stopped being angry, really. I never went to any of the original plays that trickled out of the NewTime; I've never explored their art or their music. I never learned what we looked like through their particular lens. It wasn't new works I opposed; it was their idea they had to separate themselves from us to create them. How could anything they wrote actually reflect our experience if they weren't in the community anymore?

They never came back down to live with the rest of us. My mother and I reconciled when I had Natalie, but she wasn't the person I remembered, and I'm pretty sure she thought the same about me. She came down to play with Nat sometimes, but I never left them alone together, for fear the separatist idea might rub off on my kid.

The night I saw Natalie's short-lived band perform, the night I hid in the darkness all those years ago so she wouldn't get mad at me for coming, it wasn't until I recognized "Wind Will Rove" that I realized I'd been holding my breath. Theirs wasn't a NewTime rejection of everything that had gone before; it was a synthesis.

"Wind Will Roam"

    Historical Re-enactment: Akona Mvovo as Will E. Womack:

    "My aunt cleaned house for some folks over in West Hollywood, and they used to give her records to take home to me. I took it all in. Everything influenced me. The West Coast rappers, but also Motown and pop and rock and these great old-timey fiddle records. I wanted to play fiddle so bad when I heard this song, but where was I going to get one? Wasn't in the cards.

    "The song I sampled for 'Wind Will Roam'—this fiddle record 'Wind Will Rove'—it changed me. There's something about the way the first part lifts that moves me every time. I've heard there's a version with lyrics out there somewhere, but I liked the instrumental, so I could make up my own words over it. I wrote the first version when I was ten years old. I thought 'rove' sounded like a dog, so I called it 'Wind Will Roam,' about a dog named Wind. I was a literal kid.

    "Second version when I was fifteen, I don't really remember that one too well. I was rapping and recording online by then, so there's probably a version out there somewhere. Don't show it to me if you find it. I was trying to be badass then. I'd just as soon pretend it never existed.

    "I came back to 'Wind Will Rove' again and again. I think I was twenty-five when I recorded this one, and my son had just been born, and I wanted to give him something really special. I still liked 'Wind Will Roam' better than 'Wind Will Rove,' 'cause I could rhyme it with 'home' and 'poem' and all that.

    (sings)

        "The wind will roam
        And so will I
        I've got miles to go before I die
        But I'll come back
        I always do
        Just like the wind
        I'll come to you.

We might go weeks without no rain
And every night the sun will go away again
Some winds blow warm some winds blow low
You and me've got miles and miles to go"

"*I wanted to take something I loved and turn it into something else entirely. Transform it.*"

The next OldTime started out in G. My grandmother had never much cared for the key of G; since her death we'd played way more G sessions than we ever had when she chose the songs. "Dixie Blossoms," then "Down the River." "Squirrel Hunters." "Jaybird Died of the Whooping Cough." "The Long Way Home." "Ladies on the Steamboat."

Harriet called a break in the third hour, and said when we came back we were going to do some D tunes, starting with "Midnight on the Water." I knew the sequence she was setting up: "Midnight on the Water," then "Bonaparte's Retreat," then "Wind Will Rove." I was pretty sure she did it for me; I think she was glad to have me back in the second row and punctual.

Most stood up and stretched, or put their instruments down to go get a snack. A few fiddlers, myself included, took the opportunity to cross-tune to DDAD. These songs could all be played in standard tuning, but the low D drone added something ineffable.

When everybody had settled back into their seats, Harriet counted us into the delicate waltz time of "Midnight on the Water." Then "Bonaparte's Retreat," dark and lively. And then, as I'd hoped, "Wind Will Rove."

No matter how many times you play a song, it isn't the same song twice. I was still thinking about Nelson's graffiti, and how the past had never felt like a lie to me at all. It was a progression. "Wind Will Rove" said we are born anew every time a bow touches fiddle strings in an OldTime session on a starship in this particular way. It is not the ship nor the session nor the bow nor the fiddle that births us. Nor the hands. It's the combination of all of those things, in a particular way they haven't been combined before. We are an alteration on an old, old tune. We are body and body, wood and flesh. We are bow and fiddle and hands and memory and starship and OldTime.

"Wind Will Rove" spoke to me, and my eyes closed to feel the wind the way my grandmother did, out on a cliff above the ocean. We cycled through the A part, the B part three times, four times, five. And because I'd closed my eyes, because I was in the song and not in the room, I didn't catch Harriet's signal for the last go-round. Everyone ended together except me. Even worse, I'd deviated. Between the bars of my unexpected solo, when my own playing stood exposed against the silence, I realized I'd diverged from the tune. It was still "Wind Will Rove," or close to it, but I'd elided the third bar into the fourth, a swooping, soaring accident.

Harriet gave me a look I interpreted as a cross between exasperation and reprobation. I'd used a similar one on my students before, but it'd been a long time since I'd been on the receiving end.

"Sorry," I said, mostly sorry the sensation had gone, that I'd lost the wind.

I slipped out the door early, while everyone was still playing. I didn't want to talk to Harriet. Back home, I tried to re-create my mistake. I heard it in my head, but I never quite made it happen again, and after half an hour I put away my fiddle.

I'd rather have avoided Harriet the next morning, but cancelling our standing date would have made things worse. I woke up early again. Debated showering to give her a different reason to be annoyed with me, then decided against it when I realized she'd stack the two grievances rather than replace one with the other.

We met in her quarters this time, up three decks from my own, slightly smaller, every surface covered with archival boxes and stacks of handwritten sheet music.

"So what happened last night?" she asked without preamble.

I held up my hands in supplication. "I didn't see you call the stop. I'm sorry. And after you told me I belonged in the closer circles and everything. It won't happen again."

"But you didn't even play it right. That's one of your tunes. You've been playing that song for fifty years! People were talking afterward. Expect some teasing next week. Nothing else happened worth gossiping about, so they're likely to remember unless somebody else does something silly."

I didn't have a good response. Missing the stop had been silly, sure, but what I had done to the tune didn't feel wrong, exactly. A different wind, as my grandmother would have said.

"Any word on what went wrong in the database the other day?" I asked to change the subject.

She furrowed her brow. "None. Tech said it's an access issue, not the DB itself. It's happening to isolated pieces. You can still access them if you enter names directly instead of going through the directories or your saved preferences, but it's a pain. They can't locate the source. I have to tell you, I'm more than a little concerned. I mean, the material is obviously still there, since I can get to some of it roundabout, but it really hampers research. And it gets me thinking we may want to consider adding another redundancy layer in the Memory Project."

She went on at length on the issue, and I let her go. I preferred her talking on any subject other than me.

When she started to flag, I interrupted. "Harriet, what does 'Oklahoma Rooster' mean to you?"

"I don't have much history for that one. Came from an Oklahoma fiddler named Dick Hutchinson, but I don't know if he wrote—"

"I don't mean the history. What does it make you feel?"

"I'm not sure what you mean. It's a nice, simple fiddle tune."

"But you've actually seen a farm in real life. Does it sound like a rooster?"

She shrugged. "I've never really given it much thought. It's a nice tune. Not worthy of a spot in the Memory Project, but a nice tune. Why do you ask?"

It would sound stupid to say I thought myself on a farm when I played that song; I wouldn't tell her where "Wind Will Rove" took me either. "Just curious."

"Harriet's grandson is going to drive me crazy," I told Natalie. I had spent the afternoon with Teyla and Jonah, as I did every Friday, but this time Jonah had dragged us to the low-gravity room. They had bounced, and I had watched and laughed along with their unrestrained joy, but I had a shooting pain in my neck from the way my head had followed the arcs of their flight.

Afterward, I'd logged into my class chat to find Nelson had again stirred the others into rebellion. The whole class, except for two I'd describe as timid and one as diligent, had elected not to do the new assignment due Tuesday. They had all followed his lead with a statement "We reject history. The future is in our hands."

"At least they all turned it in early," Nat joked. "But seriously, why are you letting him bother you?"

She stooped to pick up some of the toys scattered across the floor. The kids drew on the table screen with their fingers. Jonah was making a Tyrannosaurus, all body and tail and teeth and feathers. Teyla was still too young for her art to look representational, but she always used space in interesting ways. I leaned in to watch both of them.

"You laugh," I said. "Maybe by the time they're his age now, Nelson will have taken over the entire system. Only the most future-relevant courses. Reject the past. Don't reflect on the human condition. No history, no literature, no dinosaurs."

Jonah frowned. "No dinosaurs?"

"Grandma Rosie's joking, Jonah."

Jonah accepted that. His curly head bent down over the table again.

I continued. "It was one thing when he was a one-boy revolution. What am I supposed to do now that his virus is spreading to his whole class?"

Nat considered for a moment. "I'd work on developing an antidote, then hide it in a faster, stronger virus and inject it into the class. But, um, that's my professional opinion."

"What's the antidote in your analogy? Or the faster, stronger virus?"

Nat smiled, spread her hands. "It wasn't an analogy, sorry. I only know from viruses and toddlers. Sometimes both at once. Now, are you going to play for these kids before I try to get them to sleep? They really like the one about the sleepy bumblebee."

She picked Teyla up from her chair, turned it around, and sat down with Teyla in her lap. Jonah kept drawing.

I picked up my fiddle. "What's a bumblebee, Jonah?"

He answered without looking up. "A dinosaur."

I sighed and started to play.

Natalie's answer got me thinking. I checked in with Nelson's literature teacher, who confirmed he was doing the same thing in her class as well.

How wrong was he? They learned countries and borders, abstract names, lines drawn and redrawn. The books taught in lit classes captured the human condition, but rendered it through situations utterly foreign to us. To us. To me as much as him.

I had always liked the challenge. Reading about the way things had been in the past made our middle-years condition more acceptable to me. Made beginnings more concrete. Everyone in history lived in middle-years too; no matter when they lived, there was a before and an after, even if a given group or individual might not be around for the latter. I enjoyed tracing back through the changes, seeing what crumbled and what remained.

I enjoyed. Did I pass on my enjoyment? Maybe I'd been thinking too much about why I liked to study history, and not considering why my students found it tedious. It was my job to find a way to make it relevant to them. If they weren't excited, I had failed them.

When I got home from dinner that night, when I picked up my fiddle to play "Wind Will Rove," it was the new, elided version, the one which had escaped me previously. Now I couldn't find the original phrasing again, even with fifty years' muscle memory behind it.

I went to the database to listen to how it actually went, and was relieved when the song came up without trouble. The last variation in the new DB was filed under "Wind Will Rove" but would more accurately have been listed as "Wind Will Roam," and even that one re-created somebody's memory of an interview predating our ship. If this particular song's history hadn't contained all those interviews in which the song's interpreters sang snippets, if Harriet or my grandmother or someone hadn't watched it enough times to memorize it, or hadn't thought it important, we wouldn't have any clue how it went. Those little historic re-creations weren't even the songs themselves, but they got their own piece of history, their own stories. Why did they matter? They mattered because somebody had cared about them enough to create them.

I walked into my classroom on Monday, fiddle case over my shoulder, to the nervous giggles of students who knew they had done something brazen and now waited to find out what came of it. Nelson, not giggling, met my gaze with his own, steady and defiant.

"Last week, somebody asked me a question, using the very odd delivery mechanism of my classroom walls." I touched my desk and swiped the graffitied walls blank.

"Today I'm going to tell you that you don't have a choice. You're in this class to learn our broken, damaged history, everything that's left of it. And then to pass it on, probably breaking it even further. And maybe it'll keep twisting until every bit of fact is wrung out of it, but what's left will still be some truth about who we are or who we were. The part most worth remembering."

I put my fiddle case on the desk. Took my time tuning down to DDAD, listening to the whispered undercurrent.

When I liked the tuning, I lifted my bow. "This is a song called 'Wind Will Rove.' I want you to hear what living history means to me."

I played them all. All the known variations, all the ones that weren't lost to time. I rested the fiddle and sang Howie McCabe's faulty snippet of "Windy Grove" from the re-creation of his historical interview and Will E. Womack's "Wind Will Roam." I recited the history in between: "Windy Grove" and "Wendigo" and "When I Go." Lifted the fiddle to my chin again and closed my eyes. "Wind Will Rove": three times through in its traditional form, three times through with my own alterations.

"Practice too much and you sound like you're remembering it instead of feeling it," my grandmother used to say. This was a new room to my fiddle; even the old variations felt new within it. My fingers danced light and quick.

I tried to make the song sound like something more than wind. What did any of us know of wind? Nothing but words on a screen. I willed our entire ship into the new song I created. We were the wind. We were the wind and borne by the wind, transmitted. I played a ship traveling through the vacuum. I played life on the ship, footsteps on familiar streets, people, goats, frustration, movement while standing still.

The students sat silent at the end. Only one was an OldTimer, Emily Redhorse, who had been one of the three who actually turned in their assignments; Nelson grew up hearing this music, I know. I was pretty sure the rest had no clue what they heard. One look at Nelson said he'd already formulated a response, so I didn't let him open his mouth.

I settled my fiddle back into its case and left.

There are so many stories about my grandmother. I don't imagine there'll ever be many about me. Maybe one of the kids in this class will tell a story about the day their teacher cracked up. Maybe Emily Redhorse will take a seat in the OldTime one day and light into my tune. Maybe history and story will combine to birth something larger than both, and you, Teyla, you and your brother will take the time to investigate where anecdote deviates from truth. If you wonder which of these stories are true, well, they all are in their way, even if some happened and some didn't.

I've recorded my song variation into the new database, in the "other" section to keep from offending Harriet, for now. I call it "We Will Rove." I think my grandmother would approve. I've included a history, too, starting with "Windy Grove" and "Wind Will Rove," tracing through my grandmother's apocryphal spacewalk and my mother's attempt to find meaning for herself and my daughter's unrecorded song, on the way to my own adaptation. It's all one story, at its core.

I'm working more changes into the song, making it more and more my own. I close my eyes when I play it, picturing a through-line, picturing how one day, long after I'm gone, a door will open. Children will spill from the ship and into the bright sun of a new place, and somebody will lift my old fiddle, my grandmother's fiddle, and will put a new tune to the wind.

— Our Lady of the Open Road —

The needle on the veggie oil tank read flat empty by the time we came to China Grove. A giant pink and purple fiberglass dragon loomed over the entrance, refugee from some shuttered local amusement park, no doubt; it looked more medieval than Chinese. The parking lot held a mix of Chauffeurs and manual farm trucks, but I didn't spot any other greasers, so I pulled in.

"Cutting it close, Luce?" Silva put down his book and leaned over to peer at the gauge.

"There hasn't been anything but farms for the last fifty miles. Serves me right for trying a road we haven't been down before."

"Where are we?" asked Jacky from the bed in the back of the van. I glanced in the rearview. He caught my eye and gave an enthusiastic wave. His microbraids spilled forward from whatever he'd been using to tether them, and he gathered them back into a thick ponytail.

Silva answered before I could. "Nowhere, Indiana. Go back to sleep."

"Will do." Without music or engine to drown him out, Jacky's snores filled the van again a second later. He'd been touring with us for a year now, so we'd gotten used to the snores. To be honest, I envied him his ability to fall asleep that fast.

I glanced at Silva. "You want to do the asking for once?"

He grinned and held up both forearms, tattooed every inch. "You know it's not me."

"There's such thing as sleeves, you know." I pulled my wind-breaker off the back of my seat and flapped it at him, even though I knew he was right. In the Midwest, approaching a new restaurant for the first time, it was never him, between the tattoos and the spiky blue hair. Never Jacky for the pox scars on his cheeks, even though they were clearly long healed. That left me.

My bad knee buckled as I swung from the driver's seat. I bent to clutch it and my lower back spasmed just to the right of my spine, that momentary pain that told me to rethink all my life's choices.

"What are you doing?" Silva asked through the open door.

"Tying my shoe." There was no need to lie, but I did it anyway. Pride or vanity or something akin. He was only two years younger than me, and neither of us jumped off our amps much anymore. If I ached from the drive, he probably ached, too.

The backs of my thighs were all pins and needles, and my shirt was damp with sweat. I took a moment to lean against Daisy the Diesel and stretch in the hot air. I smelled myself: not great after four days with no shower, but not unbearable.

The doors opened into a foyer, red and gold and black. I didn't even notice the blond hostess in her red qipao until she stepped away from the wallpaper.

"Dining alone?" she asked. Beyond her, a roomful of faces turned in my direction. This wasn't really the kind of place that attracted tourists, especially not these days, this far off the interstate.

"No, um, actually, I was wondering if I could speak to the chef or the owner? It'll only take a minute." I was pretty sure I had timed our stop for after their dinner rush. Most of the diners looked to be eating or pushing their plates aside.

The owner and chef were the same person. I'd been expecting another blond Midwesterner, but he was legit Chinese. He had never heard of a van that ran on grease. I did the not-quite-pleading thing. On stage I aimed for fierce, but in jeans and runners and a ponytail,

I could fake a down-on-her-luck Midwest momma. The trick was not to push it.

He looked a little confused by my request, but at least he was willing to consider it. "Come to the kitchen door after we close and show me. Ten, ten-thirty."

It was nine; not too bad. I walked back to the van. Silva was still in the passenger seat, but reading a trifold menu. He must have ducked in behind me to grab it. "They serve a bread basket with lo mein. And spaghetti and meatballs. Where are we?"

"Nowhere, Indiana," I echoed back at him.

We sat in the dark van and watched the customers trickle out. I could mostly guess from their looks which ones would be getting into the trucks and which into the Chauffeurs. Every once in a while, a big guy in work boots and a trucker cap surprised me by squeezing himself into some little self-driving thing. The game passed the time, in any case.

A middle-aged cowboy wandered over to stare at our van. I pegged him for a legit rancher from a distance, but as he came closer I noticed a clerical collar beneath the embroidered shirt. His boots shone and he had a paunch falling over an old rodeo belt; the incongruous image of a bull-riding minister made me laugh. He startled when he realized I was watching him.

He made a motion for me to lower my window.

"Maryland plates!" he said. "I used to live in Hagerstown."

I smiled, though I'd only ever passed through Hagerstown.

"Used to drive a church van that looked kinda like yours, too, just out of high school. Less duct tape, though. Whatcha doing out here?"

"Touring. Band."

"No kidding! You look familiar. Have I heard of you?"

"Cassis Fire," I said, taking the question as a prompt for a name. "We had it painted on the side for a while, but then we figured out we got pulled over less when we were incognito."

"Don't think I know the name. I used to have a band, back before . . ." His voice trailed off, and neither of us needed him to finish his sentence. There were several "back befores" he could be referring to, but they all amounted to the same thing. Back before StageHolo and SportsHolo made it easier to stay home. Back before most people got scared out of congregating anywhere they didn't know everybody.

"You're not playing around here, are you?"

I shook my head. "Columbus, Ohio. Tomorrow night."

"I figured. Couldn't think of a place you'd play nearby."

"Not our kind of music, anyway," I agreed. I didn't know what music he liked, but this was a safe bet.

"Not any kind. Oh well. Nice chatting with you. I'll look you up on StageHolo."

He turned away.

"We're not on StageHolo," I called to his back, though maybe not loud enough for him to hear. He waved as his Chauffeur drove him off the lot.

"Luce, you're a terrible salesperson," Silva said to me.

"What?" I hadn't realized he'd been paying attention.

"You know he recognized you. All you had to do was say your name instead of the band's. Or 'Blood and Diamonds.' He'd have paid for dinner for all of us, then bought every T-shirt and download code we have."

"And then he'd listen to them and realize the music we make now is nothing like the music we made then. And even if he liked it, he'd never go to a show. At best he'd send a message saying how much he wished we were on StageHolo."

"Which we could be . . ."

"Which we won't be." He knew better than to argue with me on that one. It was our only real source of disagreement.

The neon "open" sign in the restaurant's window blinked out, and I took the cue to put the key back in the ignition. The glowplug light came on, and I started the van back up.

My movement roused Jacky again. "Where are we now?"

I didn't bother answering.

As I had guessed, the owner hadn't quite understood what I was asking for. I gave him the engine tour, showing him the custom oil filter and the dual tanks. "We still need regular diesel to start, then switch to the veggie-oil tank. Not too much more to it than that."

"It's legal?"

Legal enough. There was a gray area wherein perhaps technically we were skirting the fuel tax. By our reasoning, though, we were also skirting the reasons for the fuel tax. We'd be the ones who got in trouble, anyway. Not him.

"Of course," I said, then changed the subject. "And the best part is that it makes the van smell like egg rolls."

He smiled. We got a whole tankful out of him, and a bag full of food he'd have otherwise chucked out, as well.

The guys were over the moon about the food. Dumpster-diving behind a restaurant or Superwally would have been our next order of business, so anything that hadn't made a stop in a garbage can on its way to us was haute cuisine as far as we were concerned. Silva took the lo mein—no complimentary bread—screwed together his travel chopsticks, and handed mine to me from the glove compartment. I grabbed some kind of moo shu without the pancakes, and Jacky woke again to snag the third container.

"Can we go someplace?" Silva asked, waving chopsticks at the window.

"Got anything in mind on a Tuesday night in the boonies?"

Jacky was up for something, too. "Laser tag? Laser bowling?"

Sometimes the age gap was a chasm. I turned in my seat to side-eye the kid. "One vote for lasers."

"I dunno," said Silva. "Just a bar? If I have to spend another hour in this van I'm going to scream."

I took a few bites while I considered. We wouldn't be too welcome anywhere around here, between our odor and our look, not to mention the simple fact that we were strangers. On the other hand, the more outlets I gave these guys for legit fun, the less likely they were to come up with something that would get us in trouble. "If we see a bar or a bowling joint before someplace to sleep, sure."

"I can look it up," said Jacky.

"Nope," I said. "Leave it to fate."

After two-thirds of the moo shu, I gave up and closed the container. I hated wasting food, but it was too big for me to finish. I wiped my chopsticks on my jeans and put them back in their case.

Two miles down the road from the restaurant, we came to Starker's, which I hoped from the apostrophe was only a bar, not a strip club. Their expansive parking lot was empty except for eight Chauffeurs, all lined up like pigs at a trough. At least that meant we didn't have to worry about some drunk crashing into our van on his way out.

I backed into the closest spot to the door. It was the best lit, so I could worry less about our gear getting lifted. Close was also good if the locals decided they didn't like our looks.

We got the long stare as we walked in, the one from old Westerns, where all the heads swivel our way and the piano player stops playing. Except of course, these days the piano player didn't stop, because the piano player had no idea we'd arrived. The part of the pianist in this scenario was played by Roy Bittan, alongside the whole E Street Band, loud as a stadium and projected in StageHolo 3D.

"Do you want to leave?" Jacky whispered to me.

"No, it's okay. We're here now. Might as well have a drink."

"At least it's Bruce. I can get behind Bruce." Silva edged past me toward the bar.

A few at leasts: at least it was Bruce, not some cut-rate imitation. Bruce breathed punk as far as I was concerned, insisting on recording new music and legit live shows all the way into his eighties. At least it was StageHolo and not StageHoloLive, in which case there'd be a cover charge. I was willing to stand in the same room as the technology that was trying to make me obsolete, but I'd be damned if I paid

174

them for the privilege. Of course, it wouldn't be Bruce on StageHolo-Live either; he'd been gone a couple years now, and this Bruce looked to be only in his sixties, anyway. A little flat, too, which suggested this was a retrofitted older show, not one recorded using StageHolo's tech.

Silva pressed a cold can into my hand, and I took a sip, not even bothering to look at what I was drinking. Knowing him, knowing us, he'd snagged whatever had been cheapest. Pisswater, but cold pisswater. Perfect for washing down the greasy takeout food aftertaste.

I slipped into a booth, hoping the guys had followed me. Jacky did, carrying an identical can to mine in one hand, and something the color of windshield-wiper fluid in a plastic shot glass in the other.

"You want one?" he asked me, nudging the windshield-wiper fluid. "Bartender said it was the house special."

I pushed it back in his direction. "I don't drink anything blue. It never ends well."

"Suit yourself." He tossed it back, then grinned.

"Your teeth are blue now. You look like you ate a Smurf."

"What's a Smurf?"

Sometimes I forgot how young he was. Half my age. A lifetime in this business. "Little blue characters? A village with one chick, one old man, and a bunch of young guys?"

"Like our band?" He shook his head. "Sorry. Bad joke. Anyway, I have no idea what was in that food, but it might have been Smurf, if they're blue and taste like pork butt. How's your dinner sitting?"

I swatted him lightly, backhand. "Fine, as long as I don't drink anything blue."

He downed his beer in one long chug, then got up to get another. He looked at mine and raised his eyebrows.

"No thanks," I said. "I'll stick with one. I get the feeling this is a zero-tolerance town."

If twenty-odd years of this had taught me one thing, it was to stay clear of local police. Every car in the parking lot was self-driving, which suggested there was somebody out on the roads ready to come down hard on us. Having spent a lot of time in my youth leaving clubs at closing time and dodging drunk drivers, I approved this effort. One of the few aspects of our brave new world I could fully endorse.

I looked around. Silva sat on a stool at the bar. Jacky stood behind him, a hand on Silva's shoulder, tapping his foot to the Bo Diddley beat of "She's the One." The rest of the bar stools were filled with people who looked too comfortable to be anything but regulars. A couple of them had the cocked-head posture of cheap neural overlays. The others played games on the slick touchscreen bar, or tapped on the Bracertabs strapped to their arms, the latest tech fad. Nobody talking to anybody.

Down at the other end, two blond women stood facing the Bruce holo, singing along and swaying. He pointed in their general direction, and one giggled and clutched her friend's arm as if he had singled her out personally. Two guys sat on stools near the stage, one playing air drums, the other watching the women. The women only had eyes for Bruce.

I got where they were coming from. I knew people who didn't like his voice or his songs, but I didn't know anybody, especially any musi-cian, who couldn't appreciate his stage presence. Even here, even now, knowing decades separated me from the night this had been recorded, and decades separated the young man who had first written the song from the older man who sang it, even from across a scuzzy too-bright barroom, drinking pisswater beer with strangers and my own smelly band, I believed him when he sang that she was the one. I hated the StageHolo company even more for the fact I was enjoying it.

Somebody slid into the booth next to me. I turned, expecting one of my bandmates, but a stranger had sat down, closer than I cared for.

"Passing through?" he asked, looking at me with intense, blood-shot eyes. He brushed a thick sweep of hair from his forehead, a style

I could only assume he had stuck with through the decades since it had been popular. He had dimples and a smile that had clearly been his greatest asset in his youth. He probably hadn't quite realized drinking had caught up with him, that he was puffy and red-nosed. Or that he slurred a bit, even on those two words.

"Passing through." I gave him a brief "not interested" smile and turned my whole body back toward the stage.

"Kind of unusual for somebody to pass through here, let alone bother to stop. What attracted you?" His use of the word "attracted" was pointed.

If he put an arm around me, I'd have to slug him. I shifted a few inches, trying to put distance between us, and emphasized my next word. "We wanted a drink. We've been driving a while."

His disappointment was evident. "Boyfriend? Husband?"

I nodded at the bar, letting him pick whichever he thought looked more like he might be with me, and whichever label he wanted to apply. It amused me either way, since I couldn't imagine being with either of them. Not at the beginning, and especially not after having spent all this time in the van with them.

Then I wondered why I was playing games at all. I turned to look at him. "We're a band."

"No kidding! I used to have a band." A reassessment of the situation flashed across his face. A new smile, more collegial. The change in his whole demeanor prompted me to give him a little more attention.

"No kidding?"

"Yeah. Mostly we played here. Before the insurance rates rose and StageHolo convinced Maggie she'd save money with holos of famous bands."

"Did she? Save money?"

He sighed. "Probably. Holos don't drink, and holos don't dent the mics or spill beers into the PA. And people will stay and drink for hours if the right bands are playing."

"Do you still play for fun? Your band?"

He shrugged. "We did for a while. We even got a spot at the very last State Fair. And after that, every once in a while we'd play a barbecue in somebody's backyard. But it's hard to keep it up when you've got nothing to aim for. Playing here once a week was a decent enough goal, but who would want to hear me sing covers when you can have the real thing?"

He pointed his beer at one of the women by the stage. "That's my ex-wife, by the way."

"I'm sorry?"

"It's okay." He took a swig of beer. "That's when Polly left me. Said it wasn't 'cause the band was done, but I think it was related. She said I didn't seem interested in anything at all after that."

He had turned his attention down to his drink, but now he looked at me again. "How about you? I guess there are still places out there to play?"

"A few," I said. "Mostly in the cities. There's a lot of turnover, too. So we can have a great relationship with a place and then we'll call back and they'll be gone without a trace."

"And there's enough money in it to live on?"

There are people who ask that question in an obnoxious, disbelieving way, and I tend to tell them, "We're here, aren't we?" but this guy was nostalgic enough that I answered him honestly. Maybe I could help him see there was no glamour left for people like us.

"I used to get some royalty checks from an old song, which covered insurance and repairs for the van, but they've gotten smaller and smaller since *BMI v. StageHolo*. We make enough to stay on the road, eat really terribly, have a beer now and again. Not enough to save. Not enough to stop, ever. Not that we want to stop, so it's okay."

"You never come off the road? Do you live somewhere?"

"The van's registered at my parents' place in Maryland, and I crash there when I need a break. But that isn't often."

"And your band?"

"My bassist and I have been playing together for a long time, and he's got places he stays. We replace a drummer occasionally. This one's been with us for a year, and the two of them are into each other, so if they don't fall out it might last a while."

He nodded. The wolfishness was gone, replaced by something more wistful. He held out his beer. "To music."

"To live music." My can clinked his.

Somebody shouted over by the bar, and we both twisted round to see what had happened. The air-drum player had wandered over— Max Weinberg was on break too—and he and Jacky were squaring off over something. Jacky's blue lips glowed from twenty feet away.

"Nothing good ever comes of blue drinks," I said to my new friend.

He nodded. "You're gonna want to get your friend out of here. That's the owner behind the bar. If your guy breaks anything, she'll have the cops here in two seconds flat."

"Crap. Thanks."

Blue liquid pooled around and on Jacky, a tray of overturned plastic shot glasses behind him. At least they weren't glass, and at least he hadn't damaged the fancy bar top. I dug a twenty from the thin wad in my pocket, hoping it was enough.

"You're fake-drumming to a fake band," Jacky was saying. "And you're not even good at it. If you went to your crash cymbal that much with the real Bruce, he'd fire you in two seconds."

"Who the hell cares? Did I ask you to critique my drumming?"

"No, but if you did, I'd tell you you're behind on the kick, too. My two-year-old niece keeps a better beat than you do."

The other guy's face reddened, and I saw him clench a fist. Silva had an arm across Jacky's chest by then, propelling him toward the door. We made eye contact, and he nodded.

I tossed my twenty on a dry spot on the bar, still hoping for a quick getaway.

"We don't take cash," said the owner, holding my bill by the corner like it was a dead rat.

Dammit. I squared my shoulders. "You're legally required to accept US currency."

"Maybe true in the US of A, but this is the US of Starker's, and I only accept Superwally credit. And your blue buddy there owes a lot more than this anyway for those spilled drinks." She had her hand below the bar. I had no clue whether she was going for a phone or a baseball bat or a gun; nothing good could come of any of those options.

I snatched the bill back, mind racing. Silva kept a credit transfer account; that wouldn't be any help, since he was already out the door. I avoided credit and devices in general, which usually held me in good stead, but I didn't think the label "Non-comm" would win me any friends here. Jacky rarely paid for anything, so I had no clue whether he had been paying cash or credit up until then.

"I've got them, Maggie." My new friend from the booth stepped up beside me, waving his phone.

He turned to me. "Go on. I've got this."

Maggie's hand came out from under the bar. She pulled a phone from behind the cash register to do the credit transfer, which meant whatever she had reached for down below probably wouldn't have been good for my health.

"Keep playing," he called after me.

Jacky was unremorseful. "He started it. Called us disease vectors. I told him to stay right where he was and the whole world would go on turning 'cause it doesn't even know he exists. Besides, if he can't air drum, he should just air guitar like everybody else."

Silva laughed. "You should have pretended to cough. He probably would have pissed himself."

He and Silva sprawled in the back together as I peeled out of the parking lot.

"Not funny. I don't care who started it. No fights. I mean it. Do you think I can afford to bail you out? How are we supposed to play tomorrow if our drummer's in jail? And what if they skip the jail part and shoot you? It's happened before."

"Sorry, Mom," Jacky said.

"Not funny," I repeated. "If you ever call me 'Mom' again I'm leaving you on the side of the road. And I'm not a Chauffeur. Somebody come up here to keep me company."

Silva climbed across the bed and bags and up to the passenger seat. He flipped on the police scanner, then turned it off after a few minutes of silence; nobody had put out any APBs on a van full of bill-ducking freaks. I drove speed limit plus five, same as the occasional Chauffeurs we passed ferrying their passengers home. Short-cutting onto the highway to leave the area entirely would've been my preference, but Daisy would have triggered the ramp sensors in two seconds flat; we hadn't been allowed on an interstate in five years.

After about twenty miles, my fear that we were going to get chased down finally dissipated and my heartbeat returned to acceptable rhythms. We pulled into an office park that didn't look patrolled.

"Your turn for the bed, Luce?" Jacky asked. Trying to make amends, maybe.

"You guys can have it if I can find my sleeping bag. It's actually pretty nice out, and then I don't have to smell whatever that blue crap is on your clothes."

"You have a sleeping bag?"

"Of course I do. I just used it in . . ." Actually, I couldn't think of when I had used it last. It took a few minutes of rummaging to find it in the storage space under the bed, behind Silva's garage-sale box of pulp novels. I spread it on the ground just in front of the van. The temperature was perfect and the sky was full of stars. Hopefully there weren't any coyotes around.

I slept three or four hours before my body started to remind me why I didn't sleep outside more often. I got up to pee and stretch. When I opened the door, I was hit by an even deeper grease smell than usual. It almost drowned out the funk of two guys farting, four days unwashed. Also the chemical-alcohol-blue scent Jacky wore all over his clothes.

Leaning over the driver's seat, I dug in the center console for my silver pen and the bound atlas I used as a road bible. The stars were bright enough to let me see the pages without a flashlight. The atlas was about fifteen years out of date, but my notes kept it useable. The town we had called Nowhere was actually named Rackwood, which sounded more like a tree disease than a town to me. A glittery asterisk went next to Rackwood, and in the margin "China Grove—Mike Sun—grease AND food." I drew an X over the location of Starker's, which wouldn't get our repeat business.

I crawled inside around dawn, feeling every bone in my body, and reclined the passenger seat. Nobody knocked on the van to tell us to move on, so we slept until the sun started baking us. Jacky reached forward to offer up his last leftovers from the night before. I sniffed the container and handed it back to him. He shrugged and dove in with his fingers, chopsticks having disappeared into the detritus surrounding him. After a little fishing around, I found my dinner and sent that his way as well.

Silva climbed into the driver's seat. I didn't usually relinquish the wheel; I genuinely loved doing all the driving myself. I liked the control, liked to listen to Daisy's steady engine and the thrum of the road. He knew that, and didn't ask except when he really felt the urge, which meant that when he did ask, I moved over. Jacky had never offered once, content to read and listen to music in his backseat cocoon. Another reason he fit in well.

Silva driving meant I got a chance to look around; it wasn't often that we took a road I hadn't been down before. I couldn't even remember how we had wound up choosing this route the previous day. We passed shuttered diners and liquor stores, the ghost town that might have been a main street at one time.

"Where is everybody?" Jacky asked.

I twisted around to see if he was joking. "Have you looked out the window once this whole year? Is this the first time you're noticing?"

"I usually sleep through this part of the country. It's boring."

"There is no everybody," Silva said. "A few farmers, a Superwally that employs everyone else within an hour's drive."

I peered at my atlas. "I've got a distribution center drawn in about forty miles back and ten miles north, on the road we usually take. That probably employs anybody not working for the company store." There wasn't really any reason for me to draw that kind of place onto my maps, but I liked making them more complete. They had layers in some places, stores and factories that had come and gone and come and gone again.

Most backroad towns looked like this, these days. At best a fast-food place, a feed store, maybe a run-down-looking grocery or a health clinic, and not much else. There'd be a Superwally somewhere between towns, as Silva had said, luring everyone even farther from center or anything resembling community. Town after town, we saw the same thing. And of course most people didn't see anything at all, puttering along on the self-driving highways, watching movies instead of looking out the windows, getting from point A to point B without stopping in between.

We weren't exactly doing our part either. It's not like we had contributed to the local economy. We took free dinner, free fuel. We contributed in other ways, but not in this town or the others we'd passed through the night before. Maybe someday someone here would book us and we'd come back, but until then we were passing through. Goodbye, Rackwood, Indiana.

"Next town has the World's Largest Saltshaker." I could hear the capital letters in Jacky's voice. He liked to download tourist brochures. I approved of that hobby, the way I approved of supporting anything to make a place less generic. Sometimes we even got to stop at some of the sights, when we could afford it and we weren't in a hurry. Neither of which was the case today.

"Another time," Silva said. "We slept later than we should have."

"I think we're missing out."

I twisted around to look at Jacky. He flopped across the bed, waving his phone like a look at the world's largest saltshaker might make us change our minds. "It's a choice between showers and salt-shaker. You decide."

He stuffed his phone into his pocket with a sigh. Showers trumped.

About an hour outside Columbus, we stopped at a by-the-hour motel already starred in my atlas, and rented an hour for the glory of running water. The clerk took my cash without comment.

I let the guys go first, so I wouldn't have to smell them again after I was clean. The shower itself was nothing to write home about. The metal-booth kind, no tub, nonexistent water pressure, seven-minute shutoff; better than nothing. Afterward, I pulled a white towel from the previous hotel from my backpack to leave in the room, and stuffed one of the near-identical clean ones in my bag. The one I took might have been one I had left the last time through. Nobody ever got shorted a towel, and it saved me a lot of time in Laundromats. I couldn't even remember who had taught me that trick, but I'd been doing it for decades.

We still had to get back in our giant grease trap, of course, now in our cleanish gig clothes. I opened all the windows and turned on the fan full blast, hoping to keep the shower scent for as long as possible. I could vaguely hear Jacky calling out visitor highlights for Columbus from the back, but the noise stole the meat of whatever he was saying. I stuck my arm outside and planed my hand against the wind.

I didn't intend to fall asleep, but I woke to Silva shouting "Whoa! Happy birthday, Daisy!" and hooting the horn. I leaned over to see the numbers clicking over from 99999.

Jacky threw himself forward to snap a picture of the odometer as it hit all zeroes. "Whoa! What birthday is this?"

I considered. Daisy only had a five-digit odometer, so she got a fresh start every hundred thousand miles. "Eight, I think?"

Silva grinned. "Try again. My count says nine."

"Nine? I thought we passed seven on the way out of Seattle two years ago."

"That was five years ago. Eight in Asheville. I don't remember when."

"Huh. You're probably right. We should throw her a party at a million." I gave her dashboard a hard pat, like the flank of a horse. "Good job, old girl. That's amazing."

"Totally," said Jacky. "And can we play 'Our Lady of the Open Road' tonight? In Daisy's honor? I love that song. I don't know why we don't play it more often." He started playing the opening with his hands on the back of my seat.

"I'm on board," Silva agreed. "Maybe instead of 'Manifest Independence'? That one could use a rest."

"'Manifest Independence' stays," I said. "Try again."

"'Outbreak?'"

"Deal."

Jacky retreated to make the changes to the set list.

Our destination was deep in the heart of the city. Highways would have gotten us there in no time, not that we had that option. We drove along the river, then east past the decaying convention center.

We hadn't played this particular space before, but we'd played others, mostly in this same neighborhood of abandoned warehouses. Most closed up pretty quickly, or moved when they got shut down, so even if we played for the same crowd, we rarely played the same building twice.

This one, The Chain, sounded like it had a chance at longevity. It was a bike co-op by day, venue by night. Cities liked bike co-ops. With the right people running the place, maybe somebody who knew how to write grants and dress in business drag and shake a hand or two, a bike co-op could be part of the city plan. Not that I had any business telling anyone to sell themselves out for a few months of forced legitimacy.

Our timing was perfect. The afternoon bike-repair class had just finished, so the little stage area was more or less clear. Better yet, they'd ordered pizza. Jacky had braved the Chinese leftovers, but Silva and I hadn't eaten yet. It took every ounce of my self-restraint to help haul in the instruments before partaking. I sent a silent prayer up to the pizza gods there'd still be some left for us once all our gear was inside.

I made three trips—guitars and gear, amp, swag to sell—then loaded up a paper plate with three pizza slices. I was entirely capable of eating all three, but I'd share with the guys if they didn't get their gear in before the food was gone. Not ideal dinner before singing, anyway; maybe the grease would trump the dairy as a throat coating. I sat on my amp and ate the first piece, watching Jacky and Silva bring in the drums, feeling only a little guilty. I had done my share, even if I hadn't helped anyone else.

The bike class stuck around. We chatted with a few. Emma, Rudy, Dijuan, Carter, Marin—there were more, but I lost track of names after that. I gave those five the most attention in any case, since Rudy had been the one to book us, and Emma ran the programming for the bike co-op. We were there because of them. We talked politics and music and bikes. I was grateful not to have to explain myself again. These were our people. They treated us like we were coming home, not passing through.

More audience gradually trickled in, a good crowd for a Wednesday night. A mix of young and old, in varying degrees of punk trappings, according to their generation and inclination. Here and there, some more straight-laced, though they were as punk as anyone, in the truest spirit of the word, for having shown up at this space at all. Punk as a genre didn't look or sound like it used to, in any case; it had scattered to the wind, leaving a loose grouping of bands whose main commonality was a desire to create live music for live audiences.

The first band began to play, an all-woman four-piece called Moby K. Dick. They were young enough to be my kids, which meant young enough they had never known any scene but this one. The bassist played from a sporty little wheelchair, her back to the audience, like she was having a one-on-one conversation with the drummer's high hat. At first, I thought she was shy, but I gradually realized she was just really into the music. The drummer doubled as singer, hiding behind a curtain of dreadlocks that lifted and dropped back onto her face with every beat. They played something that sounded like sea chanties done double time and double volume, but the lyrics were all about whales and dolphins taking revenge on people. It was pretty fantastic.

I gave all the bands we played with a chance to win me over. They were the only live music we ever got to hear, being on the road full time. The few friends we still had doing the same circuit were playing the same nights as us in other towns, rotating through; the others were doing StageHolo and we didn't talk much anymore. It used to be we'd sometimes even wind up in the same cities on the same night, so we'd miss each other and split the audience. That didn't happen much anymore with so few places to play.

Moby K. Dick earned my full attention, but the second band lost me pretty quickly. They all played adapted console-game instruments except the drummer. No strings, all buttons, all programmed to trigger samples. I'd seen bands like that before that were decent; this one was not my thing.

The women from the first band were hanging out by the drink cooler, so I made my way back there. I thrust my hand into the ice and came out with a water bottle. Most venues like this one were alcohol-free and all ages. There was probably a secret beer cooler hidden somewhere, but I wasn't in the mood to find it.

"I liked your stuff," I said to the bassist. Up close, she looked slightly older than she had on stage. Mid-twenties, probably. "My name's Luce."

She grinned. "I know! I mean, I'm Truly. And yes, that's really my name. Nice to meet you. And really? You liked it? That's so cool! We begged to be on this bill with you. I've been listening to Cassis Fire my whole life. I've got 'Manifest Independence' written on my wall at home. It's my mantra."

I winced but held steady under the barrage and the age implication. She continued. "My parents have all your music. They like the stuff with Marcia Januarie on drums best, when you had the second guitarist, but I think your current lineup is more streamlined."

"Thanks." I waited for her to point her parents out in the room, and for them to be younger than me. When she thankfully didn't volunteer that information, I asked, "Do you guys have anything recorded?"

"We've been recording our shows, but mostly we just want to play. You could take us on the road with you, if you wanted. Opening act."

She said the last bit jokingly, but I was pretty sure the request was real, so I treated it that way." We used to be able to, but not these days. It's hard enough to keep ourselves fed and moving to the next gig. I'm happy to give you advice, though. Have you seen our van?"

Her eyes widened. She was kind of adorable in her enthusiasm. Part of me considered making a pass at her, but we only had a few minutes before I had to be onstage, and I didn't want to confuse things. Sometimes I hated being the responsible one.

"It's right outside. They'll find me when it's our turn to play. Come on."

The crowd parted for her wheelchair as we made our way through. I held the door for her and she navigated the tiny rise in the doorframe with practiced ease.

"We call her Daisy," I said, introducing Truly to the van. I searched my pockets for the keys and realized Silva had them. So much for that idea. "She's a fifteen seater, but we took out the middle seats for a bed and the back to make a cage for the drums and stuff so they don't kill us if we stop short."

"What's the mpg?" she asked. I saw her gears spinning as she tried to figure out logistics. I liked her focus. She was starting to remind me of me, though, which was the turnoff I needed.

I beckoned her to the hood, which popped by latch, no keys necessary. "That's the best part of all."

She locked her chair and pushed herself up to lean against Daisy's frame. At my look, she explained, "I don't need it all the time, but playing usually makes me pretty tired. And I don't like getting pushed around in crowds."

"Oh, that's cool," I said. "And if you buy a van of your own, that's one less conversion you'll have to make, if you can climb in without a lift. I had been trying to figure out if you'd have room for four people and gear and a chair lift."

"Nah, you can go back to the part where we wonder how I'm going to afford a van, straight up. Right now we just borrow my sister's family Chauffeur. It's just barely big enough for all our gear, but the mileage is crap and there's no room for clothes or swag or anything."

"Well, if you can find a way to pay for an old van like Daisy, the beauty of running on fry oil is the money you'll save on fuel. As long as you like takeout food, you get used to the smell . . ."

Silva stuck his head out the door, then came over to us. I made introductions. He unlocked the van; I saw Truly wince when the smell hit her. He reached under the bed, back toward the wheel well, and emerged with a bottle of whiskey in hand. Took a long swig, and passed it to me. I had a smaller sip, just enough to feel the burn in my throat, the lazy singer's warm-up.

Truly followed my lead. "Promise you'll give me pointers if I manage to get a van?"

I promised. The kid wasn't just like me; she practically was me, with the misfortune to have been born twenty years too late to possibly make it work.

I made Silva tap phones with her. "I would do it myself, but . . ."

"I know," she said. "I'd be Non-comm if I could, but my parents won't let me. Emergencies and all that."

Did we play extra well, or did it just feel like it? Moby K. Dick had helped; it was always nice to be reminded that what you did mattered. I had a mental buzz even with only a sip of whiskey, the combination of music and possibilities and an enthusiastic crowd eager to take whatever we gave them.

On a good night like this, when we locked in with each other, it was like I was a time traveler for an hour. Every night we'd ever played a song overlapped with every night we'd ever play it again, even though I was fully in the moment. My fingers made shapes, ran steel strings over magnets, ran signals through wires to the amplifier behind me, which blasted those shapes back over me in waves. Glorious, cathartic, bone-deep noise.

On stage, I forgot how long I'd been doing this. I could still be the kid playing in her parents' basement, or the young woman with the hit single and the major label, the one called the next Joan Jett, the second coming of riot grrl, not that I wanted to be the young version of me anymore. I had to work to remember that if I slid on my knees I might not get up again. I was a better guitar player now, a better singer, a better songwriter. I had years of righteous rage to channel. When I talked, I sometimes felt like a pissed-off grump, stuck in the past. Given time to express it all in music, I came across better.

Moby K. Dick pushed through to the front when we played "Manifest Independence," singing along at the top of their lungs. They must have been babies when I released that song, but it might as well have been written for them. It was as true for them as it had been for me.

That was what the young punks and the old punks all responded to; they knew I believed what I was singing. We all shared the same indignation that we were losing everything that made us distinct, that nothing special happened anymore, that the new world replacing the old one wasn't nearly as good, that everyone was hungry and everything was broken and that we'd fix it if we could find the right tools. My job was to give it all a voice. Add to that the sweet old-school crunch of my Les Paul played through Marshall tubes, Silva's sinuous bass lines, Jacky's tricky beats, and we could be the best live band you ever heard. Made sweeter by the fact that you had to be there to get the full effect.

We didn't have rehearsed moves or light shows or spotlights to hit like the StageHolos, but we knew how to play it up for the crowd. To make it seem like we were playing for one person, and playing for all of them, and playing just for them, because this night was different and would only ever happen once. People danced and pogoed and leaned into the music. A few of the dancers had ultraviolet tattoos, which always looked pretty awesome from my vantage point, a secret performance for the performers. I nudged Silva to look at one of them, a glowing phoenix spread wingtip to wingtip across a dancer's bare shoulders and arms.

A couple of tiny screens also lit the audience: people recording us with Bracertabs, arms held aloft. I was fine with that. Everyone at the show knew how it felt to be there; they'd come back, as long as there were places for us to play. The only market for a non-Holo recording was other people like this audience, and it would only inspire them to come out again the next time.

Toward the end of the set, I dedicated "Our Lady of the Open Road" to Daisy. At the tail of the last chorus, Jacky rolled through his toms in a way he never had before, cracking the song open wide, making it clear he wasn't coming in for a landing where he was supposed to. Silva and I exchanged glances, a wordless "this is going to be interesting," then followed Jacky's lead. The only way to do that was to make it bigger than usual, keep it going, make it a monster. I punched my gain pedal and turned to my amp to ride the feedback. Our lady of the open road, get me through another night.

Through some miracle of communication we managed to end the song together, clean enough that it sounded planned. I'd kill Jacky later, but at that moment I loved him. The crowd screamed.

I wiped the sweat out of my eyes with my shoulder. "We've got one more for you. Thanks so much for being here tonight." I hoped "Better to Laugh" wouldn't sound like an afterthought.

That was when the power went out.

"Police!" somebody shouted. The crowd began to push toward the door.

"Not the police!" someone else yelled. "Just a blackout."

"Just a blackout!" I repeated into the mic as if it were still on, then louder into the front row, hoping they were still listening to me. "Pass it on."

The message rippled through the audience. A tense moment passed with everyone listening for sirens, ready to scatter. Then they began to debate whether the blackout was the city or the building, whether the power bill had been paid, whether it was a plot to shut the place down.

Emma pushed her way through the crowd to talk to us. "They shut this neighborhood's power down whenever the circuits overload uptown. We're trying to get somebody to bring it up in city council. I'm so sorry."

I leaned in to give her a sweaty hug. "Don't worry about it. It happens."

We waited, hoping for the rock gods to smile upon us. The room started to heat up, and somebody propped the outside doors, which cooled things down slightly. After twenty minutes, we put our instruments down. At least we had made it through most of our set. I had no doubt the collective would pay us, and no concern people would say they hadn't gotten their money's worth. I dug the hotel towel out of my backpack to wipe my dripping face.

A few people made their way over to talk to us and buy T-shirts and patches and even LPs and download codes, even though you could find most of our songs free online. That was part of the beauty of these kids. They were all broke as hell, but they still wanted to support us, even if it was just a patch or a pin or a password most of them were capable of hacking in two seconds flat. And they all believed in cash, bless them. We used the light of their phone screens to make change.

The girls from Moby K. Dick all bought T-shirts. Truly bought an LP as well—it figured she was into vinyl—and I signed it "To my favorite new band, good luck." She wheeled out with her band, no parents in sight. I wondered if they'd decided they were too old for live music, then chided myself. I couldn't have it both ways, mad that they were probably my age and mad that they weren't there. Besides, they might have just left separately from their kid. I knew I must be tired if I was getting hung up on something like that.

"You look like you need some water," somebody said to me in the darkness. A bottle pressed into my hand, damp with condensation.

"Thanks," I said. "Though I don't know how you can say I look like anything with the lights out."

At that moment, the overheads hummed on again. I had left my guitar leaning facedown on my amp, and it started to build up a squeal of feedback. I tossed the water back, wiped my hands on my pants, and slammed the standby switch. The squeal trailed away.

"Sorry, you were saying?" I asked, returning to the stranger, who still stood with bottle in hand. I took it from her again. I thought maybe I'd know her in the light, but she didn't look familiar. Mid-thirties, maybe, tall and tan, with a blandly friendly face, toned arms, Bracertab strapped to one forearm. She wore a Magnificent Beefeaters T-shirt with the sleeves cut off. We used to play shows with them, before they got big.

"I was saying you looked like you were thirsty, by which I mean you looked like that before the lights went out, so I guessed you probably still looked like that after."

"Oh."

"Anyway, I wanted to say good show. One of your best I've seen."

"Have you seen a lot?" It was a bit of a rude question, with an implication I didn't recognize her. Bad for business. Everybody should believe they were an integral part of the experience. But really, I didn't think I'd seen her before, and it wasn't the worst question, unless the answer was she'd been following us for the last six months.

"I've been following you for the last six months," she said. "But mostly live audience uploads. I was at your last Columbus show, though, and up in Rochester."

Rochester had been a huge warehouse. I didn't feel as bad.

"Thanks for coming. And, uh, for the water." I tried to redeem myself.

"My pleasure," she said. "I really like your sound. Nikki Kellerman."

She held her arm out in the universal 'tap to exchange virtual business cards' gesture.

"Sorry, I'm Non-comm," I said.

She looked surprised, but I couldn't tell if it was surprise that I was Non-comm, or that she didn't know the term. The latter didn't seem likely. I'd have said a third of the audience at our shows these days were people who had given up their devices and all the corporate tracking that went along with them.

She unstrapped the tablet, peeled a thin wallet off her damp arm, and drew a paper business card from inside it.

I read it out loud. "Nikki Kellerman, A & R, StageHolo Productions." I handed it back to her.

"Hear me out," she said.

"Okay, Artists & Repertoire. You can talk at me while I pack up."

I opened the swag tub and started piling the T-shirts back into it. Usually we took the time to separate them by size so they'd be right the next time, but now I tossed them in, hoping to get away as soon as possible.

"As you probably know, we've been doing very well with getting StageHolo into venues across the country. Bringing live music into places that previously didn't have it."

"There are about seven things wrong with that statement," I said without looking up.

She continued as if I hadn't spoken. "Our biggest-selling acts are arena rock, pop, rap, and Spanish pop. We now reach nine in ten bars and clubs. One in four with StageHolo AtHome."

"You can stop the presentation there. Don't you dare talk to me about StageHolo AtHome." My voice rose. Silva stood in the corner chatting with some bike kids, but I saw him throw a worried look my way. "'All the excitement of live entertainment without leaving your living room.' 'Stay AtHome with John Legend tonight.'"

I clapped the lid onto the swag box and carried it to the door. When I went to pack up my stage gear, she followed.

"I think you're not understanding the potential, Luce. We're looking to diversify, to reach new audiences: punk, folk, metal, musical theater." She listed a few more genres they hadn't completely destroyed yet.

I would punch her soon. I was not a violent person, but I knew for a fact I would punch her soon. "You're standing in front of me, asking me to help ruin my livelihood."

"No! Not ruin it. I'm inviting you to a better life. You'd still play shows. You'd still have audiences."

"Audiences of extras paid to be there? Audiences in your studios?" I asked through clenched teeth.

"Yes and no. We can set up at your shows, but that's harder. Not a problem in an arena setting, but I think you'd find the 3D array distracting in a place like this. We'd book you some theaters, arenas. Fill in the crowds if we needed to. You could still do this in between if you wanted, but . . ." She shrugged to indicate she couldn't see why I would want.

"Hey, Luce. A little help over here?" I looked down to see my hands throttling my mic instead of putting it back in its box. Looked up at Silva struggling to get his bass amp on the dolly, like he didn't do it on his own every night of the week. Clearly an offer of rescue.

"Gotta go," I said to the devil's A & R person. "Have your people call my people."

Turning the bass rig into a two-person job took all of our acting skills. We walked to the door in exaggerated slow motion. Lifting it into the van genuinely did take two, but usually my back and knee ruled me out. I gritted my teeth and hoisted.

"What was that about?" Silva asked, shutting Daisy's back hatch and leaning against it. "You looked like you were going to tear that woman's throat out with your teeth."

"StageHolo! Can you believe the nerve? Coming here, trying to lure us to the dark side?"

"The nerve," he echoed, shaking his head, but giving me a funny look. He swiped an arm across his sweaty forehead, then pushed off from the van.

I followed him back inside. Nikki Kellerman was still there.

"Luce, I think you're not seeing everything I have to offer."

"Haven't you left yet? That was a pretty broad hint."

"Look around." She gestured at the near-empty room.

I stared straight at her. I wasn't dignifying her with any response.

"Luce, I know you had a good crowd tonight, but are there people who aren't showing up anymore? Look where you are. Public transit doesn't run into this neighborhood anymore. You're playing for people who squat in warehouses within a few blocks, and then people who can afford bikes or Chauffeurs."

"Most people can scrounge a bicycle," I said. "I've never heard a complaint about that."

"You're playing for the people who can bike, then. That bassist from the first band, could she have gotten here without a car?"

For the first time, I felt like she was saying something worth hearing. I sat down on my amp.

"You're playing for this little subset of city punks for whom this is a calling. And after that you're playing for the handful of people who can afford a night out and still think of themselves as revolutionary. And that's fine. That's a noble thing. But what about everybody else? Parents who can't afford a sitter? Teens who are too young to make it here on their own, or who don't have a way into the city? There are plenty of people who love music and deserve to hear your message. They just aren't fortunate enough to live where you're playing. Wouldn't you like to reach them too?"

Dammit, dammit, dammit, she had a decent point. I thought about the guy who had paid for our drinks the night before, and the church-van guy from outside the Chinese restaurant, and Truly if she didn't have a sister with a car.

She touched her own back. "I've seen you after a few shows now, too. You're amazing when you play, but when you step off, I can see what it takes. You're tired. What happens if you get sick, or if your back goes out completely?"

"I've always gotten by," I said, but not with the same vehemence as a minute before.

"I'm just saying you don't have to get by. You can still do these shows, but you won't have to do as many. Let us help you out. I can get you a massage therapist or a chiropractor or a self-driving van."

I started to protest, but she held up her hands in a placating gesture. "Sorry—I know you've said you love your van. No offense meant. I'm not chasing you because my boss wants me to. I'm chasing you because I've seen you play. You make great music. You reach people. That's what we want."

She put her card on the amp next to me, and walked out the front of the club. I watched her go.

"Hey, Luce," Jacky called to me. I headed his way, slowly. My back had renewed its protest.

"What's up?" I asked.

He gestured at the bike kids surrounding him, Emma and Rudy and some more whose names I had forgotten. Marina? Marin. I smiled. I should have spent more time with them, since they were the ones who had brought us in.

"Our generous hosts have offered us a place to stay nearby. I said I thought it was a good idea, but you're the boss."

They all looked at me, waiting. I hadn't seen the money from the night yet. It would probably be pretty good, since this kind of place didn't take a cut for themselves. They were in it for the music. And for the chance to spend some time with us, which I was in a position to provide.

"That sounds great," I said. "Anything is better than another night in the van." We might be able to afford a hotel, or save the hotel splurge for the next night, in—I mentally checked the roadmap—Pittsburgh.

With the bike kids' help, we made quick work of the remaining gear. Waited a little longer while Rudy counted money and handed it over to me with no small amount of pride.

"Thank you," I said, and meant it. It had been a really good show, and the money was actually better than expected. "We'll come back here anytime."

Just to prove it, I pulled my date book from my backpack. He called Emma over, and together we penned in a return engagement in three months. I was glad to work with people so competent; there was a good chance they'd still be there in three months.

We ended up at a diner, van parked in front, bikes chained to the fence behind it, an unruly herd.

I was so tired the menu didn't look like English; then I realized I was looking at the Spanish side.

"Is there a fridge at the place we're staying?" Silva asked.

Smart guy. Emma nodded. Silva and Jacky and I immediately ordered variations on an omelet theme, without looking further at either side of the menu. The beauty of omelets: you ate all the toast and potatoes, wrapped the rest, and the eggs would still taste fine the next day. Two meals in one, maybe three, and we hadn't had to hit a dumpster in two full days.

Our hosts were a riot. I barely kept my eyes open—at least twice I realized they weren't—but Emma talked about Columbus politics and bikes and greenspaces with a combination of humor and enthusiasm that made me glad for the millionth time for the kind of places we played, even if I didn't quite keep up my end of the conversation. Nikki Kellerman could flush herself down the toilet. I wouldn't trade these kids for anything.

Until we saw the place on offer. After the lovely meal, after following their bikes at bike speed through unknown and unknowable dark neighborhoods, Silva pulled the van up. The last portion had involved turning off the road along two long ruts in grass grown over a paved drive. I had tried to follow in my atlas on the city inset, but gave up when the streets didn't match.

"Dude," I said, opening my eyes. "What is that?"

We all stared upward. At first glance it looked like an enormous brick plantation house, with peeling white pillars supporting the upper floors. At second, maybe some kind of factory.

"Old barracks," said Jacky, king of local tourist sites. "Those kids got themselves an abandoned fort."

"I wonder if it came with contents included." Silva mimed loading a rifle. "Bike or die."

I laughed.

Jacky leaned into the front seat. "If you tell me I have to haul in my entire kit, I swear to God I'm quitting this band. I'll join the bike militia. Swear to God."

I peered out the windows, but had no sense of location. "Silva?"

"I can sleep in the van if you think I should."

It was a generous offer, given that actual beds were in the cards.

"You don't have to do that," I decided. "We'll take our chances."

I stopped at the back gate for my guitar, in the hopes of having a few minutes to play in the morning. Silva did the same. We shouldered instruments and backpacks, and Jacky took the three Styrofoam boxes with our omelets. The bike kids waited in a cluster by an enormous door. We staggered their way.

"So who has the keys?" Silva asked.

Emma grinned. "Walk this way."

The big door was only for dramatic effect. We went in through a small, unlocked door on the side. It looked haphazardly placed, a late addition to the architecture. A generator hummed just outside the door, powering a refrigerator, where we left our leftovers. I hoped it also powered overhead lights, but the bike kids all drew out halogen flashlights as soon as we had stored the food.

The shadows made everything look ominous and decrepit; I wasn't sure it wouldn't look the same in daylight. Up a crumbling staircase, then a second, to a smaller third floor. Walls on one side, railing on the other, looking down over a central core, all black. Our footsteps echoed through the emptiness. In my tired state, I imagined being told to bed down in the hallway, sleeping with my head pressed to the floor. If they didn't stop soon, I might.

We didn't have to go farther. Emma swung open an unmarked door and handed me her flashlight. I panned it over the room. A breeze wafted through broken glass. An open futon took up most of the space, a threadbare couch sagging beneath the window. How those things had made it up to this room without the stairs falling away entirely was a mystery, but I had never been so happy to see furniture in my entire life.

I dropped my shoulder and lowered my guitar to the floor. The bike kids stared at us and we stared back. Oh God, I thought. If they want to hang out more, I'm going to cry.

"This is fantastic," said Silva, the diplomat. "Thank you so much. This is so much better than sleeping in the van."

"Sweet. Hasta mañana!" said Rudy, his spiky head bobbing. They backed out the door, closing it behind them, and creaked off down the hallway.

I sank into the couch. "I'm not moving again," I said.

"Did they say whether they're renting or squatting? Is anybody else getting a jail vibe?" Jacky asked, flopping back onto the futon.

Silva opened the door. "We're not locked in." He looked out into the hallway and then turned back to us. "But, uh, they're gone without a trace. Did either of you catch where the bathroom was?"

I shook my head, or I think I did. They were on their own.

The night wasn't a pleasant one. I woke once to the sound of Silva pissing in a bottle, once to a sound like animals scratching at the door, once to realize there was a spring sticking through the couch and into my thigh. The fourth time, near eight in the morning, I found myself staring at the ceiling at a crack that looked like a rabbit. I turned my head and noticed a cat pan under the futon. Maybe it explained the scratching I had heard earlier.

I rolled over and stood up one vertebra at a time. Other than the spring, it hadn't been a bad couch. My back felt better than the night before. I grabbed my guitar and slipped out the door.

I tried to keep my steps from echoing. With the first daylight streaming in through the jagged windows, I saw exactly how dilapidated the place was, like it had been left to go feral. I crept down to the first floor, past a mural that looked like a battle plan for world domination, all circles and arrows, and another of two bikes in carnal embrace. Three locked doors, then I spotted the fridge and the door out. Beyond this huge building there were several others of similar size, spread across a green campus. Were they all filled with bike kids? It was a pleasant thought. I'd never seen any place like this. I sat down on the ground, my back against the building, in the morning sunshine.

It was nice to be alone with my guitar. The problem with touring constantly was we were always driving, always with people, always playing the same songs we already knew. And when we did have downtime, we'd spend it tracking down new gigs, or following up to make sure the next places still existed. The important things like writing new songs fell to last on the list.

This guitar and I, we were old friends. The varnish above her pick guard had worn away where I hit it on the downstroke. Tiny grooves marked where my fingers had indented the frets. She fit my hands perfectly. We never talked anymore.

She was an old Les Paul knockoff, silver cloudburst except where the bare wood showed through. Heavy as anything, the reason why my back hurt so constantly. The hunch of my shoulder as I bent over her was permanent. And of course with no amp she didn't make any sound beyond string jangle. Still, she felt good.

I didn't need to play the songs we played every night, but my fingers have always insisted on playing through the familiar before they can find new patterns. I played some old stuff, songs I loved when I was first teaching myself to play, Frightwig and the Kathleen Battle School and disappear fear, just to play something I could really feel. Then a couple of bars of "She's the One," then what I remembered of a Moby K. Dick whale song. I liked those kids.

When I finally hit my brain's unlock code, it latched on to a twisty little minor descent. The same rhythm as the whale song, but a different progression, a different riff. A tiny theft, the kind all musicians make. There was only so much original to do within twelve notes. Hell, most classic punk was built on a couple of chords. What did Lou Reed say? One chord is fine, two chords is pushing it, three chords you're into jazz?

I knew what I was singing about before I even sang it. That Stage-Holo offer, and the idea of playing for a paid audience night after night, the good and the bad parts. The funny thing about bargains with the devil was you so rarely heard about people turning him down; maybe sometimes it was worth your soul. I scrambled in my gig-bag pocket for a pen and paper. When I came up with only a sharpie, I wrote the lyrics on my arm. The chords would keep. I'd remember them. Would probably remember the lyrics too, but I wasn't chancing it.

Silva stepped out a little while later, wearing only a ratty towel around his waist. "There's a bucket shower out the back!"

"Show me in a sec, but first, check it out." I played him what I had. His eyes widened. "Be right back."

He returned a moment later wearing jeans, bass in hand. We both had to play hard, and I had to whisper-sing to hear the unplugged electric instruments, but we had something we both liked before long.

"Tonight?" he asked me.

"Maybe . . . Depends on how early we get there, I guess. And whether there's an actual soundcheck. Do you remember?"

He shook his head. "Four-band lineup, at a warehouse. That's all I remember. But maybe if we leave pretty soon, we can set up early? It's only about three hours, I think."

He showed me where the shower was, and I took advantage of the opportunity. The bike kids appeared with a bag of lumpy apples, and we ate the apples with our omelets, sitting on the floor. Best breakfast in ages. They explained the barracks—the story involved an arts grant and an old school and abandoned buildings and a cat sanctuary, and I got lost somewhere along the way, working on my new song in my head.

After breakfast, we made our excuse that we had to get on the road. They walked us back the way we came, around the front.

My smile lasted as long as it took us to round the corner. As long as it took to see Daisy was gone.

"Did you move her, Jacky?" Silva asked.

"You've got the keys, man."

Silva patted his pockets, and came up with the key. We walked closer. Glass.

I stared at the spot, trying to will Daisy back into place. Blink and she'd be back. How had we let this happen? I went through the night in my head. Had I heard glass breaking, or the engine turning over? I didn't think so. How many times had we left her outside while we played or ate or showered or slept? I lay down on the path, away from the glass, and looked up at the morning sky.

The bike kids looked distraught, all talking at once. "This kind of thing never happens." "We were only trying to help."

"It wasn't your fault," I said, after a minute. Then louder, when they didn't stop. "It wasn't your fault." They closed their mouths and looked at me.

I sat up and continued, leaning back on my hands, trying to be the calm one, the adult. "The bad news is we're going to need to call the police. The good news is you're not squatting, so we don't have to work too hard to explain what we were doing here. The bad news is whoever stole the van can go really far on that tank. The good news is they're probably local and aren't trying to drive to Florida. Probably just kids who've never gotten to drive something that didn't drive itself. They'll abandon her nearby when she runs out of gas." I was trying to make myself feel better as much as them.

"And maybe they hate Chinese food," Jacky said. "Maybe the smell'll make them so hungry they have to stop for Chinese food. We should try all the local Chinese food places first."

Silva had stepped away from the group, already on the phone with the police. I heard snippets, even though his back was turned. License plate. Yes, a van. Yes, out-of-state plates. No, he didn't own it, but the owner was with him. Yes, we'd wait. Where else did we have to go? Well, Pittsburgh, but it didn't look like we'd be getting there anytime soon.

He hung up and dug his hands into his pockets. He didn't turn around or come back to the group. I should probably have gone over to him, but he didn't look like he wanted to talk.

The kids scattered before the police arrived, all but Emma disappearing into the building. Jacky walked off somewhere as well. It occurred to me I didn't really know much of his history, for all the time we'd been riding together.

The young policewoman who arrived to take our report was standoffish at first, like we were the criminals. Emma explained the situation. No officer, not squatting, here are the permits. I kept the van registration and insurance in a folder in my backpack, which helped on that end too, so that she came over to our side a little. Just a little.

"Insurance?"

"Of course." I rustled in the same folder, presented the card to her. She looked surprised, and I realized she had expected something electronic. "But only liability and human driver."

Surprised her again. "So the van isn't self-driving?"

"No, ma'am. I've had her—it—for twenty-three years."

"But you didn't convert when the government rebates were offered?"

"No, ma'am. I love driving."

She gave me a funny look.

"Was anything in the van?" she asked.

I sighed and started the list, moving from back to front.

"One drum kit, kind of a hodgepodge of different makes, Ampeg bass rig, Marshall guitar amp, suitcase full of gig clothes. A sleeping bag. A box of novels, maybe fifty of them. Um, all the merchandise: records and T-shirts and stuff to sell . . ." I kept going through all the detritus in my head, discarding the small things: collapsible chopsticks, restaurant menus, pillows, jackets. Those were all replaceable. My thoughts snagged on one thing.

"A road atlas. Rand McNally."

The officer raised her eyebrows. "A what?"

"A road atlas. A book of maps."

"You want me to list that?"

"Well, it's in there. And it's important, to me anyway. It's annotated. All the places we've played, all the places we like to stop and we don't." I tried to hide the hitch in my voice. Don't cry, I told myself. Cry over the van, if you need to. Not over the atlas. You'll make another. It might take years, but it could be done.

It wasn't just the atlas, obviously. Everything we had hadn't been much, and it was suddenly much less. I was down to the cash in my pocket, the date book, the single change of clothes in my backpack, my guitar. How could we possibly rebuild from there? How do you finish a tour without a van? Or amps, or drums?

The officer held out her phone to tap a copy of her report over to me.

"Non-comm," I said. "I'm so sorry."

Silva stepped in for the first time. He hadn't even opened his mouth to help me list stuff, but now he held up his phone. "Send it to me, officer."

She did, with a promise to follow up as soon as she had any leads. Got in her squad car. She had to actually use the wheel and drive herself back down the rutted path; I guessed places like this were why police cars had a manual option. She had probably written us off already, either way.

I turned to Silva, but he had walked off. I followed him down the path toward an old warehouse.

"Stop!" I said, when it was clear he wasn't going to. He turned toward me. I expected him to be as sad as me, but he looked angrier than I had ever seen him, fists clenched and jaw tight.

"Whoa," I said. "Calm down. It'll be okay. We'll figure something out."

"How? How, Luce?"

"They'll find Daisy. Or we'll figure something out."

"Daisy's just the start of it. It's amps and records and T-shirts and everything we own. I don't even have another pair of underwear. Do you?"

I shook my head. "We can buy—"

"We can buy underwear at the Superwally. But not all that other stuff. We can't afford it. This is it. We're done. Unless."

"Unless?"

He unclenched his left fist and held out a scrap of paper. I took it from him and flattened it. Nikki Kellerman's business card, which had been on my amp when I last saw it.

"No," I said.

"Hear me out. We have nothing left. Nothing. You know she'd hook us up if we called now and said we'd sign. We'd get it all back. New amps, new merch, new stage clothes. And we wouldn't need a new van if we were doing holo shows. We could take a break for a while."

"Are you serious? You'd stay in one place and do holo shows?" I waited for an answer. He stomped at a piece of glass in the dirt, grinding it with his boot heel. "We've been playing together for twenty years, and I wouldn't have guessed you'd ever say yes to that."

"Come off it, Luce. You know I don't object the way you do. You know that, or you'd have run it past me before turning her down. I know we're not a democracy, but you used to give me at least the illusion I had a choice."

I bit my lip. "You're right. I didn't run it past you. And actually, I didn't turn her down in the end. I didn't say yes, but she said some stuff that confused me."

That stopped him short. Neither of us said anything for a minute. I looked around. What a weird place to be having this fight; I always figured it would come, but in the van. I waited for a response, and when none came, I prodded. "So you're saying that's what you want?"

"No! Maybe. I don't know. It doesn't always seem like the worst idea. But now I don't think we have another option. I think I could have kept going the way we were for a while longer, but rebuilding from scratch?" He shook his head, then turned and walked away again. I didn't follow this time.

Back at the building where we had stayed, the bike kids had reappeared, murmuring amongst themselves. Jacky leaned against the front stoop, a few feet from them. I sat down in the grass opposite my drummer.

"What do you think of StageHolo? I mean really?"

He spit on the ground.

"Me too," I agreed. "But given the choice between starting over with nothing, and letting them rebuild us, what would you do? If there weren't any other options."

He ran a hand over his braids. "If there weren't any other options?"

I nodded.

"There are always other options, Luce. I didn't sign up with you to do fake shows in some fake warehouse for fake audiences. I wouldn't stay. And you wouldn't last."

I pulled a handful of grass and tossed it at him.

He repeated himself. "Really. I don't know what you'd do. You wouldn't be you anymore. You'd probably still come across to some people, but you'd have the wrong kind of anger. Anger for yourself, instead of for everybody. You'd be some hologram version of yourself. No substance."

I stared at him.

"People always underestimate the drummer, but I get to sit behind you and watch you every night. Trust me." He laughed, then looked over my shoulder. "I watch you, too, Silva. It goes for you, too."

I didn't know how long Silva had been behind me, but he sat down between us now, grunting as he lowered himself to the ground. He leaned against Jacky and put his grimy glass-dust boots in my lap.

I shoved them off. "That was an old man grunt."

"I'm getting there, old lady, but you'll get there first. Do you have a plan?"

I looked over where the bike kids had congregated. "Hey, guys! Do any of you have a car? Or, you know, know anybody who has a car?"

The bike kids looked horrified, then one—Dijuan?—nodded. "My sister has a Chauffeur."

"Family sized?"

Dijuan's face fell.

Back to the drawing board. Leaning back on my elbows, I thought about all the other bands we could maybe call on, if I knew anybody who had come off the road, who might have a van to sell if Daisy didn't reappear. Maybe, but nobody close enough to loan one tonight. Except . . .

"You're not saying you're out, right?" I asked Silva. "You're not saying StageHolo or nothing? 'Cause I really can't do it. Maybe someday, on our terms, but I can't do it yet."

He closed his eyes. "I know you can't. But I don't know what else to do."

"I do. At least for tonight."

I told him who to call.

Truly arrived with her sister's family-sized Chauffeur an hour later. We had to meet her up on the road.

"It'll be a tight squeeze, but we'll get there," she said. The third row and all the foot space was packed tight with the Moby K. Dick amps and drums and cables.

"Thank you so much," I said, climbing into what would be the driver's seat if it had a wheel or pedals. It felt strange, but oddly freeing as the car navigated its way from wherever we were toward where we were going.

I was supposed to be upset. But we had a ride to the gig, and gear to play. We'd survive without merch for the time being. Somebody in Pittsburgh would help us find a way to Baltimore if Daisy hadn't been found by then, or back to Columbus to reclaim her.

With enough time to arrange it, the other bands would let us use their drums and amps at most of the shows we had coming up, and in the meantime we still had our guitars and a little bit of cash. We'd roll on, in Daisy or a Chauffeur, or on bikes with guitars strapped to our backs. No StageHolo gig could end this badly; this was the epic, terrible, relentlessness of life on the road. We made music. We were music. We'd roll on. We'd roll on. We'd roll on.

— *The Narwhal* —

One week after she was hired for what had to be her best Oddjobz gig yet, a whale arrived at Lynette's door.

So many things could go wrong answering Oddjobz ads. Lynette had taken enough sketchy jobs that she'd learned how to protect herself. She arranged to meet Dahlia at a crowded hipster coffee shop, with her best friend, Paula, hiding in plain sight in case the stranger turned out unbearably creepy. Paula enjoyed the subterfuge, positioning herself spy-thriller style behind the *Baltimore Sun*, front-page headline blaring STUPENDOUS SUPERS SAVE NEW YORK AGAIN. She'd bought an actual print newspaper just for the purpose.

Dahlia had not set off any alarm bells. She arrived looking friendly and sad, fitting for the circumstances, a fiftyish white woman with an air of freelance life coach/yoga instructor. She had laid out her plan to drive her recently deceased mother's car to her home in Sacramento, talking up the route highlights, which were the main selling points for Lynette, and the eight days they'd have to make the drive. She'd pay for a hotel room for Lynette every night. When Lynette accepted the gig, Dahlia bought the one-way air ticket from Sacramento back to Baltimore on the spot, to prove she was serious.

A week later, at 9 AM sharp, Dahlia texted from the street:
Outside
Not leaving car

Surrounded by children
Time to go

Lynette opened her front door to a double-parked whale. The neighborhood kids had been drawn across the street from the playground, but they weren't surrounding it so much as clumping a few feet in front, staring. Who wouldn't stare? She took a moment herself.

The whale's blue-silver body looked like fiberglass. It seemed to have been built on a station wagon's chassis, the tail arcing up off the wide back end. The only art cars she'd seen, at festivals and fairs, had looked like they were happier standing still than moving; this one looked ready to dive into the road. One painted eye gazed back at her beatifically from above the passenger window.

"You riding in that, Miss Lynette?" asked Case, her neighbor's oldest, inching closer. He wore a T-shirt emblazoned with a photo of Astounding Man's perfect face, and his slogan, "Another day, another city saved."

"I guess I am," she said, trying to sound casual, then abandoning that idea. "All the way across the country."

The kids looked suitably impressed.

The interior resembled a station-wagon interior; she'd half been expecting a ribcage. She tossed her bags into the backseat beside Dahlia's bags and boxes, then slid into the front passenger seat. The dashboard had the usual buttons and dials and levers you'd expect someone's mother's station wagon to have, and then a whole bunch of mystery buttons.

"If you don't know what it is, don't touch it," Dahlia said. "I have no clue what any of these do."

Lynette was about to protest that she wasn't going to touch anything, but then decided not to start a long drive on the defensive. "I've always liked whales," she said instead. "You didn't say the car was a whale. This is awesome."

"We should get moving. We've got a tight schedule to keep if I'm going to be back at work on Tuesday."

Lynette didn't know how to respond to that either, so she stayed silent as Dahlia pulled away from the curb. The kids followed. Their wonder reminded Lynette of when the circus used to parade their animals down Lombard from the arena to the train yards on their way out of Baltimore. She and her friends would be playing on the stoop and suddenly an elephant would come into view. It had always been unexpected and magical. The circus didn't come anymore.

Like her, none of these kids had ever been anywhere. The farthest she'd ever travelled was to DC, on one class trip to the Capitol. On that trip, she'd bought a commemorative coin which she still kept in her pocket: a lucky charm and a promise to herself that she'd someday be the kind of person who collected spoons or coins or magnets to show all the great places she'd been.

People in movies were always heading out on epic road trips, but they seemed to have more money and time than she did, not to mention cars. This whole trip, with its benefactor, its employment factor, was as much of a miracle as a whale appearing at her door or an elephant walking west on Lombard.

The junkie teenagers panhandling on the corner of MLK missed a whole light cycle watching them idle at the red. As the whale merged onto the highway, other cars honked and waved. A strange celebrity; it would get old if cars honked at them for three thousand miles, but for a little while it would be fun.

"Does this always happen?" she asked.

Dahlia looked over, giving her full attention to Lynette, even as the whale plunged forward. "No clue. This is the first time I've ever driven this thing."

"Oh! You said it was your mother's. I figured you grew up with it."

Dahlia laughed. "It's a funny picture, isn't it? My mother running her errands in this? I don't know if I would've been proud or mortified."

Watch the road, please, Lynette didn't say.

"As far as I knew, she drove a maroon Camry, but she left that to charity. This is the one thing she left me in her will. She said 'I don't have money and you don't need money, so I thought I'd give you the only thing I ever made that mattered.' I figured I'd take it home with me and then figure out why she gave it to me and what to do with it. I had to trek halfway to Delaware to find the garage where she kept it, too. It might be our old family station wagon underneath but I'm not sure."

Dahlia returned her attention to the road, and Lynette made a mental note not to ask any more questions unless they reached a straightaway. She busied herself downloading an app that showed all the tourist highlights along the route, setting up notifications for everything she hoped to see.

Ten miles before they reached the spot where her app told her the Appalachian Trail footbridge crossed over the highway, Lynette asked Dahlia if they could pull over to take a picture with the marker.

"It's just a sign." Dahlia picked a hair off her sweater, lowered her window a few inches, and flicked it out.

"But a cool sign! I've always wanted to hike the Appalachian Trail," Lynette said. "People walk it, and it's almost as far as we're going to be driving, and even the drive takes a week. I'd love to document that I made it this far. Twenty seconds. That's all."

Dahlia again shifted her entire body around in the driver's seat to address Lynette. "I'd really rather not stop this early since I don't want to drive this car after dark. I have no idea how well it's been maintained, and I don't feel like getting stranded. Let's just get to Ohio today. Then we can talk about places to stop."

I-70 banked and climbed, and the car juddered as two wheels met the shoulder. Lynette, watching the road from the passenger seat while the driver watched her, gave up.

"Sorry. Never mind." She tried to take a picture with her phone as they passed, but it came out blurry.

In that moment, Lynette started thinking of Dahlia as "Boss" instead of her name, to remind herself that this woman was paying her to help with the drive, not sightsee. Lynette didn't have a vote. They weren't friends. Maybe Dahlia'd be less tense once they were farther along.

But, no. Even when Lynette drove, the Boss's schedule ruled. She knew exactly where and when she wanted to stop for meals and sleep. She left a little leeway for bathrooms, but not much. Over the next two days, they zoomed past Fallingwater, a giant coffee pot, the John & Annie Glenn house, and dozens of assorted parks and museums. Lynette spotted Vandalia's water tower from the highway, but not the Kaskaskia Dragon somewhere below it, waiting for her to drop a coin in the slot and make it breathe fire.

On the first night, at a roadside motel in Ohio, eating takeout burger and fries on her bed, Lynette had still held out a little hope. She'd taken tourist brochures from the lobby and spread them in front of her, mapping them on her phone as she ate. Nothing within walking distance. The Boss would never let her use the car to go sightseeing, and no place would be open by nightfall in any case.

Anything Lynette wanted to see, she had to see through the car window. Maybe it had been her own fault for assuming "see the country" meant "stop along the way through the country" and not to watch it all stream by the windows. Maybe it was her fault for not questioning why someone wouldn't have a friend willing to make the journey with her. She knew all the things she'd clarify if she were ever offered this opportunity again.

"There's got to be something you want to stop for," Lynette said as they passed signs for the Model T Museum. She was behind the wheel, but she knew better than to pull over. "A waterfall. A tourist trap. The Grand Canyon."

"A big hole in the ground."

"Something else, then?"

"It's not a tourist thing."

"What, then?" This was the first time Dahlia had mentioned interest in anything at all. Lynette tried not to get her hopes up again.

Dahlia pulled a photo out of her purse, then replaced it before Lynette could see it. "This was in my mother's top drawer. It says 'Baleful' on the back, and I found a town called 'Baleful' along this highway. I wanted to drive through and see if the movie theater in the picture is actually there."

"Drive through? You don't even want to stop?"

"If we're on schedule, we'll reach there halfway through the day. It'll be too early to stop."

Of course.

At least driving the whale was fun. It was bigger and heavier than anything she'd driven before, like it wanted you to feel like you had earned that lane change, and the dorsal fin and tail caught wind, creating a rudder effect. It would be hell to park in a city, but out on the road it just took muscle and spatial awareness.

She liked driving; the rest frustrated her. The tight timeline, the rigidity. The only small rebellion Lynette found was in pressing random buttons and turning mystery dials. Dahlia had made it clear that neither of them should touch anything before they knew what it did, but Lynette found it easy enough to reach for the radio and knock something else instead. She tried to figure out some of the extra features before she tried them; the puzzle killed time. The one with a pig icon opened a panel of ham radio controls, though she didn't get enough time with them to see how to use them before Dahlia made her close the panel again. The redundant defrost icon on the arm console activated a radar jammer.

"Aren't those totally illegal?"

"Maybe you shouldn't turn it on, then."

She always apologized immediately after; by now Dahlia probably thought she was completely incompetent, pawing at random buttons instead of asking for what she needed. She took comfort in that deception.

"Would you be more careful?" Dahlia asked after she flipped a switch that made the entire car squeal like an abused megaphone, spooking the horses in the adjacent field.

Lynette tried to change the subject. "Did your mother do all this herself?"

"I have no idea. I told you, I didn't even know this car existed. I wouldn't have said she was the kind of person to drive a whale around town, and I wouldn't have said she was the kind of person to modify a car with secret buttons to deafen the passengers. She had an engineering degree, so I guess she could have done it? She always said it was impossible for a woman to get an engineering job back then, so she engineered me instead. She was just a normal mother. We didn't get along well—she always pushed me to do more with my life—'If you're going to be a lawyer, can't you at least be a lawyer for good, not evil?'—but a car like this doesn't fit at all. I guess she had a secret artistic side."

"Are you an evil lawyer?"

"Not from my perspective," Dahlia said, without elaborating or inviting follow-up. At least that explained how she had the money to pay Lynette and fly her home.

"What do you do, Lynette?"

"This."

"You drive? Like a ride share?"

"No, you need a car to do that," Lynette said. "I do Oddjobz."

"That's enough to make a living?"

"It's enough for me to cover my bills and pay my parents some rent. I'm still trying to figure out what I want to do." She tried not to get defensive.

"You're what, twenty-three? You've got time to figure it out."

Definitely time to change the subject. "Can we stop for dinner soon?"

The Boss sighed. "I'd like to get a little farther west first. Granola bar to tide you over?"

Lynette reached for her fast-emptying snack bag. After this trip, she planned never to eat another granola bar again.

As the Boss opened and closed her window for the two-hundred-and-twenty-first time, Lynette looked around for a button that would blow out the window once and for all. Sure, they'd be stuck with highway noise and wind for another fifteen hundred miles, but at least Lynette's ears would stop popping.

She thought she'd been a gracious companion. She listened to music in earbuds. She tolerated the relentless schedule, the ridiculous refusal to take any joy from the trip. Still, it was hard to keep all the little irritations from magnifying.

"Why do you do keep opening and closing the window?"

"I don't," said the Boss, turning her attention away from the road. She did that a lot too, turning her whole attention to Lynette whenever either of them spoke, no matter the traffic or the road condition, so that Lynette had mostly stopped talking altogether. She'd picked a two-lane straightaway to ask, no cars ahead or behind, but she still dug her nails into her seat and watched the road, as if she'd have any control in the passenger seat.

"Never mind. I must've imagined it."

No point in arguing. How do you convince someone they are doing something when it's clearly so habitual they don't even know they're doing it? You don't. You mind your own business, concentrate on the road or the view, and maybe, maybe, you start keeping track on your phone, sending text updates to your best friend, fifteen hundred miles of open-close behind. The return text, which Lynette casually shielded from Dahlia's wandering gaze, read "OMG how can you stand it?" followed by a silent scream GIF.

The window opened and closed again. Lynette felt an unbearable need to do something. She reached over and jabbed at a button they hadn't hit before. It lit up.

The whale surged forward.

"What did you do?"

"I don't know." Lynette hit the button again, but the light didn't turn off.

Dahlia gave her a panicked look. "The pedals aren't responding."

The speedometer edged up to eighty. Ninety. They approached a semi, and Lynette braced for impact, but the whale swerved around it.

"I didn't do that! The car did. What the hell did you press?"

Lynette looked at the button. "It's a flower."

"I told you not to press anything. Shit."

"Can you pull the emergency brake?"

"Not at ninety miles an hour."

"Call the cops? So that if they clock us they know we're having technical difficulties?"

"Officers, please come catch me speeding . . ."

"Runaway-truck ramp?"

"Those are only in the mountains."

They both sat silently for a minute. Lynette resisted the overwhelming urge to apologize. If Dahlia hadn't been so annoying, she wouldn't have hit the flowery button of doom. "At least we'll make good time?"

"This isn't funny."

Lynette kind of thought it was funny, as long as they didn't die: the car was even more deadline oriented than the Boss. She reached into her pocket and wrapped her fingers around her lucky coin.

The miles ticked away. After a while, Dahlia started fiddling with her phone. Lynette wondered what would happen if they passed a cop while the driver checked her phone with no hands steering. She pictured a chase, cops lobbing harpoons out their windows, tossing nets at them, shouting, "Thar she blows." She had to admit she felt safer than when Dahlia was in control and took her attention off the road.

"It's got to stop soon," Dahlia said after a couple of hours. "We're running out of gas."

They didn't get to the end of the gas; at thirty miles to empty, something went wrong in the engine and the whale shuddered and slowed to a stop in the middle of the lane, all lights flashing.

"You're going to have to get out and push before we get hit," Dahlia said, putting a hand on the wheel. "I think I've got steering back again at least."

Lynette searched for her sneakers under the granola-bar-wrapper sea that surrounded her ankles. When she got out, there was another surprise.

"Ah, Boss—Dahlia? Can you come out here a sec and tell me if this was here before?"

Dahlia flung her door open and got halfway out. "Huh."

The whale now sported a ten-foot unicorn horn, deployed from a hole in the head above the windscreen that Lynette hadn't noticed before. "I guess it's a whadayacallit. A narwhal, not a whale. I'm not sure it would be legal to drive a car with a spear sticking out the front. It's kind of *Mad Max*-y."

"A narwhal is a whale too, and I think that's the least of our concerns. Push. We'll deal with that when we can drive it again." Dahlia shook her head and ducked back into the car.

It took Lynette a few tries to find a good place to push from, since she couldn't get purchase on the smooth body or the tail, but they eventually managed to guide the narwhal off the road.

Dahlia fished under the dashboard until she found a latch for the hood, which unhinged the whale's jaw. Lynette hung back; she didn't really know cars. She was a good driver—the only reference the Boss had actually asked for was a copy of her clean driving record—but she had no idea how to change a tire, and while she could find the oil dipstick, she didn't know what you looked for when you took it out and stared at it. Not to mention, who knew what lurked under a narwhal's hood. Krill, maybe.

"Dammit," the Boss said from the vicinity of the engine. "Some belt's shredded."

"Hmmm. Do you want me to look online to see what to do?"

"No. I. Dammit. Dammit. I need to call a tow truck."

She slammed the hood shut. She looked genuinely distraught as she dialed a number and marched off in the direction they'd been traveling. Lynette wondered whether Dahlia would keep walking in her determination to stay on schedule. Let Lynette and the car catch up when they were ready to do their part again.

She returned, frowning. "They said they couldn't send anybody all the way out here for a few hours. I offered two hundred dollars to put us next in line and they said they'd see, but it'll be forty minutes at least. Honestly."

Lynette tried to imagine what it would be like to have enough money to drop two hundred dollars that casually, or to offer that money before knowing how much the car repair would cost, or to expect that money would let you automatically jump the line.

A tractor-trailer whooshed by, shaking the car and blasting them both with hot, gritty air. Lynette spit and looked around. She'd never seen an emptier place. On either side of the road was rocky, grassy plain. Ahead and behind, the same. The sun burned June-hot, directly overhead in a cloudless sky, and everything smelled like what she guessed was cow. It figured that when they finally stopped, there was nothing worth seeing.

"I'll be back in a few minutes," she said, then quickly added, "I promise I'll be back before the truck gets here. I need to pee."

She set off through the field. Five minutes, ten. The landscape was so flat, ten minutes didn't take her out of sight. From a distance, at a standstill, the car looked like a landmark rather than a vehicle. A small whale beached on the highway. Narwhal. If the truck had arrived early she would have sprinted back, since she had no doubt she'd be left behind if she made them wait. She made it back to the car with time to spare.

The driver was a Jesus man and made sure they knew it. After his initial wonder at transporting a whale, and did they know the Jonah story, and wasn't God good to have brought him to this day, he was all thank God they'd called him, thank God he'd gotten to them, thank God it was only a belt, thank God he was out with the flatbed instead of the other tow. Lynette sat in the middle, sandwiched between the driver, named Haskell, and Dahlia.

Whatever shock absorbers the truck had possessed were long gone, so Lynette folded her arms around her backpack, braced both feet against the center console, and practiced being as small as possible so her thighs wouldn't graze the thighs beside her. A large cross decorated with macaroni and spray-painted gold dangled from the rearview mirror, and it whacked her forehead every time the truck hit a bump.

Dahlia kept fiddling with her phone, scrolling west on a map, as far as Lynette could tell. After about ten minutes, she looked up. "What town did you say you're taking us to again?"

"Springfield."

"Is there a repair shop in Baleful? It looks like it's only ten miles farther west. I'd love for you to take us there instead."

"There's a shop, but it's not my shop. It's farther than your insurance pays for, too."

"I'll give you cash for the difference, and for whatever you think the repair would've cost."

"Okay. Cash. Yes, ma'am." He picked up his own phone and called a dispatcher to explain the change in plans.

Lynette watched longingly as they passed Springfield. The ride took them an endless, thigh-grazing, cross-whacking ten miles farther west, made better only by the fact that the windows were open. Thank God.

The driver took the Baleful exit north, then turned left—west again—and traveled through what was presumably the town named on the exit sign. Main Street looked abandoned except a bar and a real estate office, windows papered with property ads.

When they reached the shop, Haskell pointed them to the waiting room. Lynette went in; the Boss stayed outside to supervise the whale's lowering. The vending machine was broken, but a blue cooler beside it had "HELP YOURSELF" written in permanent marker on a piece of printer paper taped to the top, the sign itself water-stained. She fished a generic orange soda from the ice water it floated in.

There was nobody else in the waiting room, not even a receptionist. Lynette took a grape lollipop from a bowl on the desk and fanned out the magazines. Nothing looked worth reading. A brochure display stood under the desk, and she browsed those instead, selecting a couple as souvenirs. If she couldn't visit places, at least she'd have proof she'd gotten close.

The Boss came through the door from the garage, her movement so purposeful that for a moment Lynette thought she was an employee. A mechanic followed.

"A fan belt takes twenty minutes to fix," the Boss was saying.

"Yes, that's if there isn't another car ahead of you in line, which there is, and if it doesn't do any other damage when it snaps, which yours did, and if there aren't really bizarre modifications to your engine making me second-guess myself at every step, which yours has, and if we have the right one in stock, which we don't. They'll have one in Springfield, but I can't get over there again until tomorrow morning."

"Then let me borrow a car from you and I'll go get the part myself."

"Nothing here I can let you borrow."

"Rent, then?"

The mechanic shook her head. "I'll have you on your way tomorrow, if the damage isn't any worse than it looks, I promise."

The Boss scowled, then looked Lynette's way. "You see? This is why I didn't want to stop frivolously. You never know when something's needlessly going to make you lose an entire day."

She seemed to have forgotten they'd just travelled two hundred miles as prisoners of a speeding automated whale. Lynette and the mechanic exchanged a look.

The Boss pulled out her phone and jabbed at it for a minute. The mechanic pulled a buzzing phone from her own pocket. "You're on Oddjobz, too, huh? I don't think anyone else is going to take you up on this. I'm the only one in town who claims parts runs. How about you check into the motel down the road and kick back for a night?"

The Boss looked so distraught, Lynette felt momentary sympathy. "We're ahead of your schedule, Dahlia, and you'd wanted to check this town out in any case. I'm sure the garage will look out for your car, right?"

The mechanic gave another grateful look. "Of course. I'll even lock the gate out front tonight so nobody messes with it. We'll take good care, I promise."

The Boss exhaled. "Okay. Okay."

Both women took their overnight bags from the car. The Boss shouted back over her shoulder as they reached the sidewalk. "If you don't know what it does, don't touch it."

"You'll see her tomorrow," the mechanic responded from the far bay.

Lynette followed Dahlia, who set off as if she knew exactly where she was going. West, of course. Always west. Immediately past the garage, a thrift store and a small discount grocery shared a parking lot. The sidewalk was cracked, with grass invading the spaces between buckled slabs of concrete. Beyond the stores, the sidewalk ended abruptly, leaving them walking the shoulder.

A grassed-over parking lot followed, and beyond it a long chain-link fence surrounding a crumbling movie theater. Not the majestic kind that people fundraised to revive; it looked bland and suburban. The beige brick façade and its flat marquee were all that remained, and whatever the name had been, the letters had been removed at some point. The left side listed THE LAST STARFIGHTER and

MATINEE: THE MUPPETS TAKE MANHATTAN, and the right side promised COMING SOON: PURPLE RAIN.

Dahlia dropped her bag and stood staring.

"Are you okay?" Lynette asked.

"The movies are still the same. The movies are still the same as in the photo." After a moment, she nodded and grabbed her bag's handle again. "I'm fine. I'm fine."

The White Diamond motel was another quarter mile down the road. One story in a U surrounding an empty pool, one car in the parking lot.

The motel lobby held two folding chairs and another brochure rack, which Lynette paged through while Dahlia attempted to negotiate down from an already reasonable nightly rate. Why did rich people always try to get better deals? She pretended not to know the other woman, taking one of every brochure, then walking out again to wait outside.

Dahlia emerged dangling two keys on diamond-shaped keychains. Lynette was relieved at the thought of her own room; she needed a break from her travelling companion. She dropped her bag inside the door and spread the brochures on her bed, hoping to find something within walking distance, since it wasn't yet too late in the day to go out, for once.

Most were too far to reach by foot, attractions she'd never be able to convince the Boss to go for when they got moving again. Scenic routes would take too long, even the kind you drove through on your way to your destination. Ditto state parks and national monuments and reptile museums. She added them to her collection, for another trip she'd take someday. She'd spend two months, she told herself. She'd stop at every historic house, every kitschy roadside attraction. Every single one.

Only one brochure offered an address in Baleful. "The Museum of the Incident." More a bookmark than a brochure, really, black ink on yellow cardstock. It didn't say what incident. Just the name and an address and the hours, 2-7 PM on Fridays. No phone number, no website.

Lynette had to look at her phone to figure out that it was, in fact, Friday; she'd lost track on the road. According to her phone, the address was a mile east, which probably put it in the deserted downtown area. She dumped her backpack's contents on the bed, repacked it with wallet, phone, and room key, and headed out the door. She was going to do one touristy thing on this trip. One, and she could say she'd been somewhere.

Dahlia sat in a deck chair by the empty pool. Her bag still lay next to her; it didn't look like she'd gone to a room at all. Lynette desperately wanted some time alone, but the slumped posture twinged her guilt.

She approached the low wire fence. "Hey, I'm going into town. Do you want to come?"

Dahlia's face was puffy. It reminded Lynette that she had only recently buried a parent. "No. I'm good, thanks. Have fun. I'll text you in the morning when the car is ready."

Lynette stopped in the grocery to buy some granola bars to replace her dwindling supply and a microwave soup she'd eat for dinner if she didn't find someplace with food.

Past the garage, where the whale rested inside the open middle bay. She fought the urge to wave to it. Past the bar and the real estate office, with signs declaring it the place to find acreage PERFECT for cattle. Then one left turn, and she found herself on a residential street. The houses stood one story tall, each with a peaked roof hinting at attic space and a truck or bald-tired sedan parked in front of an attached garage. A grain silo a few blocks away dominated the neighborhood.

The house matching the brochure address was smaller than the others, stone rather than wood, with no garage. A small tree grew in the rain gutter. It didn't look like a museum. Disappointment again; the only chance she had to see anything, and it didn't exist.

No sign marked it as a museum, but beyond the screen, the door was open.

"Hello?" Lynette called.

"Hello?" somebody repeated.

"Is this the museum?"

"Is this the museum?"

The door opened when she tried the latch, and she stepped into a tiny foyer with a coat tree and a mirror. The mirror reflected the room to the right, which showed her the response had come from a green parrot in an enormous cage. An old man slept, face up and snoring, on a couch under the front window. She rounded the corner to get a look at the room and decide what to do. Every museum she'd ever visited had a reception desk where you paid, and maps, and signs, and souvenir counters. She still wasn't sure if this was even the right place.

"Hello?" she said again, daring the parrot to repeat. It eyed her but kept quiet. "I'm here for the museum."

The parrot shrieked, and the man opened his eyes. He was younger than she'd first thought, though not by much, and his skin had the leathery look of someone who'd spent a lot of time in the sun. He levered himself to a seated position. Shaggy white hair took off in several launching trajectories around his face. "For the museum? Excellent. That'll be eight dollars. Five if you're a senior or student."

She still had her community college ID for the current year, even though she'd withdrawn before the spring semester. On the other hand, this place looked like it needed the money, and she'd spent way less than she'd expected to on the trip so far. She reached for her wallet.

"So, what's 'the incident,' anyway?" she asked, counting out a five and three ones.

He reached for her money, but cocked his head, looking a little parrotish himself. "You're here but you don't know? I think that's a first."

"My car broke down and I'm stuck here overnight. Your museum was the only attraction within walking distance of the motel."

He looked a little miffed, and she realized that could be taken badly. "I'm happy it's here," she said in all honesty.

He gestured toward the room's closed second door, labelled "Museum" on a wooden sign she hadn't noticed before. "Hit the wall switch when you go in."

The door swung closed behind her faster than she expected, leaving her in total darkness. It occurred to her she had just walked into a strange house without telling anyone where she'd gone. She groped for the wall switch.

The room came to life. A lighted diorama dominated most of the room, like a model-train set without a model train. It showed the town of Baleful, obviously. She recognized the motel and the movie theater and the garage, though the garage had a different name. The motel's pool was full of plastic water. The tiny cinema marquee offered the same tiny movie options as she'd seen today. If possible, there were even fewer cars on the roads and in the parking lots. The back of the movie theater was a bubbling crater.

She looked around the town again. Everything else looked roughly the same. Nobody was inside the discount store. Lights were on in the downtown stores and the apartments above them, too, but all the stores and streets stood empty. The detail on the buildings amazed her: tiny letters carved into the tiny post office said "Established 1903"; tiny placards in the window of the real estate office advertised acreage perfect for cattle; tiny beer logos hung inside the miniature bar. She found the museum, which looked like a small house, sans gutter-tree, and the silo she'd noticed from the road.

Back to the bizarre centerpiece, then: the shimmering hole in the movie theater, swallowing brick and plaster and screen and toppled seats. The thing emerging from the hole, a blur of teeth and eyes, made even more unsettling by the fact that Lynette couldn't make sense of it. Layered translucent shapes, filaments like cilia. She blinked to focus her eyes, but everything else remained in focus, and the shape of the thing remained obscure.

There was only one person in the whole diorama: a woman standing in front of the blurred thing, a device in her hands the relative size of an Etch-a-Sketch. Beside the woman: a narwhal-shaped car pretty much exactly like the one Lynette was driving across the country. A narwhal-shaped car that hovered above the ground, hanging from the top of the case by an almost invisible wire. A narwhal-shaped car with a red LED at horn's tip, and something coming out of it, and it occurred to Lynette that when their trip resumed, maybe she should be more careful which buttons she pushed. She stared for a long time, eventually giving up because staring didn't help anything make more sense.

Another illuminated case stood along the room's far wall. This one held newspaper clippings: TOWN EVACUATED; NONE HARMED IN CONTROLLED EXPLOSION; BALEFUL CINEMA LOT FOR SALE. That was it. None of the articles explained the bizarre diorama in the center.

A third case held a bowl of dirt, a small popcorn box with a hole burned through it, and a device that looked like an old Nintendo controller, but larger, the size of an Etch-A-Sketch, silver-blue, and covered with buttons and knobs. She recognized some of them.

The old man sat on the couch waiting for her when she returned to the front room. "Let me guess: You want your money back?"

Lynette shook her head. "No, but what is it? I don't understand."

"I think it's pretty self-explanatory. What you see is everything I know."

"The articles say the town was evacuated and the movie theater blew up. Nothing about a . . . whatever that is."

"That's all anybody knows."

"Then how do you know it happened?"

He grunted and hoisted himself off the couch. She followed him back into the museum, where he pointed at the southeast corner of the cinema. A tiny figure she hadn't noticed before peered around the corner. "That's me."

"You?"

"We still had a weekly paper back then. I was the only reporter. I wasn't going to miss the only interesting thing that ever happened in this town. Everybody evacuated except me; I hid my car in a barn and doubled back to see what was going on. Except I should have known they'd never let me publish any of it. Someone bought the paper before the evacuation was even lifted, and I got canned. Nobody else would take the story."

"Did you take pictures? Your figure has a camera."

"Of course. But the negatives went missing before I had a chance to print them. It wasn't like today, where you upload your phone's photos to the cloud."

"Huh," Lynette said. She wouldn't believe the man at all if it weren't for that one strange detail. The one she had to ask about. "What's with the whale car?"

He looked away from his miniature. "Narwhal. I don't know. I don't know who she was; I never managed to track her down. I guess the big heroes all had their own cities to defend and couldn't be bothered with little towns. Anyway, that car was hard to forget. The rest of the scene is, uh, dramatic re-creation, I guess. The closest I could get to truth."

"Huh," she said again. "So, who comes to your museum? People who live here?"

"Nah. Nobody comes." He laughed. "I keep it open a couple hours a week, but nobody comes. Nobody here believes it happened, and nobody else cares. It's a pretty lousy museum."

Lynette searched for a compliment. "Your diorama is fantastic. I'm sorry nobody believes you."

"Do you?"

She considered. "Yeah. I think I do. Truth is always too weird to be fiction, right? In high school I told people that once a year circus elephants walked down my street, but nobody believed me. You don't have any postcards, do you?"

"No. I thought they would look like a joke."

Oh well. She'd keep the brochure as a souvenir, anyway.

Unless. "Look, um, I know this might sound strange, but would you let me borrow that controller thing that's in the case? I'll bring it back to you tomorrow."

The man frowned. "Why would I let you do that? I told you they already took my photos. Where did you say you were from again?"

"I swear. I'll bring it back. You can keep my student ID for the night. Or my driver's license. Or"—she fished in her pocket—"this is my lucky coin. It's not worth much, but you can see where I've worn it down playing with it in my pocket. I'm not leaving town without it. I promise I'll be back in the morning, and I'll make it worth your trust. Like you said, they already took your photos. The awesome part of your display is the diorama. An old controller doesn't say much to anyone unless you know what it is, and I think I know what it is."

"You do?"

"I think. Maybe."

She wasn't sure she had convinced him, but he crossed to the case and swung it open. It hadn't even been locked. She handed over her lucky coin and accepted the device he handed to her. It was heavier than it looked.

"See you tomorrow?" He sounded resigned. She had a strange desire not to disappoint him.

The fence around the repair shop had been closed and locked as promised, but the narwhal's bay stood open, probably because the horn extended a few feet beyond the garage door. It still looked friendly. She looked around, but the mechanic seemed to have left, and nobody else was on the street.

Hopefully the device didn't need batteries. The directional toggle was self-explanatory, and the antenna, and the on/off switch. She examined the icons, trying to match them to the ones inside the car. The one with a horn on it seemed obvious, but she looked over her shoulder and realized it was aimed at the window of a two-story building across the street. Better to be careful.

Finally, she chose a button with two wings on it. Took a deep breath. Pressed it. Nothing happened at first, so she pressed again, for a little longer. A chuffing noise came from the garage. The whale chassis rose on its tires, then lifted, tires and all. Just a couple of feet. She lowered it as gently as she could back to the ground.

She walked back toward the motel, heading west into a setting sun, low enough and bright enough she had to turn her head slightly rather than watch where she was going. Her sunglasses were still in the whale. The narwhal.

The grocery and thrift store had both closed for the night. Beyond them, the ruined cinema. The chain-link fence stood seven or eight feet high, but there didn't seem to be any security. No cameras, no razor wire at the top, nothing to say anybody was trying to keep anybody else out particularly badly. She walked perpendicular to the road until she drew parallel with the building, then scaled the fence.

The cinema's wall was intact until it wasn't. Wall, wall, wall, then a crumble of beige bricks and stucco. Beyond that, a large circular area that indented slightly, filled with dirt.

"Not much to look at." Dahlia sat in an unanchored velveteen seat. She beckoned. Lynette flipped the seat beside her, which fell off its hinge. She sat cross-legged in the dirt instead.

"I think my mother came here once when I was a kid, but I can't figure out why." Dahlia held out the photo from her purse. "It has to be this place. The movies are still the same."

"I think she was here, too."

The Boss's habit of turning her whole attention to the person beside her was much less terrifying when they weren't driving. Her surprise showed clearly on her face. "What makes you say that?"

"Something happened here. There's a museum about it in town."

"What?"

"Yeah. Only open Fridays, but he'll open the door for you. Your mother's car is in his diorama. You'd probably make his decade if you drove up in it tomorrow."

"Maybe I'll do that, if we're not running too late."

They sat for a while in silence, the sun setting over the filled hole.

The Boss chewed at her nails and flicked them toward an imaginary window. "She used to disappear sometimes, but my dad always said 'She's off making sure there's enough good to go around' or 'She thinks if help doesn't come it's because you're supposed to be the one doing the helping.' I thought she went gambling or something. There was this one time, just once, when I was a teenager, where she kissed me goodbye like she wasn't sure she would see me again. I asked my dad where she was going, but he wouldn't say, or else he didn't know. She was gone for days. And here we are."

"Here we are," Lynette repeated, like the museum guy's parrot.

She reached into her pocket for her lucky coin, but it wasn't there. She took a deep breath. "Not maybe. We're definitely going to knock on the museum door tomorrow, both of us. We've got time. We're running early by your schedule. We're going to knock on the museum door, and I'm going to show you both something awesome. Then we're going to keep driving, and we're going to stop at Arches National Park, and I'm going to get out of the car and actually see the arches, and then I'm going to buy a T-shirt or a postcard or one of those pressed-penny things. Or all of the above. I haven't decided."

Dahlia didn't agree, but she didn't say no either. Lynette thought that was progress.

The ground didn't shimmer. There were no heroes on hand, no monsters either, nothing remarkable about this place to put on a postcard, not anything that anyone would believe, anyway. Nothing to see, nothing to write home about. Still, for the first time on the trip, she felt like she'd been someplace.

— *And Then There Were (N-One)* —

I considered declining the invitation. It was too weird, too expensive, too far, too dangerous, too weird. Way too weird. An invitation like that would never come again. I'd regret it if I didn't go. It lay on our kitchen table for three weeks while I argued out the pros and cons with Mabel. She listened, made suggestions; I countered her, then argued her part, then made both arguments, then reversed them again.

"How do I know it's not a hoax?" I asked, studying the list of backing organizations for the twentieth time. "The website looks legit, but how could it not be a hoax?"

"Look at it this way," Mabel said. "Either you'll be part of a groundbreaking event in human history, or a groundbreaking psych experiment. Someone benefits either way. And you've never been to eastern Canada, so at least you get to see someplace new even if you just end up standing in a field somewhere looking silly."

She always had a way of making an adventure out of things that would otherwise stress me out. Four months later, I flew to Nova Scotia, took a bus to a seaside town too small for a dot on a map, boarded a ferry to Secord Island, and stepped through the waiting portal into an alternate-reality resort-hotel lobby swarming with Sarah Pinskers. At least two hundred of us by my estimation, with more straggling in.

It was easy to tell who had just arrived. We were the ones planted in the lobby, bags in hand, eyes wide and mouth open. My body and face, even my expression, reflected back at me in two hundred funhouse mirrors. Stranger even than that, an energy in the air that I couldn't quite explain, a feeling that every single Sarah had stepped through to the exact same thought, to the same curious-amazement-horror-wonder, to the same rug-yanking confirmation that the invitation had been real and we were no longer alone, or maybe we were more alone than we had ever been.

Large groups gathered around the hotel check-in desk and Sarah-Con registration, no doubt trying to pick themselves off the long lists of near-identical names. A third faction, which I decided to join, had adjourned to the lobby bar, hoping to use alcohol to blunt the weirdness of coming face-to-face with our multiverse selves. I found a barstool and shoved my suitcase and backpack under my feet. Space was tight amid the other suitcases and backpacks.

"The stout," I said when I caught the bartender's attention, pointing at the third tap handle.

He grinned and held up a glass. "Seventh one in a row. You all go for the stout or one of the good whiskeys."

I filed that information away. Took a sip. The Sarah next to me did the same. We both put our glasses down at the same time. Both raised eyebrows at each other.

The bartender hovered. "Room number for your tab?"

"I haven't checked in yet. Cash isn't okay? Oh. The cross-world currency thing."

"You can put her drink on my tab," said the me next to me. She wore her hair in a long braid down her back. I'd worn mine that way when I was thirteen.

I lifted my glass and toasted in her direction. "Thanks. Appreciated."

"My pleasure. I've never bought myself a drink before. Well, not like this, anyhow. Do you know how many there are altogether? How many of us here, I mean."

I shook my head. "No clue. You could ask someone at registration."

A third Sarah, maybe a decade older than me, joined our conversation. My parents were married years before they had me. I'd always wondered if I'd still be me if they hadn't waited. "I'm sure she'll tell us the numbers in her opening address."

"She?" asked One Braid. "Sorry if it's a stupid question. I checked into my room but I haven't braved convention registration yet. I hate lines."

Older Sarah rummaged in a SarahCon commemorative tote bag and pulled out a program. She turned to a bio page and started reading. "'Sarah Pinsker [R0D0]'—I don't know what 'R-0-D-0' means—'made the discovery creating the multiverse portal. She is a quantologist at Johns Hopkins University.'" She looked up. "I think that's her over there. She's been rushing back and forth as long as I've been sitting here."

We followed her pointing finger to a Sarah bustling through the lobby, walkie-talkie to her lips. Her hair was pixie-short, defeating the frizz that plagued me. She looked harried but better put together than most of us, elegant in a silk blouse and designer jeans that fit and flattered. I had never been anything approaching elegant. Never had the guts to cut my hair that short, either.

"Quantologist," I repeated.

Older Sarah paged through the program. "It looks like there are four other quantologist Sarahs on the host committee."

One Braid scratched the back of her neck. "I've never heard of quantology. I don't think it's a real field of study where I'm from."

"Not where I'm from, either. Where are you from? I mean, answer however you want."

"I'm from all over the place," One Braid said. My usual answer. "But I live in Seattle."

Eerie. "Me, too. I went out for a job after college and stayed."

"Same! Summer job, then I met my girlfriend and settled for good. I'm in West Seattle. How about you?"

"Ballard." I raised my glass to clink hers, though that particular girlfriend and I hadn't lasted.

Older Sarah chugged her beer and waved for another before turning back to us. "Our Seattle was destroyed in an earthquake."

We both stared at her. She sipped her fresh beer and continued. "I never got out west myself, so it wasn't a personal thing for me, but it was horrible. Four thousand people died. The city never recovered."

I pictured our little house bucking and buckling, our yard splitting down the middle. Mabel, my friends and neighbors, the coffee shop up the street. Shuddered. It was too much to imagine. "This is so damn weird."

Older Sarah waved her program at me. "That's the name of the first panel. 'This Is So Damn Weird: Strategies for Navigating Sarah-Con Without Losing Your Mind.'"

One Braid and I both reached for our beers.

The registration line thinned as a programmed cocktail hour began in some lounge somewhere. Since I'd already been drinking for a while, I took the opportunity to check in and register.

"Find yourself on the list," said the Sarah behind the convention registration table. I could tell she was fried, like she was already too tired to remember how to put expressions on her face. I knew that feeling.

Looking at the list, it was easy to see why she'd had a long day already. My mind was still boggling at the handful of Sarahs I'd met; she'd come face-to-face with all of us.

The list grouped us by surname first. Mine the most common, a trunk instead of a branch. I paged past, curious. Mostly Pinskers like myself. Made sense if we were the closest realities to the Pinsker who had invited us. There were other random surnames I chalked up to marriage. A full page of Sarah Sweetloves. I'd never really considered changing my name for anyone, even Mabel, but apparently others had.

After surname came city, divided evenly between Seattle, Toronto, and Baltimore, with a few outliers in Northampton, Somerville, Asheville, New York, Pretoria. After that came birthdate, occupation. The occupation list read like a collection of every

"What do you want to be when you grow up?" I'd ever answered. Geneticist, writer, therapeutic-riding instructor, teacher, history professor, astronomer, journalist, dog trainer, barn manager. I was the only insurance investigator. In fairness, it had never exactly been on the greatest-hits list.

Address messed with me the most for some reason. Someone else here shared my full name, birthdate, and address. She worked as a program director at a non-profit. That was the only place our lines on the list differed. Where else did we diverge? Did we move around our house in the same ways at the same times? Had she fallen in love with the kitchen first, too? Did she live with an alternate Mabel?

"There's a Making Connections board over there." The volunteer behind the table pointed to a poster on the far wall of the lobby. She sounded like she'd said it a hundred times already. "In case you come across somebody you absolutely have to meet. Judging from your face, you just found somebody on the list who intrigues you. Somebody who wears the same life as you, or near to it."

It brought to my mind those grade-school puzzle pages with six or nine near-identical cats or robots drawn in a grid, where you were supposed to find the matched pair hidden among the ones with slight differences. In the same moment I had that thought, a Sarah perusing another copy of the list said it to me.

I looked her over. The invitation had said, "Be yourself." We both wore jeans and *Wonder Woman* T-shirts, hers with a graphic from the 70s TV show and mine from the 2005 Gina Torres movie. We both had our hair pulled back in messy ponytails. The only difference I noticed was that her skin was much better than mine.

The volunteer didn't bother to look down at the list when I highlighted my name and returned it to her. She handed me a program and a tote bag. "You can decide whether you want to bother with a nametag."

I looked at the markers and stickers piled on the table. "Is there a point?"

"Not with a name like yours, unless you have a nickname you think is particularly original. Though it probably isn't. There are a few non-Sarahs. They're the only ones who really need to bother. Right at the beginning we tried making people choose a nickname, but the first eight tried their identical middle names, and then four had the same roller derby name, and three asked for the name they all used as counselors at Girl Scout camp, and we gave up."

It didn't seem worth it. I went over to the hotel check-in line, made slightly easier with individual registration numbers. The desk clerk was one of us too, in a business suit and a manager's gold nametag that suggested this was probably her home reality.

"The credit card you registered with will be charged by a third-party billing company that's handling the cross-world weirdness. Bill anything you buy to your room." She spoke with an accent I couldn't place.

"Where are you from?" I asked her.

"I live just over on the mainland. You?"

"Seattle."

A sympathetic look crossed her face.

I tried to change the subject before she told me Seattle was gone in this reality too. "So why is this being held on Secord Island?"

"Everyone asks." She smiled, showing gapped teeth. She'd never gotten braces. "It's a sovereign island off the east coast of Canada. You know Canada?"

I nodded, wondering what variation had prompted that question.

She continued. "Sovereign island, at least in this reality, so the organizer didn't have to worry about visas or passports. You're all allowed here, then back to where you came from."

"What if someone tried to skip off this island? Not that I would. I'm an insurance investigator. Professional questioner of motives."

Another grin. "That's why all the boats were sent away for the weekend. We're stuck with you, or you're stuck with us."

She put a keycard in a paper sleeve and pulled out a pen. "Do you have keycards in your world?"

"Yeah." I glanced at the number she'd written, committed it to memory, pocketed the card, and handed her back the sleeve to discard.

"You're the only one so far to do that," she said. "Congrats on being original."

I gave her a little salute and went to find my room in the annex, the cheapest room available when I'd registered. Her directions led out of the original building and down an L-shaped hallway tacked onto the back. I passed a stressed-looking housekeeper pushing a cart full of cleaning supplies, then two Sarahs trying to wrangle a cot into a tiny room, under the direction of a third, who looked up and waved. They must have taken advantage of the room-sharing option in the questionnaire that followed the RSVP. I'd liked that offer; it meant the Sarahs who attended wouldn't only be those with the time and privilege to do so. That had even gotten Mabel to tone down some of her teasing about the whole event.

Around the next bend, a different type of cold than the air-conditioned lobby, that of Canadian November penetrating a closed system. Someone had propped open the fire door at the hall's end. I unlocked my door, dropped my bags in my bathtub, then went to get a look outside.

When I leaned out the fire door, I found two Sarahs smoking, shoulders hunched against a biting wind. A vivid bruise of a cloud-bank pressed down overhead, making it seem much later than it was. The air tasted like cigarettes and salt water. We had a dramatic land-locked view of a loading dock and a couple of dumpsters, but I felt the sea lurking nearby. I felt oddly displaced, jet-lagged without the jet. Portal lag, maybe.

"Join us?" The curls spilling down her shoulders were dyed carrot orange, a color that said it was not trying for anything natural. They looked wild and luxurious, when I only ever managed feral at best.

The other looked less healthy. Beneath her toque, her cheeks were gaunt, and the No Good Deeds T-shirt under her bomber jacket swam on her. She held out a pack of American Spirits.

"I'm good," I said. "But hey, No Good Deeds. They were a cool band."

She grinned, showing yellowed teeth. "ARE a good band. Bam! Divergence point! In my world they're on album number six and still awesome."

"The hall isn't getting too cold, is it?" Orange Curls asked. "The door locks if we shut it. I had to walk around the whole building earlier. It's huge."

The other lit a new cigarette off her old one, then stubbed out the butt with a worn combat boot. "I've got to go back inside in a minute anyhow."

She didn't look like she was in any hurry. I assured them it wasn't too cold, mostly because I didn't want to be That Person, which they probably knew. We didn't like to inconvenience people.

"So why are you here?" Orange Curls was the chattier of the two.

"What do you mean? I got an invitation."

No Good Deeds shook her head. "She's asking what made you accept. Excitement, curiosity, wonder, a desire to exploit? Not that you're limited to those choices."

I thought about it. Mabel had said the whole thing was an exercise in narcissism.

She'd read the invitation, then tossed it on the table, laughing. "Who discovers how to access infinite realities and then uses that discovery to invite her alternate selves to a convention?"

"Some other me, apparently." As I'd said it, I'd known it was true. "Why, what would you do?"

Her response came easily. "Talk to world leaders or scientists. Find out why one reality is running out of water and another is doing fine, or how one made the transition from fossil fuel to solar. Check in on the state of democracy. Something useful. Anyway, you hate decisions. This'll just make you question every choice you ever made. Should you have gone to grad school? Should you have stayed with this ex or that one? How would your life be different if you'd managed to buy that horse you loved as a teenager? If I were you, I wouldn't want to know the answers. I mean, you've got to go, obviously, but it's a wasted opportunity if you don't talk about some of that stuff."

Everything she'd said was true, like usual.

I looked back at Orange Curls. "Curiosity. I guess I'm here because I'm curious. And maybe a little because if I stayed home I'd always wonder about it."

The smokers shot each other a satisfied look.

"She's asked twenty-one Sarahs that question now," No Good Deeds said, "and that's been the answer every time. Even the same phrasing."

I retreated to my room. Stripped the bedspread, checked the mattress for bedbugs. Searched the room and the bathroom for cameras and peepholes in case we really were all part of someone's psych experiment.

Concerns assuaged, I dumped my backpack's contents onto the table and repacked the stuff I wanted to carry with me for the evening, then flopped onto the bed to read the program. It contained a basic explanation of the multiverse theory, a welcome note, a sponsor page, a thank-you page, a map, and "Fun Statistics!" based on the questionnaires we'd filled out prior to arriving. Ninety-two percent of us played instruments. Five percent of us owned horses, thirteen percent owned cats, eighty percent owned dogs. One person lived in a world where dogs had been rendered extinct by a virus. So much for fun.

A program schedule took up the rest of the pages. Some of the serious stuff Mabel had wanted to see was mixed in: "Let My World Solve Your World's Water Problem," "Climate Change Strategies That Actually Worked," "The Way It Could Have Been: Political Divergence Points."

Alongside that, the topics piquing my own curiosity. "Gender, Sexuality, and Me." "Driving Forces: Favorite Cars, Stolen Cars, Those Who Never Learned to Drive." "Let's Talk Family." "The Babysitting Incident and Other Divergence Points." "Why We Live Where We Live." "Horses and Dogs and Cats, Oh My." "Outliers." "Yes, Another Horse Panel." "Music and Art." Some were listed as panels, others as moderated large-group discussions.

The second evening was filled with concerts and readings and art shows by the more creative among us. Tonight featured a keynote speech by the host, followed by a DJ'd dance. Normally that wouldn't be my thing, but the thought of a dance with a self-curated song list—I pictured upbeat soul, Bowie, 80s pop—and an entire room full of enthusiastic but uniformly terrible dancers, excited me more than I'd admit. There'd be nobody to watch who wouldn't understand. Maybe I wouldn't even be the worst dancer in the room. A girl could dream.

I glanced at the clock on the table. Enough time for a nap before dinner. The organizers of "This Is So Damn Weird" were probably sitting in an empty room, sighing to themselves, wishing they could grab a few minutes' sleep too.

We had all just started on our salads in the banquet hall when the Sarah from hotel registration approached my table. Her uniform still made her one of the easier ones to recognize.

The hotel employee knelt by the Sarah to my left, who had my haircut and who was wearing the same T-shirt as me, only with a long-sleeved shirt underneath it. She was the only one I'd seen with a prosthetic hand. It was a good prosthetic; I wouldn't have noticed it if we hadn't stood at a washroom sink next to each other before the meal. Other than the hand, she'd looked more like me than most; I desperately wanted to figure out where we'd diverged, but hadn't worked up the nerve to ask her yet.

"Pardon," said Hotel Sarah. "Did you say earlier you were a detective?"

Prosthetic Hand shook her head. "I wouldn't have said that. Not anymore. Go fish."

I traced the scar on my own left wrist and wondered how many worlds you had to travel away from mine before you reached one where Go Fish wasn't a game.

Hotel Sarah straightened up, put her hands on her hips, scanned the room. I debated not identifying myself, just to observe how she approached the problem of discreetly finding the sole detective in a room full of functionally identical people. My curiosity over why she was looking for me won out. Curiosity and pity; I recognized the panic just under her surface. Everyone at the table recognized it. It rippled over us like a wave.

"Right table, wrong person," I said in a low voice. "How can I help you?"

Her relief was so obvious I felt guilty for having considered withholding. "Would you mind coming with me?"

Seven faces watched as I stood up from the table: prosthetic-hand Sarah, left-handed Sarah, bearded Dare, bearded Josh, stubble-faced Joshua—the three of them had sat together to compare notes, they'd said—and two random Sarahs I hadn't yet managed to meet or distinguish because I was more interested in the others. They reopened questions I had closed for myself. From the way we had all allowed them to center conversation, I guessed that was the case with everyone else who'd sat down at this table, too.

All seven had pushed the olives to the side of their salads, as I had. I pictured dishwashers scraping the entire room's worth of olives off our plates at meal's end. Wondered how the organizers had proactively made the entire weekend vegetarian, but forgotten to tell the kitchen we didn't like olives. Maybe whoever had set the menu was an outlier who assumed they were in the majority.

I stuffed a dinner roll into my bag in case I missed the entire meal. The others all nodded approvingly, knowing we didn't work well when hungry.

Hotel Sarah led me through the lobby and down another dog-legged corridor, this one in the opposite direction of my own. I pictured the building's aerial footprint, a sprawling figure. We passed a tiny convenience store, a shuttered boutique, a small arcade where a lone Sarah manipulated a claw machine. An elevator waited open at the end of the hall. Once inside, she used a key to unlock it and pressed for the third floor, the top.

The elevator was the slowest I'd ever ridden. I waited for her to tell me where we were going, or why. When no explanation came, I concentrated on figuring out the observable differences between us. There were none, or none beyond the superficial. Her tailored uniform, her short, tight curls versus my shaggy ponytail. She was sizing me up in the same way; I wondered what she saw.

The elevator opened onto a dark room. An enormous nightclub, I realized, as my eyes adjusted. There was a long bar down one side, and on the opposite side a row of well-dressed folding tables holding some kind of display. In the center of the room, dozens of small tables ringed the perimeter of a dance floor. Beyond the dance floor, a high stage with a single podium and a DJ table. It took me another few seconds to notice the slumped figure in the stage's shadow.

As I approached, I saw what had the hotel manager so spooked: a dead Sarah.

Not me, my logic brain understood, even though some tiny part of me screamed something was wrong. I'd made it through the entire afternoon talking with people who were more like me than an identical twin would be, but the body was somehow more real. The others down at dinner all had stories to remind me I was still myself, that I could still be differentiated. Absent stories and quirks, absent a person talking at me to prove we were not the same, the vacuum came rushing in. Who was she? In what ways was she me, in what ways was she not? Who would mourn her? I tried to imagine the shape of my own absence from my own world. It was an impossible exercise.

I struggled to regain control over myself. "You know I'm an insurance investigator, right? Dead bodies aren't my area of expertise."

"You're the closest thing we've got. None of us are medical doctors, and it's too late for one anyhow, and I figured you investigate things. I couldn't find any of the organizers, so I thought I'd look for you." She must have had a good memory for details, if she managed to find me in that dining hall based on one short conversation. Maybe that was a thing we all had in common.

Anyway, she was right: I did like a good puzzle. Not that I had any idea if this even was one yet. "Are there lights in here?"

She disappeared from my side, and the house lights came up a moment later. The room looked much smaller without the depth of shadow.

The body wasn't me, I told myself. I concentrated on the differences rather than the eerie familiarity. Her cheeks were hollower than mine. She had more freckles, close-cropped hair. My empty stomach lurched.

She was starting to cool to the touch. I felt for a pulse, though I didn't expect to find one. Her eyes were open, her pupils tiny in the blue. For some reason it brought the 90s John Lennon song "Change Your Tune" into my head, lyrics twisted. *You'll change your eyes, dear.*

I shook the song away. Focus. She slumped against the stage, half sitting, head leaning back against the stage. She wore a silk dress with a hibiscus flower print, louder than anything I'd wear, but not in a bad way.

"What's your story?" I asked her under my breath.

I crouched to examine her hands and arms, trying not to move her too much. The nails had been bitten painfully short, but there was nothing under them that implied a fight. Some bruises and track marks on the insides of her arms, not all of them scabbed over, but nothing to suggest she'd tried to protect herself from the fall. I didn't see any blood anywhere, but I didn't want to move her until police or a coroner came.

Hotel Sarah stared at the body, absently chewing on her thumb.

"Why me?" I asked.

Not the question she'd expected, or else she'd tuned me out. "Pardon?"

"I know you said I was the closest thing to a detective, but why do you need someone to investigate? Aren't the police on their way?"

She shook her head. "Gale winds on the Sound tonight. They can't make it out here by boat or helicopter."

"What about a medical team? Surely there's a medic here."

"We paid a paramedic team to come out to the island this weekend, but they turned around because of the weather, too. My staff have basic CPR and first aid, but, well . . ."

I finished her sentence. "But she's obviously already dead."

"Yeah. I thought maybe you'd be the next best thing to police, until they can get here. If she had a heart attack or stroke or just fell off the stage, it's sad but nothing to worry about. If it was foul play"—the phrase sounded funny, like something on television—"we're stuck with a murderer all weekend. If the police don't get here in time, we can't keep people from the portals. They're timed precisely."

"How about security? Surely you have security staff."

She dismissed them with a wave. "They've never had to handle anything worse than kids setting off the fire alarms."

"And I know I said this already, but you understand I'm in insurance? I investigate fraud. People lying about whiplash, that kind of thing. Not even the glamorous cheating-spouse stuff."

She shrugged. I decided not to give her any harder time about it. She'd made a decision, never my strong point. She was probably already questioning herself, wondering what other option she hadn't considered.

I was what they had. Right. So until police got here, I played coroner, law, and order. Not a role I was comfortable with at all, made weirder by the circumstance. Victim: Sarah. Investigator: Sarah.

Suspects: all variations on the theme, other than the hotel staff. Hard to imagine one of us murdering; I knew I didn't have it in me to kill someone. Also hard to imagine the hotel staff bothering; most murders involved somebody the victim knew.

I summoned up my inner TV detective. "Just to rule this out, nobody on your staff has any beef with you that you're aware of? Nobody would be driven to kill by an entire hotel full of your dopplegangers?"

"I think we're all weirded out by that, myself included. But I don't think any of them hate me, and I don't think I work with any killers, though I guess that's what everybody says. 'He was such a nice man. He kept to himself.'" She touched her nametag. "Anyway, if they hated me, I'd think they go after me, not one of you. I'm easy to spot."

"True enough. I'll put them aside for now." Though that meant focusing on the Sarahs again. "Were you the one who found the body?"

"No. The DJ did. She called me." She held up her walkie-talkie.

"The DJ is one of us, right? Not your staff?"

"All the performers this weekend are attendees."

"And where is the DJ now?"

"She went back to her room. She was a little freaked out." Understandable, if her reaction to seeing her own dead twin was anything like mine.

"Has anyone else been up here?"

"The Sarah running sound and lights came up to check the system earlier for the host's speech."

"The host. Have you told her yet?"

Hotel Sarah chewed at her thumb again. "That's the thing. Like I said, I haven't been able to reach her. The organizers are all on walkie-talkies since your phones don't work here, but she's not answering hers. Nobody on the committee is answering, actually. That's why I took matters into my own hands. Last I saw her, she was down in the

Operations room, but she'd been up here earlier, so she could have come back for something."

I looked down at the body. Tried to remember the woman who had breezed through the lobby earlier. "Are you saying you think this might be the organizer?"

She didn't say anything, so I continued. "Do you remember anything specific about her? Anything to differentiate her?"

Her look suggested the question was a pointless one. "She was a little thinner than most. I think she runs marathons. Most of the committee do."

The body was freckled and thin. She could have been a runner. A runner with a possible drug problem seemed a little counterproductive, but maybe she had pain issues or something.

"How about her clothing? Do you remember what she was wearing?" The woman I'd seen earlier had been in a blouse and jeans, not a dress, but she'd had time to change her clothes.

She shook her head. "I have a pretty good memory for detail, but everyone's blending together . . ."

"You don't have a registration list, do you? That might be useful. We need to try to identify the body before anything else."

"I'm sorry. I didn't think to bring one up here. That couldn't be her, right? Should I try to find her again? She's going to need to notify the next of kin, and create a procedure to bring a body crossworld. Nobody's ever died in the wrong world before."

Infinite permutations. Surely someone must have. Except that for all the individual crossworld expeditions, according to the program this was the first gathering of its kind. Our host, one of us, the Sarah who had created the crossworld portal. It made me feel like I had wasted my life, in comparison. What would I have had to do differently to become a scientist? Her branch of science didn't even exist as a field in my world. And now she was possibly lying dead in front of me.

Focus. If I hadn't been carrying a backpack, I'd have put my ID and my keycard into my front right pocket. Her silk dress had a shallow pocket at the hip. When I slid my hand into it, I came up with a driver's license. Her ID gave her name as Sarah Pinsker, which wasn't much help. An address in Baltimore; the host worked at Johns Hopkins.

I held up the license. "Do you know how many here this weekend live in Baltimore?"

"Forty or fifty? There would be more if so many hadn't been lost, from what I understand."

"Lost? Baltimore?"

"A bunch of Seattles were lost in tsunamis or earthquakes. Some of us moved from Baltimore to Seattle or Seattle to Baltimore . . ."

I followed her train of thought, pictured a giant wave swallowing my house. Shuddered, brought myself back to the situation at hand.

"So this might still be our host. One in forty or fifty in that city, but maybe we can narrow it down when names and addresses come into it. It probably isn't the sound person, since she's dressed up a bit. Isn't the DJ, since the DJ found her. The host wasn't working alone this weekend, was she? The registration desk, entertainment, programming . . . She had a committee, you said?"

"Yeah. Four others pretty similar to her. They'd all been on the verge of making the same discovery, so they were the first ones she reached out to."

Next question, if I was acting sheriff. "I don't suppose this bar has a walk-in fridge or freezer?"

"Why? Oh God. Shit. Yeah, there's a walk-in fridge."

"You take the legs and I'll get the arms?"

She nodded.

As I positioned myself, the body's head tipped forward, and I saw what I would have looked for earlier, if I were a real detective: a sickening, deadly deep indentation at the back of the skull. A cave-in. The hair was matted and sticky-looking, blood and—I didn't want to look closer.

"I think I found the cause of death," I said. "And I think we can rule out natural causes. Fuck."

I didn't want to touch the head any more than I wanted to look, but we still had to move the body. I grabbed a towel from the bar and wrapped her like she'd just stepped out of the shower. It still lolled against me as I lifted, and I fought the urge to be sick. She wasn't heavy, wasn't yet stiff. Rigor mortis started two hours after death. An odor came off her; a body doing body things, I told myself.

We put her in the walk-in in a re-creation of the position she'd been sitting in. I inspected her exposed parts. No blood other than the back of her head. No bullet holes. Some bruises, as I'd noted earlier, but none that looked like they came from a fight or a fall. I wasn't comfortable looking any further than that. After, I waited while Hotel Sarah rummaged in a drawer for notepad and tape and made a thick-markered "Do Not Open" sign for the fridge door.

"So, do you think she just fell and hit her head?" she asked. "Or do you think she was murdered?"

There was a hopeful note in her voice on the first option, but below that, I could tell she didn't believe it any more than I did. "*You* do, or else you want me to reassure you that the track marks suggest she overdosed and stumbled off the stage. Otherwise you wouldn't have asked me up here. You would have dealt with it quietly, to keep from scaring the rest of the guests or harming the convention. You still want to deal with it quietly."

She shifted from foot to foot. I recognized her restlessness. She felt helpless. Wanted something concrete to do, a decision made for her, a plan.

"Okay, here's what I need from you," I said, taking pity. I didn't know my next step, but I could give her a task. "Go back down to registration, make me a copy of whatever you've got down there. Um, and what time was that dance supposed to start? They can decide if they want to have it in some other space, but they probably shouldn't have it in here, in case there's still evidence to be found. And, you know, out of respect. I'm going to look around right now, but I'd think the police would still want this left untouched."

"I think they'll cancel the dance. The DJ didn't look fit to play."

"I'm going to need to talk to her, too. But maybe downstairs, so she doesn't have to come back in here? And the sound person."

She nodded and left.

There really wasn't anything else to do without the registration list. And it wouldn't do any good to interview people without the right questions. Hard to ask who else was up here, when everyone looked the same. Hard to ask "Where were you at x o'clock?" if you didn't solve for x. I could at least guess at that.

Or start with the crime scene; I walked back over. The stage was about chest high. I'd only had eyes for her before, but looking now, there was a blood smear on the stage's lip just above where the body had been. The spot where she'd hit her head? No, the lip wasn't the right shape to have caused the damage, I didn't think. I pictured myself tripping or slipping off the edge of the stage, but I couldn't imagine a way I would have fallen that would have had that result. No scuff marks, no chips in the wood, no bone fragments or hair. Just the one small smear and a deeper bloodstain where her head had been resting when we got to her. The wound itself hadn't bled a lot. Maybe a forensic expert could see more.

A coroner would be useful, too. They'd be able to say if she'd fought someone, though I didn't think so. She hadn't looked scared or angry or horrified or even distressed. Dead. An absence of her, an absence of me.

The stage had two narrow curtained wings, and stairs on both sides. I walked to the front of the stage, to the spot where she must have slipped off or fallen after being hit. I tried to imagine falling from here. If someone had hit me from behind, I'd have put my hands out, fallen forward, unless they had dropped me in my tracks. There was no scenario I could think of that would result in stepping straight off to hit the back of my head on the stage. Maybe if I was looking behind me as I walked, and missed the edge? Even then, I'd expect more of a twist, a person trying to catch herself as she went down.

Something caught my eye a few feet from the stage, under the pedestal foot of the first table. I hopped down carefully. A keycard, still in its envelope. Room 517. The dead Sarah's pockets were shallow enough that it could have fallen from her pocket, though the trajectory didn't seem quite right. I dropped it into my bag and looked around to see if the floor held any other secrets, but didn't see anything. Back to the stage.

The far wing was packed with music equipment and PA speakers. I hefted one of the mic stands. It had a pedestal base, heavy enough to hit someone with. There were six of them in a row, and any of them could be a murder weapon, though I didn't see blood, and they were rounded, where the wound had looked angular.

The wing closer to the DJ table was empty except for the top of a travel case. It was black and silver, all the edges and corners reinforced with metal. I hefted it: heavy, and this was the unpacked half. The underside was foam, cut to fit the turntables. It had a small dent in one corner, and I flipped it to look at it closely. The shape was right, but it would be an awkward thing to wield. Still, I mentally added it to the list.

I felt around the edges and found a luggage tag. Sarah Pinsker. The unmoored feeling caught me again; it was getting more familiar. Seattle address, in Rainier Beach, if I was right about the zip code. One of the cheaper neighborhoods to rent in the city, at least in my world.

The DJ equipment was set up on a table in front of the alcove. Under the table, two full record crates. I thumbed through them, amused I'd guessed the genres correctly. On the table, two fancy-looking vinyl turntables with a mixing console in between, all cushioned in the other half of the travel case. I knew nothing about DJ gear, didn't know if this was expensive or cheap equipment. There were two records already on the turntables, the Sharon Jones/ David Bowie cover of Bowie's "Modern Love," and Stevie Wonder's "Signed, Sealed, Delivered, I'm Yours." I'd have had fun dancing to those. Too bad the dance wouldn't happen now.

There was an "SP" in silver marker at each record's center, and on each piece of equipment. I pictured tomorrow's lineup of musicians, all with the SPs that normally differentiated their gear from others'.

I ran my finger over a spot where the foam had separated from the protective casing. Some glue would stick it back, an easy repair, except as I touched it I realized something had been pushed down in between. I crooked a finger into the gap and felt around until I snagged a tiny envelope. Tapped it out into my palm: eight tiny pills. I didn't recognize them, but I didn't have any knowledge of narcotics. They could be ibuprofen, for all I knew, though most people didn't go around slipping envelopes of ibuprofen into secret cubbies. In my world, anyway.

"Hello?" someone called from the back of the room.

I tucked the pills back in the envelope and the envelope into my pocket alongside the keycard. "Over here."

A Sarah made her way over to me. She wore cargo shorts, black combat boots, and a T-shirt for a band I didn't recognize. She walked with a swagger. Interesting to consider how we might have developed different walks.

"They asked me to bring up a copy of the registration list." She held a red three-ring binder out to me.

I hopped off the stage to take it from her. "Thanks. Are you the sound tech?"

"Yeah. I'd introduce myself, but it hardly seems worth it."

I smiled. "Hardly. But I wouldn't mind if you pointed out which name is yours, so I can start taking notes."

She took the book back from me and flipped to the last page in one sure movement. "Mine is easy, since I took my wife's last name. Yarrow. Last person in the whole book."

I grabbed my pen off the table where'd I left it and circled her occupation to remind myself who she was. "Do you mind if I ask you a few questions?"

"Go ahead."

"What time did you come up here?"

"Three-thirty. There wasn't a whole lot to set up, but it always takes a little longer when you're not working with your own gear. I soundchecked the DJ, then the keynote speaker. Figured out how to run her slideshow. After that I took some time to get situated with the light board. I'm not really a lighting person, but it's pretty well labeled. I think I was out of here by four-thirty."

"Were they both still up here when you left?"

"No. The DJ left after we tested her gear through the PA. She'd managed to haul her big case and one crate of records up here in one go, but she said she had to get a second crate from her room on the other side of the hotel."

"And she didn't come back?"

"I figured she got to talking to someone, or took a nap or something. She didn't come back while I was here."

"And the host stayed? The, ah, keynote speaker?"

"She said she wanted to go over her speech while nobody was in the room."

"Did anybody else come up?"

"Not that I saw."

I paused to consider what else I needed to ask. "Would you recognize the keynote?" She cocked her head, and I amended my question. "You don't have to be definitive. But if you know it's NOT her, that would be helpful."

I led her to the fridge. "I should have asked: Are you okay looking at her? I can warn you it's a little freaky looking at a dead person who looks like you."

"This whole thing is freaky. I'll be okay."

We approached within a couple feet of the body. The vertiginous feeling hit me again.

"It could be her?" she said, half statement and half question. "But, uh, she was wearing something else. She had on jeans, not a dress. Maybe she left and changed into what she was going to wear tonight and came back?"

That made sense. Or the manager's fear that this might be the host was unfounded.

"That definitely helps," I said. "You can go if you need to."

She nodded. "They're going to have to find someplace else for tonight's programming, so I should probably find out where they want me. But, hey, it's good to have something to do, right?"

I hadn't considered it until then, but it was true. As disturbing as the idea of a dead me was, something about the whole weird weekend became more concrete now that I had a purpose. No wonder so many had signed up to run sound and registration and play music and lead discussions. The other volunteers must have been self-aware enough to recognize it before they arrived.

I sat down on the stage's edge with the list. Flipped to the "Sarah Pinsker" section, the big section, and put stars next to the ones who lived in Baltimore. The host and eleven others, since several Baltimore Sarahs had taken other surnames. Five of the remaining Sarahs were Quantologists. They all had a big *C* after their name. Committee, I guessed. All five lived at the same address, the address on the license in the deceased's pocket. The lone difference between them on paper was a designation in the last column. R0D0, R1D0, R0D1, R1D1, R0D1A. No clue what that meant, but the program had listed a parenthetical R0D0 after the host's name, so I circled that one.

I paged through the book for a while, making notes beside the entries for the DJ, the hotel clerk, the sound tech, and a few others I'd met who stood out from the pack. It would have been really interesting reading material any other day; now it was a headache.

I still hadn't finished my circuit of the room. I searched the bar for something with the right shape and heft to be the murder weapon. A couple of the bottles might have fit the bill, but I would have thought they'd smash on impact.

My desire for diligence didn't extend to alone-time with the body, so I decided against searching the fridge. I wandered across the floor. The back of a chair or barstool? Or the leg? Possible, and a pain to check them all.

On the far side of the room, four folding tables covered with velveteen tablecloths. A printed sign hung on the wall behind them: Sarah Pinsker Hall of Fame.

Each table held a series of objects. A few had explanatory note-cards in front of them, but most spoke for themselves. I remembered the questionnaire: "Do you have any special awards or achievements you'd like to show off? Bring them for our brag table!" I'd have thought they'd have better security, but then again, up until now I would have thought I could trust my other selves.

If the list of occupations had made me feel like an underachiever, this display reinforced it. A Grammy for Best Folk Album 2013, a framed photo of a Sarah in the Kentucky Derby winner's circle, a Best Original Screenplay Oscar, a stack of novels, a Nebula Award for science fiction writing, an issue of *Quantology Today* containing an article with a seventy-word title that I guessed amounted to "Other Realities! I Found Them!" A few awards I didn't recognize, though I wasn't sure if that was because they didn't exist in my reality or I just hadn't heard of them.

Two of the awards looked like they had the shape to be the murder weapon, and one of them looked like it had the weight as well: the Nebula, a three-dimensional rectangular block of Lucite, shot through with stars and planets. What did you call a three-dimensional rectangle, anyway? I didn't want to pick it up without gloves, but I used the back of my hand to push it gently backward. It was heavy enough, for sure.

As I touched the award, I felt a strange certainty this was it. That if I were to murder someone, which I absolutely wouldn't do, this would be the weapon of choice. Not the mic stands, not the chairs, not the turntable case: this glittering block that would travel back to another reality at the end of the weekend with its owner none the wiser. I shuddered and shook the thought off.

Stooping to examine it closer, I didn't see any sign of blood or hair. In fact, there wasn't a single fingerprint on it, which was odd enough in itself. The other statuettes had fingerprints, but this one looked like it had been polished clean.

If this was the murder weapon, what did that say about the murder? Was it an act of passion, carried out with an item at hand? Was there any significance to the choice? If it was premeditated, that would narrow the list of suspects to the people who knew it would be up here: the host committee and the writer who had brought it. The list of people who had seen it here was probably more or less the list I'd already made of people who had been up to the room. Not much help.

Nobody else came upstairs, and after a while I got sick of waiting. I headed back down to the lobby. Passed the arcade, now empty, and the convenience store, now closed. The registration table, cluttered with nametags and markers, otherwise abandoned. A few people sat in the lobby, but the mood was markedly different than it had been before dinner. I gathered word had spread.

A new clerk was working the front desk, an acned non-Sarah in his late teens or early twenties. I held up my registration binder like an overlarge badge, trying to look harried and committee-bound. "I don't suppose if I gave you a name and ID code, you'd tell me what room someone is staying in? Official business?"

He nodded. I flipped to the DJ's name and pointed. After a moment's typing, he looked back up at me. "107. That's in the annex. Do you know where that is?"

My room was in the annex, but if the committee members were all staying in the tower, I didn't want to break the illusion. I let him point me in the direction of my room. Her door was a few down from my own.

I knocked a few times before she heard me. When the door swung open, I recognized the person on the other side. "That makes sense! I didn't realize you were the DJ."

She smiled blankly. I pointed at her T-shirt. "We met outside earlier? When you were smoking? No Good Deeds?"

"Oh, yeah." She replaced the empty smile with a warmer one. "It's hard to keep everyone straight. Can I help you?"

"I'm, uh, investigating the death of the Sarah you found. I'm a detective. Do you mind if I come in and ask you a few questions?"

She opened the door wider, and I followed her into the room. The first bed's bedspread lay in a heap on the floor. Her duffel's contents were scattered across the second bed, in some sort of half-organization. A pile of grayed-out underwear, a few T-shirts, neatly folded, a pile of tampons, pack of cigarettes.

"Sorry," she said. "I always spread out in hotels. You can have the chair." She flopped down on the first bed. "Did you say you were investigating her death? She looked like she fell off the stage to me. Not that it wasn't freaky to see her, you know?"

"Yeah," I agreed. "But the hotel manager asked me to look around a little. Because of the circumstances."

"Oh. Okay."

"Are you alright with me asking you some questions?"

"Go ahead. It's all a little upsetting, though. I'm not sure I'm thinking straight."

That might be chemical, if the pills I'd found were hers. "Can you walk me through the afternoon?"

"I loaded my stuff into the room around four. Set up, sound-checked. Came back down here to get my second crate of records. When I went back, that's when I saw her."

"Do you know how long you were gone?"

She shrugged. I tried to remember when I'd run into her. She must have gone out for a smoke before going back with the crate.

"Where were you when you saw her? Where in the club, I mean?"

"As I was coming down the aisle toward the stage. She was just sitting there. I thought she had sat down, but then I realized the posture was funny."

"And—sorry—was she definitely already dead by then?"

She bit her lower lip, bringing it to the white of her teeth. "Her eyes were open. I nudged her leg, but she didn't respond, so I checked for a pulse."

"Was she warm or cold to your touch?"

"Warm. I've never seen a dead person before, and she looked so . . ." She shuddered. I did too.

"And then you left her there? To go for help?"

"No! I made a call on her walkie-talkie. I figured the other people in charge would be on the other end, and maybe someone from the hotel."

I closed my eyes to mentally revisit the scene. "There wasn't a walkie-talkie there."

Her eyes widened. "There was. I swear, I called on it. Ask the manager. It was next to the body. She'd been carrying it around before, complaining it dragged her jeans down."

"Her jeans? Before she changed into the dress and came back?"

She gave me a quizzical look.

There wasn't really much point to asking her anything else if she couldn't even get basic details right. Her confusion felt genuine. "Thanks for letting me in. 'Questions lead to questions lead to answers lead to answers,' right?"

"I hope so," she said absently, standing up and ushering me out. "I hope you get her home okay."

She'd completely ignored the No Good Deeds lyric I'd used as a peace offering. Second and last album in my world, their one hit single. I wondered if it was the drugs or the shock, or she just wasn't the fan I'd thought she was earlier.

Back in the hallway, I dug in my bag for a pen. I'd normally have taken notes while she talked, but I'd had a feeling it would have shut her up. Instead of a pen, I came up with the dinner roll I'd taken earlier. I ate it in two bites. Diving in again, my fingers settled on the key card I'd found in the nightclub. Room 517. In the tower, I guessed. Might as well check it out.

I rode the tower elevator—much faster than the one to the nightclub—with two Sarahs who were making eyes at each other in a way that made me deeply uncomfortable. I was happy to escape.

Room 517 was around the corner and down the hall. My shoes sank into plush carpeting. Pushing a luggage cart through it wouldn't be any fun, but maybe tower people paid bellhops to do the grunt work. The halls up here had actual wallpaper, tasteful stripes, in contrast with our bare-walled wing.

I paused for a moment outside the room, trying to hear if there was anyone moving inside, preparing myself to find . . . I didn't know what. I hadn't gotten clearance to do this. Then again, nobody had told me not to, which was basically permission. I knocked, waited for an answer, knocked again.

The swipe card worked on the first try. I stepped inside. The light had been left on. The furniture looked like hardwood instead of plywood, and the room was maybe a foot or two wider, but I didn't really see anything to justify the cost difference between this space and mine.

Three dresses hung in the open closet, in styles similar to the dead woman's. Worn gym clothes lay crumpled in the corner next to the first bed, a pair of sneakers half buried underneath the pile. The closer bed had obviously been slept in; if she was the organizer, she'd probably been here a night or two early to get situated before the rest of us arrived. She'd dumped her suitcase—mostly underwear and bras—out on the second bedspread. Maybe in her world hotel bedspreads got washed along with the sheets.

A toiletry bag had been emptied on the bathroom counter. Ipana gel toothpaste, the exact same product I used. How much could toothpaste change from world to world? The makeup was an assortment of familiar and unfamiliar brands, so maybe I was wrong. A damp towel hung over the shower curtain rod. So far, this was the room of someone who had assumed she would be coming back. I flushed the toilet for her, as a courtesy. Immediately regretted it as disposing of evidence.

The room door clicked shut, startling me. Had I left it open? I didn't remember closing it when I'd entered. Maybe someone had gone into another room on the hall and the wind had pulled this one closed. I'd lived in houses where that happened. I opened the door and peered down the empty hallway.

I'd left her second bag for last, under the hope there was a clue waiting somewhere for me. A clue, like I was a real detective, not somebody who flushed away evidence. The bag was an expensive-looking leather satchel. My style, if I had the cash for it.

There were a few things I was expecting to find and didn't. I'd expected a registration binder like the one I had in my bag. I didn't see a walkie-talkie or charger, though maybe the charger was in the convention's Ops room the manager had mentioned earlier, wherever that was. I did find a program, with a couple of items circled. Not the ones I expected. "Sarahs in the Sciences" on Sunday morning and a penned-in Information Desk shift from 12–4 PM on Saturday. Not the keynote. Maybe she didn't have to circle it because it went without saying.

The rest of the bag was filled with the usual odds and ends I carried: pens, gum, emergency flashlight, loose change. A dog-eared paperback novel called *Parable of the Trickster*.

No wallet. I looked in all the places I'd have left a wallet if I were her: all her bag pockets, the TV stand, the nightstand, even the sink. There wasn't a room safe, so it couldn't be there.

I wouldn't have noticed it at all if I hadn't kicked it on my next circuit of the room, hidden half under the second bed. Maybe she'd tossed it in the bed's direction in a hurry and missed? Or knocked it to the ground as she left? It was unlike me. I wasn't the neatest person in the world, but I was careful with the important things.

I kept making assumptions she'd think like me, and they kept paying off. Still, I had to keep reminding myself we weren't the same person. We were and weren't. Our experiences had shaped us, the differences in our worlds. Something had convinced her to become a quantologist, but whatever had driven her would have had a different effect on me, in my quantology-free reality. Given all that, it didn't seem unreasonable we would have different opinions on where to leave your wallet in a hotel room.

The other option, obviously, was that somebody else had been in here. How hard would it be to flash the desk clerk an ID and say you'd lost your room key? Or even without ID, to rattle off one of the numbers the hotel had used to differentiate us? Whoever it was might even have still been in the room when I entered. That would explain the door shutting while I was poking around the bathroom. In which case, the question now wasn't only what could the room tell me, but what couldn't it tell me? I would never know if something was missing.

I opened the wallet. No cash, but that wasn't unexpected since we couldn't use it here. No driver's license, since that was in the body's pocket. Two credit cards, car insurance, Johns Hopkins ID, some store discount cards. The university ID could be important, if only a few Sarahs worked there.

The only thing personal—the only thing personal I'd noticed in the whole room, really, if you didn't count fashion—was a cropped photo tucked behind her health insurance card. I tapped it out, sucked in my breath. It was a picture of her—not me, I told myself—standing with my friends on a mountaintop at what I was fairly sure was the Grand Tetons. I had gotten somewhat used to the surreality of seeing my face on strangers, but there was something even odder about seeing a picture of myself, with my friends, in a place I'd never been. Mabel, my Mabel, with an arm wrapped tight around another Sarah's waist. All in someone else's wallet.

It was impossible to tell which details were piquing my interest because they were pertinent, and which were piquing my interest because they were me. What would it be like to be this Sarah? I remembered my own professors' homes, pictured myself coming and going from a majestic old house with a glassed-in sunroom. Did she live with alterna-Mabel? This Sarah lived in Baltimore, not Seattle; I couldn't imagine Mabel leaving Seattle.

If I stayed any longer I'd start trying on the dead Sarah's clothes, and I was pretty sure they wouldn't fit, mentally or physically. I left everything where I'd found it.

The Sarah in the room across the hall and I both closed the doors at the same time. I panicked for a second before realizing I was supposed to be there. Or at least I wasn't doing anything wrong.

She gave me a curious look. "Are you the detective?"

"Yeah. How did you know?" I looked her over. Another flowered dress, freckles, runner's build. Another short haircut. She'd either had her breasts reduced or run all the fat off her body. The body of somebody with a whole lot more determination than I had. One of the quantologists from the committee, I guessed.

"I'm in charge, and you're coming out of her room." She gave extra weight to the word "her." "The hotel manager said she'd called you in. Thank you for your help."

"You're in charge? In place of the, ah, host? The quantologist?"

"In place of? Everyone on our committee is a quantologist, but I'm the one you'd call the host. I'm the keynote speaker." She waved a sheaf of handwritten papers in my direction.

"Wait—is the speech still going on?"

"We moved it, obviously. It'll be in the dining hall. The dance is cancelled, out of respect." Her walkie-talkie squawked and fed back, loud enough to generate an echo. She dialed the volume down without looking at it. "And I rewrote my speech, of course."

"But we were looking for you—the manager thought you were the dead woman. Do you know who she is?" As I asked, I understood. "Oh, I had the wrong one. She's one of the others from your committee."

Her face crumpled for a second, like she was trying not to cry. She pulled herself together. Bit her lip until it turned as white as her teeth. "Yes. We hadn't known each other that long, obviously, but she was tremendously helpful. Working with her, well, it was like working with myself, if that doesn't sound too narcissistic. We were on the same page about everything. They said they'd given you a registration list? She's the one from R1D0, by our designation. I'm R0D0. I ID'd her when the manager took me up to look a few minutes ago."

"It's not my fault you're identical," I said, a little angry with myself for not having considered the possibility. "I'm not even this kind of detective."

She patted my arm. My feeling of inadequacy blew over as soon as I said it, leaving her gesture as sincere commiseration, not condescension. Her smile was genuine, sympathetic. "I wouldn't have suggested getting you involved in all of this, but I wasn't there when the hotel manager panicked. I think she must have fallen off the stage and hit her head, but we'll bring in the authorities as soon as the weather lets up. No need for you to worry about it."

Everything I'd learned was still lurching and settling into new positions. The clothing change made sense if it was a different person. Everything I knew about the one fit the other.

"How close are your worlds? I mean, do you know the divergence point? I don't think I'll get the science of it, but I get the divergence-points concept."

"I'd love to talk more," she said, "but my speech is supposed to start in a few minutes."

"Do you mind if I walk with you? I have a couple more questions I wouldn't mind asking. Even if you think I don't need to investigate."

She shrugged and started walking. I followed. "Why didn't you answer your radio when they called for you?"

"I was in the shower. I must not have heard it."

"Do you know what she was doing in the nightclub?"

"No clue. Looking for me, maybe? Or adding something to the Hall of Fame display? A few people brought items they hadn't mentioned on the questionnaire."

We waited for the elevator. A couple more Sarahs joined us, giving the same curious once-over we were all giving each other. If they were staying in this tower, they were likely on the richer side of the spectrum. Both were dressed the way I'd dress if I could afford nicer clothes, but one had cut her hair shorter than I'd ever cut mine before, the back shaved, the top still curly. It looked good; I wished I had the guts. Neither wore glasses. Contacts or surgery or some fluke of genetics? I'd have asked if I wasn't more interested in the host.

I didn't want to question her much in front of strangers without knowing what had already been said to the general public. I searched for a more neutral topic. "Why did you choose this hotel?"

The elevator chimed and let us in. We stood silent while it descended; I used the time to study the others. Hair and clothes had been the easiest ways to catalogue differences at first, but I was starting to see that we fell into a few different basic phenotypes. The host and the other athletic Sarahs on one side of a spectrum that ranged lean to soft. Still no way to suss out anything beyond the superficial without asking.

Once the other Sarahs had walked away, the host answered my question as if there had been no gap. "Secord Island is a tiny dot in the Atlantic. I won't bother getting into the geopolitics, but it's independent in nine identified worlds. Three are home to private mansions, six to private resort hotels. In this one and only this one, one of us is manager, though she's one of the more distant iterations I identified, from a subset who went to university in Nova Scotia and then stayed in the east. This place was perfect. So inhospitably perfect we were able to guarantee to our sponsors and grantees that nobody would go AWOL. One weekend, in and out. No risk." She flashed a rueful smile.

"What do sponsors and grantees get from this?" Mabel had asked me, and I'd wondered ever since. I repeated Mabel's question.

"The usual name recognition, for those in worlds where they exist. And if it goes well—if it had gone well, I guess—the chance to explore doing it for other purposes: recreational, educational. There're a couple of travel companies, a couple of charitable foundations, a couple of think tanks. I'm hoping I'll still be able to convince them her death would have happened anywhere, nothing to do with the event."

I nodded. "One more thing. Is there a way for me to talk to your other committee members? You're the ones who would have known her best."

She looked for a second like she was going to say no, but then she lifted her walkie-talkie to her lips. After a brief back and forth, they agreed to meet me at registration after the keynote.

"Anything else?" she asked. "I still say there's no point in you investigating before the police get here, but if you think there is, I'll cede to your expertise."

I wasn't sure if that was a dig or not. She was probably right. I had no idea why I was still asking questions. Except I did like having something to do, and I was suspicious of anything dismissed too easily. If I were lying in a hotel fridge, I'd want someone asking questions for me.

A crowd bottlenecked at the dining-hall entrance; I guess none of us liked arriving too early. We didn't like jostling either, so the result was a polite alternate-right-of-way situation that worked itself out pretty quickly. The room was still arranged in a constellation of eight-person tables, but a microphone had been set up on one end of the room. I peeled off to find standing room beside the entrance, where I could watch the speech and the crowd at the same time.

The host walked to the microphone. She wore small heels with her dress. Heels always made me walk like a moose on a frozen lake, but she came across comfortable and confident. I couldn't help coveting her poise. She glanced at the clock above the door—for a moment I thought she was looking at me—and then started to speak without consulting her notes.

"Welcome, friends. First, I think by now many of you have heard we've had a death at the conference. One of my committee members, perhaps the person who worked most closely with me, Sarah Pinsker. It's so strange to say that name, my own name, the name that many of you call your own, in this context. We're still waiting for the authorities to arrive to tell us what happened. We're also working to inform her family, and to find the proper way to memorialize her. I'm sure she's in all our hearts.

"I say 'in all our hearts,' and I know it sounds clichéd, but it's literally true. She is every one of us. So we can imagine what her loss will mean to her own world and her own family. At the same time, it's impossible to imagine. Even now, when I say her name, you picture yourself, not her. Not the things that made her distinct from you or me. In that way, we grieve her as friend and family, not a stranger, even those of us who didn't know her as an individual."

The door creaked, and I looked over to see the DJ slipping from the room. The speaker continued.

"You all took such pains to get here, it didn't feel right to cut the weekend short. I'm sure she would have wanted it to go on, because I know I would have wanted it to go on, after all our work. Tonight's dance is cancelled, out of respect. There'll be rooms available tonight and tomorrow for support groups if anyone needs to process in that setting. There will also be a Shabbat service in the chapel tomorrow morning at ten if anyone wants to say kaddish for her, led by Rabbi Sarah Pinsker. Stand up, Rabbi?"

A Sarah stood, raised a hand in solemn greeting, then sat again. The only rabbi, I thought. Was there a panel on our more unexpected career choices? I knew what had led me down my road, but not what had led her down hers.

"Without invalidating anyone's grief or confusion, I have to say that this death, tragic as it is, highlights the reason we're here: to learn from each other. I've got a panel tomorrow where I'll explain in more detail how this all works, but I think this is a fitting moment to explain the basics, to explain how we are all different and the same."

Her tone changed, as if she was now on more comfortable ground. "It's human nature to center ourselves in the narrative, but I encourage us all to consider the larger picture. I'm standing here before you not because I am the first, or the best, or the trunk of a branching tree. I'm here due to two things I can own: a discovery and a decision. I'm the one who figured out how to open a door; I'm the one who invited all of you to walk through it. Nothing more, nothing less.

"There are others among us who are as accomplished in their own fields, who could invite us through other doors, figuratively speaking. There are others among you who made ordinary decisions that nonetheless changed you significantly: leaving school, pursuing higher education, adopting children, or not. Even the smallest decisions, like kissing someone instead of waiting to be kissed."

I wondered how many of us thought of Mabel.

"I'm sorry I'm not feeling up to doing my whole intro-to-quantology speech, but I can leave you with one more thing to think about, something that may provide comfort on a night like tonight. Not only can I say nobody here is prime, I can also say all of us have always existed. It's hard to wrap your head around, but it's true. Those divergence points, where we discuss pets and girlfriends and boyfriends, wrong turns and big decisions? They work backward and forward. The moment a divergence point sparks, the new one has always existed too.

"I tried to invite Sarahs with some variety, to learn from each other, but Sarahs who are still recognizably us. This conference exists in infinite variations: some where I invited a different group of Sarahs, some where you chose a different dessert, where you sat next to someone else at dinner, some where my friend Sarah is still with us. They are no more or less valid for having diverged, no more or less real. You are all you, we are all we, constantly shaped by and shaping worlds."

It was a good line, delivered by a good speaker, meant to buoy everyone. What would it be like to be a good public speaker? To be a discoverer of worlds? We all clapped, both for her speech and her attempts to reconcile the moods of the occasion. That was why I clapped, anyway. I kept extrapolating outward from myself.

I spotted the older Sarah I'd had a drink with earlier, and went to stand beside her as the crowd started to file from the room. "In the bar a few hours ago, you pointed at someone and said she was the host. How did you know?"

She shook her head. "Sorry, that must have been somebody else. I haven't been to the bar. Sober ten years."

There was more than one older Sarah, or more than one who looked older than the rest of us. A good reminder not to make assumptions, even here.

Three Sarahs stood clustered around the registration desk, as promised. I didn't see the host, but I was pretty sure she was still behind me in the dining hall. I'd already spoken with her anyhow. So a committee of five, minus the host and the dead woman. They all wore silk; I guess they didn't sweat the dry-cleaning bills.

They agreed to talk to me one at a time, in the lounge seating area between registration and the bar. The bar was starting to fill up again, but it wasn't yet too noisy for conversation. A knot of Sarahs with guitars gathered on the other bank of couches, but the odd timbral similarity of their voices made them easy to tune out. They'd found a way to eke joy out of the situation, and for a moment I envied them.

I'd have saved time by talking to them all together, though; their answers might as well have come from the same mouth.

Q: Where were you between four-thirty and six PM?

A: Registration, then the cocktail party, then up to take a nap and shower. I figured a shower would be worth being a little late for dinner.

Q: Were all of you at the cocktail party?

A: Yes! I think. At the beginning, anyway.

Q: Including the one who passed away?

A: Yes. I think. It's hard to say. We were mingling.

Q: When did you first realize something was wrong?

A: When the hotel manager came to find us, toward the end of dinner.

Q: Us?

A: The committee. She found all of us except—her.

They all gave the same weight to "her" that the host had upstairs.

Q: What did you do then?

A: Figured out which of us she was. Cried. Freaked a bit. Talked about what to do next.

Q: How did you figure out which of you she was?

A: Um, a roll call. I know that sounds silly, but I can't tell any of the other four apart without asking them questions or knowing what they're wearing. I had friends in seventh grade who were identical twins, and I never had a doubt which of them was which. This is different.

Q: Did anyone use the radios to contact any of you?

A: Not that I heard? I might have been in the shower.

Q: Is there anything else you know about her that might be helpful? Anybody who she was angry with? Anybody who was angry with her? Jealousies, rivalries?

A: There's no point in a cross-world rivalry. We were all a little jealous of R0D0, of course. She made the breakthrough we were all trying to make. But not R1D0.

Q: Do you know your divergence point from the others on your committee?

A: Eleven days before the big discovery, R0D0 and R1D0 made a mistake in an equation. The rest of us got it right. It was the mistake that was the key. The three of us differ in ways barely worth mentioning, all within a month of each other: a hospital visit, a sprained ankle on a run, a birthday party the rest of us skipped.

Q: What about R0D0 and R1D0, then? Where do they diverge? Would there be any reason for the host to be jealous of the deceased?

A: If anything it would be the other way around. They diverged an hour before the discovery. R1D0 went out for an anniversary dinner with her girlfriend; R0D0 cancelled dinner and stayed in the lab. If I were R1D0, I'd have carried a little resentment over that, but if she did, she never showed it. Anyway, someone said it was an accident, right? Is there any chance it was anything else?

"She hasn't been examined," I said. "She's got one hell of a knock to her head."

I left it deliberately vague, to see if any of them gave anything away. They all gave me the same look, stressed and relieved, hopeful and guilty about that hope. I found myself wishing all of my insurance interviews were with Sarahs. My job would be much easier if I recognized every expression on everyone's face.

I was desperate for something to break one of them from the pack, but nothing came. Even their divergence points were mundane. They were the same person. I thanked them for their help and let them go. They had all looked genuinely upset. I had believed all of them, and the identical answers were as good as corroboration. They were all willing to help, but convinced it was an accident. They couldn't figure out why I was still asking questions when the answer seemed obvious.

In their shoes, I'd be desperate to believe it was an accident too. Better than thinking somebody might have it in for me. If I were one of them, I'd be terrified and trying to hide it. I'd be looking around every corner for a killer, trying to live up my last moments, to settle accounts, just in case; except we were all trapped for the weekend, unable to contact anyone we loved or go anywhere.

I was one of them. Without the science background, without the urge to be the first or the best or whatever it was driving them. Which was an interesting line of questioning I hadn't followed at all: What was driving them? Why were they so ambitious, when the rest of us weren't? What had made them go into quantology? Could any of them still make the same discovery, for their world, or had the host Sarah spoiled it for everyone? I looked over to see if they were still standing by registration, but they had all gone.

The bar was half full, and when I slid onto the nearest empty stool, the bartender handed me a tumbler of bourbon, neat, without my needing to ask. The guesswork was gone from his job: there was a plastic cup over the handle for the stout. I hoped he had another keg somewhere that he hadn't had time to tap yet. Down the row, six other Sarahs sipped from identical glasses.

"Cheers," said the Sarah next to me, holding up her drink. She was wearing a *Wonder Woman* T-shirt too, an Alex Ross illustration, deflecting bullets. She looked exhausted, like she'd spent the evening deflecting bullets herself. "It's hitting you too, huh?"

"Hitting me?"

"The difference question. You've noticed a thing about yourself, or a thing about someone else here that isn't true of yourself. You can't quite tell if you should feel bad about it, if it's a flaw in you, if there's something you did wrong along the way. You thought one more drink might let you fall asleep without it keeping you up all night."

We clinked glasses.

I wandered back to my room still mulling it over. Wind whipped down the chilly hallway, but I saw only one figure silhouetted against the open door, with her mass of flaming curls.

"Where's your friend?" I asked, leaning out. A gust hit me hard enough to knock me off balance; in its wake, the air was heavy with the promise of rain. The smoker whirled to face me when I spoke. "Sorry if I scared you. I was the one who chatted with the two of you out here earlier, in case you can't tell."

She shrugged. "Haven't seen her. I heard she found the body. Maybe she needs some alone time. I know I would. Drink?"

She held a flask out to me, and I took it with a nod of thanks. Bourbon. Cheaper than the stuff the bartender had served, but still decent. Another gust of wind tore the top of a dumpster off its hinges and sent it tumbling over the loading-dock wall. We both watched it cartwheel away.

"New question for tomorrow," she said, taking her flask back. "You get to test it first. What are you most afraid of?"

My answer was instant. "Everything. Earthquakes. Bombs. Random violence. Falling tree branches. Losing people I love. Cancer. Being in the wrong place at the wrong time. This storm. Missing out on something because I didn't want to make a fool of myself. Missing out on something because I'm afraid. I try not to let it control me—my job helps desensitize me a little—but . . . yeah. Long answer to a short question. You?"

She took a long drag on her cigarette. "I'd have stopped at 'Everything,' but, yeah, same basic theme. Pretty amazing that we're all here despite being chicken. Afraid to ride bicycles but willing to step out of our own reality completely for a weekend."

"Maybe it falls under 'Afraid of missing out on something because I'm afraid'? We all push ourselves in the same ways?"

"Maybe. I guess I'll see what everyone else answers tomorrow. You know what you didn't list, in that long list of things you were afraid of?"

"What?" I replayed my answer in my head to figure what I might have missed.

"Dying alone, far from the people you love, surrounded by strangers who wear your face and mirror your thoughts. I would think that would make your list, since it makes mine."

I considered. "The first part, maybe. I'm starting to get used to the second part. And I'm still more afraid of the storm than the other Sarahs."

Lightning cracked the sky open to punctuate my sentence, close enough to make the hairs on my arms stand on end.

"Bam. Divergence point," she said, with less enthusiasm than her smoking buddy had earlier. "I'm getting a distinctly bad vibe from all this. Do you have Agatha Christie in your world? Isolated island, bad weather. I'm still waiting for us all to be picked off one by one."

"And yet you were standing out here all alone. So either you're not as scared as you say, or . . ." As I said it, I wished I hadn't. If I was joking, it wasn't funny. If I was implying she was a suspect, well, everyone was except me, since I knew I hadn't done it. That didn't make it a smart move to address the subject directly.

"Or I'm the killer, in which case you're the one in trouble, not me." She gave me a look that told me she agreed my comment had been in poor taste, and held out the flask, daring me to take it. "I'm not a killer. I can't prove it, of course, but I know I'm not. Which makes me pretty sure none of us are, because I can't imagine the circumstance that would bring me to kill someone."

"I can't imagine killing someone, but I also can't imagine the circumstance that would have turned me into a smoker." I swigged whiskey. "Or a hotel manager, or a quantologist, or a DJ."

She took one more drag, then dropped the butt and crushed it with her boot. "It's the storm and the island that made me say the Christie thing. I'm way more nervous about this storm than being killed by a serial Sarah, at least while there's still only one body. Hopefully I won't have cause to revise that. In the meantime, there's facing fear and there's being stupid. We should probably go inside before we get hit by lightning."

As if in response, the sky opened up. We were both drenched in the two feet to the doorway.

"If the lights go out, start counting Sarahs," Orange Curls said before squelching off down the hall.

Back in my room, I stripped my wet clothes off and replaced them with another T-shirt and boxer shorts. The whiskey didn't do the job I'd hoped it would, so I spent the night in imaginary conversation with Mabel. The rain battering the window filled in her side of the dialogue. I walked through the order of events, everything I'd found. I had ideas, but they weren't cohering. The timing was important, I knew that. Murder weapon would be lovely, but I didn't expect a forensic report anytime soon. As for suspects, for all the people giving me alibis and vouching for themselves and each other, it could still have been anybody.

I drifted away from the case itself. The host said she wasn't the Prime, wasn't the trunk of a branching tree, but she'd labeled us all in relation to her. We were all in close proximity. Even the most distant of us were still recognizable. Tiny differences. I hadn't run into anyone who lived in a post-water-shortage America, or post-flu, or post-oil. We all knew how to flush toilets.

What would it look like if we had radiated out from me instead of the host? Or if we had all radiated out from the hotel clerk, who the quantologist had said was one of the further iterations? There were other realities between these, ones she hadn't chosen. N Sarahs, in N realities, where N was unknowable and constantly changing. Why had she chosen us and not others? Was I the most interesting of a string of insurance investigators, or the only one available this weekend? I had more questions than I'd had before I arrived.

Why did I go into detective work, not one of the sciences? I hated my calculus teacher, dropped it after a few weeks; because of him, I didn't get far enough in math to pursue a college major in bio or physics. Maybe he didn't exist in the other worlds, or maybe the science Sarahs hadn't let him get the better of them. Maybe they pushed themselves to spite him. Some went on to become geneticists or researchers or science fiction writers. Same mind, applied differently. Choices, chances, undecisions, non-decisions, decisions good and bad.

Maybe I shouldn't have come. Maybe one of me was sitting at home with Mabel right at this very moment, another me, another Mabel, another reality where my curiosity hadn't won out. But if I'd stayed home, who would be asking questions for the Sarah in the fridge? If nothing else, I was good for that. Even if I hadn't yet found any answers.

It was still raining when I woke. The thin carpet felt vaguely damp, like the weather had come up through the foundation. My head hurt. I had a vague sense that I had unlocked something in my sleep and forgotten it again.

I took a quick shower, hoping it might clear my head. No luck.

Breakfast was served buffet style, which was good since I was ravenous after only eating a roll the night before. I built a tower of eggs, potatoes, and toast, a second tower of fruit, and deposited both plates on the nearest empty table. When I came back from the tea station, the table was full.

"How are you enjoying the weekend?" asked the Sarah next to me. I didn't think I'd met her before. "Other than . . . You know."

"I haven't had much time to do anything," I said between mouthfuls. "Duty called. Well, not a duty I expected to have, but I'm trying to figure it out."

"Oh, were you the one who got pulled away from the table last night? It would be a shame if you didn't get to go to anything." That was Dare; I remembered him from dinner, with his copper and silver beard and mustache. His talk on gender was one I'd circled when I thought I'd get to actually attend programming. "It's not like we'll have this chance again."

"You don't think so?" another asked.

Dare shook his head. "No. Somebody died. That's not exactly an encouragement to the backers to bring us back for a sequel. Even if it was an accident, the logistics of explaining her death on the other side of the portal will be a nightmare."

"Infinite variations," said another Sarah. "Maybe next year we'll get invitations from an iteration where she didn't die."

That made my head hurt. "I think I need to get back to work after I leave breakfast. I still need to interview the hotel staff, and anyone who talked to her yesterday afternoon . . ."

My neighbor speared a chunk of pineapple and waved it at me. "Stay. One talk won't hurt you. We've got a big-group discussion on 'Horses and Dogs and Cats, Oh My' in this room right after breakfast. All you have to do is not stand up."

Her argument on its own might not have been persuasive, but inertia won out. Inertia and jealousy and a bad feeling I shouldn't have eaten as much as I did and I might still be sick if I moved very quickly. Besides, everyone else had already had a chance to get to know each other a bit, and all I'd talked about was one unfortunate dead person whose death I wasn't even supposed to be investigating anymore. I lingered as the mics were set up and the buffet tables cleared.

The setup was loosely structured, with a leader and a few planned speakers to kick things off. The first storyteller sat to speak. She was trim, polo shirt tucked into worn jeans. She looked like she'd spent time in the sun.

"When I was a teenager, I spent my summers working at a trail riding stable in upstate New York." Several Sarahs snapped their fingers. I realized a system had developed while I was snooping around. Snap to say that had been your experience too. Too late for me to snap with them, but so far this story was mine as well.

"I had a favorite horse, Smokey. An Appaloosa." I snapped along. She didn't bother describing his color, like a white horse that had rolled in dirt, or his dustbroom mane and tail. I had loved him even though he was ugly as anything.

"One afternoon, a man drove up with a little girl, maybe five or six years old. My boss put the little girl on Flicker. Flicker wasn't the first choice for someone that small, but the kid-friendly horses were both out with another guide. There wasn't even a children's-sized saddle left, so we had to run the stirrups all the way up to the top hole and then flip them over. Even then, she had to stretch her toes to reach."

We all snapped quietly. We knew this story.

"I took them on the usual circuit: through the woods, circling the pond and the far field, back into the woods, then looping out to the dirt road. The road was the problem. We sometimes raced the horses home that way when we were goofing around. It was a dumb thing to do, teaching the horses to rile themselves up and anticipate the run back to the barn, but all the teenagers working there had been doing it for as long as anyone could remember.

"I spent the whole hour thinking about ways to avoid trouble. I decided to take them back through the field so they wouldn't race, but we still had to cross the road. Smokey jigged a bit as we crossed, but listened to me. It was Flicker who bolted toward home. She probably didn't even realize there was someone on her back, the kid was so small.

"Make your horse WALK," I remembered shouting to the father before I took off after his child. "Don't let him race us."

It wasn't hard to catch up with Flicker: Smokey was much faster. The problem was stopping a running horse from the back of another running horse. I couldn't think of a safe way to do it. If I tried to grab Flicker's reins, I'd pull her head to the side, and her body would bow away from me, and the kid would be thrown.

Even after a summer of tossing hay bales, I knew I wasn't strong enough to pull her onto my horse. The only thing I could do was reach over and steady the girl, who was clinging like a burr to the saddle. I kept picturing her little body slipping off onto the hard-packed dirt, or the barbed-wire fence that ran parallel. All I could do was hold her where she was.

I held the girl up there until the horses reached the top of the road and stopped, just like that, race over. Flicker dropped her head to graze. The father came up the road just behind us, grabbed his daughter, called me a hero. When we got back to the barn, he explained to my boss as if I had saved his kid from a freak occurrence. I would have said I minimized the damage in a totally avoidable near-catastrophe.

At summer's end, my boss offered to let me take Smokey home for the off-season, as thanks. I wanted to say yes so badly, but I knew it was impractical. I did the research, visited a dozen barns, worked out the expenses, and finally called the barn, weeping, to say I couldn't afford to take him. The next summer when I went back to work, he wasn't there. I couldn't bear to ask where he'd been sold, since I knew I'd blown my chance at any claim on him.

"In the end, I found a way to make it work to bring him home with me," the storyteller said, going off the script as written in my head. I had forgotten she was still talking. Up until she changed the story, she'd sounded just like my own interior monologue. "I found a barn that let me give lessons on him to cover board. I saved enough to buy him the next spring. He was my extracurricular, my only extra-curricular, the joy my whole life revolved around. When I decided to go to community college for large animal management instead of going to university, it was for him. From talking with all of you, I'm pretty sure this was a major divergence point, so I thought I'd tell you I had him until he died of old age at thirty-two."

I wiped a tear from my eye. The sniffles around me suggested others were doing the same. One was openly weeping, another holding her. "It wasn't your fault," the second one said, loud enough for me to hear. "You couldn't have saved her. We couldn't all save her."

Something nagged at me. She had left out a few things, to the point where I didn't know if they had only happened to me. My boss had sat me down after the father and daughter had driven away. We spent an hour going over what had happened, with him suggesting different phrasings, different ways of thinking. "If anyone asks, you don't need to mention that Flicker isn't normally a kid horse, right? Or that the stirrups were too long?"

That was the seed of my investigative career: the hour where we sat at the picnic bench and massaged the truth into something litigation-proof. I was exhausted, drained of adrenaline, at once sickened and fascinated at the way the story changed before my eyes. I understood the need for the lie, understood that he'd lose the business if he was successfully sued, went along with it. At the same time, his casual erasure of the truth horrified me.

All these other Sarahs had either missed that moment or internalized it in some other way. Was the rabbi here? Maybe this was the incident that started her search for meaning. Maybe the quantologists had launched their careers looking for a way to do that day over again.

Part of me wanted more than anything to trade places with this barn manager. To have had sixteen years with a horse I loved, to have made a decision based on gut instead of practicality. I knew that ship had sailed, but I still wanted it. That one change had defined her life. She was happy. I was happy too. I'd left that incident alone as a disappointment but not a defining one, or maybe a defining point but one that had shaped me without tearing me down. The weeping Sarah might argue otherwise. Divergence points. Divergence points were the key to everything.

"I'm sorry," I whispered to the woman who was still crying over the little girl, as I got up to leave.

The hotel manager was standing in the lobby talking to a couple of her employees when I passed. I debated telling her where I was going, decided against it. Probably stupid, I reflected without slowing, as I walked down the mildewed-smelling hall to knock on a murderer's door. I heard footsteps inside, and the door swung wide; she opened it without checking who was on the other side.

"I know." I didn't need to say more. She'd believe me.

I pictured her hitting me over the head, running down the hall and out into the storm. That was the movie scenario, the dramatic culmination: the two of us wrestling on some wind-wracked cliff. Why wasn't I afraid of that? I knew she had considered it and rejected it in the same moment. That wasn't the kind of person we were. I was pretty sure of that, though not as sure as before I figured out what had happened.

She let me in. She was still wearing the No Good Deeds T-shirt, which looked even more rumpled than before. When she turned away there were sweat stains under the arms and all down the back, like she'd been exercising.

"I was going to take a quick shower," she said. "Do you mind? You can look around."

I nodded, let her go. She didn't bother to close the bathroom door, or left it open out of courtesy to show me she wasn't plotting anything.

I poked through the DJ's stuff, scattered on the second bed. An ancient laptop, an ancient MP3 player, decent-looking headphones. More pills. A twist-tied baggie with a brown lump in it, another baggie of what looked like ground coffee. A few T-shirts, one pair of ragged jeans.

She emerged from the bathroom in a towel, the picture of good health.

"Do you mind?" she asked, and I moved aside for her to take a pair of underwear off the pile. She poked her finger through a hole in a seam. "I didn't think about this part. How I'd have to wear someone else's used underwear."

"Was it worth it?"

She cocked her head, gave me a sad, unstained smile. "That's kind of up to you, I think."

I hadn't considered it that way, but as she said it I knew what she meant. If I told the authorities—whatever that meant in this context—the real DJ would still be upstairs in the fridge wearing someone else's clothes. It would all have been for nothing.

"Why?" I asked. "Why her, specifically? What's the divergence point?"

"There are a hundred thousand divergences between her and me. She wasted herself, wasted her life. She was a decent DJ, but she was otherwise a total fuck-up. Tried a hundred times to get clean. It never stuck."

"She was nice to me," I said, thinking about our brief interaction, her jittery enthusiasm. "Seemed pretty cool."

She pulled on the jeans from the bed. They fit, but not as well as the designer pair she'd worn the day before. "I researched her for a while. Trust me. She may have been nice, but she was a four-alarm fire. Smoked everything in her life other than music."

"But just because she was a mess doesn't mean she deserved to die. I mean, you've still got a lot going in your life, right? You invented cross-dimensional travel. Why would you want to take on her life if you think it's so shitty?"

She reached into the backpack on the bed and withdrew the DJ's wallet. Pulled out the ID and tossed it in my direction.

Oh. "Seattle's gone in your world." It wasn't a question.

She nodded, tears in her eyes. "Not only Seattle. Everyone. I lived in a house with five of my closest friends during grad school. I was visiting our parents back east when it happened, but everyone else was in the house when the earthquake hit. I was on the phone with Kelly when it happened—they were all watching *Labyrinth*—and I heard the whole thing. It took ten days to dig them out. Too late, of course. They all still exist where the DJ's from, and she sits in her shitty apartment pretending they're not out there. Ignoring their calls when they try to check in on her. Estranged from our parents and sisters. She never even met Mabel. There are a million Sarahs I could have chosen and wouldn't have because they still had people."

"But you still have other people," I said. "What about them?"

"My lab staff might miss me, but that's about it. Mabel left me the night I made my big discovery, when I skipped out on our anniversary dinner because I was on the verge; I got home to tell her and she was gone. Our family would have felt terrible, of course, and I felt terrible about leaving them. But they would have been comforted by the way I lived and died, I think. Knowing I did everything I had set out to accomplish. It was a good life. They knew I loved them."

"A good life you're willing to leave behind?" I was still trying to imagine that. "You'll trade tenure and fame and everything for whatever she's got left?"

"That stuff is good for my ego, but it doesn't matter. Not like having a home. Not like people. I'll trade it all in a second for a world where everyone and everyplace I love still exists. Where I could find her world's Mabel—they never even met!—and see everyone else again."

"Even if they hate you?"

She didn't hesitate. "Yes. Relationships can be repaired. Even if they hate me, I know they're still out there hating me."

"And that was worth bashing her head in?"

I watched her face carefully. I could imagine the horror I'd feel if I'd lost everyone in such a terrible way, and the guilt of knowing

I'd have been there with them if I hadn't been out of town, and even sitting on one side of that haunting phone call, but I still didn't think it would drive me to murder.

"She didn't feel it. Dropped like a stone. She doesn't even own a bra," she said, rummaging in the bag. "I haven't gone out without a bra since I was twelve years old."

"You did last night. I saw you in the back at the keynote." I watched her pull a T-shirt over her head for a band I didn't recognize. "Why did that other quantologist take your place? The real RID0?"

She sighed. "If I say we're exactly the same, I mean we are exactly the same. Literally the only difference in our lives is that the night I actually made the discovery, she went out for an anniversary dinner with Mabel, and I cancelled dinner and stayed in the lab. That's our divergence point. She's pissed she didn't stay in the lab that night. She wants the glory. She's let that supersede everything else, thinks she'd be happy if only she were in my shoes. That's all. I mean, I'd be pissed too, but I don't think she's seeing clearly. She's still with Mabel. That matters way more than a name on a paper, even one this huge."

"Her decision must have been spur of the moment," I said. "I think she heard the call you made, and switched clothes with the body when she realized she was the first one there. I'm not sure why she took both radios, but maybe that was panic. I heard the second one inside her room when I was standing in the hall with her. Anyway, I saw her speak last night. She could be you perfectly."

"She is me. Nobody will know the difference. She can have them. Now I don't have to feel guilty about leaving my family, even; it's her world that'll have to deal with her absence. Anyway, she might have been headed up to the club to do exactly the same thing I did."

I shuddered to think that was true, and how many murderous Sarahs actually existed in that case. "Was that your whole motivation for going into quantology? To switch places?"

"No! We were already in a physics masters program, so finishing that degree and going into quantology wasn't a stretch. We wanted to know if there really were realities where Seattle still existed. Where

Kelly and Taylor and Allison and Scott and Andrea were still alive. Not to go there, just to know."

I didn't know who Andrea was, but Kelly and Taylor were my best friends other than Mabel, and we'd all lived in Scott and Allison's house in Capitol Hill when I first moved to Seattle. I couldn't imagine the guilt of living in a world where they had all died and I had been spared by some quirk of timing. And Mabel had broken up with her on top of that. She'd lost all of them. Even hearing her say it, it hit my gut as if I'd lost them myself.

"So you weren't always going to kill someone?" I was still having trouble imagining this ambitious Sarah ditching everything she had to become a DJ, but it didn't seem as far-fetched anymore. Something else bothered me too. I believed everything else she'd said, but I still couldn't picture myself bashing in somebody's head, or taking the time to position her beneath the stage in the hopes of making it look like an accident. Every step screamed intention.

She ran her hands over her short hair, smoothing the flyaways. "I only decided for certain when she came back with her second crate. She must've gotten herself messed up in between; she could barely answer my questions when I tried to talk to her. Anyway, I'm sure there are other realities spawned at that moment where I decided not to."

She believed what she was saying, I could tell, but I didn't. I was certain she'd waited up there, taken the time to pick the perfect weapon from the show-and-tell table. She might even have picked in advance, when the questionnaires had come in, researching the offerings until she found the award that she could turn into a weapon; that would explain why the Hall of Fame was in the nightclub instead of someplace people could browse it throughout the weekend. It was disorienting, to hear her lying to herself and recognize it for what it was. I wasn't her, I reminded myself again. We'd made different choices to bring ourselves to this point.

"And in case you're wondering, I wouldn't have killed you for your Seattle, either. You haven't squandered it. Most haven't. Anyway, when I started my research I thought I would be happy if I just proved that they were out there somewhere, in some other reality. That's why we all got into quantology, to prove there were other possibilities, not to change places. And that felt like enough until I started researching all of you to figure out who to invite. Until I found her"—she pointed at herself—"and realized there was a way to make it happen. If I didn't try, I'd always wonder about it. You'd do the same thing, right?"

I didn't answer. I didn't think so. I hoped not.

She kept talking. "When I reached out to the other quantologists, I picked ones who had diverged before I had that idea. Or so I thought, anyway. Maybe I was wrong about that, at least in the case of R1D0. I didn't think about the ways they'd diverge because of the influence of my inviting them to help plan this. That was short-sighted. Do you think the others know I switched?"

"I don't think so." None of them had mentioned it to me. If they didn't know, that meant they hadn't thought of it; if they hadn't thought of it, that left only one or two capable of murder.

"Yeah, I hope not. I want to think I'm the worst of us, other than her." She stood before me, wearing the clothes of the DJ I'd met the day before, wearing her life. "So what are you going to do? Are you going to tell them? Turn me in?"

"Did you ever chase down a runaway horse?"

She looked confused, then nodded.

I thought about divergence points. I'd never felt I could have done anything else in that moment on the road, which was a good thing. Even the tiniest choices paralyzed me; I tried to play out every decision's every repercussion. Better not to have time to think.

Up until I came here, I'd tried to tell myself that once I made a choice it was done, I had to own it. We all built the future with our choices every day, never knowing which ones mattered. Now I still had to own it, but I knew others were stuck living the other side of my decisions, or I was living theirs. I wasn't even sure yet if that was paralyzing or freeing. If I let her go, if she was anything like me, guilt might wear her down to nothing. That was a punishment in itself. If I turned her in, would it be justice for the DJ, or merely proof I could solve a crime?

"If you turn me in," she said, as if I had spoken out loud, "there's going to be a whole lot of confusion in a whole lot of places. I have no idea how any authority will deal with it. There'll be a dead body in one world, an accused killer in another. If you let me go, think of all the good I can do. I can repair her relationships with our friends and family. I can find her world's Mabel. This Sarah was never going to pull out of her spin, I swear. She would be dead tomorrow or next week or next month. And she'll still be dead tomorrow. I could do some good there in her world."

Somewhere out there, iterations were sparking. Variations on the host, deciding and not deciding to go through with her plan. Killing the DJ, changing her mind and walking away. More iterations yet: the second quantologist, making and unmaking her split-second decision to leave her life and slip into one that was identical in all ways but a crucial one. Somewhere, another me turned in the second but not the first, the first but not the second. Both. Neither.

Some other place, the DJ had never died. She put another record on her turntable, slowed the beat to match the song already playing, shifted seamlessly from one into the other. Some other place, a hotel nightclub full of Sarahs danced awkwardly to their favorite music, shaped by their worlds, shaping new ones.

— *Acknowledgments* —

I don't know how many authors walk around from childhood harboring the dream of a short fiction collection, but I need to start by thanking Small Beer Press for making this book a reality. My love for short fiction is an unseemly love, and if I started thanking all of the writers whose work inspired me, it would be a book of its own.

My wife, Zu, deserves her own acknowledgment page. She keeps my heart steady and whole.

My fiction is always better for someone pushing me to ask the next question. My deepest thanks to everyone who critiqued these and other stories, including Sherry Audette Morrow, Rep Pickard, A. C. Wise, A.T. Greenblatt, Fran Wilde, Siobhan Carroll, Karen Osborne, Richard Butner, Christopher Rowe, Kelly Link, Gavin J. Grant, Kiini Ibura Salaam, Maureen F. McHugh, Karen Joy Fowler, Molly Gloss, Ted Chiang, Meghan McCarron, Carmen Maria Machado, James Patrick Kelly, John Kessel, Andy Duncan, Jessica Reisman, Christopher Brown, Nathan Ballingrud, Matthew Kressel, E. Lily Yu, Carolyn Ives Gilman, Dale Bailey, my mother, my sisters, and everyone at the Baltimore Science Fiction Society critique circle. If I left anyone off that list, my most profound apologies.

Thank you to the original editors of these stories—everyone at *Asimov's, Uncanny, F&SF, Lightspeed, Strange Horizons,* and

Apex—and to all the magazine and anthology editors there and elsewhere who gave my stories homes, encouraged me, traded Twitter puns, and provided edits that make me look smart. A special shout out to Sheila Williams, whose early and ongoing support and friendship mean the world to me.

Thank you to everyone who invited me to workshops and retreats for providing mental space and actual space and good beer and fantastic company.

Thank you to the Red Canoe for letting me sit in your lovely cafe for uncountable hours.

Thank you to my father for the Red Canoe gift cards that funded my second office, and for making sure that every single "year's best" anthology and Le Guin collection was on our shelves when I was a kid.

Thank you to SFWA and Codex and the most well-hydrated Slack and my beloved Treehouse and BSFS and AN and EF and all the reading-series-runners and all the Baltimore writers and musicians for community and friendship and support.

Thank you to my writing buddy K. M. Szpara for his advice and company. If you don't have a friend at a similar career point whose work ethic complements yours, I highly recommend it.

Thank you to all my writing and history teachers, but particularly Judith Tumin, teacher and friend.

Thank you to all my family members who are not otherwise thanked above, for unwavering support, and to all the friends who are as close as family.

Thank you to all my music friends for being patient while I do the splits over this faultline. It's all storytelling, but the beat varies.

Thank you to my agent, Kim-Mei Kirtland, for expertly helping me to steer this ship.

Thank you to everyone who reads stories.

— *Publication History*—

"A Stretch of Highway Two Lanes Wide," *The Magazine of Fantasy & Science Fiction*, 2014

"And We Were Left Darkling," *Lightspeed*, 2015

"Remembery Day," *Apex Magazine*, 2015

"Sooner or Later Everything Falls into the Sea," *Lightspeed*, 2016

"The Low Hum of Her," *Asimov's Science Fiction*, 2014

"Talking with Dead People," *The Magazine of Fantasy & Science Fiction* 2016

"The Sewell Home for the Temporally Displaced," *Lightspeed*, 2014

"In Joy, Knowing the Abyss Behind," *Strange Horizons*, 2013

"No Lonely Seafarer," *Lightspeed*, 2014

"Wind Will Rove," *Asimov's Science Fiction*, 2017

"Our Lady of the Open Road," *Asimov's Science Fiction*, 2015

"The Narwhal" appears here for the first time.

"And Then There Were (N-One)," *Uncanny Magazine*, 2017

— *About the Author* —

Sarah Pinsker's stories have won the Nebula and Sturgeon awards, and have been finalists for the Hugo, the Locus, and the Eugie Foster Memorial Award. Her first novel, *Song for a New Day,* will be published in autumn 2019. She is also a singer/songwriter with three albums on various independent labels and a fourth she swears will be released someday soon. She was born in New York and has lived all over the US and Canada, but currently lives with her wife in Baltimore in a hundred-year-old house surrounded by sentient vines. Her website is sarahpinsker.com.

"The variety is tremendous, exhilarating. Each one is differently excellent."
—Ursula K. Le Guin

AT THE MOUTH
OF THE RIVER
OF BEES

~ stories ~

Kij Johnson

★ "Strange, beautiful, and occasionally disturbing territory
without ever missing a beat. . . . Johnson's language is beautiful,
her descriptions of setting visceral, and her characters compellingly
drawn. . . . [S]ometimes off-putting, sometimes funny, and always
thought provoking." — *Publishers Weekly* (starred review)

Includes the Hugo and Nebula Award winner
"The Man Who Bridged the Mist."

paper · $16 · 9781931520805 | ebook · 9781931520812